latitude zero

ALSO BY DIANA RENN

Tokyo Heist

latitude zero

DIANA RENN

VIKING
An Imprint of Penguin Group (USA)

VIKING
Published by the Penguin Group
Penguin Group (USA) LLC
375 Hudson Street
New York, New York 10014

USA ///// Canada ///// UK ///// Ireland ///// Australia
New Zealand ///// India ///// South Africa ///// China

penguin.com
A Penguin Random House Company

First published in the United States of America by Viking,
an imprint of Penguin Group (USA) LLC, 2014

LIBRARY OF CONGRESS CATALOGING-IN-PUBLICATION DATA
Renn, Diana.
Latitude zero / by Diana Renn
pages cm
Summary: Tessa, an aspiring investigative journalist, travels to Ecuador as she investigates the sudden death of young cycling superstar Juan Carlos Macias-León at a charity bike ride.
ISBN 978-0-670-01558-0 (hardback)
[1. Bicycles and bicycling—Fiction. 2. Bicycle racing—Fiction. 3. Murder—Fiction. 4. Investigative journalists—Fiction. 5. Reporters and reporting—Fiction. 6. Organized crime—Fiction. 7. Ecuador—Fiction. 8. Mystery and detective stories.] I. Title.
PZ7.R2895Lat 2014 [Fic]—dc23 2013043837

Printed in U.S.A.

1 3 5 7 9 10 8 6 4 2

Set in Amasis MT Std Designed by Kate Renner

For Jim

latitude zero

PART 1

latitude forty-two

MASSACHUSETTS

1

WE RODE through the busy parking lot and looked for the easy way out. Riding close to Jake's back wheel, I followed his crooked path through the cars circling the lot and the cyclists unloading their gear. And the bikes! I'd never seen so many, not even at Jake's races.

Some guy opened a car door right by me. I sucked in my breath and swerved hard.

"Hey, watch it!" Jake shouted at the driver. "You okay?" he asked me, softer. "That idiot almost doored you."

"Still breathing."

"This place is an accident waiting to happen." Jake stood on his pedals and scanned the crowds. "This way." He steered toward the edge of the parking lot, bunny-hopped his bike onto the sidewalk, and entered into the street.

As I followed him toward the starting line, I tried to ignore the passing cars, whose heat I could feel on my legs. I focused on the positives. We were gliding down brand-new asphalt: a black licorice whip of a road. And it was the perfect morning for a bike ride. A milky June sky, a breeze at our backs, miles of training rides stored in our muscles. The warm air was drying out last night's rain, and steam swirled up from the road.

But my front tire wobbled. My breath came fast. This was my first time bandit riding with Jake. It wasn't exactly breaking the law, but it was the closest I'd come. We were unregistered riders who'd raised zero dollars for this charity ride.

A few minutes later, we reached the edge of a middle school parking lot. It had been transformed into the cyclists' staging area. And a party. Music from a live band pulsed from speakers. Balloon clusters danced in the breeze. A red-and-white banner stretched between two poles announced the name of the ride: CHAIN REACTION. FIGHTING CANCER BY THE MILE!

Hundreds of cyclists swarmed like bugs riding or walking their bikes toward the starting line, organizing themselves into zones. The zones were separated with yellow tape and signs displaying average speeds: 12–13 MPH, 14–16 MPH, 17+ MPH.

My heart pounded out of sync with the music. I'd known this event would be big, but now it really hit. Ten professional cycling teams from all over the United States would race the one-hundred-mile route. The top three teams would donate their prize money to cancer research. The regular fundraising riders—"recreational" riders—would start the charity ride shortly after the race, riding one hundred miles or one of the shorter route options.

Not that "shorter" was short. Jake and I would be doing the thirty-miler. Jake could knock out those miles like nothing, but I'd never done more than twenty. Still, when Jake had casually suggested I join him on this ride, I'd jumped at the chance. He'd be off to UMass at the end of August. I still had one year of high school to go. I wanted to be the one he'd come back to. To be gritty, daring, tough as steel. The fun roadie girl of his dreams.

As we wove through the crowd, the professional team vans and trailers at the opposite end of the parking lot caught my eye. An electric thrill buzzed through me as I read the names on the trailers: Team Velo-Olympus. Bose Pro-Cycling. Team Trident-Crisco. We'd get to ride in their wake!

I gripped my handlebars and sucked in my breath as a group of cyclists strolled past the cycling gear expo booths, wearing cycling kits or uniforms I was all too familiar with. White spandex shorts and white jerseys, with a writhing pattern of green jungle vines.

Team EcuaBar.

Of course they'd be here. They did charity rides all the time. And this one was in their backyard, starting in the town of Cabot and lacing through Boston's western suburbs.

I glanced at Jake. His shoulders hunched as we passed those cyclists. I couldn't read his expression.

"Looking for el Cóndor?" Jake's words zinged at me. "Is that why you wanted to ride with me today?"

"What? God. No. I'm here for *you*. I am riding with *you*."

"Good to know."

I fixed my eyes on the road as Jake pulled ahead. "Great. Here we go again," I muttered.

Juan Carlos Macias-León was a name we steered around like a downed power line. Jake couldn't stand his former rival from the EcuaBar junior development team. Jake was a sprinter, Juan Carlos a climber. The way Juan Carlos attacked the hills, passing teammates and competitors, had earned him his nickname el Cóndor, the national bird of his native Ecuador. Back in January, when he turned eighteen, Juan Carlos snagged a coveted spot on EcuaBar's pro cycling team, even though most riders didn't turn pro until they were in their twenties.

I swallowed hard. On some level I'd known Juan Carlos would compete today. Maybe that was why I'd tried on five cycling jerseys before finally going with the black extra-fitted one.

And the shorter cycling shorts.

I caught up with Jake and rode by his side.

"I'm sorry," said Jake. "I shouldn't have said that. I know riding in big crowds isn't your thing. And I'm glad you're here."

"Thank you." I relaxed a little. This ride was supposed to bring us closer together, after all the hard stuff we'd been through lately. I was not going to keep an eye out for el Cóndor.

The band paused between songs. Hundreds of biking shoes clopped on asphalt. Gears clicked and clattered, and tires hummed.

My head turned automatically to watch a woman with a prosthetic leg pedaling by. *Survivor* was inked in black marker up and down her real leg. I looked down, suddenly self-conscious. Unlike almost all of the recreational riders, we weren't wearing the official red-and-white Chain Reaction jersey. Dressed in all black, with no rider numbers pinned to our backs or our bikes, we stood out here. And this was a big-deal fundraiser. Maybe we could get in trouble.

I stared at a girl with no hair and no eyebrows, waving a handmade poster that read: THANKS TO U I AM 10 TODAY! GO CHAIN REACTION RIDERS!

I let out a long breath. "Jake, some of the riders and spectators here today are survivors," I said loudly, as the band started up again. "I mean, this event is a huge deal. I was thinking. Maybe we could do the ride, then fundraise later and send in money." I'd wanted to raise the $1,500 minimum, but Jake had only mentioned this ride a few days ago. There was no way I could have raised that kind of money so fast. "I don't get why you can't suck it up and do the fundraising for all these charity rides you're hijacking."

Jake sighed. "Because for *each* ride, there's a fundraising minimum. Let's say I busted my ass and raised the fifteen-hundred-dollar minimum for Chain Reaction. Okay, fine, I could do that. But how I could I ask all the same people for another five hundred dollars for burn victims? And then multiple sclerosis?"

"But we could at least try to—"

"Babe," Jake interrupted. "There are over three thousand riders here today, not counting the pro teams that are going to race. If you're going to freak out, you shouldn't be here."

I lifted my chin. "I'm not freaking out. I can do this ride. I just don't want to get caught."

"So don't get caught. Act like you belong. If we do get questioned, don't worry. I'll do all the talking."

"And if we get separated?"

"Just be your honest self. Maybe they'll let you off easy. Or"—he flashed me a grin—"maybe your honesty'll buy you a nice view from the backseat of a cop car."

"Oh my God. My parents would *kill* me."

His face softened. "Hey. Don't worry about bandit riding. Worst that happens is some ride official asks us to leave. It's not that big a deal."

I chewed my lip. This *felt* like a big deal. I was the kind of person who sat in the front row at school and took notes. I never cut classes. Or corners. Or lines. And I was in the media, the host of a popular kids' TV show about young social activists and kidpreneurs. I'd always loved the way Jake brought out my inner rebel and steered me away from everyone else's expectations. But maybe this cancer ride was going too far.

Jake pulled ahead again. I churned my pedals to try to catch up, then swerved to avoid slamming into a girl carrying baskets of free samples.

"EcuaBars! Free EcuaBars!" the girl called out, not seeming to notice our near collision. She had a heart-shaped face and voluminous red hair—like someone from a shampoo commercial or one of those podium girl models who give flowers to bike race winners. She shook a basket of energy bars at me. Beside her stood a tall, superskinny guy with stooped posture, a long brown ponytail, and bushy eyebrows. He also waved baskets of bars.

Both wore white pants and white EcuaBar T-shirts with PURE ENERGY, NO ADDITIVES spelled out in green letters. The guy and the girl looked college-age. I felt a flicker of envy. It looked like a fun volunteer job, handing out free samples. Something I'd probably do with Sarita and Kylie, if I weren't bandit riding with Jake.

"New flavors!" the ponytail guy called out, jogging after me. "Chocolate Chipotle and Sweet Tomatillo! Dulce de Leche Delight! Great fair trade product! EcuaBar gives back. Eat one and help the rain forest and its native cacao farmers!"

I shook my head and pedaled on, though I would have loved one. I was an EcuaBar junkie. I hoarded them—in my backpack, my locker, my room. These bars were a delicious cross between an artisanal chocolate bar and a sports energy bar, with more instant energy than a cup of espresso, thanks to a superfood—leaves from the guayusa plant—which was grown in the Ecuadorian rain forest. (Why, yes, I'd memorized the ads.)

But I couldn't eat one in front of Jake. The other day, at Jake's house, we'd seen the new print ad in *Bicycle* magazine: Juan Carlos, drenched in sweat, tearing the wrapper off a bar, the scar at his neck neatly Photoshopped out. Jake had pitched the magazine into the trash.

As I left the free samples behind, I could see our goal not far ahead: the edge of the parking lot, Great Marsh Road, and the woods beyond. Jake's plan was to cut through a patch of conservation land. We'd join Great Marsh Road again on a quiet stretch where it curved left, merging with the ride about a half-mile from the ride's starting line. There wouldn't be any ride marshals or spectators there to notice our lack of rider numbers.

Jake slammed on his brakes, so I did, too.

"Damn. I forgot my drinks," he said. "I have to go back to the car."

I looked down at the two empty bottle racks attached to his frame. It wasn't like Jake to forget something like that. "It's already eight twenty. Can't you take some sports drink samples?"

"I need *my* home brew. It's all measured out."

This was true. He always concocted his special mix of blueberry-flavored electrolytes and water like a chemist, measuring out every molecule. "But Jake . . ."

"I'll find you right here. Ten minutes, tops." Jake hooked an arm around me and pulled me into a sideways hug. He touched my chin, lifting my face toward his, gazing at me with his piercing green eyes. "Hey," he whispered.

"Hey," I whispered back.

"It's us," he said. "Remember? We're on our own ride. Forget all these idiots around us here. This is about you and me today."

I managed a smile. I reached out to tuck a stray lock of dark hair behind his ear. He'd been growing out his hair lately—it looked good, windblown and below his chin—but he sometimes forgot it was there.

Jake pressed his lips to my bike helmet, then turned around and curled over his drop handlebars. He downshifted smoothly, fingers barely tapping the gearshift. His lanky body, all angles and bones, with smooth shaved legs, looked like an extension of his bike frame.

I'd had that exact same thought when I first met Jake last summer, for that *KidVision* interview. I'd first seen him on a high-speed circuit training course. The way Jake leaned into his turns, or descended hills in a full tuck, had left me breathless. I couldn't tell where his bike ended and his body began.

Now, as Jake rode off against the stream of cyclists, I imagined derailleurs in place of kneecaps, well-oiled chains for legs. When he saw an opening in the crowd, he shot forward, as if he had springs in his calves. My sprinter. I smiled. There he was.

The athlete I'd cheered from the sidelines. The smart strategist, the fierce competitor. Not the mopey cynic who'd taken over his body the past two months. If bandit riding was what it took to relight his fire, then fine.

In the mirror attached to my handlebar, I noticed two men watching me with apparent interest. One held a microphone. The other shouldered a TV camera with GBCN on the side.

GBCN—oh, no. My employer!

I breathed hard, as if I'd been riding for miles, not yards. My sunglasses and bike helmet should have disguised me. Still, I felt exposed. I couldn't be caught on film. A viewer might recognize my trademark hairstyle, my long sideways blonde braid draping over one shoulder. Surely someone would figure out I was Tessa Taylor, teen host of *KidVision*. Maybe Jake didn't care if anyone recognized him, but I did. Kids looked up to me. They sent me emails and handwritten notes. They assumed I was someone who Had It All Together, and who set a good example. What would they think if it leaked out I hadn't raised a dime for this cause? And why hadn't I even *considered* that there'd be a major media presence here?

I hopped back on the bike saddle and shoved off, heading into the thick of the crowd.

2

YOU'D THINK the Best Girlfriend Prize would have already been awarded to me. I'd practically written my acceptance speech. As I pushed through the crowd, away from that GBCN guy, I mentally reviewed all the points I'd racked up over the past few months:

1. I supported Jake during his hearing before the USA Cycling Board.
2. I comforted him when his racing license got suspended and again when he got kicked off his team.
3. I rode his roller coaster of moods (whee!), from depths of despair to vows of vengeance at whoever had framed him for distributing drugs.
4. I insisted on his innocence to anyone who would listen. Those syringes they found in his bag at a race? The banned "energy supplements"? The Adderall? Not his. Random drug tests were done all the time, and Jake always tested clean. He trained rigorously and monitored every calorie, logging his weight, body mass index, and energy levels.

As I looked up now, the sight of all those team vans and trailers at the far end of the parking lot filled me with rage. His team had turned on him. He'd been written up for the intent to distribute drugs. Lance Armstrong's loss of all his Tour de France titles had done serious damage to pro cycling's image, as had other doping scandals. Tyler Hamilton, Floyd Landis, George Hincapie—so many other famous cyclists had tested positive for doping, or confessed as well. A shadow had fallen over the sport.

Now competitive cycling, from pros to juniors, was trying to get the public, and potential sponsors, to believe in it again. So Jake's team coaches and managers had showed him no mercy. Zero tolerance. End of the ride.

They kicked Jake off the team. First he lost his racing license, then his cycling scholarship at Colorado Mesa U. That was when he started jacking New England charity rides. His new plan was to go to his backup school, UMass Amherst, and apply for a racing license in a new age bracket as soon as next year. Meanwhile, riding in crowds, taking advantage of the marked routes and traffic control, would help him keep his skills sharp.

He still loved his sport, but not all the machinery behind it. The managers, the coaches, the team owner—he felt like they'd betrayed him. I could understand. But these Chain Reaction riders today were out fighting cancer. While Jake and I weren't hurting anyone, using their route suddenly seemed wrong.

Light-headed, I jumped off my bike and walked it through the crowd, diagonally, like a swimmer escaping a riptide. I needed air. Fast.

I stopped before a set of metal barricades. They separated the professional racers' starting line from the rec riders' staging area. In this zone, elite riders and junior cyclists were stretching out, swigging sports drinks, consulting with teams and coaches. Like Jake, they were lean, not an ounce of fat on them. And, like Jake, they moved cautiously, protecting their joints, like elderly people. But I'd seen enough races to know how those bodies concealed hidden powers. Legs that seemed sticklike and frail when walking could pound the pedals for miles. Streamlined bodies could lean close to the ground, taking tight curves, carving the air.

A few of the cyclists were chatting with reporters. I scanned the TV cameras and vans. Fortunately, Greater Boston Cable News wasn't yet among them. Not that it mattered now. Who would be interested in a kids' TV host when they could talk to champion cyclists? I was safely invisible here.

Jake's former teammates, dressed in green to separate them as juniors, were huddled around head coach Tony Mancuso. They burst into laughter and high-fived each other.

Near them, the professional riders of Team EcuaBar, looking fresh in their green-and-white cycling kits, were assembling for a team photo.

A woman with tattooed vines writhing around her arms and legs, black-rimmed glasses, long black hair, and dyed blue bangs was arranging the pro cyclists into rows. She didn't look like a cyclist type, despite the Chain Reaction tank top she wore with ripped cargos. But she seemed like an experienced photographer—and as the daughter of one, I had to admire how she quickly got the fifteen riders into neat rows.

Fifteen. Not sixteen. Juan Carlos wasn't in the shot. Maybe he was sick or sitting this one out. A mix of relief and disappointment ran through me. Jake wouldn't cross paths with him. That was good. But it meant I wouldn't see him, either.

The photographer beckoned Coach Mancuso and two other men to come stand on either side of the team. One man I immediately recognized: Preston Lane, the Team EcuaBar owner, and one of my school's most famous alumni. Instinctively, I stood up straighter.

I'd met Preston before, for a *KidVision* interview last year, and I'd seen him only two weeks ago, at the Shady Pines graduation ceremony. There he'd delivered a rousing keynote speech. He'd brought the audience to tears with his talk about turning around the lives of struggling cacao farmers in Ecuador. He'd received a standing ovation, accepted the Shady Pines Corporate Responsibility Award.

Preston was dressed in full cycling regalia, including a Team EcuaBar cycling jersey. As a former Olympic hopeful, he liked to pretend he was part of the team, Jake said. He also liked to pretend he was twenty years younger than he was, back-slapping and high-fiving, and constantly saying "awesome." But now his lips were pressed together, his gaze faraway. He looked, suddenly, older.

As the pro cyclists squished in closer together, I turned my attention from Preston to the other bookend in the photo: a balding, heavyset man. He wore khakis and a striped polo shirt that didn't exactly flatter—or cover—his overhanging gut.

"Excuse me, Mr. Fitch?" the photographer said to him.

"Please, call me Chris," said the large man, a grin cutting into his doughy face.

"Chris. Can I get you to face front? You're kind of standing out."

He grumbled, but in a good-natured way, and rotated to face front. "Hey, where's the banner? Who's got the banner?" he called out.

"Right here, Mr. Fitch." A cyclist in the front row held up a rolled-up banner. His front-row teammates helped him unfurl it, and together they held it up. ANNOUNCING TEAM CADENCE-ECUABAR. PROUD PEDAL PARTNERS!

The name change jolted me. The team must have gotten a new co-title sponsor and bike supplier: Cadence Bikes. I suddenly remembered that Airborne had pulled its sponsorship, and its bikes, back in April. Jake had been sure it was because of his situation.

Any whiff of doping scandals sent sponsors running these days.

Chris Fitch looked down at the banner and beamed. I figured he had something to do with Cadence Bikes, even if he didn't look capable of riding one himself.

"Everyone ready?" The photographer adjusted the camera on the tripod.

"No." One of the front-row cyclists held up a hand. "El Cóndor. He's not here yet."

So Juan Carlos *was* here today. Somewhere. My heart beat a little faster.

"Photoshop him in later," said Chris Fitch, with a dismissive gesture. "We don't have all day to wait for somebody running on Latin American time."

Several riders chuckled, and Coach Mancuso laughed loudly. "Yep. He's probably busy styling his hair. For his fangirls." He winked at Preston. "What do you say, Preston? How much would you bet on that?"

Preston frowned. I did, too. That wasn't a nice way to talk about the team's star rider.

"But this photo's for the new website," another cyclist protested. "El Cóndor needs to be in it."

"You're right. He's always front and center," Coach Mancuso explained to Chris Fitch. "That's what gets our website hits. He brings all the ladies. Nobody wants to look at our ugly mugs."

Another wave of laughter rolled through the group. Preston smirked but still looked distracted. He pulled a cell phone out of his jersey pocket and started scrolling through it.

My stomach lurched. Maybe *I* was the one who'd driven up those website hits, circling back to the Team EcuaBar site as often as I had.

"Maybe he's with Dylan?" another cyclist suggested. "Someone should check the trailer."

The trailer. Where the team's bikes and gear were stored. Dylan must be the new team mechanic. Jake had mentioned that the original mechanic, Gage Weston, had been replaced recently, but he didn't know why.

Preston put his phone back in his pocket, an annoyed expression on his face. "If he doesn't show his face in five minutes, we'll have to ride without him," he said. "Who's our backup leader?"

On the junior team, that would have been Jake. But among the pros? I had no idea.

"Matt can lead," said Coach Mancuso, though his expression looked doubtful.

Chris Fitch folded his arms across his chest. "This is ridiculous. The media and spectators are here to watch Juan Carlos ride. I saw him a half hour ago, suiting up. I'm sure he's just lost track of time, or is chatting up some girl. I'm organizing a search party." He called some of the junior riders over and talked to them. They grabbed their bikes and took off in different directions.

Seeing everyone spring into action made me itch to do the same. I'd seen Juan Carlos before races all last summer and into the fall. I had a good idea of what he was doing. If I found him, I could get him to that photo. It would be an excuse to see him one last time, before his whirlwind of international races and product endorsements sucked him away. I'd never had a chance to wish him luck or even say good-bye. If I did it fast, Jake would never have to know that I'd slipped off to see el Cóndor in person.

8:30. Jake would be back any moment. But a moment was all I needed. I pedaled away from the barricades, out of the parking lot, and crossed Great Marsh Road, toward the woods.

3

IT TOOK me a minute of riding back and forth to spot him at the edge of the conservation land, where he sought refuge from cameras and crowds. With his olive skin and his green-and-white jersey, the trees almost camouflaged him. But there, beneath a maple tree, stood Juan Carlos Macias-León, his eyes closed, his head bowed in prayer. A breeze danced the branches around him. With one hand, he held his white bike helmet by the straps. The other hand was raised to his chest, clutching the gold crucifix necklace that he wore all the time.

I approached as quietly as I could, afraid to startle him in the middle of his prayers. But the sound of my brakes squeaking made him lift his head and turn. His dark brows knitted together as he looked around. Then he smiled. "Tessa?" His smile widened, displaying his even, white teeth. *"¡Qué sorpresa!"* His voice was as rich as I remembered, with so many notes contained in it, and a musical lilt. "You are doing this ride?"

I brought my bike to a stop in front of him. "Yes. I mean, no. I mean, I'm not riding." For a moment I forgot I was a bandit. For a moment I forgot I had come here with Jake. For a moment every rational thought flew right out of my head.

I was three feet away from el Cóndor.

I knew the details of his appearance, of course—those chocolate-brown eyes flecked with gold. Those high cheekbones.

That long, arched nose. That thick black hair, slicked back with gel, immune to the dreaded helmet head. As the Great New Hope for road cycling, Juan Carlos had been profiled in every bicycling magazine lately. And ever since the new EcuaBar campaign had launched, all I had to do was drive down I-93 to get my sixty-five-miles-per-hour Juan Carlos fix. He was larger-than-life on a billboard, tearing into an energy bar.

But here, up close, he was real. I could see a light sheen on his skin—the damp post-rain air settling on him. I was acutely aware of every water droplet that swirled in the mist around us. He was about three inches shorter than me, and a wild thought ran through my mind—would I wear flats if we were together?

I'd forgotten how nervous I could feel around him. Looking down, I noticed an angry black mark on my right calf, almost like a bruise. The imprint of gear teeth, caused from leaning against the chain ring. A year into road biking and I was still getting these stupid grease tats, the mark of an amateur rider.

"You are here for *KidVision*?" Juan Carlos guessed.

"Yes," I lied, grateful for his assumption. "I'm covering the event for the show. Hey, I think your team's looking for you. They're doing a photo shoot."

Juan Carlos slapped his forehead. "*¡Ay! Miércoles.* I forgot all about it!" He emerged from the stand of trees. He tucked his crucifix necklace inside his cycling jersey, then zipped up his collar. The top of the jersey partially covered the slightly raised pink scar that cut a jagged path up the right side of his neck. "How did you know where to find me?"

I shrugged. "You said you always look for a quiet place and a tree where you can talk to God before races."

He looked impressed. "You remembered that?"

"Sure."

"And you came by yourself? Why didn't you tell my teammates to come find me here?"

"I thought you wanted your privacy." I didn't add that Jake and the other junior riders used to joke, behind his back, about el Cóndor's need for quiet and prayer while the rest of the team revved up. Nor did I mention they'd sometimes called him "the altar boy." As someone who got called PBS Princess by Jake's school friends, because of my goody-goody TV image, I'd always sympathized with Juan Carlos. We were both more than our nicknames.

He smiled. "You are right. Thank you."

"Anytime." We stood awkwardly for a moment, until I realized I was blocking his way with my bike. I maneuvered the front wheel to let him pass by.

But Juan Carlos didn't move. He looked at me. *Into* me.

I shivered, even though the heat and humidity were starting to burn through the haze.

"I am happy to see you here," he said. Then he added, almost under his breath, "You are the perfect person."

"What?!" Could he hear my heart hammer? "Perfect? Me?"

"Perfect to talk to. You listen. You remember things."

"Oh. Right." Of course. Perfect to talk to. Because I interviewed people on TV.

Juan Carlos looked around, even though the only person within possible earshot was one of those EcuaBar volunteers, the redhead girl I'd seen earlier, walking with her basket across the road from us. She stared from afar like a starstruck fan.

"Can we meet somewhere? And talk?" Juan Carlos asked in a low voice.

I shrugged, as if meeting him was no big deal. "Sure. I'm around this week. I guess we could meet up somewhere?"

"Actually, for me it would be better today. This afternoon.

Right after the race. Okay?" There was an urgency in his voice that I'd never heard before.

"This—this afternoon?"

"The team flies to Bogotá on Friday for the tri-country Pan-American Cycling Tour," he explained, talking quickly. "We will be three weeks in South America. We will not return to Boston until August."

"Can you meet sometime before Friday?"

"I can't. I will be busy with trip preparations and meetings."

"Sure. Okay. This afternoon." I massaged one elbow, pinching my skin. Was I betraying Jake by making a plan to talk to Juan Carlos?

"Do you have your phone with you?" Juan Carlos demanded.

"Um. Sure." I got my smart phone out of the saddle pouch strapped beneath my seat. As soon as I turned on the phone it began to vibrate. I saw Jake on the caller ID. I sucked in my breath and hit END before pulling up my contacts list and handing the phone to Juan Carlos.

"Call me at two," he said. "We can meet and talk right after the awards ceremony." He typed on the touchscreen. "I cannot believe my luck, to find you like this today." He looked up. "Do you have a laptop with you?"

"A laptop? Why would I have a laptop here?"

"For work."

"Oh, right." I was "working." For *KidVision*. "Yeah, I can probably find one."

"Perfect," he said, and returned to his touchscreen typing.

My heart galloped. Juan Carlos had said he was "happy" to find me. He wanted to talk as soon as possible. And I had hung up on my boyfriend, who was probably looking for me in the crowd right now. I was planning a crazy scheme. Where was I going to come up with a laptop computer, and why did he need one? Would I even be done with my ride by two? I'd be a sweaty mess. I'd have to make it look like I'd been interviewing riders all day for *KidVision*. I'd also have to find a way to separate myself from Jake long enough to talk to Juan Carlos. At least I had thirty miles to come up with a plan.

Juan Carlos handed back my phone. Our fingers brushed. An electric tingle ran through me. The phone still felt warm from his hand. I slid it into the back pocket of my cycling jersey. I swear I could feel the phone burning through fabric, warming my skin.

"I have to run," said Juan Carlos. "You will call? Please? It is very important."

"Yes. I will call. Definitely. At two." My phone buzzed again. I ignored it.

Suddenly Juan Carlos reached up toward his neck and unhooked his necklace in one swift movement. "Will you do me one more favor?" He gestured for me to hold out my hand. I did, and he poured the thick chain into it, slowly, like water. The crucifix, about three inches tall, felt heavy in my palm. "Can you take care of this for me? While I am on the ride?"

I stared at the gold cross, at the small figure of Jesus. It was a fairly simple cross, with bands of filigree running across all the ends. "You always wear this," I protested, handing it back.

"Not today. It is better that I do not."

"Oh. Is there some regulation about what kind of jewelry you can race in?"

"Something like that. I can explain you later. Here. Let me to help you." He plucked the necklace from my hand, his fingers stroking my skin and sending a spark through my whole body. "Turn, please?" He put the chain around my neck, lifted my braid in the back, and clasped the chain together. His breath was warm on my neck, and small shivers traveled down my back, all the way down my legs.

Oh my God.

"See you soon?" he said, a hopeful smile playing at his full lips when I turned to face him again.

"See you soon," I echoed, trying my best not to melt and become one with the asphalt. My eyes flicked down, taking in the top of the jagged pink scar at his neck, then up to his face again. "Good luck out there today!"

"*Gracias. Suerte, chica.* Have fun with your interviews. *Chao!*" And he ran off to join his team.

"Chao," I whispered, tasting the word. It tasted sweet. I put my hand up to the necklace and squeezed the gold cross. It felt warm and solid against my skin. My family wasn't religious. I'd never worn something like this. I imagined it protecting me. Not because it represented God or anything, but because it was from Juan Carlos. It had carried him through so many races. Maybe it would carry me through my ride today.

A new worry stabbed me. I couldn't let Jake see the necklace. He'd completely freak out.

I tucked it under my jersey, as I'd seen Juan Carlos do, and I zipped up the jersey as far as it would go. Then I got back on my bike and crossed the road, back toward the staging area.

I didn't have far to travel. Jake was pedaling toward me, a sour expression on his face.

4

JAKE CRUISED across the street, toward the woods. How much had he seen? I couldn't tell.

"I saw GBCN cameras," I told him, following. "I had to get away. So I came here."

He just kept riding. Silent treatment. Fantastic.

About ten feet from where I'd discovered Juan Carlos, Jake's wheels left the pavement, and he entered the woods. I turned to follow his path. As my wheels churned through dirt and gravel, my mind churned over possible explanations and excuses I could give him, to explain why I'd been talking to Juan Carlos, why I wasn't where Jake had left me.

About five minutes into our off-road riding, I couldn't watch him anymore, or even think. I fought to control my bike. The woods were closing in, choking the trail. There were slick patches of mud, probably oozing in from the great marsh that had earned Great Marsh Road its name. A mountain bike or a hybrid could handle this stuff, but not our skinny road-bike tires. After nearly skidding out, I hefted my bike over one shoulder and jogged after Jake.

When Jake dismounted a moment later, he didn't even stop moving. He slung his bike over one shoulder in one graceful movement, a tactic he'd perfected riding cyclocross on the off-season. While I got whacked in the face and scratched on the arms by every tree branch I passed, Jake glided between the trees, angling his bike so it didn't get scratched. He was careful that way. About his bike.

"Hey! Wait up!"

Jake turned and peered at me through the rear wheel of his bike. The spinning tire spokes changed his face, shuffling it through a Wheel of Fortune of expressions.

When I was about five steps behind him, the wheel stopped, and I saw the face I'd won. *Pissed.* So he'd seen Juan Carlos and me talking. Suddenly that necklace I was wearing felt enormous. Alive. Like the telltale heart ticking under the floor in the Poe story we read for English class.

"It's eight forty-five already," Jake said, his voice flat. "The race starts in fifteen. Better keep up."

"I'm *trying* to keep up."

"Oh, really? Is that why you took a little scenic detour to say *hola* to your old *amigo*?"

"There's nothing between us. You don't like him because he's confident. And lucky."

"Jesus, Tessa. You have such a blind spot about him. I've seen how he looks at you. I notice he's always popping up the moment I turn my back. And I'm not stupid. I see how you look at him, too. You're both waiting for me to disappear, so you can finally hook up."

"Did you seriously just say that? Because that is completely crazy."

"Is it?" He raised an eyebrow. "I know you've talked before, behind my back. Remember Harvard Square last month? Maybe you talk all the time."

That hurt. The Harvard Square meeting last month was actually about Jake. I was trying to get to the bottom of the doping allegations, to help him out. I thought Juan Carlos might have some clue who framed Jake for drugs. But no matter how much I'd insisted, Jake did not believe me. He'd almost punched Juan Carlos in the face after he ran into us there—I'd had to restrain his arm—and then he'd threatened to get Juan Carlos sent back to Ecuador if he moved in on me again. We'd broken up for two weeks about this stupid misunderstanding.

"Jake. I—"

Jake held up a hand. "You know what? Save your breath. You'll need it for the ride. Stay on the wheel out there." He turned and followed the path around a bend.

My feet remained rooted. Tears stung my eyes. As soon as I was sure Jake couldn't see me, I sank to the ground, holding my breath, trying not to cry. When Jake turned cold like that, it felt like getting slammed against ice.

I took a few deep breaths, trying to pull myself together. *Think, Tessa, think.* The best thing to do? Bail. I could walk back to the official starting line and sign on as a volunteer. In an hour, I could be at the first checkpoint, serving sandwiches and water to hungry riders. That would undo the lie I'd told to my parents. And when Jake cruised by the food table at the first water stop? I'd throw a sandwich right in his face and call him a—

No. What I should do was call Kristen, my *KidVision* producer. I could pitch a show idea about young riders and volunteers. I'd always wanted to do my own story, to say words that weren't scripted for me.

My mind raced with new ideas. If I called Kristen with a pitch, that would undo the lie I'd told Juan Carlos. I'd legitimately be here working for *KidVision* today. Then I could easily meet up with him after the race, hear what he wanted to tell me—*my God, what could it be?* I could give him back his necklace.

I stood up again and turned to peer through the thick trees behind me. I could still make out dots of red-and-white cycling jerseys at the starting line. In five minutes, if I pushed my bike and ran, I could be right back there. And maybe I could go back even further, back to my pre-Jake life. Was that my real starting line?

I dared myself to imagine a permanent breakup. I'd get my best friends back, full-time. Jake had thought Sarita and Kylie were loud, unambitious, and boring. They'd said he was moody and took up all my time.

And they had a point. If I wasn't out riding with Jake, I was hanging out at his races, even toughing it out at cyclocross meets in the fall and winter, standing in the rain. I'd paid for that time with my social life and my grades. My parents were freaking out.

But. If I ditched Jake, I'd lose the good stuff, too. The guy who had patiently coaxed me off my clunky hybrid and reliable old bike paths, and shown me the excitement of the open road. He had nudged me out of my comfort zone in so many ways. My past relationships had taken a long time to get off the ground. Maybe because everyone knows everyone's business when you go to a small school like mine, and people are leery of labels. But with Jake—I guess because we went to different schools—things had been intense from the start. He'd asked me out, to a bike gear expo, within minutes after that *KidVision* interview. He called and texted all the time. He'd called me his girlfriend after our third date.

Things with Jake had moved fast physically, too. Sometimes in our first weeks together, Jake and I would veer off-road on a country bike ride—here in Cabot or in neighboring towns—and find a patch of grass in a meadow. We'd mess around for a while, kissing while our hands explored, and traffic, oblivious to our bliss, rushed past on distant roads.

"You're so good for me. You remind me life isn't always a

race," he said to me one day late last summer, coiling my braid around his fingers as we lay side by side in the grass. "It's like, I don't know, I can stop and see the view with you. Pay attention to stuff around me more, instead of always looking over my shoulder to see who's coming up behind. When I'm with you, I don't care who's behind me. I just care who's next to me. You. I love that."

"Me too," I'd confessed, my whole body thrilling at his words. "Sometimes I feel like my whole life's been mapped out for me. School, college, everything. But you—"

He'd grinned. "I'm the unscheduled stop on your map."

I'd laughed. "A diversion. Right."

"No," he'd murmured, rolling toward me and cupping my face in his hands. "No way. Not a diversion. The *destination*."

That connection between us was powerful. I couldn't give up on us now. We just had to get through this ride together.

I hefted my bike and slung it over one shoulder. Then, in the bushes off to my right, a few yards away, something shiny caught my eye. I backed up a few steps and looked.

A bike wheel was sticking out from behind a cluster of shrubs. Bizarre.

I set down my bike and leaned it against a tree. I had to see what this thing was.

Sidestepping a patch of poison ivy, I circled the shrubs and saw what that wheel was attached to: a black bike frame with streamlined streaks of white and green paint. Its drop handlebars were wrapped with white bar tape, its carbon wheels black and shiny. I wasn't much of a gearhead, but I knew this bike did not belong off-road. I slowly extracted the bike from the bushes. It felt featherlight compared to mine. It was a fancy racing bike, with Kevlar tires, at high pressure, rock-hard. CADENCE was emblazoned on the frame.

This bike wasn't abandoned on someone's scenic detour. It had been *placed* here. *Hidden.*

Cadence made high-end consumer bikes, but they also supplied teams like EcuaBar with custom-made racing bikes. Could this be one?

Then I sucked in my breath, sharply, as I saw something else on the downtube. A white decal, with a border of green vines.

J. MACIAS

As in, *Juan Carlos Macias-Léon.* As in, oh my God. What was *his* bike doing here?

Team mechanics were supposed to supervise the bikes. Gage Weston had always guarded the bikes like a pit bull. Jake used to complain how the riders had to sign the bikes in and out of the trailer and the team's storage garage. But maybe this new mechanic, Dylan, was more relaxed . . . and maybe his casual attitude had resulted in the star rider's bike getting stolen.

I let out a long breath, trying to process this and figure out what to do. Just minutes ago, Juan Carlos had been praying, having no idea one of his bikes was stashed in the woods less than five hundred feet away!

But why would a thief *hide* the bike here, instead of riding away? Or stashing it in a car?

I knew from Jake that all the EcuaBar pros had two racing bikes. Their spares always had white-taped handlebars. So this had to be Juan Carlos's spare. Maybe a bike thief had thought the spare would be an easier target. Also, Juan Carlos would still have his main bike fitted and ready to ride. A stolen spare bike wouldn't throw off his whole race.

Still, I had to let Juan Carlos or someone on Team EcuaBar know what I'd found. But how? I couldn't run, with my bike and his, back to the staging area to find him before the professional race began.

Then I remembered that I had gold: Juan Carlos's number.

I carefully leaned the bike against the bushes where I'd found it. I took out my phone, pulled up my contacts list, scrolled to *J*, and found the name and number he'd typed there. I called. No answer. Not even voice mail. So I texted him as fast as I could.

> Hey, ur spare bike is in woods near where we were just talking! Walking path. Someone should pick it up or should I

Startled by a sudden noise, I accidentally hit SEND before I could finish the message.

Swish, snap.

I sat back on my heels and listened. Birds twittered in branches. I must have heard Jake, ahead on the path, snapping twigs as he walked.

Swish, snap. There it was again. The sound came from behind me, from the direction of the road I'd come from. That couldn't be Jake. Footsteps through underbrush distinctly came from off to the right, a few yards from the walking path—and from me.

SwishSNAPswishSNAPswishSNAP.

"This can't be the right place. I didn't see a spray-painted boulder anywhere." A man was speaking in a low voice. Talking on the phone, I guessed; I heard only one set of footsteps. "Why here? *Mumble.* No. Check again."

Crouching low, I scuttled a few feet away to the big tree where my own bike was propped, hoping the generous branches would conceal me from this guy's view.

"Any chance he's lying about where it is? Trying to *mumble mumble*? . . . I don't know. Put him on. What? *Mumble?* What do you mean he won't talk to me? What—no! Lock it. Tie *mumble mumble* if you have to."

I missed a bunch of words, but it sounded like he was up to something. Lock what? Tie what? I turned on the video camera on my phone. I didn't know if it would catch anything, or if the audio would pick up the conversation. But I was an obsessive viewer of *Watchdog*, the investigative reporting show on GBCN. And I knew from its host, reporter Bianca Slade, that ordinary citizens could help prosecute criminals. On her list of Qualities of Good Investigative Reporters, the first one was Being Observant. *Note details in your surroundings and your day-to-day life. If you can safely and legally capture suspicious details on film, even better.* Details. Yes. I made sure to capture the bike on film as I panned the area. I also filmed the walking path I'd come up, and I rotated slowly 360 degrees.

Through the screen, I glimpsed a blue bicycle helmet through the trees. The guy wearing it came closer, into view. He looked huge—broad shoulders, biceps, thick neck.

"Fine. I'm calling *mumble*," said the guy in the blue helmet. "He should know."

I heard the sharp beep of a hangup. Then, after a pause, "Hello?"

The start of a second phone call.

"Mangoes," the guy said in a low voice, "are best at this time of year."

Mangoes? In New England? Was that what he was looking for—a secret mango grove? We didn't grow mangoes anywhere near here. Maybe he meant mangoes at the grocery store. Or maybe the guy was just deranged. An escapee from some institution.

I had zero desire to meet him in person.

Still holding my cell phone in one hand, the video still recording, I stood up, grabbed my bike, and slung it over one shoulder. I tried to get back to the walking path as quietly as I could.

"*Mumble mumble* call you back." The guy's phone beeped again. "Hey!" the man shouted.

It took me a moment to realize he was not talking on the phone anymore. He was talking to—and staring at—me.

I spun around and ran down the path, away from him, my bike wheels banging against my body.

5

"STOP! RIGHT now!" the guy shouted, thrashing through underbrush.

I glanced back and saw him leap easily over a felled log.

I stopped short. I was an idiot, running with my back to him. The guy could have a gun.

We stood about five yards apart and stared at each other. Remembering Bianca Slade's advice about details, I tried to memorize everything about this creep in case I had to report him. Assuming I got out of these woods alive.

He looked to be in his mid to late twenties—thirty, tops. His brown hair was cut close to his head. A Bluetooth device with a blinking light was attached to one ear. He wore cycling shorts and a Chain Reaction jersey. He looked like a cyclist at first glance. But he had a football player's physique, not a cyclist's. He wore mirrored aviator sunglasses instead of cycling shades. Gleaming white tennis shoes, not cycling cleats.

A bike would help the look, too. Only he didn't have one.

His nostrils flared. "Take off your helmet," he said, his voice harsh. "Your sunglasses."

With shaking hands, I set down my bike and removed both those items. I hoped that was all he'd ask me to remove.

Even though I couldn't see his eyes, I felt the force of his gaze as he looked me up and down from behind those mirrored shades. "Tell me why you're here."

"I'm doing the cancer ride. Chain Reaction?"

"You don't have an official jersey."

"I didn't buy an official jersey."

"And why not?"

"I-I-I only wear organic cotton." My tongue felt thick and dry. Could this guy be a ride official, checking out my story? No. Ride officials didn't skulk around in the woods. They were out on the ride.

"Did you follow me here?" he asked next.

"No!" Wait. Maybe he was a bandit rider, too. "I am doing the ride," I insisted. "I was just on a cut-through."

"A cut-through." The man smirked. "Now I get it. You're a cheater."

"I'm *not* a cheater. I'm just—"

"You're wasting my time. Give me your phone."

I looked down at the phone, still recording. My hand was so hot and sweaty, the phone almost slipped out.

He snatched the phone, then wiped it on his jersey with a look of disgust. He looked at the screen and jabbed the button to stop the video recording. He played back what I'd recorded, then hit PAUSE. "That bike. Where'd you see it?"

I pointed in the direction we'd run from. "Back there. Down the path." Juan Carlos's bike. Was he an undercover detective trying to bust a bike thief? He didn't seem like a cop. Then again, I hadn't had many encounters with police. Or any encounters, actually.

"How far back?" he asked.

"I—I'm not sure."

"Try to recall."

I squinted helplessly into the woods behind him and the curved walking path. I swear more trees had sprung up, fairy-tale style, in the two minutes that we'd been talking. "Maybe ten yards back? It was near that big rotted-out tree stump. I found it in a bunch of bushes."

"Okay. You've done me a favor. I'm going to let you go. But here's the deal." His eyes locked on mine. "You were never on this path. You never saw me. You never saw that bike."

Mutely, I nodded. That wasn't how cops generally talked. He definitely wasn't a cop.

"You breathe one word about this bike or our little chat, and you will pay. I can screw things up for you bad. Do you understand?"

"I got it. Can I have my phone back?"

"In a moment." He reached into his jersey pocket, checked his own phone as if for a message, and repocketed it. Then he looked through my phone for a minute or two, scrolling and typing, before handing it back to me between two fingers, as if it were something dead.

"I took the liberty of deleting your little home movie," he said. "Now go. Go! Before I change my mind!"

I didn't need any more urging. I lifted my bike and ran. As soon as I got back to the walking trail, I jumped on my bike and rode. My teeth chattered as I pounded the pedals, over rocks and sticks, in the direction that Jake had gone.

6

THE WOODS thinned out, revealing an eerily quiet Great Marsh Road, closed to traffic for the ride. No spectators, no ride officials, no cameras. No witnesses, if that mango-loving madman decided to burst out of the woods and kill me.

I checked my watch. 8:56. Jake and I had been apart for only eleven minutes. It seemed like so much longer. Where was he anyway?

I rode a few yards down the road, following it around a bend. There Jake stood, straddling his bike, adjusting a biking glove. I wanted to throw my arms around him. Any doubts I'd had about Jake minutes ago suddenly didn't matter. I'd made it out of the woods.

"Well, howdy, stranger. Long time no see," he said in a flat voice as I pulled up beside him.

Legs wobbling, I dismounted. "Jake. Something happened back in the woods. I found—"

"My glove?" He held up a bare hand. "Forgot to zip my saddle pouch. Must've fallen out."

First the forgotten sports drinks and now this? He was off his game today. But that wasn't important right now. "No, I found something else. Jake, I'm really scared."

He finally turned to look at me. His face softened into concern.

"You do look pretty rattled. Okay, take a deep breath. Calm down. What happened?"

I spilled the facts: the bike in the bushes, the angry man, the threats he'd hurled at me. I left out the detail about the bike belonging to Juan Carlos. I couldn't quite bring myself to say Juan Carlos's name to Jake. "Did you see the bike? Or the guy?" I finished.

"Nope. Nothing. No one."

"So what does this sound like to you? Did I see a bike theft in progress?"

"I bet you did," Jake agreed. "A thief probably left a bike at a drop point, and you ran into the fence."

"I ran into the what?"

"The fence. Oh, I forgot. While you're making quality television programming for kids, the rest of us are rotting our brains on cop shows. A fence picks up and sells stolen goods."

"A middleman. Okay. That makes sense," I said. "From the phone conversation I overheard, it sounded like he was trying to pick up something that had been left for him in the woods, like at a drop point. He mentioned a spray-painted rock, and how the bike hadn't been there. But aren't fences used for big-ticket items, like cars? This is just a bike."

"Not just a bike," said Jake. "A *high-end* bike. And bikes get stolen at charity events."

"Why?"

"Rich bastards with their fancy steeds get all caught up in the moment. They wander off and forget to lock them. That frame will show up on eBay or Craigslist. I guarantee."

But this was *el Cóndor's* team bike. "What if the bike belonged to a team?" I ventured. "A person couldn't just sell that on eBay. It would obviously be stolen."

"Team names can be painted over. Decals can be scraped off," said Jake. "Why? You think this was a team bike?"

I hesitated. Mentioning Cadence meant steering us into Juan Carlos territory again. "I don't know."

"Actually, you *could* sell a stolen team bike," Jake went on. "Some people pay thousands of dollars for sports equipment used by pro athletes. Like a baseball bat used by David Ortiz, or anything touched by an NFL player. There's a legitimate market for stuff like that, but also an underground one."

"Underground? Like a black market?"

"Yeah. There's serious money to be made by people willing to loot sports items and move them to private buyers."

So the guy in the woods could have hired a thief to do the dirty work of stealing Juan Carlos's bike. The thief could get it out of the staging area and to a drop point in the woods. Then the fence—the guy I'd run into?—could pick it up, transport it away after the race started, and sell it.

"I think we should call the police," I said. "But what if this guy, this *fence*, finds out I reported him? After he warned me not to? Because of *KidVision*, I'm not exactly anonymous." I pressed my lips together, thinking. "Hey, what if *you* called and said *you* saw a bike hidden in the bushes?"

"No way," said Jake. "I am so done talking to cops."

"I'm going to go back to the staging area and find a police officer there."

"I would remind you that we cut through the woods on a charity ride. We're going to look bad just being here. They might think we had something to do with it."

"But we didn't! And it's our duty as citizens to share information about possible crimes."

"And it's our right not to incriminate ourselves. If we talk to a cop, he'll take down our names. Then we're on the record as kids looking for trouble. The police are not our friends. Anything we say can be used against us. Didn't your lawyer dad teach you that?"

I glared at Jake. "He taught me that it's a crime not to report a crime."

"You don't have any proof. Look"—Jake scratched his neck—"I went through hell with this doping allegation stuff. Nothing good comes from talking to cops. The more you say, the bigger the hole you dig for yourself. Anyway, the race is about to start. And guess what? Bikes get stolen. It's not our problem. We don't even know the people involved."

"But we do," I blurted out. "I mean, we might."

Jake gave me a long look. The kind of look he gave me when he knew I was holding back.

I plunged ahead. A theft was in process, and we did know the victim. This was bigger than us. "It's a Cadence bike. The decal said 'J. Macias.' The bike belongs to el Cóndor."

Jake kicked the ground and swore under his breath. He looked past me down the road, cutting me out with his gaze.

"Talk to me," I pleaded. "This has nothing to do with us. It's about doing the right thing. Don't you think we should help him get his bike back?"

BANG.

I jumped and glanced back at the woods behind me.

"Starting gun. The race is on." Jake clipped one foot into a pedal.

I clipped a foot into a pedal, too, even though riding this event was now the last thing I wanted to do. But no way was I going to turn around and go back through those woods.

Two police motorcycles zoomed past, too fast to flag down. They were almost immediately followed by a SAG wagon—a flatbed truck with a support crew and equipment—and a media truck. The cameras were trained on the peloton of professional cyclists, now fast approaching. The bicycle wheels thrummed like cicadas. Heads bowed, backs hunched, legs pumping, the riders whizzed by. There went Firestone-Panera. Velo-Olympus. And Team EcuaBar, in third place, shot past like a green-and-white comet.

I didn't see Juan Carlos. And I'd always been able to spot him in the peloton, even when they went upwards of thirty miles per hour. I'd been to a lot of races by now. Juan Carlos always stood out, and not just because he had the darkest skin on the team. How many times had I let my gaze drift from Jake to Juan Carlos at races—even as I cheered myself hoarse for Jake?

Jake rode like a machine designed for maximum efficiency. He pounded hills, pulled back on descents, leaned into curves with precision. His gaze was intense, his smile a grimace. Juan Carlos was different. He always seemed calm, even joyful, when riding. Grinning like a kid. Light on the wheels. Jake knew how to handle his bike, but Juan Carlos rode the air.

The women's pro teams zipped by. The fastest group of rec riders would be coming next. Because I was new to this, Jake had planned for us to merge with the medium-speed group. Even so, we were looking at a two-lane road with a narrow shoulder, not much space to maneuver, and almost no time to get up to speed.

The fast recs shot by in a red-and-white blaze.

Still no sign of Juan Carlos. Clearly I'd missed him going by.

Jake nudged his bike onto the road.

"Wait!" I said. "Wrong group! They're way too fast for me."

"Good luck, *chica*," Jake sneered as he shoved off and joined the riders.

7

"JAKE! WAIT!" I shouted. I jammed my foot into a pedal clip and bore down hard, slanting toward the advancing peloton of highly skilled recreational riders. The road, still wet, was slick and slippery. My front wheel skidded out. Water sprayed my back as I rode through a puddle.

"Hey! Learn how to ride!" a woman yelled at me. A sign taped to the back of her jersey fluttered. "Squirrel," she spat at me as she passed. Then she gave me the finger.

Squirrel. That hurt. That's what cyclists call panicky riders who can't hold their line. I pedaled hard, still veering right, trying to hold my line as I approached the peloton and then rode alongside it. I scanned for a break where I could dip in. I found that break and merged.

I couldn't see Jake. I couldn't believe he'd ditched me because of Juan Carlos.

Or was Juan Carlos really the reason?

I held my breath. Maybe he'd planned to merge early all along, and then catch up with the professional race. Maybe Jake wanted to get attention from the Firestone-Panera managers or someone else. To be a wonder kid again. Or maybe doing the recreational ride as if it were a race—his own race—was all a weird way of protesting against Preston Lane, Coach Mancuso, everyone. *Thanks for nothing, assholes. Look what Team Cadence-EcuaBar missed.*

Whatever his reason for jumping the gun, it was clear that he wasn't doubling back. He'd dropped me. I was on my own.

I stood on my pedals, pumping hard, fueled by pure rage. My braid slapped against my shoulder. When my thigh muscles strained, I pulled up on the handlebars as Jake had taught me, and felt a little relief. Minutes later, I took a hill full throttle and even passed a rider.

Jake had always cautioned me about pacing myself so I didn't bonk. But now I didn't care. Grinning, I pumped the pedals in my easiest gears. I felt like a nine-year-old kid again, on my old hybrid bike that I'd nicknamed Columbus. For an instant, I was back on the Minuteman bike path, free and easy, imagining that my bike was enchanted and might take me to places unknown. Riding for pure fun.

On a long descent I kept pedaling, gaining even more speed. The energy of the other riders carried me along. I smiled at the funny helmet decorations some teams had chosen—wings, antennas, children's toys. A fleet of penguins atop helmets zoomed past on my right, a team of stuffed green Kermit the Frog helmets on my left. I could totally get through thirty miles with all this entertainment.

After that descent, the road shoulder widened and crowds appeared. "Go, Chain Reaction riders!" they shouted, jangling cowbells and waving homemade signs. Kids held out their hands for the riders to slap as we passed.

All that energy went into my body. *Pure energy.* Like EcuaBar.

But I wasn't remembering that slogan—I was *seeing* it. On the back of a green-and-white cycling jersey a few yards ahead. I passed another rider and got a bit closer to make sure.

It was Juan Carlos!

He rode a black, green, and white Cadence bike, identical to the one I'd seen in the woods, only this one had green handlebar tape. His main ride.

What was he doing so far back? In a road race, a team's *domestiques*, or "servant" riders, were supposed to protect the lead cyclist, to help him save energy for strategic moves like breakaways, hill climbs, and attacks. Team cycling was all about strategy. And no one could ride all-out for one hundred miles.

So had Juan Carlos not started the race with his team? Or had his team dropped him?

Juan Carlos was getting farther away from me, passing riders, making up for lost time. My legs burned. I sucked wind. I couldn't maintain this pace.

I scooted left and got behind a paceline. Six women were riding in a straight line, close to one another's back wheels. They all wore paper signs pinned to the backs of their jerseys. The signs said TEAM MAUREEN and showed a photo of a smiling woman. I recognized one of the women in the paceline as the woman who'd called me a squirrel.

There was only one way I could attempt to chase Juan Carlos. Drafting.

Jake had told me about how drafting works on our very first "date" last year. "The leader in a paceline generates most of the energy and blocks the wind for everyone else," he'd explained, standing close behind me as we watched a video of one of his races at the Boston Bicycle Expo. "The rest of the riders in the line get pulled in the slipstream, increasing their speed a few miles an hour without having to spend more energy. Then they take turns pulling up front and leading. The whole team can gain five or ten miles an hour that way."

Now I came within inches of the bike wheel in front of me, just as I'd watched Jake and his team do in that video and, later, in countless live races. I checked the gear that the rider in front of me was in, and I shifted into the same gear. That was it. I was drafting!

It felt as close as I'd ever come to flying. I instantly felt the pull, the boost.

I tried to keep Juan Carlos in sight. Then I glanced down at my wheel. Oh, no. I was overlapping the wheel in front of me. And we were starting another descent. I feathered the brakes instead of squeezing them hard, to try to stay in control. Then I downshifted, matching the gears of the paceline again. Success. I grinned. I was keeping up! The paceline hadn't accelerated and dropped me. Maybe they didn't know I was there.

But my conscience nagged. Drafting strategically in a race was legit. Drafting a paceline, without ever taking a turn at the lead? That made you a "wheelsucker." A "leech."

A yellow diamond sign with the words SLOW DEAF CHILD distracted me for a moment. I felt sorry for whoever that was, his or her disabilities announced to the world.

I caught sight of Juan Carlos off to my right, toward the road shoulder. Oh my God. I was *passing* him now, with the help of my poached paceline. Either I was riding faster than I'd ever ridden, or Juan Carlos was in some kind of trouble.

He was grimacing, looking down at something. Was something wonky with his bike? God, I hoped not. Unless he'd gotten my half-finished text and sent someone to retrieve that spare bike in the woods, he was screwed if his main bike had a mechanical problem.

Was he going to pull over? Had he lost contact with his team? The pros all wore earpieces and two-way radios to communicate with their coaches, but sometimes things went wrong. Could I give him my phone? Could I help?

I swerved back. He thought I was here with *KidVision*, not riding. What could I do?

Stay on the wheel, Tessa.

I looked straight ahead, blinked, and focused on that photo on the jersey in front of me. The woman pictured smiled warmly, one arm slung around a golden retriever. Beneath her marched somber black numbers. *1974–2014.*

The woman was Maureen. The woman was dead. This team rode to honor her memory.

My mind flashed to Kylie's mom. Beth Sullivan had been diagnosed with breast cancer last fall. I hadn't been such a good friend to Kylie all the months her mom was in chemo. A couple of weeks ago, I'd seen her mom at an end-of-year academic awards assembly. I'd been so startled, I could hardly look at her, even as I gave her a hug and asked how she was feeling. She had lost her hair and her eyebrows. She had dark circles under her eyes. I'd said some cheerfully optimistic things, then escaped as fast as I could. I didn't know how Kylie did it—kept up her spirits, her grades, her activities, with the fear of losing her mom always hanging over her.

Seeing that image in front of me—which might as well have been Beth Sullivan—I could not be on this ride anymore. Game over. I was out.

The hill got steeper and started to curve. What had Jake done on curves? He'd brought up one knee higher so the bike would lean and turn, and not shoot forward. Right knee or left? When? No. I had to get out before the turn got too sharp. I had to get out now.

Without sparing even one second to glance behind me, I jerked my front wheel toward the right road shoulder. I dropped out of the slipstream. And slipped.

8

KALEIDOSCOPE. SHARP images. Spokes and derailleurs. Tires and chains. Everything spinning, spinning, spinning. A high-pitched whining sound.

Then I was on asphalt, spitting dirt.

That whine, and scraping sounds, went on and on. It took me another moment to realize it was the sound of bikes falling. People behind me continued to crash.

I eased myself up on one elbow. My cleats had come out of the pedal clips. My bike was several feet away.

"Riders down! Riders down!" people shouted. More approaching cyclists swerved, way out to the opposite road shoulder. Some got off their bikes to help people; others kept going. I hoped Juan Carlos was one who kept going. I hoped he wouldn't see me like this.

Juan Carlos. The necklace. I reached up and felt the cross outline beneath my jersey, and the gold chain firmly clasped. Still there.

I checked in with my arms and legs, my fingers and toes, and, lastly, my head. Everything moved. I crawled over to my bike, then dragged it to the road shoulder. My beautiful Bianchi. The pretty mint-green frame was scratched up. Two spokes were bent in the front wheel. How could I have been so stupid not to look behind me when I pulled out?

I turned and took in the full horror of the scene. Another paceline had stopped short to avoid me. Some cyclists ahead of me had crashed, too, maybe startled by the noise. I counted ten riders down behind me, eight up ahead—including some from Team Maureen. Riders were groaning, holding knees and elbows, surveying damage to bike frames.

I knew I should help people. Instead, I froze. What if someone recognized me as the girl who had *caused* this pileup? Sure, the road was wet. But that was all the more reason for me to have been more careful riding outside of my skill area.

A huge gray shark, jaw flapping, made its way up the road, hovering above the crowds. Hallucination? Head injury? I blinked. No. It was an inflatable shark, like for a swimming pool, lashed to the top of a support van. All the support vans, sponsored by various bike shops, had animal or fish floaties for visibility. Jake had told me to watch out for them. Support vans carried mechanics but also ride officials.

The van's horn blared. Cyclists, still coming up to the crash scene, veered right to let it pass. COMPASS BIKES, CAMBRIDGE, MA, I read on the side of the van. In smaller letters: TAKING YOU PLACES. The store logo was an old-fashioned compass rose on a bike wheel.

The van stopped when it got to the pileup. A girl who looked to be around my age jumped out of the driver's side. She wore a green Compass Bikes T-shirt with the short sleeves rolled up. She scanned the downed riders and, spotting me, frowned and ran to my side.

"Are you okay?" The girl dropped to her knees. Her short brown hair barely made it into a ponytail. She blew her long bangs out of her eyes in order to look at mine. "Did you hit your head?"

"No. I landed on my side."

"Can you move your arms and legs?"

I demonstrated.

She held my right arm and inspected it. She looked tough, like she might lift serious weights. Her fingers were blackened with bike grease. Yet her face was pretty, her features soft. She had large brown eyes, full lips, olive skin, and a look of intense concern on her face. I hoped she'd sympathize with me and not ask too many questions.

"You're lucky. Your brain bucket worked." She reached over and tapped my helmet. "Looks like you're walking out of this with just a nasty case of road rash. That must kill."

It didn't, until I followed her gaze. My right arm and leg looked like raw meat spiced with sand. Then the pain hit all at once. I sucked in my breath.

"I'll take you back to the medical tent." She offered an arm.

"N-no, thanks," I stammered. "No medical tent. Really. I'm fine."

"They can give you something for the pain. And you'll want to get those scrapes irrigated. Let's get you up. Go easy." She was shorter than me by several inches but pulled me to my feet with her strong arms. She looped one of my arms over her shoulder and helped me limp toward the van, pushing my bike along with her free hand. "I'm Mari, by the way. What's your name?"

Clearly she didn't recognize me from TV. Still, a fake name—Teresa—flew out of my mouth. "I can't get medical services," I added, thinking fast. "My rider number flew off."

"No worries. We'll look you up in the system," Mari said. "So what happened out there anyway?" She suddenly looked a little less friendly. Her gaze was intense. Was I imagining it, or did she suspect me of being the cause of all this?

"I saw people suddenly wipe out in front of me. I couldn't stop in time." I winced. What was wrong with me? I went to a school founded on Quaker values, a school that launched people like Preston Lane into the world. And here I was, leaking lies all over the road.

Mari lowered me into a seat in the van, giving me a long look. "Where's your friend?"

"What friend?" I felt dizzy.

"That guy you were with. He was wearing a black jersey like yours."

She'd seen us together. I *knew* we'd attract attention.

"I don't know what you're talking about. I wasn't with anyone," I managed to say. Part of me wanted to rat Jake out. Payback for having dropped me. But the old instinct to protect him kicked in.

"I'm sure I saw you on the road together earlier. Who is he? And where is he?"

"I really don't know who you're talking about. I was doing the ride alone." That was almost true. I got dropped. I *was* doing the ride alone, in the end. "I swear," I insisted, when she crossed her arms. "A friend of mine was going to do it with me, but he—he changed his mind."

"So your guy's not somewhere out on the course now."

"Honestly? I have absolutely no idea where he is." No lie.

Mari's gaze lingered on me a moment longer. Then she glanced back at the cyclists on the road shoulder. "Okay, then. I have to go scoop up more roadkill. Be right back."

Relieved she no longer seemed interested in Jake, I caught sight of myself in the rearview mirror as I took off my helmet. I did look like roadkill. Sweaty. Streaked with dirt and blood.

I felt like bolting and rejoining the ride. But my bike was a mess. Make a run for it? No. My arm and leg killed. I'd just get my wounds cleaned up and find somewhere to wait for Juan Carlos.

The van filled up with six other riders complaining of injuries and busted bikes. Everyone tried to piece together what had happened as Mari turned around and drove back down Great Marsh Road, past the ride still in progress. One woman said a novice rider probably started the crash. "People ride outside their skill area and their speed group; it's a recipe for disaster," she said, and everyone murmured their agreements.

I shrank into my seat and stared out the window. The trees at the edge of the conservation land seemed more crowded together than before, concealing all their secrets.

Was Juan Carlos's spare bike still in those woods? Doubtful. Unless Juan Carlos had gotten my text and sent someone in to retrieve the bike, the fence must have found it by now.

One thing was for sure. Even with this road rash, I'd find a way to talk to Juan Carlos after the race and tell him what had gone down in those woods. I pictured the look of gratitude on his face when the police brought the mango man into custody and returned Juan Carlos's stolen spare bike.

Then at least one good thing would come out of this horrible day.

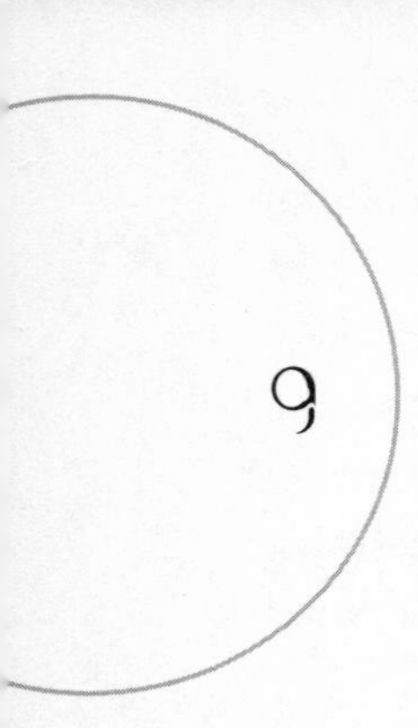

9

IN THE medical tent, Mari helped me into a folding chair and handed me a bottle of cold water. I gulped it down gratefully, forgetting that, as a bandit, I was not even entitled to an ice cube.

"So I'm going to go look you up in the system and get your medical release form," said Mari. "What was your rider number again?"

"292."

"Okay. Patricia here will take care of you." She seemed warmer now, but still wary of me, as she turned me over to an EMT, an unsmiling woman who immediately set to work cleaning my wounds. I hoped Patricia worked fast. Partly because the pain was excruciating. Partly because Mari would discover soon enough that I'd given her a fake registration number.

A siren wailed in the distance. My whole body tensed. What if someone were really hurt badly, all because of my dumb split decision?

Patricia switched on a bright lamp and inspected my scrapes. "Twenty-one?"

"I'm seventeen."

"No. Miles per hour. I'm guessing how fast you were going when you went down." She squirted my leg wound with a syringe of antiseptic.

"Not sure." God, that stuff stung. I gritted my teeth and closed my eyes. I pictured the slick asphalt and those few thrilling moments of near-flight when I'd drafted.

"You're lucky it's not worse," said Patricia. "At least it's only skin abrasions. I'll put on some antibiotic dressings after we clean everything. You can use vitamin E oil for scarring prevention. It's not like, you know, *cancer*," she added, plunging into my leg with the tweezers. "Whatever you're going through right now, it's not chemo. There are survivors among us."

I nodded, feeling smaller by the second.

"Hey." The woman looked up and studied my face. "Have I seen you before? Maybe in a TV commercial or something?"

"I doubt it."

"Hmm." She studied me, then shrugged and continued harvesting dirt from my leg.

With my good arm, I unwound my long braid and shook out my hair, letting it fall messily around my face in a lame attempt at disguise.

Mari returned with a skinny, fortyish guy wearing a green Compass Bikes T-shirt like hers, and a Chain Reaction baseball cap, backward. He had salt-and-pepper hair and an eyebrow ring. An aging hipster type.

He was also someone I'd met before. Gage Weston. The former mechanic from Team EcuaBar.

I averted my face. My heart thudded. We'd met only a handful of times, at races and one party. I hadn't seen him since October, the end of racing season last year. Maybe he wouldn't remember me.

"This is Gage, my boss," said Mari. "He's the manager of Compass Bikes. And he's one of the ride marshals. Gage, this is Teresa."

Gage looked down at his iPad. "What'd you say your rider number was?"

"292."

"Nothing's coming up."

"Maybe it was 291? Or 293? I'm so bad at remembering numbers."

"I checked all the 290s. You're under eighteen?"

The air in the tent felt close. "Yeah. But I'm going to be a senior in the fall?" I added, as if that might compensate. I tipped my head and flashed him my *KidVision* smile.

"Congratulations. But if you're a minor, we need a medical release form signed by your parents. Plus a consent and liability form. You filled those out when you registered?"

I looked down at my lap.

Finally, Gage looked at me. "I've seen you before. Aren't you Jake Collier's girlfriend?"

My cheeks burned. I nodded, even though I wasn't sure what Jake and I were right now. And I could feel Mari's laserlike stare. Judging me. Hating me. I felt so small. Other people nearby—people being treated for injuries or waiting for friends—also turned to look. Including that redheaded EcuaBar girl I'd seen before, still carrying her basket of samples.

"Yeah," said Gage, sizing me up. "I thought you looked familiar. Jake's girl."

Jake's girl. That's what some of his teammates had called me. I'd embraced "Jake's girl" like a cool shirt that wasn't my style. Now I didn't love it. I had my own name. I had my own life.

A muscle twitched at Gage's temple. "You know what I think?

"What."

"I think you were bandit riding."

Goose bumps. *How did he know?*

"And bandits usually ride in teams. Anyone else on the course I ought to know about?"

God knew where Jake was on the course. Again, I was

tempted to rat him out. But I didn't want to go down that road again, dealing with Jake and accusations. And even though I was mad at him, there was no point getting him in more trouble. I didn't need revenge.

I glanced at Mari, who looked like she was about to speak up. "I'm on my own," I said before she could talk. "But bandit riding isn't illegal." I met Gage's gaze. "We all pay for the roads. It's a free country." That was one of Jake's favorite arguments in favor of bandit riding.

"You're right," said Gage. "God bless America. It's not a crime to be on the ride. But it sure as hell is a safety issue during a major cycling event. Allow me to educate you, young lady. The ride organizers hire support staff like EMTs, police officers, and bike mechanics. They reroute traffic and close down roads. All these safety precautions are based on the number of registered riders. Having extra riders out there puts everyone in jeopardy. Especially when unregistered riders engage in reckless behavior."

"I didn't mean to hurt anyone," I protested. "I swear, I had just decided to quit the ride."

"You had no business on the route at a big event like this." Gage's voice rose. "And imagine if you'd been hurt worse. Unconscious. We wouldn't have known who to contact. Mari here left the support vehicle to help you. You've taken one of my top mechanics off the road."

I stole another glance at Mari. She stood with her hands in her shorts pockets, all the warmth and sympathy drained from her face.

"You're wasting our time and resources," Gage said. "Maybe you thought hijacking was all for yuks, but there are serious riders out there still, who may have equipment failures or other medical issues going on, and we're here babysitting a teenage bandit. You've let down those riders, their sponsors, and every individual volunteering today."

"I'm so sorry," I whispered. No lie. I wanted to go back on the course and apologize.

Out of the corner of my eye, I noticed a woman at the station next to me, holding an ice pack to her elbow. Staring at us. The woman from Team Maureen. The one who'd seen my unsafe merge. I turned my head away.

"You've said sorry," said Gage, "but words won't erase what you've done. As soon as you're cleaned up, why don't you high-tail it out of here. Got a ride?"

I shook my head. Jake? Forget it. Besides, I couldn't leave. The awards ceremony was just a few hours away. I had to stick it out and meet with Juan Carlos, like we'd planned.

"So get busy. Call someone." Gage looked like he wasn't going to budge until I made that call. What was I supposed to do? Calling Jake was out of the question. I was too mortified to call my best friends. Kylie would be horrified, given how she felt about cancer these days. Sarita, the world's Oldest Living Girl Scout, would lay the guilt on thick. My dad? I was the apple of his eye, and might have his sympathy. But he was at a weekend men's retreat, drumming in the woods, under a doctor's strict orders to "explore stress reduction techniques."

That left only one person.

When I got my mom on the phone, I was sure everyone in the tent could hear her freaking out. ("You did what? I need to pick you up where? This is unbelievable! We are going to have a SERIOUS TALK.") After she was through with me, my mom was going to need to explore a few stress reduction techniques herself—and maybe I was, too.

"I'm sorry," I said to Mari, after Gage stomped off to deal with some other crisis.

Mari glared at me. "You crash cancer rides? Why would you do that?"

"Not *rides.* Just this one. It's . . . complicated."

"I'm sure it is."

It was one dumb mistake, I wanted to tell her. *Can't a person make one dumb mistake?* Patricia got up to get more supplies.

"So. Your boyfriend," said Mari. "Or whoever he is. He's out there, isn't he? Riding."

I hesitated. "He is."

"He's Juan Carlos's old teammate?"

"Yep."

"He's just bandit riding? That's it?"

I hesitated. "What else would he be doing?"

"I don't know. You tell me."

"He's training. It's a secret. He's planning a big comeback. He's not taking any ride resources. I swear."

Mari tipped her head, considering this. "All right," she finally said. "Whatever drama you guys have going on, I won't spill it."

"Thanks. And hey. I want you to know, I was bailing on the ride. I—"

Mari held up a hand and walked away.

Patricia came back and dove into my leg again with the tweezers, with renewed zeal, and the pain took my breath away. I bit down on my thumb.

I thought of Juan Carlos.

He'd seemed different out on the course. Usually when he rode, I pictured wings streaming behind him. The way he held his shoulders back so proudly always stirred something inside me. Watching Jake ride made me feel proud, too, but tense, as if I were the one burdened with looking after his worries, an emotional coat-check girl. Watching Juan Carlos ride had made me feel joy. As if the wind he left in his wake stirred up possibilities in my soul and made me want to fly, too. Especially when Jake and I hit our rocky patches.

But not today. Today Juan Carlos had seemed broken. Off his game.

I wished I could ask him what had happened out there. But clearly our after-race rendezvous was off. My mom was on her way to get me right now.

At least I could text Juan Carlos and let him know I couldn't see him. And I could tell him properly about his bike and the fence. I took my phone out of my pocket again, noting the battery warning sign flashing red. Weird. I was sure I'd charged it up before the ride. I went to my text message app.

But the text I'd sent to Juan Carlos in the woods wasn't even there. Maybe I hadn't sent it after all. It was possible I'd accidentally deleted it when I got startled in the woods.

I went to my contacts list and to *J*. But Juan Carlos's number wasn't there now, either. I frowned. I checked *M* for *Macias* and even *E* for *el Cóndor*. Nothing. *Nada*. I'd somehow deleted all his contact information. Another stupid move today.

Then my phone went dark. Dead battery. With a sigh, I repocketed it.

"Squirmy one, aren't you," Patricia commented as her tweezers probed my arm.

"You really don't have to keep working on me." I clenched my teeth through the pain.

"Don't be ridiculous. I'm not letting you walk away with abrasions like this. Regardless of what brought you on the course, I am morally obligated to treat you. Hey!" She pointed at me with the tweezers. "I just figured it out!"

"Figured what out?"

"Where I've seen you before! You're that character! On *KidVision*!"

I wanted to sink into the floor.

"You're the host! Yeah! My daughters, they're eight—twins—they watch that show every Saturday morning."

I raised my hands in surrender. "You got me." *That character.* Was that what I was? Maybe I was delusional, thinking someday I'd have more say in the direction of *KidVision.*

"The pizza boxes! Yeah! Last week, that was a terrific show. Who knew all those things you could make out of pizza boxes? My kids made the desk and chair set."

"Glad they liked it." My eyes tracked Gage and Mari, who both passed by again, heading toward the tent's exit. Gage was frowning as he listened to someone on a cell phone. "Yep. Okay. Call you right back." He reached for a remote control. He turned up the volume on a TV in the corner of the tent, where GBCN was showing nonstop event coverage.

The screen showed an ambulance and a figure being loaded onto a stretcher. The reporter's words filled the tent. Everyone in the tent stopped talking. Patricia turned to see, too.

"The crash victim has been identified," said a familiar-looking male GBCN reporter. The same guy who'd tried to stop Jake and me for a pre-ride interview. "He is eighteen-year-old Juan Carlos Macias-León, an Ecuadorian citizen, and a cyclist for Team Cadence-EcuaBar."

Juan Carlos! No! I leaned forward, ignoring the stabbing pains in my right side. My hand flew to the necklace. I squeezed it through the cloth of my jersey.

"Witnesses say he had become separated from his team even before the race began," the reporter went on. "The young cyclist has already led the local upstart team to victory this season, in a number of national races. He's been predicted to do so again at the upcoming Pan-American Cycling Tour, a tri-country series of road and circuit races that will culminate in his hometown of

Quito, Ecuador. But it looks like this young cyclist's racing future will be an uphill battle. He has sustained injuries to his head and neck and remains in critical condition."

Somebody cried out. Mari. She stared at the screen, which now showed the stretcher being loaded into the ambulance.

And a familiar yellow diamond sign in the background. SLOW DEAF CHILD.

Oh, no. Juan Carlos had crashed maybe ten yards behind me. Close enough to have been affected by the pileup.

The pileup *I* had caused.

10

BACK AT our house, my mom helped me into loose-fitting shorts and a tank top, easing them over my wound dressings. Her touch was soft. Her words were harsh. She launched into a lecture, which might have been titled "How Could You Lie to Us—We Raised You with Values!" At least it was better than the stony silence I'd endured on the half-hour car ride from Cabot to Cambridge.

"Tessa? Are you even listening?"

"I'm listening." I glanced at her, then looked away, unable to face her angry expression. Not to mention the glittery alien antennas she wore. My mom had left her portrait studio so fast to come get me she hadn't removed the prop she wore to get little kids to smile.

The antennas reminded me of the fun things Chain Reaction riders mounted on their helmets. "You might want to lose the antennas," I mumbled.

"What?" She felt the top of her head. "Oh." She snatched them off and flung them aside. Then she pointed at my chest, almost accusingly. "Speaking of odd accessories, what's that?"

I looked down. Juan Carlos's necklace was now exposed, as I wore a scoop-neck tank top. My hand flew to my chest and covered the cross. "Nothing." The necklace. Fresh worries. How was I going to give this back to him? Could I get to the hospital? He probably needed this necklace now more than ever.

"It's not nothing. Let me see that." She moved my hand away and looked more closely at it, tracing the body on the cross with one finger. "Why are you wearing a crucifix?"

"Why not? Is it a crime or something?"

"Of course not. It's just not like you."

"Mom, *chill.* It's just a friend's necklace, okay? I borrowed it. I thought it looked cool."

My mom pressed her lips together.

After she delivered Lecture #2 ("You Will Use Your Own Money to Donate to This Charity, Young Lady, Oh Yes You Will"), I limped over to the screened-in porch, like a dog slinking off to lick its own wounds. A sprinkler hissed in the neighbor's yard. Kids played ball in the driveway. An ice-cream truck cruised down the street, its music unusually shrill. Everything seemed false and wrong while Juan Carlos was in the hospital, his life in the balance.

News. I needed news.

I sat in the wicker love seat, wincing from pain. I propped my hurt leg on the coffee table and turned on my laptop. While it booted up, I tore open an EcuaBar that I'd grabbed from the stash in my room. Mocha-Cinnamon Fiesta. It melted in my mouth.

I went to the GBCN site and learned Chain Reaction had not been canceled. There were still hundreds of riders out on the course. Team Firestone-Panera had won the competitive portion of the event, with Team Trident-Crisco taking second and Bose Pro-Cycling in third. Cadence-EcuaBar, thrown off by Juan Carlos's ride, had not even placed on the podium.

I clicked on a link to eyewitness accounts of the crash and forced myself to watch.

"I was ten feet or so behind the guy," one out-of-breath man said, as he was interviewed at the mile fifty water stop. "He'd slowed down, but then he started going faster, maybe twenty-five miles per hour on a downhill curve. A bunch of us tried to give him room to do what he needed to do, especially since the road was wet. We figured he was trying to catch his team."

"I heard this horrible sound up ahead," said a woman. "I was cresting the hill, and I didn't even realize what I was seeing at first. People falling off their bikes. Arms and legs . . . flailing."

An older cyclist said, "I saw el Cóndor go down, right in front of me. It was like his bike blew apart. He must have been going even faster than I thought."

"Did an endo. End over end, right over the handlebars," said a teen cyclist.

I could hardly breathe. Juan Carlos had never passed me. His crash had to have been a result of my own.

My hand shaking, I clicked on "Team Cadence-EcuaBar Reacts." Juan Carlos's equally stunned teammates could barely stammer out sentences.

"El Cóndor always rode on the edge, man. But he always stayed in control. I don't know what went wrong for him today."

"He seemed okay in the morning. He was amped for the race."

Coach Mancuso, his face lined with worry, added, "But he never showed up for the team photo. Or to the starting line. We had to make the tough call to start the race without him."

I gasped and replayed that statement to make sure I'd heard him correctly. He'd never made it to the team photo? He'd started the race late?

So where had he gone after talking to me by the woods on Great Marsh Road?

The next clip was an interview with Dylan Holcomb, the heavily tattooed and pierced team mechanic. He spoke from the team trailer. He looked shell-shocked. "He came running up here after the race had already begun," he explained to the reporter when she asked about the last time he'd seen Juan Carlos. "There wasn't time to talk, so I don't know what made him late. After he rode off, I saw he'd dropped his radio earpiece." The camera zoomed in on the device in Dylan's palm. "I guess that's why he couldn't reach anyone once he was on the course."

Dylan didn't say where he thought Juan Carlos had come from. Nor did he mention a missing spare bike. Maybe Dylan didn't even know yet that Juan Carlos's spare bike was missing. *He's the person I should tell about what I saw in the woods. I should find a way to get in touch with this guy.*

But I couldn't resist watching another video clip. An interview with Preston Lane.

The dazed and bleary-eyed EcuaBar entrepreneur faced the camera in front of Mass General Hospital.

"I heard you were signed up to do the recreational ride. Where were you on the route when you heard the team leader was down?" the reporter asked Preston.

He glanced away, his eyes watering. "I never made it out there. Some of the junior riders and I were looking for him, right up until race time. Then the race started without him. I couldn't fathom why he wasn't with the team in time." Lines appeared in Preston's forehead. "I mean, it doesn't make sense. The Chain Reaction event was important to Juan Carlos. You see, he lost his own mother to cancer."

He did? Juan Carlos had mentioned his mom's cooking to me once, something about her perfect *empanadas.* He'd told me he had two younger sisters and a dad who worked in a factory that manufactured windows. He'd mentioned a best friend nicknamed el Ratón, or the Mouse, whom he'd raced with in Ecuador. He'd never said a word about his mother having cancer. Yet he'd probably been through everything Kylie was going through now.

The waiting and worrying. I felt an ache of sympathy for him.

"He was airlifted from Emerson to Mass General, because of the severity of his head injury," Preston went on. "So I immediately left the race site and followed him here."

The reporter murmured something vaguely sympathetic. "And how long do you plan on keeping vigil here at the hospital?"

Preston ran his hands through his hair. "As long as I need to. We're trying to reach his family in Ecuador. I doubt they'll be able to fly out here. It's the least I can do."

The last link I clicked on was to an interview between my idol, Bianca Slade, and Chris Fitch. I sat up straighter, ignoring the throbbing pain in my limbs. Bianca's interview was sure to be different. *Avoid the obvious. Look for the unusual angle. Dig deep, and you'll hit the truth eventually,* she'd advised in her blog post about investigative reporting.

"Mr. Fitch, we understand there have been complaints about Cadence bikes," said Bianca. "Two product liability lawsuits, for which settlements were reached, and a recall on the Cadence Navigator two years ago. Could el Cóndor's bike have played a role in this crash?" Bianca demanded.

"Absolutely not," said Chris, practically glaring at her. "First of all, those were consumer bikes, not racing bikes, and they came out of a factory we no longer use in Hong Kong. Team Cadence-EcuaBar bikes are custom-made in our factory right here in Massachusetts. They are rigorously tested for quality control. And Cadence has a strong record of proactively addressing potential safety issues. We have the highest standards for quality and integrity." He looked directly at the camera. "Cadence owners should have no cause for alarm. Whatever caused this incident had nothing to do with the integrity of the bike frame."

Bianca pursed her lips. "This accident must bring up a lot of emotions," she said. "Your brother, of course, the founder of the company you took over, died tragically on a bike. It must be unsettling, to be so close to two bicycle crashes involving head injuries. One of them fatal."

"Yes, this crash hits uncomfortably close to home," Chris said, robotically, as if he'd said these words a hundred times before. "But my brother was hit by a car, so at least we knew the cause. My heart goes out to this young cyclist's family in Ecuador. We all want to figure out what caused Juan Carlos to go down in the way that he did. And our prayers are with him for a speedy recovery."

I should just come forward. That was the right thing to do. But what if someone accused me of negligence? Was Jake right that I could incriminate myself and get into worse trouble? When Bianca advised reporters to "*dig deep,*" she probably didn't mean "*dig one's own grave.*"

Normally information calmed me. News comforted me. I'd been falling asleep to the murmur of news on a tiny radio on my nightstand since I was eleven years old. Knowing was better than not knowing, I always told myself. Even when news was horrific—bombings, tornadoes, airplane crashes—there was something about journalists trying to find the human stories in the chaos that always made me feel better. But now these testimonies from people in Juan Carlos's inner circle just fueled my guilt. I massaged my stomach to calm my nerves.

My emotions must have shown. When my mom came in to check on me, she promptly closed my laptop. "Media break," she announced. "Sorry, hon. Obsessing about this crash isn't healthy. You've just been through a shock. Your body needs rest. So does your mind."

"But I want to know what's going on with Juan Carlos."

"You mean that guy Jake raced with? From El Salvador?"

"Ecuador. And yeah. He crashed. He's still in critical condition at Mass General. Unconscious, with a head injury."

"Oh, my. Well, I'm sure he'll pull through," she said, sitting opposite me on the wicker ottoman. "Cyclists are tough. Though it does seem strange how one of the most skilled cyclists out on that course got hurt the worst."

"I know."

"I wonder if something went wrong with his bike," my mom suggested.

I remembered Juan Carlos looking down with a grimace, as if the bike were handling funny. Jake had taught me about how picky cyclists could be about seat and handlebar adjustments, down to the millimeter. The slightest difference could throw off their game.

But he was riding his main bike, with the green handlebars. That bike should have been fine-tuned and ready to ride.

"Or he could have been sick," my mom went on, reaching for a Mexican blanket on the floor and folding it neatly. She was weirdly obsessive about that blanket, a threadbare souvenir she'd bought on a trip to Mexico approximately one hundred years ago.

"But when he beat Jake in Colorado at the junior nationals last summer, he had strep throat *and* a sprained wrist," I pointed out. "If something were wrong, it would be serious."

"Well, maybe it was. Like a bad reaction to something." She paused. "Like drugs."

"God, Mom. Can you give it a rest? You and Dad are always assuming drugs and bike racing go hand in hand. They don't. El Cóndor rides clean. Everyone on Team EcuaBar does." Team EcuaBar was actually created to counteract the doping stigma. Several years ago, Preston Lane had bailed out a struggling, upstart cycling team, then added the junior development team.

Combined, they'd be "the pure team"—a new generation of untainted cyclists.

"I know. 'Pure energy, no additives.' Just like the energy bars. It all sounds good. Still"—my mom shrugged and set the Mexican blanket on the arm of the love seat—"the scrutiny of crowds, his sponsors, the media, his team—it seems like so much pressure."

I wanted to buy my mom's theory. If he had reacted badly to some drug, then I was less responsible. But I just couldn't believe Juan Carlos was doping! He visited schools. He was deeply religious. His faith, his training, and his natural talent all combined to make him win.

If he had doped, only drug tests could confirm that. Or an autopsy report if he died.

If he died . . .

I curled up into a ball on the love seat, drew my mom's wool Mexican blanket over my head, and tried to shut out the world.

If he'd crashed because of the domino effect of my swerve, I was, in some way, responsible for his hospitalization now. An invisible fault line connected our crashes.

And if he died? I would be responsible, too.

11

A RHYTHMIC scratching and snapping sound startled me awake—I must have drifted to sleep on the love seat.

The scratching was on the porch screen. I didn't know what the snapping was.

I remained frozen under the Mexican blanket, suddenly thinking of that guy in the woods, and the snaps of the underbrush as he had chased me.

"Tessa!" a girl's voice called out. "Are you awake? Didn't you hear the doorbell?"

I emerged from under the blanket and sat up to find Kylie and Sarita outside the porch. Kylie was scratching the screen with a twig to wake me up, and Sarita was loudly snapping an enormous piece of gum. Behind them, parked at the curb, was the Fingernail: Kylie's ten-year-old maroon Ford Taurus. The car had earned its nickname due to its uncanny resemblance to a press-on nail. It was our portable home away from home, where we'd had heart-to-heart conversations, taken crazy road trips in search of New England's best ice cream, and collectively consumed about a billion lattes.

All that stuff suddenly seemed a lifetime ago. Even my friends standing there didn't seem real. Sarita's black curls were damp against her brown skin. I could see the tie of a bathing suit halter around Kylie's sunburned neck, and her auburn, pixie-cut hair looked recently towel-dried. They smelled of chlorine and coconut sunscreen. They'd been having a normal summer day. I wished I'd been on their ride.

"Oh my God! What happened to you?" Kylie pointed to my arm and leg bandages.

"Long story." I limped to the front door and let in my friends. They joined me on the porch, where we took up our usual perches: Sarita sprawled on the chaise longue, Kylie cross-legged on the ottoman, and me, curled up on the love seat.

"Nice necklace," said Sarita. "I've never seen you wear crosses or anything like that. You're not becoming Catholic, are you?"

Kylie reached out and touched it. "Is that real gold?"

"I think it is. It's heavy."

"I'm not sure. Kind of seems like metal."

"Well anyway, it's not mine. It's a loaner." For some reason I felt funny telling them who'd given it to me. I slid the crucifix on the chain so that it hung over my back instead, and so they'd stop staring at it. "It's jewelry, guys. It's not that weird."

"Not judging. Just noticing," said Kylie, not taking her eyes off the necklace.

We were together now, yet separated by an invisible screen. Something had shifted in me at Chain Reaction. I was now a person capable of doing devious and harmful things.

"You look like hell. What happened?" asked Sarita.

I sighed. "Did you hear about the big bike crash on the cancer ride in Cabot?"

"I did." Sarita's eyes widened. "I saw the news on my phone when Kylie was driving here. I thought of you right away. I heard el Cóndor got hurt. Didn't we meet him, when you dragged us to one of Jake's races?"

"You did meet him. And yeah. He got hurt. Bad." I took a deep breath and plunged in to the whole story, since my mom was in her photography studio out back and couldn't hear the details. As I talked about bandit riding on the cancer ride, I couldn't meet Kylie's eyes. I would have understood if she walked out.

But she didn't. Neither did Sarita. They both hugged me. They expressed alarm about the man in the woods, and agreed with my theory about him: he was a fence, a middleman between a bike thief and a black-market sports memorabilia collector who wanted the young cycling protégée's bike.

"So what happened to Jake?" asked Kylie.

"I didn't see him again after he took off. My phone battery died, so we didn't talk."

"Asshole." Kylie glowered.

"May I?" Sarita pointed to my phone, charging in the wall.

"Go for it."

Sarita scrolled, wide-eyed. "Fifteen messages! All from Jake. Stalker."

I took the phone from her hand, and Sarita and Kylie read over my shoulders.

The first text from Jake had come in at 10:05. I'd have been leaving the medical tent with my mom around then.

> **Hey. Where RU? Hit mile 20 and realized u weren't there.**

"It took him *twenty miles* to realize you weren't behind him?" said Kylie.

That did kind of hurt. I had to force myself to read the next messages.

> **What happened 2U? Heard there was big crash.**
> **Tessa? U OK? Call or txt me.**

OK I stopped by med tent. They said girl w ur de-
script went home w mom. Wouldn't give name but
sounds like u. Hope its u. Call me OK??

RU home now? Almost called house. Trying to respect parental situation. CALL ME.

Tessa. I'm so sorry. PLEASE get in touch. Let's fix
this.

Call me as soon as you get this, K???

"Please tell me you're not going to call him," said Kylie.

"I'm not. He can wait for me now and see how it feels being dropped."

"Good," said Sarita. "Put us out of our misery. I know he's got this romantic side with those moonlight picnics, and he's adventurous, and smart. But I hate the other side of him. The side that makes you feel so bad about yourself. It's not right."

A new text buzzed in.

Sarita lunged for my phone. "I'll get rid of him for you." She frowned. "Who's this?"

I looked at the screen. The message came from a number I didn't recognize. It had a whole bunch of zeros in it, and no name.

YOU LITTLE LIAR.

Then a second buzzed in:

YOU DECEIVED ME. YOU WILL PAY.

I chilled. I'd never gotten any kind of message like that before.

"Oh my God. Who sent you this?" exclaimed Kylie, leaning in to see.

"I don't recognize that number. It's not in my contacts list. It doesn't even look like a real phone number." Maybe the message was a wrong number.

The phone vibrated again.

YOU MADE A BAD, BAD MOVE.

AND I KNOW WHO YOU ARE.

So much for the wrong number theory. I reached for the Mexican blanket and hugged it.

"You're sure it's not Jake texting from someone else's phone?" said Kylie.

"I'm sure. This doesn't sound like stuff he'd say." My throat tightened. Who would have gotten my number and sent me something so creepy? Who hated me that much? Not Gage or Mari. I hadn't left my phone number in the medical tent.

You made a bad, bad move. Someone might have known about my stupid swerve. *You will pay.* I was already paying, wasn't I? I felt terrible, worrying about Juan Carlos. But *you deceived me*—that made no sense. Unless—a new idea flew into my head. I sat up straight. "You guys! What if it's from that guy who chased me in the woods? The guy who was looking for Juan Carlos's spare bike?"

"The fence? How would he have gotten your phone number?" asked Kylie.

I thought for a moment. "He held my phone. He deleted the video I took. Maybe he saw my number and memorized it."

"That's possible. But why would he call you a liar? You didn't lie," Sarita pointed out. "You showed him where you'd seen the bike. He told you not to report him. And you didn't."

"I think this is a spambot," said Kylie. "Remember that scary text that was going around last year, where you had to forward it to ten people or you'd die? It's like that. *You will pay.* They'll probably ask you for money if you respond."

"Kylie's right. Delete it," said Sarita.

I hit the DELETE button. Maybe it *was* random spam. I desperately wanted to believe that.

"You seem like you have a lot on your mind," said Kylie. "We should go. I'll take a rain check on the mock interview."

"What mock interview?"

Kylie took a file folder out of her tote bag, its edges damp and curled from her day at the pool. "You were going to coach me this afternoon for my Lane Scholarship interview." She stared at me with a hurt expression. "You didn't forget about that, did you? You already rescheduled our practice once to go bike riding with Jake."

"No. Of course I remember." An elevator dropped in my stomach. How could I have forgotten about this? The Lane Scholarship was a huge opportunity for Kylie. Preston Lane would pay an entire year of Shady Pines tuition for a student who demonstrated commitment to social issues combined with an entrepreneurial spirit. Sarita, who was captain of our school's nationally recognized debate team, was supposed to help her come up with talking points. And I'd agreed, weeks ago, to coach her on interviewing techniques—eye contact, voice modulation, stuff I knew from *KidVision*—since Kylie was on the shy side and often froze under pressure.

Kylie really needed this money. Her mom's cancer treatments had eaten through their savings. There was a chance, if she didn't get the scholarship, that she'd have to transfer to another school for her senior year.

Kylie stuffed the file back into her tote bag. "Never mind. I know you forgot all about it."

"I didn't—"

"No, you did. If you hadn't crashed, you'd still be out there on that ride."

"Kylie, I'm so sorry. I've been trying so hard to patch things up with Jake, and when he suggested we do this ride together, and try to reconnect, I jumped at it. And forgot everything else. I completely suck."

Kylie shrugged. "We'll find time." She managed a small smile. "The important thing is you're not hurt worse. Let's do this when you're not in mortal pain or thinking of a million other things."

"What's there to think of?" Sarita asked.

I sighed. "The other people I hurt. I'm responsible for a bunch of people's injuries. Including Juan Carlos's."

Sarita raised an eyebrow. "Now how could that even be possible?"

I explained how people stopped to avoid the pileup, and what witnesses had said. "He wasn't that far behind me," I concluded. "My crash caused his crash."

Kylie leaned forward and scrutinized the gold chain more closely. "Wait. Is that *his*?"

"I ran into him before the ride and he told me to take care of it for him. He couldn't ride with it for some reason. Anyway, he said he wanted to talk to me about something after the award ceremony. Obviously we didn't get to that."

"Wow. Most guys go out with you at least a few times before they hand over the bling," said Sarita, a sly grin spreading across her face. "How long was it before Jake gave you jewelry?"

"Jake wasn't into jewelry. He said it was too materialistic."

"Right." Sarita gave me a knowing look.

"Don't go there, Sarita. This is totally different."

"Still. Now I see why you're taking that crash so hard," said Sarita. "That's intense."

"But accidents happen," said Kylie. "Especially on wet, crowded roads. People crash and die on the Tour de France, don't they? His crash is not your fault. You can't sit here dwelling on it. Life's for living. Not worrying. My mom tells me that all the time now."

"And I'm sure he'll pull through." Sarita patted my good knee.

"Okay," I said, but the word sounded hollow. "How's your mom, by the way?" I asked Kylie. "I'm sorry I haven't been over more lately."

Kylie shrugged and looked down. "She has her good days and her bad. She's tired a lot. But her spirit's strong."

"Talk about an inspiration," said Sarita. "Beth Sullivan. She's my hero."

"Hey, can you two come over for dinner on Tuesday?" asked Kylie, brightening a little. "It's actually her birthday. We were going to keep it simple, just family—but you guys, you're like family, too." Her eyes watered. "My dad said he'd come and help out, but I don't know. My bro and I—we're kind of on our own with this. I guess I could use some moral support. People to take pictures, sing—make it seem more like a party, you know?"

"Oh, Kylie, I can't." Sarita looked crestfallen. "I wish I could. I have to present my service project idea at a Rotary club meeting. It's too late to reschedule."

"Tessa?" Kylie looked at me. "My mom was just asking about you this morning. She'd love to see you."

Beth Sullivan had asked about me that morning. While I'd been busy crashing a cancer ride, in more ways than one. "Sounds fun," I managed to say. "I will be there."

"Really? You'll really come?" Kylie's face lit up.

I managed a smile, too, even though Beth Sullivan's illness scared me. From now on I would do only good things. "I will absolutely be there," I said. "I wouldn't miss it for the world."

12

SOON AFTER my friends left, my dad came home from his retreat. After he and my mom talked in hushed voices in the kitchen, he called a family meeting in the living room, where he handed me a legal pad. "Here. Draw everything you remember about the crash scene, while it's fresh in your mind," he said. "We should be prepared for all possible outcomes."

I sighed. Possible outcomes and worst-case scenarios were a popular topic in our house. My parents always tried to help me steer clear of anything that could hurt my chances of getting into a good college and having a perfect and successful life.

"Possible outcomes? What are you getting at, Randall?" my mom asked, evidently thinking along similar lines.

"Police may want to question Tessa as part of the crash scene investigation."

My stomach lurched. Police? Investigation? *No, no, no, no.* I'd wanted police to look in the woods and stop a *bike theft.* I didn't want them looking for the cause of a crash: me. Jake's words haunted me. If I reported the bike in the woods now, the police might start wondering what I was doing on the route, so close to Juan Carlos when he went down. They'd ask more questions. I'd have to explain the unsafe merge. The leeched paceline. The reckless pullout. I was pretty sure I'd broken no laws, but maybe I could get in serious trouble for negligent riding.

I should tell my parents the truth. Especially my dad. He practiced environmental law, but still he'd know what to do. But what they thought I'd done today—sneaking off with my boyfriend, riding for charity without raising money—was bad enough. My dad had already had one heart attack and bypass surgery. The death of his father and his grandfather at age sixty weighed on his mind; my dad had turned sixty last month. Even my mom suddenly looked older: silver glinting through her brown hair, shadows under her eyes.

I couldn't let them down or make them worry anymore.

"Tessa?" my dad prompted gently. I took the pen and paper. I sketched a basic diagram of the crash site. I added the SLOW DEAF CHILD sign, and the downhill curve on the map. I made sure to put me, crashing, behind a downed paceline.

"It all happened so fast," I explained. "The road was wet. Other riders went down. I couldn't stop in time. People were swerving all over the road."

"Rider errors are inherent risks of this or any sport." My dad pressed his fingertips together. "And Chain Reaction is a reputable organization. But maybe parts of the course were not well maintained."

"That's true," I said, even though I couldn't recall obvious road hazards, other than the rain-dampened asphalt. No sand patches, no stray rocks. The road was newly paved.

"We'll want to have you checked out by Dr. Ellis tomorrow," my dad went on. He scrawled notes on a legal pad. "If Dr. Ellis thinks you have any lingering issues, we can discuss possible next steps."

I swallowed. Would my dad sue Chain Reaction? Then I'd have to retell this story and relive this day, and drag Jake into all of it. I'd be back on his emotional roller coaster. I wished I'd never gotten on a bike that morning.

"What happened to Jake out there anyway?" my dad asked, as if reading my mind. He lowered his glasses to look over the rims at me. "Your mother said he roped you in to this crazy stunt."

"Which is completely bizarre to me, by the way, since you told us you guys were through," my mom chimed in. "You've been sneaking around seeing him? That is just not okay."

I picked a thread on a sofa cushion. "He didn't make me do the ride. He mentioned it'd be fun to do together, and I chose to go. Okay? I *chose*. And he got way ahead of me. I don't even think he knows that I crashed."

My parents exchanged a look, confirming their suspicions: Jake was a champion asshole.

"Fine. I did lie to you guys about breaking up with Jake," I said, "and I'm sorry about that. But I didn't think you had the right to tell me to break up with him. It's my life."

"We were worried. *Are* worried," my mom corrected. "I mean, he was accused of doping! Someone like you—a media personality, a role model—you can't be dating a doper."

"It wasn't a doping charge, Mom. It was possession. And he's—oh, forget it."

My mom sighed. "Jake may be a great, fast bike rider, but honey, he's going nowhere. I always thought he had character flaws, and now I really see it."

"Okay, okay. I get it." I got it. I couldn't be with a guy who'd drop me on a ride, and I was sick of him jerking my emotions around. I just didn't want my mom to think she was the one who convinced me.

My mom smiled sadly. "Maybe the silver lining of this whole incident is that you'll get some clarity from it. I'm sure you'll go on to make good decisions, like you usually do."

"You mean like *you* usually do." The words flew out on their own. "Don't you guys make all my good decisions? What classes and extracurriculars to take? How to budget every second of my time?"

"Tessa. That's enough," said my dad. "What your mother's trying to say is, you're our only child, and we want the best for you."

"I thought you wanted me to open my eyes to people's struggles. You've been pounding that into my head since I was in preschool, and you made me give my birthday presents to a charity of my choice."

"Yes, of course. We think having a social conscience, and awareness of inequalities, is very important," said my dad. "But we don't want *you* to struggle. It isn't necessary. Your mother and I have worked hard to help you avoid just that."

"Yeah, but I'm just so tired of—oh, forget it." I sighed. "Can I go to my room now?"

"That sounds like an excellent decision," my mom said in a clipped voice. "Then later we'll talk about consequences."

"Consequences?"

"Of riding in a charity event without raising any money."

"Awesome. I cannot wait." I stood up, with some difficulty.

"One more question," my dad said. "Did you hear about the downed Team EcuaBar cyclist?"

I felt a weird rushing sound in my ears. "Yeah."

My dad gave me a long look. "Did you know him?"

"Not really. I mean, sort of. I'd met him a few times. At Jake's races. They rode on the junior team together."

"I thought his name sounded familiar. Were you anywhere near him when he went down?"

I hesitated, then shook my head.

"Good. Promise me," he said, "if the police contact you with questions about the ride, don't answer without me or your mother there."

"Okay. But why not?"

"You were with Jake. Jake's got a rap sheet now, and I just think we should be careful. I'd like to keep you far away from this investigation, with college applications on the line."

College applications! I wanted to throw something. It was summer. I'd just caused a huge pileup at a bike event. I didn't care about college right now.

"Oh, Randall. This all sounds a bit extreme, don't you think?" said my mom.

"It's not extreme. When there's a fatal accident, an investigation follows. Anything out of the ordinary will be looked at. Tessa and Jake bandit riding? That could attract attention."

"Wait. Fatal accident?" said my mom. "Aren't we being prematurely catastrophic?"

My dad looked from my mom to me. "You mean, you two don't know? Isn't the news always on in this house?"

"Your daughter was overdosing on it. I enforced a media break."

The room was swaying. "Dad," I said. "*What happened?*"

"Oh, honey." My dad crossed the room and came over to me. He put his hands on my shoulders and looked into my eyes. "The doctors couldn't revive him. He . . . he died."

My mom's hands flew to her mouth.

I snatched the remote from the coffee table and turned on GBCN. The reporter was now in front of Mass General. BREAKING NEWS: CYCLING TRAGEDY ran across the bottom of the screen, in red, like pooling blood.

13

I WOKE the next morning twisted in my sheets, my eyes salted with dried tears. All night I'd had crazy dreams of looking for Juan Carlos after the race. I was pushing through crowds, calling his name, seeing the back of his jersey but never his face. As I pushed, the green rain forest vines shown on the cycling outfit started to grow around my feet, pulling on my legs and tripping me.

Now I sat up and gazed at a box of Tres Leches EcuaBars I kept on my desk for late-night study snacks.

Juan Carlos was dead.

Never again would I see him fly down the road on his bike.

Never again would I see him pray before a race. Or bump into him after to offer congratulations. Or shoot the breeze—in Spanish, so I could practice—about school or movies or *KidVision* or bikes.

And I would go the rest of my life without knowing what Juan Carlos Macias-Léon wanted to talk to me about so urgently.

I swung my legs out of bed and felt a weird pain in my chest. Then I looked down and realized what it was. I'd fallen asleep with that crucifix necklace, turned the wrong way against my chest, and it had left marks in my skin. I adjusted it and promised myself not to fall asleep with it on again. Much as I wanted to wear it forever, close to my heart, it was too awkward and painful to sleep with it on at night.

How did he race with this thing on anyway? Wouldn't it fly up and hit his face, or bang against him if he unzipped his cycling jersey, as most of the cyclists did to cool off?

I swallowed hard as another reality hit me. Now I would never get the chance to return the necklace to him.

I reached for my laptop at the foot of my bed. I'd finally fallen asleep last night after hours of crying alternating with chasing Juan Carlos—online anyway. I'd watched race videos, where he seemed very much alive. I'd viewed shots from his most recent races. Astonishing breakaways. Stunning wins. In each case, he overtook competitors at the last minute, passing them on hills and flying over the finish line. His sudden speed seemed to come out of nowhere. I could hear the crescendo of spectators' cheers every time he flew by. Sports commentators said he raced with an ease and confidence far beyond his years, and was proving himself to be, potentially, as great a climber as the young Colombian cycling star Nairo Quintana.

I'd left off my tearful viewing last night with an archived *KidVision* video. It was the story we'd done on the EcuaBar junior development team last summer.

I took a deep breath and fast-forwarded to the end of the segment, where I'd introduced Juan Carlos as the hotshot rider recruited from Ecuador who shared the team's mission of community service. Off-camera, before the shoot, Juan Carlos had been nervous, I now remembered. I'd told him—in Spanish—to talk directly to the kids.

"I can talk to kids," he'd said, flashing me a grateful smile. The camera rolled, and when he spoke, he looked straight into it and relaxed. "*¡Hola, KidVision! ¿Cómo están? Me llamo Juan Carlos, y soy de Ecuador.* In my home city, Quito, I worked with an advocacy group. This group is called Vuelta. We work hard to make the streets safe for bikes. We also teach kids how to ride and we have a racing club. I hope to continue this work in some ways, now I am here to Boston."

He'd traveled so far to change his life. Not to end it. What was the point of coming all the way to New England to develop his racing career, only to wind up at eighteen in a hospital morgue? What good was it to fight to make public streets safe for biking if he couldn't survive a crash on a controlled route for a charity race?

I toggled over to Juan Carlos's fan page, which swelled with comments and condolences.

Mi más sentido pésame.

You were a shining inspiration to others. *Vaya con Dios, el Cóndor.*

Condolencias a la familia y los compañeros del equipo.

My hands hovered over the keyboard. Then fell to my lap. What could I possibly say? He was gone. He wouldn't be reading this page. Words wouldn't undo anything.

I managed to get dressed, despite my awkward wound dressings, and limped down to the kitchen, where I found ibuprofen and a note on the table.

Your dad had a client to visit this morning. We're seeing Dr. Ellis at ten. Please be ready to go by 9:40 and let me know if you need help. I'm in the studio. xoxo mom.

I took the ibuprofen and brewed coffee. I peeled a banana. I focused on the positives. It was a new day. The rest of the summer sprawled out before me. I had not been killed or seriously injured in a bike crash.

I switched on the TV and flicked through channels as I ate, lingering on the Spanish station. I closed my eyes, just listening to Spanish pouring over my head like water. Commercials for cars, cleaning products, and cereal. Urgent pleas to call now and take advantage of limited offers. *¡Llame ahora mismo!* I kept listening for words Juan Carlos had used, or voices that sounded remotely like his, trying to feel closer to him or bring him to life just by listening to his native language on a TV station he might have turned on every day.

The banana was tasteless, mushy. I almost gagged. I looked down and saw it was almost black inside, rotting from the inside out. The sticker on the peel said FAIR TRADE BANANAS. PRODUCT OF ECUADOR. Everything reminded me of another product of Ecuador, Juan Carlos Macias-León. El Cóndor, the great bird. Downed. All because of me. I threw the banana away.

I slipped on my flip-flops and limped out the back door. I paused at the addition on our Victorian house, and the KATHERINE TAYLOR PHOTOGRAPHY sign on the door. My mom was talking to a guy around my age who was standing in the doorway, probably picking up his graduation portrait package. Sure that I looked as putrid as I felt, I snuck past them and padded onward, across the driveway.

I lifted the garage door open awkwardly with my left arm and limped inside. Shadows clung to spiderwebs in the overcast morning gloom. I quickly switched on a light.

The first thing I saw was my busted bike leaning against the wall next to my mom's Lexus. I wheeled it outside. The spoke repairs were beyond me. The wheel needed truing, too. I didn't know how to true a wheel.

I put one leg, my good leg, over the bike frame, testing myself.

I hoisted myself onto the seat. My eyes swam. The ground felt like it was rising to meet me. I quickly dismounted, breathing hard. In an instant, the full horror of the crash had returned. The scrapes, the whines, the frantic cries of "Riders down!"—it all came back again. And the news report on Juan Carlos's death. I shivered. Who ever came up with the crazy idea of riding at high speeds on skinny tires and pieces of metal? This wasn't a harmless sport. It was lethal.

I pushed the bike back into the garage and let it fall against the wall.

Then I noticed something strange.

The back door to the garage, which led out to a small storage area for our back yard, seemed to be cracked open an inch. We never opened that door. I couldn't remember if I'd ever seen it open at all. I walked to the door and pushed on it. It swung wide with a creak.

I inspected the old lock on the outside. There were scratch marks around it, as if a sharp object had been used to pick the lock.

I scanned the garage. My dad's tools looked intact. The leaf blower and lawn mower were there. The kayak still hung from the ceiling. Big-ticket items, all worth stealing, all left undisturbed.

I shivered. Someone had broken into our garage.

14

BREATHING HARD, I half limped, half lurched into my mom's studio. The guy at the door had left, and my mom was glued to her computer. She didn't even seem to hear me come in. She was going through proofs of seniors' graduation pictures; the packages had to be delivered to clients soon, and she'd been stressing about it. Now it pained me to see all those smiling kids in their caps and gowns. Kids sailing on to their promising futures, without a care in the world.

What would my graduation portrait look like next year? Would I still look haunted from being the cause of Juan Carlos's death? No amount of Photoshop could remove that scar.

"Oh, good, you're up," my mom said, still clicking on proofs. "How are we feeling?"

"Better. I took the ibuprofen you left me."

She turned in her chair and looked at me with real concern. "And emotionally? I know you took the news of that crash hard yesterday. I heard you crying in your room late last night." She scooted her office chair over to me and held my hand. Squeezed it. "It's hard. I know. You knew this guy. And he was so young . . . oh, Tessa. I'm sorry you have to deal with all this. It's an enormous burden."

You have no idea. "I'm okay," I managed to say, extracting my hand from hers. I didn't feel like sharing an emotional moment with my mom over this right now. I couldn't explain to her why el Cóndor's death had hit me so hard. "The back door to the garage was open."

"What? Are you sure? That's strange."

"I know. Do you think Dad might have opened it this morning? Or recently?"

"I don't know if we even remember where the key is. But maybe. I'll ask." She sent him a quick text on her phone. "Did you hear anything unusual outside last night?"

"No. Nothing."

My dad's reply chimed in, jolting me, an instant reminder of the creepy texts I'd gotten yesterday afternoon.

"He says he didn't touch the door," said my mom. "Gosh, I hope we don't have a neighborhood prowler. Did anything seem to be missing?"

"Nothing. But you should check, too, just in case."

"I'll do it now. And I'll call the police and report a break-in."

As she did so, I took a seat at the extra desk across the room and twirled in the swivel chair, gazing at all the portraits of babies, kids, and families on the walls.

Who could have come by and worked their way in? And why the garage, of all places?

Why not the house? Or this studio, with its expensive camera and computer equipment?

I thought of my usual nocturnal visitor. Jake wasn't the type to break and enter. Or was he? I'd also never pegged him as the type to leave his girlfriend by the side of a road, stuck between a madman in the woods and an approaching cyclone of cyclists.

But what would Jake be looking for? All I had of his were some CDs, two shirts, and some cycling books, and he knew those were all in my room. I didn't even have my own car yet. There was no reason for him to poke around in our garage.

I rubbed my forehead, as if to erase these crazy thoughts. We'd been randomly targeted for a break-in, just like that text spam I got on my phone was random. Bad luck. And everything was rattling my nerves since the crash.

My mom squeezed a little squeak toy she used to make babies laugh. "Hey! I'm talking here."

"Sorry. What were you saying?"

"The police will come by this afternoon to take a report."

"Great." I felt dizzy. Police would be coming. Why did I feel like they were going to lead me away in handcuffs, for killing Juan Carlos?

"Also, I'm sending in a check to Chain Reaction today, to cover your fundraising minimum."

"Wow, that's really generous of you. Thank you."

"Oh, it's not a gift. You're going to be paying me back in weekly installments. Time to start looking for a summer job, kiddo."

I kicked the floor and spun the chair around. "I have a summer job. With *KidVision*."

"That money all goes to your college fund. You'll need to find something on top of that. Maybe we can brainstorm a list of places you can apply to work."

I stopped spinning. I stared at her. It was like she was talking in another language. I had *killed* Juan Carlos, for God's sake. I didn't care about getting a job.

It took me a moment to remember she didn't know the whole story.

I looked away from her intense gaze and stared at the photo above the desk instead, a picture that had always fascinated and disturbed me. It was a black-and-white image of ramshackle homes—slums, really—clinging to a steep hill. I never understood why she hung something like that in a children's photography studio. It was kind of depressing.

"I have an idea," my mom said in that bright, chirpy voice that usually signaled an idea I would not like. "Why don't you work for me this summer? Don't give me that look. I really could use an assistant. You could pay off your debt to me. With your time."

I pictured a summer spent making silly faces at kids to get them to smile, tickling babies with feather dusters, cleaning up Cheerios and puke, all the while tormented by endless replay memories of my bike crash, of Juan Carlos sprawled on the ground. "Thanks. But no, thanks."

"Why not? It'd be fun. You and me. Working together. Bonding." My mom patted my unhurt leg. "I'm just happy you've ended it with Jake and you'll have more time. I've missed—"

At that moment, a car pulled up in our driveway, tires crunching on gravel.

"It's Kristen," my mom said, looking out the window. "What's she doing here?"

"I have no idea."

"You're not filming a show today, are you?"

"No. Next week." I followed my mom outside and to the front porch, a pit of dread in my stomach. If Kristen was here making a house call, when she was supposed to be at her summer house, I knew it couldn't be good.

15

KRISTEN STRODE up the walkway. Instead of her usual business attire, she wore her Don't Anyone Bug Me I'm Off to My Beach House uniform: white capris, a lime-green tank top, flip-flops with little palm trees on them, a belt with tiny lobsters. A ponytail was firmly cinched high on her head, a sign of her further determination to have fun.

"Off to the Cape?" my mom guessed, smiling weakly.

"Eventually. I needed to see Tessa in person first. We have a situation."

My mom glanced at me, then got Kristen a wicker chair. My mom and I sat on the porch swing opposite her. Kristen took a tablet out of her canvas tote bag and pulled up an online newspaper. *The Daily Commonwealth Online News.* "You're familiar with this?" she asked.

My mom and I both shook our heads.

She scrolled down to the headline of an article. KIDVISION HOST CAUGHT BANDIT RIDING! This was followed by an image of me in the medical tent, my hair wild, my expression surly.

I read the article with a deepening sense of dread.

> In addition to being an off-the-beaten path, ear-to-the-ground, renegade reporter, I'm also a former nanny. The kids I took care of are addicted to the popular

GBCN show *KidVision*. I've been subjected to countless hours of watching this relentlessly cheerful teenage host spouting perky tips for saving the world, and introducing us to an endless string of young talents and altruists.

I must admit, even though I'm twenty-four and well out of the show's demographic, *KidVision* has always elicited a sense of skepticism in me. With all these aMAzing kids with aMAzing ideas, and all their well-intentioned social responsibility, the world should be a much better place, right? But the world still seems pretty messed up to me. That's not necessarily the fault of the host or its subjects. Yet there is a note that rings false in this show.

So I wasn't entirely shocked when I saw host Tessa Taylor in the medical tent and heard an argument going on with one of the ride sponsors. Looks like she's not the golden girl she appears to be on TV. This girl had not registered to do the ride or raised any money for cancer. Unconvinced? Have a listen.

An audio file icon followed. When Kristen clicked on it, we could hear the entire conversation I'd had with Gage about the hazards of bandit riding. She'd recorded every word.

All I could think of was the injured Team Maureen rider next to me in the medical tent. She must have recorded the whole conversation on her phone. The camera angle was strange on the photo, though. I could see the back of the EMT working on me, not the side. It was like the photo had been taken by someone else in the tent, someone in front of me.

"This is ridiculous," my mom snapped. "It's not even real journalism. It's a blog post masquerading as a tabloid article. Thank goodness nobody really reads these things."

"Oh, but they do." Kristen showed us a sidebar. "This electronic rag's got quite a following. Nearly four thousand subscribers, not to mention their followers on social media."

My mom sighed. "Tessa's father is an attorney. I'll have him send a cease and desist letter. They can't throw her image and voice up there without our consent. She's a minor."

"Yes. By all means, have him do that," said Kristen. "But I'm afraid it won't erase the thirty-plus comments so far. Or the retweets and links to the article that are already out there."

"Comments? From whom?" I asked.

"Cancer survivors. Parents. *KidVision* fans. Well, former fans."

She showed me a few. That was enough. Each one popped a hole in my soul and let the air out. All this stuff about how I'd let them down, I was a hypocrite, I didn't really care about people, I was a complete and total fake. I was mean-spirited. Selfish. Narcissistic. Cold. I was a symbol of everything that was wrong with teenagers today. I was using *KidVision* for self-promotion and self-gain. I didn't live by the values the show sought to promote.

I took a deep breath. "I want to respond. I want to record something we can put up on the *KidVision* website right away."

"No need," said Kristen. "Our Community Relations representative will issue a statement on behalf of the show."

"So I don't get to speak up about my own behavior? You think I should continue with the show like nothing happened? Show up for taping next Tuesday and not address it?"

Kristen gave me a long look. "You know, a chain is only as strong as its weakest link."

Panic rose in my throat. "What are you saying? That I'm a weak link?"

"What I'm saying," she said gently, "is that a show with controversy doesn't look good for the network. Under the circumstances, we feel you should take a little hiatus from the show."

"A hiatus? Like, a break? For how long?" I asked, gripping the edge of the seat. The whole porch seemed to be spinning.

"Her contract's up for renewal," my mom added. "There's that meeting next week."

Kristen pursed her lips. "Actually. We were thinking. It might not be best to renew." Her eyes shifted, averting my stony glare.

Kristen wasn't talking about a hiatus. I was being *fired*.

"*We*?" I burst out. "Nobody asked me how I felt about it. I'm the host of the show. I've been the host for five years! Don't I have a say in this?"

"Ratings have been down lately," Kristen went on. "And given that GBCN is a prominent Chain Reaction sponsor, we feel this is a controversy we should steer clear of."

"But this is totally undemocratic! Don't I even get to defend myself? To explain?"

"Tessa," my mom said, laying her hand gently on my arm. "Raising your voice won't help. Let's talk about this rationally. I'm sure we can find some compromise."

"We really feel this is the best decision for all involved," Kristen said smoothly.

I shrunk into the chair, teeth clenched. Sure, I had my frustrations with the show at times. True, lately it had nagged at me that I'd gotten the show because of my dad, who knew someone at GBCN. But *KidVision* was what I was known for. And now everyone would know why I'd gotten kicked off.

Turning to Kristen, I ventured a wild idea. "You know, I'm a huge fan of *Watchdog*, and I want to be an investigative journalist someday. Maybe I could work for Bianca Slade, as an intern?"

"That show?" My mom frowned. "It's so negative, don't you think? That's a big turn from *KidVision*."

I ignored this. "Could you help me work something out?" I pleaded with Kristen.

"I'll see what I can do," Kristen said, through the thinnest of smiles.

I knew, from her tone, that she wouldn't help. I was radioactive. A teen star screwup.

"So how does someone recover from something like this?" my mom asked Kristen. "That footage is out there, for anyone to see, forever. Those college admissions committees, they Google kids now."

College admissions committees. The least of my problems. But maybe Kristen had some idea of what I could do to make up for the mess I had caused. "I just want to make this right," I said, fighting back tears. My mom nodded, assuming I was talking about bandit riding, but I was really thinking of the pileup and of Juan Carlos. "What can I do?"

Kristen pondered this, lips pursed, manicured nails tapping on her white pants. "Going to the opposite extreme to restore a good image might help."

I leaned forward. "Okay. How?"

"Run a guerrilla campaign of community service. Visit sick kids in cancer hospitals. Do some cancer fundraising on your own. I'm sure you'll find the right path."

AS SOON as Kristen left, I went up to my room to get my phone from the wall charger. I found three more messages from Jake, sent late last night, wondering why I wasn't responding. *Delete,*

delete, delete. I'd have to deal with him at some point, but right now wasn't the time.

Suddenly a new text buzzed in. From that number with all the zeros again.

WHERE IS THE BIKE.

Fear zapped through my body, as a new message sent the phone vibrating again.

IT'S NOT IN YOUR GARAGE. WHERE ARE YOU KEEPING IT?

I dropped the phone onto my bed and stepped back, as if the thing might explode. This was no spambot. These texts, like the one yesterday accusing me of being a liar, were from the guy in the woods. The fence. He'd tracked me down. He'd broken into our garage.

The guy, the bike in the woods, yesterday's creepy texts, the open garage door—all these things were linked. The fence must have memorized my name and number when he looked at my phone in the woods. From that information, maybe he could figure out where I lived.

But why would he think I had Juan Carlos's bike?

I picked up the phone and typed back, with trembling fingers:

I don't have that bike. I told you where I'd seen it.

The reply came fast.

NOT THERE. YOU MISDIRECTED ME. YOU WENT BACK AND REMOVED IT.

What? If this guy thought I'd deliberately set out to mess up his plan, he really was crazy!

I typed back, more boldly now:

> **You have the wrong person. I'm just a high school student. Please stop texting me.**

There was a pause, then a text that I swear buzzed in with even more insistence:

> YOU'RE NOT JUST A HIGH SCHOOL STUDENT.
>
> YOU'RE IN THE MEDIA.
>
> WE KNOW ALL ABOUT YOU.

We? So he wasn't acting alone. And did he know I had some connection to Juan Carlos? Had he seen us talking on Great Marsh Road? Oh my God. Maybe that's why he thought I had Juan Carlos's bike—because we'd spoken, privately, just minutes before! And I'd been texting Juan Carlos just before the fence took my phone. Texting him about that bike. I'd even started to type something about arranging for someone to go pick it up.

I should shut off my phone right now. That would stop these insane texts from coming. But it might not stop the fence. He'd already been to my house. I didn't want to see him in person again.

I looked up at the signed 8×10 photo of my idol, Bianca Slade, taped to the wall above my desk. Bianca, in the photo, wore a black blazer as well as her game face: pursed lips, a gleam in her eye. Her glossy dark bobbed hair, with a silver streak on one side, was shellacked into obedience. She was the perfect mix of glamour and grit.

My eyes flicked to the printout from her blog. Qualities of Good Investigative Reporters #4: Never Stops Asking Questions. *If you hit a dead end, find fresh questions.*

A new text buzzed in.

WELL????

I texted back, trying to channel my inner Bianca Slade.

Who are you? I won't write back unless you tell me your name.

After a pause, his reply came:

YOU CAN CALL ME DARWIN.

BRING THE BIKE TO THE MEMORIAL SHRINE ON GREAT MARSH ROAD BY 6:00 PM ON THURSDAY. ONE OF MY ASSOCIATES WILL BE WAITING FOR IT.

Memorial shrine? What was he talking about?

"Tessa?" My mom tapped at the door. "Ready to go see Dr. Ellis?"

"Um . . . yeah. Mom?" I had to tell her what was going on here. The police were coming later to check out our garage. I could show them these texts and tell them to go get this guy. They could look for footprints in our yard and the garage, and then find ones that matched in the woods in Cabot, connect them to my crazy texter, show up at the memorial, whatever that was, and haul him into custody.

"Yes, sweetie?"

I stared at my phone as one more message buzzed in.

> DO NOT MENTION ME OR THE BIKE. NOT TO PARENTS, NOT TO THE MEDIA, NOT TO COPS. IF YOU DO, OR IF NO BIKE ON THURSDAY, YOUR MOM WON'T BE SITTING PRETTY IN THAT STUDIO OF HERS.

Then an image appeared: a photo of a kid who looked to be my age. The same guy I'd seen standing outside my mom's studio door.

My grip tightened around the phone. Had Darwin—or some associate—been lurking around our house, with a camera? I rushed to my windows and slammed my shutters closed.

"Sweetie?" my mom said again, anxiously. She tapped at the door again. "You all right?"

"Uh, yeah. Just a sec." I studied the picture Darwin had texted.

My mom was talking to the kid in the picture, but she'd been caught in a weird gesture, as if beckoning him inside. And winking. I knew it was totally innocent—my mom always squinted one eye when she smiled—but in the wrong context, it could look really bad. Like she was kind of coming on to this kid.

"Mom, did some guy come by your studio this morning to pick up a graduation portrait packet?" I called through the door.

"Not to pick up a packet. To ask about senior portrait prices for the fall."

"Did you get his name or address or anything?"

"No, just gave him a brochure and a price list. Why?"

A text buzzed in.

> SEE THIS KID? HE WORKS FOR US. HE LOOKED AROUND YOUR GARAGE BEFORE PAYING A VISIT

TO YOUR MOM. HE'S NOW IN A POSITION TO FILE A COMPLAINT AGAINST HER, ALLEGING MISCONDUCT WITH A MINOR. DON'T MAKE US ACTIVATE HIM.

Then the picture and the messages—my entire correspondence with Darwin—got wiped away. Erased. As if our whole conversation had never happened at all.

16

LATER THAT afternoon, after seeing Dr. Ellis, and after my mom returned to her studio, I paced in the living room, waiting for my friends. I kept the shades drawn tight and my phone turned off. Every few minutes, I peered out of the corner of the window shade, expecting to see shadowy figures darting in and out of the bushes with cameras. Every time I saw a car pass, I dropped the shade back in place with a sigh of relief.

When the Fingernail finally pulled into the drive, I limped out to the car as fast as I could, got in the backseat, and slammed the door. I sunk low in the seat so I wouldn't be visible from the windows. If Darwin or someone was snapping incriminating pictures near our house, I didn't need to be modeling for one.

"Route 2 west," I said to Kylie.

"What am I, a taxi?"

"I thought we were doing Kylie's mock interview here," Sarita added.

"We can mock on the road. Now go."

I sprawled out in the backseat of the Fingernail, breathing in the familiar smell of mildew, vanilla air freshener, and the sour milk of a thousand spilled lattes. Once we got out of Cambridge, onto Route 2, I pulled myself back up to a sitting position and relaxed a little.

/////

"YOU HAVE to tell someone about this Darwin guy," Kylie said when I'd finished explaining why I'd called her and Sarita in a panic, from our land line, as soon as I was home from the doctor's appointment. "Your mom. Police. Tell someone."

"No. He specifically told me not to. And now he could wreck my mom's business by framing her for sexual misconduct with a juvenile. I'm not going to piss him off."

"So is all this the reason I'm speeding down Route 2?" asked Kylie.

"If you can call going five miles above the speed limit speeding," Sarita grumbled.

"I told you. I have to have a perfect driving record. My mom can't afford our insurance going up."

"I'd drive, but my leg hurts too much," I said. "Look, the truth is, I have to go to Cabot. And I need your help. Three of us can search better than one."

"Cabot?" Sarita twisted around to stare at me. "Where the bike thing was?"

"What are we searching for?" Kylie asked.

"I need to go to the woods where I found the bike and ran into Darwin. If I can at least get a lead on Juan Carlos's stolen bike, and prove I had nothing to do with it, then he'll leave me—and my mom's business—alone."

"You mean get a lead on Juan Carlos's *twice* stolen bike, right?" said Kylie.

"Right," I said.

"Wait, what?" said Sarita. "Twice stolen? Head spinning. Explain."

"A thief took it from the team trailer to leave it for the fence," I reminded her. "And then I think while Darwin was interrogating me in the woods, someone else found it and swiped it, screwing up his plan."

"So after he let you go, you think he went to find the bike where you told him it was, and it was gone? And now he blames you?" Sarita asked.

"Exactly. And now he must think I'm hiding it somewhere or I know someone who is. That's why he tracked down my house and went through the garage. And sent someone to my mom's studio to set her up, as more ammo against me."

"Maybe the original thief took it back," said Sarita. "Like, to make a fast buck for himself and cut out the middleman."

"Maybe. So then how could that bike still be in the woods, Tessa?" Kylie asked, as the speedometer needle inched up a notch. She was now seven miles over the limit. I could tell she was getting excited about all this, despite her skepticism

"Actually I'm pretty sure it's *not*," I said. "But maybe there's some clue there. Something that might tell us who Darwin really is. Or something that would point to the person who messed up his plan and took the bike out from under him."

"Or a clue that points to the original thief," Sarita added.

"I don't know," said Kylie. "It's not really our job, is it? It's not like we're trained forensics experts. And we probably shouldn't tamper with a crime scene."

Sarita sighed. "It's not an official crime scene. There's no 'official' crime. Nothing's been reported. Come on, Kylie. Remember when we all used to read Nancy Drews? If we were in a Nancy Drew book, we wouldn't even be debating this. We'd just go look."

"If this were a Nancy Drew book," said Kylie, "we wouldn't have to poke around in the woods. The clues would be more obvious. Like a sign of a twisted candle or something."

"Or the Inn of the Poison Oak," Sarita said in a spooky voice.

"How about the Grove of the Poison Ivy?" I said. "There was a lot of that in the woods."

"Great. That's what we all need. Poison ivy," grumbled Kylie.

But she shifted to the right lane, and took the exit to Cabot at ten miles per hour over the limit.

IT WAS eerie, driving through Cabot again. The parking lot by the elementary school where Jake and I had parked yesterday was now completely empty. So was the middle school lot where the staging area had been. There were no banners, no sponsor signs, no discarded pamphlets. The only sign of a recent event was a flatbed truck pulling out with portable toilets.

I'd half expected to see crime scene tape strung up everywhere. And a sign with my face on it: WANTED: CHARITY BIKE RIDE BANDIT. CAUSER OF MAYHEM.

But this wasn't a crime scene, I reminded myself. No one knew a bike had been stolen. And no one knew—yet—that I'd made a stupid move on the route.

I clutched my seat belt as we passed the last place I'd seen Juan Carlos. "Stop here," I said. "This is near the trail into the conservation land, where Jake and I went in."

Sarita led the way into the woods, down the walking trail, with Kylie close behind. I lingered a moment, staring at the place where I'd last seen Juan Carlos. I knelt down and looked at the grass for signs of his footprints, anything he might have dropped, any physical memory I could hold on to. I found nothing. I held the cross in my hand, pulling at the chain until it cut into my skin, forcing me to remember what it had felt like to have him put it on me.

You will call? Please? It is very important.

"Tessa!" called Kylie, a note of panic in her voice. "Where are you?"

"Coming!" I stood up and hurried to catch up with my friends.

We spread out and looked around, off the trail, in other bushes, hoping some clue would turn up. A tire track. A footprint. I saw the bush where I'd found the bike, and the patch of poison ivy. No bike. And no sign of anyone having been there. No footprints, no trampled grass, no bike parts. Nothing. It was as if the woods had erased any secrets as swiftly as Darwin had erased all those texts.

KYLIE CONTINUED driving down Great Marsh Road, heading back toward the highway. I cringed when we passed the place where Jake and I had joined the ride. We drove a little farther and I saw the SLOW DEAF CHILD sign ahead. "Can you pull over?" I asked.

Kylie did. "Whoa," she said as we came over the hill. "Check that out."

There was already a bike there, attached to the street sign, painted entirely white. The shrine had sprung up all around it. Flower bouquets. Flowers in vases. Living plants. Teddy bears. Angel figurines. Cycling jerseys. EcuaBars. Votive candles flickering softly in jars.

"Why's the bike all white?" Kylie asked in a hushed voice. "It's beautiful. But kind of haunting, don't you think?"

"It's supposed to be haunting. It's a ghost bike," I said. My voice was hushed, too. Ghost bikes were things of beauty and dread. Reminders of cycling's freedoms and dangers.

I'd seen a ghost bike once before, on a busy Boston street, where a college student had been hit by a truck. A sign at that memorial had explained how ghost bikes were constructed by mourners, bolted to signs or fences near where a cyclist had been killed. They were meant to raise awareness of the need for bike-friendly streets. My heart raced. This had to be the memorial shrine that Darwin had mentioned in his text message that morning. The place where an "associate" would expect me to hand over the bike on Thursday evening.

"I want to go see it close up," I said.

"Do you want us to come, too?"

"No. That's okay. I just need a moment."

"Be careful," Sarita urged as I got out. "There's a lot of traffic here."

I approached the shrine. I reached out and touched the bike. Then I knelt down for a closer look. What if this was Juan Carlos's twice-stolen spare bike?

No. That would be too easy. And I could see, beneath the coat of white paint, that this was an older-model Cannondale, not a Cadence. Just something the Ghost Bikes organization had donated to the cause.

While I was kneeling down, I read personal notes and hand-painted signs, in both Spanish and English.

¡Eres un ángel más en el cielo ahora!

You ruled the roads, el Cóndor. Rest in peace.

Que descanses en paz.

I let my tears fall and wiped my nose on the back of my hand. I wished I'd brought something to leave for him there, some way to pay my respects.

"I'm so sorry," I whispered. To Juan Carlos. Or the air. "I'm sorry for crashing and for making you crash. And I wish I knew what you wanted to talk to me about. After the race."

Birds twittered. Traffic whooshed. I guess I'd been hoping for some kind of sign, an otherworldly communication. But Juan Carlos's spirit didn't speak to me, in any language.

I saw a dark brown streak on the pavement. I hugged myself and looked away. "I'm sorry," I whispered, and listened intently, as if the breeze or the rustling trees might send back a response, a reassurance.

Instead all I heard was the indifferent rush of passing cars.

I shuddered as I turned away, wondering what—and who—Thursday would bring. Would I return to this spot with a bike? With information about who really had it? Or with nothing at all? And what would happen to my mom if I showed up empty-handed?

KYLIE DROVE a couple of exits east and pulled up at our favorite farm stand, which had the best ice cream in New England. "We need a break from all this," she said. "You're a wreck."

We sat at a picnic table and ran Kylie's mock interview.

"You don't need two weeks. You could face Preston Lane today," said Sarita once we were done. "Especially with all your answers about ethics and business and corporate responsibility."

Kylie swatted her arm. "You should like them. You wrote them." She grinned, then looked worried. "Maybe I shouldn't use your words so much. Isn't it kind of cheating? I mean, what if Preston asks me some follow-up question that I can't answer?"

"The ideas are yours, Kylie," I said. "Sarita didn't say anything you wouldn't say yourself. She just made it all concise and sequenced, and threw in some business vocab. You'll do great."

"Just win this thing. Okay?" said Sarita.

"Okay." Kylie smiled nervously. "I just hope I don't freeze up when I meet Preston Lane. He's kind of intimidating."

"What do you think, Tessa? You've met the man. Is he intimidating?" Sarita asked.

I thought a moment. He shouldn't be. Preston Lane represented everything Shady Pines stood for. We wrote letters to our state reps starting in second grade. We lobbied to get products with non-sustainable palm oil out of our vending machines, to save chimpanzees in Indonesia. We were highly advanced recyclers. Our whole school was in love with the guy because of the good work EcuaBar did. From afar, he seemed totally down-to-earth. Up close, I knew from my *KidVision* interview with him, he seemed less approachable. Distracted.

"He seems like he's always thinking of a million other things, like you're not sure if you have his full attention," I admitted. "And powerful people can be intimidating, I know. But he's a pretty regular guy."

"Who just happens to be one of Boston's ten wealthiest men," added Sarita. "And *Forbes* magazine's top pick for this year's most socially responsible executive. Did you see that article?"

Kylie and I shared a knowing smile. Sarita, obsessed with business, had subscribed to magazines like *Forbes* and *The Economist* since she was thirteen. "Um, I think I missed that one," I said. Then, to Kylie, I added, "Imagine Preston Lane in cycling clothes. You can't possibly be scared of someone in spandex."

Then I remembered how scared I'd been with Darwin in the woods. He'd been a man in cycling gear. Nothing funny about him.

Thinking of Darwin, and his texts, I remembered my phone, which had been powered off for hours, a record amount of time for me. Hopefully Darwin hadn't left me any more messages. But maybe Jake had. Maybe having my phone off this long was driving Jake crazy.

I pushed the power button, even though I knew I shouldn't. I just wanted to check to see if anything had come in from Jake. I wouldn't reply. And I'd turn off the phone immediately.

The text that buzzed in shocked me. Darwin. He was back.

ANY NEWS?

"Who's that?" Kylie asked, leaning over to see. "Not Jake, I hope."

SO HOW'S THAT ICE CREAM? YUM.

Darwin. *Where was he?* I looked around wildly, at happy families at picnic tables, and kids lining up at the ice-cream stand. I saw no one with aviator sunglasses, a buzz cut, a thick neck.

I HAVE OTHER EYES AND EARS.

My God. It was like he was reading my thoughts! I spun around again, scanning the crowds for anyone who looked like a potential associate. I didn't even know what I was looking for. Trench coats? Fedoras? Darwin had tried to dress like a cyclist at Chain Reaction. Any of these moms and dads mopping ice cream off kids' faces could be working for him. Or anyone serving up ice cream. Or maybe there was some kind of webcam trained on us!

The texts vanished, all at once, as before.

"Tessa? You okay?" asked Sarita.

"Darwin's back. Texting me. He knows we're here." I stood up so fast I knocked over my ice-cream dish. "We have to get out of here. Now."

We piled into the Fingernail, and Kylie peeled out of the lot.

While Kylie drove, fast, back to Route 2, I explained the latest texts, while looking behind us every five seconds. No cars seemed to be following us, and near the exit for Cambridge, we all finally relaxed. A little.

"So no clues, no bike—what now?" asked Sarita. "And you've got spies," she added grimly, as if I had head lice.

"Why is this guy keeping tabs on you anyway?" asked Kylie.

"He's monitoring her," said Sarita. "Making sure she doesn't slip up. Or hoping she'll just lead them to the bike directly."

"Tessa, it's time to call the cops," said Kylie. "You didn't do anything wrong."

I'd done everything wrong.

I shook my head. "Not so simple. I don't know how many of these 'eyes and ears' Darwin has. I'm going to keep looking for the bike or for leads and get him off my back."

"And we still have until Thursday to find something," Sarita pointed out.

"No," I said. "*We* don't. *I* do. You guys should keep your distance from me until this thing is over."

"What? No!" said Sarita. "We're not abandoning you to this creep."

"Seriously. Don't text or call my cell phone and don't come by the house. I don't want him tailing you, too. From now until Thursday, my phone is a direct line to Darwin."

17

TAPPING SOUNDS at my window woke me up that night.

I glanced at my nightstand clock. It was just after midnight.

The tapping grew louder. Insistent. The windowpane shook. I sat up and drew the covers up to my chin, like a kid in a picture book frightened by monsters. There could be a monster out there. Darwin. Could he have come back to the house, and located my *room*?

The slats of my bottom shutters were down, but my top ones were open enough so that I could just make out a baseball cap shape in the moonlight.

Through the shutter slats I saw the movement of an arm reaching up, as if the person was looking for some way to open the window.

My heart in my throat—I now understood what that expression really felt like—I glanced at my cell phone, plugged in to the wall charger. Across the room, out of reach.

I glanced at Bianca Slade's photo. And in the moonlight, I read the second item on the list of Qualities of Good Investigative Reporters: Having courage. *You may find yourself under attack, legally or personally. Believe in what you're doing and find the courage to carry on.* No more games. I'd confront Darwin head-on and make him believe I had not intercepted his stolen bike.

I got out of bed and crept up to the window. At the last second, I grabbed from my bookshelf a trophy I'd received last year, when *KidVision* was honored at the National Academy of Television Arts and Sciences. It was heavy, made of brass, and might function as a weapon.

I took a deep breath and threw open my shutters.

And stared into the face of a guy wearing a Red Sox cap and a startled expression. Jake.

I stared at him, my fingers tightening around the trophy base. Even though I'd rather see Jake than Darwin at my window, my anger at him came back in a rush.

"Can I come in?" he asked through the window.

I set the trophy down on the desk, opened the window, and let him in. We did need to talk. Might as well get it over with.

Jake was no stranger to my window. He'd even stayed over half the night in my bed a couple of times. But now we stood awkwardly facing each other, our hands at our sides.

"Hey," he said. "You up for a moonlight picnic?" He gestured outside. "I have fruit and a blanket. And brie. Oh, and this." He reached into his back pocket and took out a spray of baby roses. "I'd have sprung for the big ones, two dozen, but it's hard to bike with those."

I stared at him, and the roses. How could he show up and act like nothing had happened?

"And this?" He reached into another pocket and pulled out an EcuaBar. My favorite flavor, Jungle Gem, with real cacao nibs. The ultimate peace offering. "I think I may have overreacted," he said. "A little." He set the EcuaBar down on my desk.

Those were welcome words, long overdue. Something sharp lodged inside me softened. But only for a moment. Now Juan Carlos was no longer a threat, out of the picture. Is that what freed Jake up to finally say words I wanted to hear?

"You know he died, right?" I said.

He looked down. "What a freak accident. I don't get how it happened."

"You're probably happy about it."

He frowned. "I'm not. Do you really think that? Yeah, I didn't like the guy. But I definitely didn't want him to die." He shuddered. "I can't imagine what he must have gone through out there. It's freaky. It's every cyclist's worst nightmare, that kind of crash."

I glanced at my nightstand, where the necklace I'd removed just before falling asleep gleamed in a beam of moonlight slanting through the shutter. I didn't feel like explaining that to Jake. I backed up slowly and picked up a sweater. I casually tossed it toward the nightstand so that it covered the cross.

Jake stepped forward and gently touched the gauze pads taped to my right arm and right leg. "Babe. You're hurt," he murmured. "You really were in the crash yesterday. I'm so sorry."

"Not as sorry as I am." I flinched and pulled away. "You have five minutes."

"To do what?"

"To tell me why you dropped me on the ride."

Jake sunk into a beanbag chair. "What happened to 'hello'?"

"Okay. *Hello*, you dropped me on a ride? *Hello*, what was the point of doing the ride together if we weren't going to actually do the ride together?"

"I was pissed. Okay? Pissed. Is that a crime? Am I allowed to have an emotion? Or are you the only one?" He glared at me a moment, then sighed. "Okay. See? My emotions took over just now. And they did on the ride, too."

"Yeah, that seems to happen to you a lot lately. Maybe you should get some help."

"What, like talk to someone? A professional? Please." Then he stood up again and reached for my hand. Held it. Caressed it softly. "I don't need to talk to anyone except you, babe. You're the only one who truly understands me. You're like a part of my soul. You know?" His eyes teared up. That couldn't be faked.

But he was wrong. I didn't truly understand him. Sometimes I felt like I didn't even know him. And he definitely did not understand me. I snatched my hand away. "You now have three minutes to wrap up your story about what happened to us on that ride."

"Fine. I made it to the first water stop, at mile twenty. You weren't there."

"Mile twenty? God, Jake. You left so fast, did you really think I'd be right on your wheel? And make it that far without saying a word?"

"I got caught up in the moment," Jake insisted. "Besides, you're a better rider now. I trusted you weren't far behind me."

"Really? I think your guilt didn't catch up with you until mile twenty."

He ignored this. "Anyway, then I heard there was this big pileup back at the six-mile mark. I got really scared that you might have been caught in it. I couldn't get all the way back because they were turning people away. I went out to the main road and rode back to the medical tent at the staging area."

"Why?"

"Why? Are you kidding? Because I was worried sick about you. I looked for you everywhere. Finally some EMT in the medical tent said you'd gone home with your mom. Tessa." He ran one finger down the inside of my unhurt arm. A movement that used to send electric thrills through my whole body, now just made me recoil. "I feel so terrible that this happened. It's all my fault. I should never have asked you to ride bandit with me."

I pulled away. "I don't get it. Why did you ask me to do that ride in the first place?"

"Because I just wanted to ride with you. I want you in my world, okay? Why is that such a crime? It was supposed to be fun. Then it got . . . complicated. That's all."

Complicated. Like so many things with Jake these days.

There's a beautiful moment in bike racing. The breakaway: when a rider breaks out of the line of riders in the peloton and charges toward the front, taking the lead. Now was my moment. I looked him right in the eye. "You left me on the ride. And you *dismissed* everything I was worried about. Like getting caught. Or the stolen bike and the guy in the woods."

"It won't happen again. I'll do better. I'm willing to fight for us, Tessa. Aren't you?"

"No. I'm not."

He stared at me. "We have something really rare and special. You know it. You're probably not going to find something like this with anyone else. But if you want to throw it away, everything we've worked for, fine. Be a quitter."

My face burned. *Quitter.* He knew I hated that word. But I stood my ground.

As he opened the window and put one leg over the sill, I stared at his shaved calf muscle. I stared at it for the last time. Never again would it brush over my own leg. Then I saw a constellation of red blisters on his ankle. I pointed. "What is that?"

"What? Oh. I had a little brush with poison ivy." He slung that leg over the sill. "I'm not sure why the hell you care."

My stomach seized. Could *Jake* have stolen Juan Carlos's bike and left it for the fence? I looked at him, hard. Was he the kind of person to steal something like that—or anything?

"Jake," I said. "Wait."

He paused, one leg over the sill.

"Did you see Juan Carlos's spare bike in the woods when we were cutting through?"

"For real, Tessa? Is that a serious question?"

"It's a serious question."

"*No.* God no. If I'd seen it, I would have stopped and looked, same as you."

"Did you *put* Juan Carlos's spare bike in the woods?"

"You mean, did I steal his spare bike from the team trailer? And hide it in the woods?"

"Yes. And did you leave it for that guy I ran into? The fence?"

"Of course not! That's ridiculous!" he burst out. "You were with me the entire time."

I glanced at my door. "Shh. You'll wake up my parents. And no, I was *not* with you the entire time. You rode off to get your sports drinks from the car. Remember? We were apart for almost fifteen minutes." I looked closely at him. "Did you really go get those sports drinks?" I wished I could remember seeing bottles on his frame. I'd been so freaked out about Juan Carlos giving me his necklace, and then about the guy in the woods, I hadn't bothered to look.

"Of course I did," he said. "And how would I have had time to get back to my car and then go steal and hide a bike?"

He had a point. Then again, Jake was a champion racer. Maybe he could have accomplished all that in ten or fifteen minutes.

"You still think I did it? Tessa. What would I want that asshole's spare bike for?"

"I don't know. To sell to some black-market sports collector? You said sports memorabilia from famous athletes are worth a lot of money."

He let out a long breath. "Wow. Just, wow." He smirked. "If I were in that business? I might have waited until Juan Carlos was dead. Then the bike would be worth a lot more."

"Look, I'd almost understand if you did." I used the voice I always used during the doping scandal. Soothing and vaguely cheerful. "I know things have been tight financially. I know you need money for UMass. I know your mom works two jobs."

"Great. One rash on my leg, and now I'm a bike thief?" Jake's eyes blazed. "And an impoverished one? I don't need your pity party. I thought you were on my team."

"I didn't call you a thief. Don't put words in my mouth. I just want to find out—"

"Oh. Sorry. Isn't that what you like? Other people's scripts?" he shot back. "Sorry you lost your job, by the way. Heard about that. Maybe now you'll know what it's like to be a regular person who isn't handed everything on a platter."

"Get out." My voice shook.

"My pleasure," he shot back.

I turned my back. I heard him lift the window, then the soft thud of his jump to the ground. Bike wheels churning on gravel. Then silence. It was over.

I felt something lift off my chest. I felt like I was at a higher altitude. Like the air was crisp and clean and, finally, I could breathe.

I sank into my desk chair, trembling. Now I couldn't rule out Jake as a suspect. I glanced at Bianca's Qualities of Good Investigative Reporters #6: Having a Passion for Truth and Justice. *Good investigators are committed to looking at all sides of a problem and working tirelessly to uncover the truth.* And quality #5: Thinking Logically. *Organizing and thinking through ideas and rationales is key.* I picked up a pen and a notebook and wrote my rationale.

Bike Theft Suspect: Jake

1. He could have asked me to do the ride with

him as a cover. He was away from me long enough to do the job.

2. He could have stolen Juan Carlos's spare bike from the Team EcuaBar trailer. He'd know where to find it.
3. He could have hidden the bike in the woods, thinking he'd pick it up later, after the ride, and sell it. Or Darwin could have paid Jake a flat fee for the job.
4. Even if Jake was the thief who originally took the bike from the trailer, that doesn't mean he's the one who intercepted it from Darwin. Or that he knows who intercepted it.
5. Jake isn't a strong enough lead (yet) to refer Darwin to. Much as I'd love to get revenge.

I sighed and set down my pen. I ate the Jungle Gem EcuaBar Jake had brought me, and concentrated on Bianca's Qualities of Good Investigative Reporters #3: Being Flexible. *If you hit a dead end, be prepared to take a turn with your research and your questioning.*

Other people had been around the starting line that day. People who might have seen suspicious activity. People who might have been able to cover a lot of ground.

I knew just who I needed to talk to.

18

COMPASS BIKES, taking up most of a warehouse, was one of the biggest and busiest bike shops I'd been in. Gripping the handlebars of my scraped-up Bianchi, I breathed in the strange stew of smells: leather, rubber, metal, grease. Aisles of bike frames stood at attention. More hung from the walls. All around me, people were checking out equipment or browsing for clothes and accessories. Conversations and laughter echoed off walls, punctuated with the sounds of chains whirring, tools grinding and clicking. It felt like standing inside a machine. Everyone had a place to be, a role to play.

Except me. I was an outsider to this world. Anytime I'd needed work done on my Bianchi, Jake had done it for me. The one time I'd needed something bigger fixed, Jake had asked his team mechanic for free help.

His team mechanic. Gage Weston. I remembered something Mari had said about him: he was now the manager of Compass Bikes, where I, a known bandit, probably wasn't welcome.

I glanced out the window at my mom's departing car. If I ran now, I could catch her, and she'd be all too happy. "I don't love this neighborhood," she'd said when we first arrived in the stark industrial area near MIT. "Why don't I wait outside while you ask about bike repairs and volunteer opportunities? Better yet, I'll go in with you."

"Mom. I'm blocks away from the Kendall T station," I'd argued. "There are MIT summer session students everywhere around here."

"I don't know, honey. . . ."

"*Mom.* This is a great chance for me to get some ideas for a vlog I want to start. About volunteer work. You know, like for college applications." I told her about my brainstorm idea that morning: starting a vlog about teen volunteering. I didn't need GBCN to keep doing what I was already good at: talking to people and listening. The vlog would help restore my public image and also get me closer to people who'd known Juan Carlos.

Volunteer work. College. Those two key words had instantly won me a day of freedom.

So there was no turning back now. I pushed my bike deeper into the store, desperate to find Mari without attracting the attention of Gage.

I remembered Mari's strong reaction to the news that Juan Carlos had crashed. It made me think she knew him personally. So she might have some insight into who would want his bike. And Mari had swept the whole Chain Reaction route in a support van, passing the woods more than once. Maybe she'd seen something or someone odd.

I reached under my lightweight scarf and squeezed Juan Carlos's necklace for luck, then arranged the fabric to conceal it. I didn't want to answer questions about it.

I scanned the crowds. Most people were in the mechanics shop area, behind the counter. They were clustered around bike repair stands or putting together parts strewn out on the floor.

Where was Mari?

Backing up to get a better view, I knocked over a display of water bottles.

As I scrambled to reconstruct the Great Pyramid, I looked up and saw a girl glaring at me, hands on her hips. She had grease streaks on her face, and a blue bandanna holding her bangs off her forehead. But even without the name tag on her Compass Bikes T-shirt—MARISOL VARGAS, ASSISTANT MECHANIC—I knew who she was.

Mari smirked. "You. The bandit rider."

"My name's Tessa, actually. Tessa Taylor. I think I told you it was Teresa, but—"

"I know who you are now. My little sisters used to watch your show. They always liked your character. Said you were like Dora—older, of course. And better dressed."

"Dora?"

"Dora the Explorer. The cartoon? They said you were like Dora for big kids. The way you always listed information in threes. And the map gimmick—locating the volunteers on that little map by spinning around—three times, right?—and throwing a dart in it? They thought that was cute." She smirked. "Dora the Explorer, she has a map, too. And a backpack."

"I'm not a character," I informed her. "That was really me on the show." The comparison to Dora—a character who amused preschoolers—that stung. I was Bianca Slade now, here to ask tough questions.

"Well, whatever. It doesn't really matter now, right?" Mari shoved her hands in her jeans pockets and regarded me with a trace of amusement.

I could tell she'd heard the word on the street. She knew I was media roadkill.

"So. You hijacked the cancer ride, and now you've come to trash our store?" She raised an eyebrow as I placed the last water bottle back on the top of the wobbling pyramid. "How nice of you to include us on your wanton path of destruction."

"Actually, I'm here to get my bike fixed."

"Urgently? We're finishing our bike drive today and have to process these donations."

"I guess it's not so urgent. Hey, why don't I donate my bike instead? Can you use it?" I pushed it toward her. It's not like I was ever going to ride it again. And the donation could win me points. I might get more information from Mari if I proved we were on the same side.

She walked around my bike, inspecting it. "The spokes are hopeless in front, but the wheel can be replaced. Nice steel frame—no obvious cracks or dents, but we'll have to take a closer look before we can donate it whole. If there's any doubt, for safety reasons, we'd strip it for parts. It's a good bike. You're not serious about giving it up."

"It has bad memories."

"Because of Chain Reaction?"

"Because of my boyfriend. I mean, my ex."

"Ah. The ex-boyfriend and also the ex-racer, right?"

"Right." I was about to ask her if she'd seen Jake before the race without me, but she kept on talking. "That's a little extreme, don't you think? I mean, you can ditch a guy anytime. Another one comes along eventually. Right?"

"Sure," I said, looking away. Would another come along?

"My advice?" she went on. "Lose the guy. Keep the sport."

"Thanks. Duly noted." My Jake wounds were still too raw, too exposed. I didn't want to go there. I changed the subject. "Where are all these bikes going anyway?"

"Ecuador."

"Why Ecuador?" I asked, trying not to betray my excitement. Mari *must* have known Juan Carlos personally! "Don't they have bikes there?"

"They do, but they need more *decent* bikes, and parts," said Mari. "Like in poor sections of Quito—that's the capital city—

and in villages. There are places in the rain forest where kids stop going to school because they can't get to the middle schools or high schools that are ten miles or more away. But if they have bikes, they can get to school, finish their education, and avoid taking crappy jobs or getting married and pregnant at age fifteen. Bikes change lives."

She spoke so passionately, I knew I'd found a safe topic, a way to get her to put her anger toward me to the side and to open up. At the same time, I felt something stirring inside *me*. I wished I could do something so helpful myself, instead of always interviewing everyone else about their visions, their causes. What would it be like to find a cause of my own?

"So we've got a forty-foot shipping container coming tomorrow afternoon, and we have to get the donated bikes prepped and loaded by Thursday afternoon," Mari went on. "We're hurrying to get this shipment down there."

"Why the hurry?"

"It's in honor of Juan Carlos. This was a project he started." Mari blinked, her eyes glassy. "And of course we want to get them there in time for the Pan-American Cycling Tour."

The PAC Tour. When we'd talked at Chain Reaction, Juan Carlos had mentioned leaving for Bogotá soon. "Isn't it in Colombia?" I asked.

"It starts there, but it goes to three countries. Colombia, Venezuela, and Ecuador," said Mari. "Plus, Ecuador's capital city, Quito, is doing a big cycling exposition timed with the tour. We want this delivery to be a beautiful thing, the unloading timed with the bike tour finish and the expo. Good advertising for Vuelta, and a fitting tribute to Juan Carlos. That was Gage's idea."

Now I understood the fast-paced mechanical dance going on in the shop, the choreography among bikes and people, parts and tools. Time pressure.

"The bikes that are damaged or too old we're stripping for usable parts," Mari went on. "And the good bikes have to be partially disassembled for shipping. We have two days to prep and pack four hundred bikes into a box."

"That's a lot of work." It looked like interesting work, actually, but I tore my eyes away from the busy mechanics and got back on track. "So, um, did you know Juan Carlos pretty well?"

Her face suddenly closed. "Why so many questions, Dora?"

"I'm starting a vlog about young adults who do volunteer work." My mind whirled. "And I want to profile Juan Carlos on it. As a kind of memorial tribute thing."

Mari tipped her head. "Huh. That's nice," she said cautiously. "Okay. He'd been volunteering with our Earn-a-Bike program. Don't you want to take some notes?"

"No. I'll remember. Go on. What'd he do with your program?"

"He dropped in, even after he went pro, whenever he had time. He loved teaching bike mechanics to kids and helping them build their own bikes."

"He adored children," I remembered out loud.

"Yeah. He really connected with the kids."

I followed Mari's gaze to a glossy photo of Juan Carlos, tacked to a wall near the door. It was an official team portrait, autographed. Beneath it, attached to a memorial poster that people were signing to send to his family in Ecuador, was a collage of snapshots taken in the store. I bent closer to see. Juan Carlos helping a little girl oil a bike chain, the girl looking up at him with adoration. Juan Carlos showing a teen guy how to true his wheel.

I felt a pang inside me. A sour plucked string from a broken part. Juan Carlos had been a force for good. The kind of person I was before Jake. The kind of person I wanted to be again.

One snapshot showed him standing with younger riders,

against a background of rolling green hills and snowcapped mountains. "Wow, gorgeous," I murmured.

"Wasn't he?"

"I meant the place. Where was this picture taken?" I tried to ignore Mari's slip, but I couldn't. She'd liked the guy. A lot. That was clear.

Mari flushed. "Oh. Right. Quito. That's his hometown."

"Have you ever been there?"

"Not yet. But I have cousins there—my dad was born there and moved here when he was a kid. I'm flying there this weekend, actually. As a Vuelta volunteer."

"Vuelta! Juan Carlos was involved with that group, wasn't he?"

"Yeah. And they're a big deal. They've helped turn Quito into this huge biking city."

"So you're going there. That's awesome. What are you going to do with Vuelta?"

"Teach bike mechanics to girls and women." She couldn't hold back her proud smile.

I marveled at her confidence. She was someone making her own way in the world, without pushy parents or coaches behind her. I wondered what that must feel like, to be so committed to something big, so sure of where you were going. To be able to say, "It's my life" and know exactly what that meant. Nobody had scripted those words for her.

Mari reached behind the front counter and handed me a bilingual brochure. "You should mention Vuelta in your vlog." She smiled briefly. "Put that in your backpack, Dora."

My face burned at the Dora reference again. But I just said, "I'll mention it," and slid it into my tote bag.

"Hey, can I ask you something else?" I said. The store was getting even busier. I couldn't lose my chance to ask the most important question of all. "You were driving that support van yesterday. At Chain Reaction. Did you notice anyone near the woods on Great Marsh Road, or anywhere near the woods, before the ride?"

She thought a moment. "No. Why do you ask that?"

I almost told her about the stolen bike in the woods, and about Darwin and his threatening texts. But Gage appeared behind the counter and was now looking our way. Because he was a ride official, probably involved in the investigation, I had to watch what I said. "Where were you from about eight in the morning till the start of the race?"

"Oh my God. Do you think I did something? What are you getting at?"

"No! I'm just curious. I heard there was a crash scene investigation."

But her pause made me pause. Could Mari—not Jake—have been the bike thief working with Darwin? Maybe. I listed reasons in my mind. She had a van—the perfect place to hide a bike, and the perfect cover if anyone caught her. She needed money to finance her Ecuadorian adventure. If she'd stolen the bike for a fee, working for Darwin, that money could go a long way. Literally.

I thought of a test I could run. Darwin had said something on the phone in the woods when he made that second phone call. Something about fruit—mangoes. Yes. Maybe the mango thing was a way to identify his contact person.

"You know, mangoes are best at this time of year," I ventured, watching her carefully.

"Good to know," she said, staring at me like I'd lost my mind.

I realized my test was stupid. If Darwin's statement was some kind of code, I didn't know the desired response. "Sorry. Just stating, um, a random mango fact. I do that sometimes. It's like a tic."

Mari shrugged. "Whatever, random mango girl." Her eyes

flicked to the photos of Juan Carlos again, and I immediately erased my suspicion. Mari had strong feelings for Juan Carlos, that much was clear. Why would she have taken his bike?

Still, she might have seen something. I asked again where she was before the race.

"I was in my van that whole hour before," she said. "Why are you asking all this?"

I glanced at Gage and lowered my voice to a near-whisper. "I heard a rumor he might have been missing his spare bike," I explained. "And Preston Lane said in a TV interview that Juan Carlos was late for the ride. I'm trying to figure out why."

"So you think he was looking for a missing bike?"

"Maybe." If he'd gotten my half-finished text, which had just enough information to go on, he could have. Crap. Maybe he'd gone back for the bike himself. Maybe *I'd* made him late for the start, by texting him. Fresh pangs of guilt stabbed at me. If he'd started on time, with his team, and not back with the recreational riders, he'd never have been affected by my crash. He'd still be alive.

Mari frowned. "I didn't hear anything about a stolen bike."

"When did you start sweeping the route in your van?"

"About quarter past nine. After the professional race started and the rec riders took off."

"And you saw no one going in or out of the woods?"

"No one," she insisted. "Why?"

Gage strode over to us. "Is this girl bothering you, Mari?"

Mari started to explain. "She's—"

"Donating a bike," I interrupted. "And I want to help out. With the bike drive." I could not get kicked out of this store.

Mari stared at me. "You want to what?"

"I'd love to help out. It'd be good for my vlog if I had firsthand experience."

Gage looked down his long nose at me. "Can you replace a chain? Tune a wheel?"

"No. But I can learn."

Mari looked doubtful.

"Please, give me a chance. I really want to do this."

Gage studied me a moment longer, then smiled. "Okay. If you're looking to serve some time for last weekend, and honor a great cyclist, you've come to the right place. This bike drive's gone gangbusters because of all the interest in el Cóndor. While Mari gets your bike donation processed, Tessa, let me show you how to break down a handlebar." He handed me an Allen wrench.

I felt powerful, taking that tool, seizing a chance to finally do something good.

19

AFTER MY long day at Compass Bikes, I trudged toward the Kendall Square subway station, my right arm and leg throbbing and itching. I'd clearly pushed myself too far, working all afternoon. But it had felt good to be doing real work, supporting Juan Carlos's cause.

I still had questions for Mari. But it had been impossible to talk one-on-one the rest of the afternoon. Bikes had steadily poured into the shop, dropped off by Boy and Girl Scout troops, by churches and temples and Rotary clubs.

Gage and three younger mechanics had kept me busy "flattening" bikes. That involved turning the handlebars and pedals inside out so they'd fit better into the shipping container. My hands felt clumsy at first. I kept dropping tools. But then I got the hang of it. Gage eventually stopped hovering over my shoulder.

Pizza appeared. I paused just long enough to inhale a slice. EcuaBars were passed around for dessert. I couldn't eat more than one bite of one, though. It tasted more bitter than sweet.

I'd been disappointed when Mari grabbed her courier bag and left the shop promptly at five. Fortunately, I'd redeemed myself with Gage. He'd invited me to come back to help out with the container load in two days, and film the load-in for my vlog.

About a block away from Compass Bikes, I took my phone

out of my bag, thinking I'd call my mom and tell her I was on my way home. But my battery was almost out again. And sure enough, a text buzzed in.

WELL??????

Another insistent buzz.

WHERE IS THE BIKE?

I typed furiously.

No idea! Tell me why you want it.

His reply:

NOT YOUR CONCERN. JUST GET ME THE BIKE BY THURSDAY. NO MEDIA CONTACT, NO POLICE TIP-OFFS.

MY EYES AND EARS ARE EVERYWHERE. WE CAN DESTROY YOU.

Then the messages vanished.

I TOOK the subway from Kendall to Harvard Square and went straight to the phone store.

"My battery's not holding a charge," I explained to the technician. "And I've been getting some weird texts from an unknown sender. Can you trace them?"

"That's probably a job for the police," said the tech. "But I can take a look, see what I can find." He scrolled through. "What text messages? I don't see any record of messages here."

"Yeah, that happens. They go away. Could someone be controlling my phone?"

"Very possible. Someone could control it remotely and wipe data."

Wipe data. Like Juan Carlos's phone number, which he'd typed into my phone the morning of Chain Reaction. And my half-finished text to him. And my exchanges with Darwin. All that was gone.

No wonder Darwin thought I might have something to do with the missing bike. I'd implicated myself by texting Juan Carlos and mentioning the bike in the woods. And he probably took Juan Carlos's number out of there so I couldn't warn him with any more details.

"Yeah, your phone's infected with malware." The tech made a clucking sound as he scrolled through a computer screen. "This model's been particularly vulnerable to attacks. I see you're still under warranty. Give me a half hour. I'll wipe it, go back to factory settings, and install an antiviral for you."

I wandered outside to wait and strolled through Harvard Square, down JFK Street toward the Charles River. It was a relief to be free of the phone for now, even for thirty minutes. I could almost feel normal again. Almost, but not quite.

Juan Carlos was dead. That was not normal.

My thoughts veered back to this reality every few moments. I resented all the cheerful people—tourists, students, moms with kids—who went about their daily business as if the earth had not been jolted off its axis. As if a good guy had not left this world.

I paused at a boutique, determined to distract myself even for a minute. I couldn't walk around weeping all the time.

A rack of sundresses caught my eye, especially a red dress at the front.

"Looking for anything special?" a saleswoman asked.

"Oh. Um. No, thanks." I had no business doing something as frivolous as shopping. The last time I'd shopped for a new dress was for Jake's prom. I'd bought that silvery, shimmery column dress and gone to that prom less than a month ago. How long ago that seemed. A happy night, even though my parents had thought we were broken up, and I'd had to lie and say I was at Sarita's. Jake had actually danced. We hadn't talked about the bike scandal all night. *You're a snowflake,* he'd murmured into my neck as we swayed under hot lights on the dance floor. *Don't melt. Promise me. Don't ever go anywhere.*

I won't, I promised. *Don't go anywhere, either. Okay?*

He hadn't answered. Of course he was going somewhere. College. Cycling again. And I'd be going places, too. Hopefully to study journalism. The whole conversation now seemed absurd, begging someone not to go. But a kind of enchantment had come over us that night—maybe from the dress—and being in his arms had felt right.

"That one would look darling on you," said the saleswoman, nodding at the red halter dress. "Want to try it on?" She took the hanger off the rack and danced the dress toward me.

A soft breeze played at the skirt. Sunlight caught the beading around the neckline. This was not a dress for a high school prom night in New England. It was a dress for salsa dancing. A dress for flirting in the moonlight. In South America. Not here.

"No, thanks. Just looking." I walked down to the Charles River. Standing in the middle of my favorite footbridge, leaning over the railing, I took Mari's Vuelta brochure out of my tote bag. The photos showed people biking through green and gold hills, snowcapped mountains rising up in the background. Couples strolled down cobblestone streets, past white and pastel-colored colonial buildings topped with red-tile roofs. Indigenous women with embroidered white blouses, long black braids, and layers of gold necklaces hugging their necks held out handwoven baskets, embroidered shirts, fruit. I drooled over cloud forest pictures, enormous blue butterflies, chocolate-brown rivers, and jungle vines. Banana plantations. A land of colors.

I tore my gaze from the brochure and looked down the river at the buildings of Harvard, white spires rising out of red brick. I watched the joggers along the footpath, the scullers on the river, the summer school students with backpacks. Cambridge had been my world for as long as I could remember. Here, I'd thought I was marching down a straightforward path to success. But now my path was no longer sure.

I looked at the brochure again, reading the words this time.

> Volunteer for Vuelta! Come to latitude zero, the middle of the world, and give your time and skills. Have the adventure of a lifetime! Contact: Wilson Jaramillo.

An email address and a phone number for their Quito office followed.

My breath caught in my throat. Was changing the direction of my life as easy as calling a number or emailing this guy? Could I go to Ecuador, like Mari, as a Vuelta volunteer? Even film for my vlog there? Could I ditch Darwin and those creepy texts, put some serious miles between me and that crash scene—not to mention Jake—and flee to the middle of the world? Maybe

I'd free myself of this nightmare. I'd come back to a fresh start, having done some good in the world.

Right. Like my parents would ever let me go. This Vuelta advertisement might as well have been a brochure to the moon. I folded up the paper and shoved it deep into my bag.

BACK IN the phone store, the tech handed my cell to me between thumb and forefinger, as if its infection was catching. "Just as I suspected: loaded with malware. That's what ran the battery down. You've got the best antiviral now, but a sophisticated hacker can get full remote access and subvert the antivirals."

"Oh my God. How did this happen to me?"

The tech shrugged. "Hackers manage to stay ahead of us all the time. If you're within a few feet of someone's mobile device now, a hacker can install malware that pulls your data without even touching your phone."

"Could someone track down where I am?"

"Oh, absolutely, if your phone is turned on," said the tech. "Your phone has GPS activated. Listen, if you're worried, tell your parents. And they should call the police."

I thanked him and turned off the phone before shoving it deep in my tote bag. What I really wanted to do was chuck it into the Charles River—but then I'd have to explain the loss to my parents, who paid for the phone. And throwing out the phone didn't rid me of Darwin. I had no doubt he'd find more direct ways to stay in touch with me.

Now I knew how Darwin had tracked down my house. I'd had my phone off at Compass Bikes to save the battery, so at least he hadn't known I was there all day. But he had known I was at the ice-cream stand near Cabot yesterday. He could have seen my location on the phone and assumed I was eating ice cream, then worded his text as if he were watching, just to freak me out.

If he could get into my phone and manipulate texts, and figure out where I was anytime that phone was on, I had no doubt he could follow through on his promise to wreck my mom's business. And more.

20

DURING DINNER, much as I wanted to tell my parents about Darwin, I couldn't. Instead, I gushed about my day of volunteer work at Compass Bikes and the idea I had for my vlog. My parents seemed intrigued. They even agreed to let me return to the shop in two days to help with the container load and film interviews with volunteers. It felt good to see their proud smiles again.

After dinner, we turned on the living room TV and caught up on the latest news updates. The medical examiner spoke at a press conference. "Toxicology tests are in. Mr. Macias's blood levels were normal," she said. "Hematocrit level was normal. There is no evidence of ingesting any performance-enhancing substances, either legal or illegal."

No doping. That was good, right?

"The cause of death was a brain hemorrhage, a result of the impact of the crash."

I buried my face in my hands and stifled a sob.

His reputation was intact. Juan Carlos was riding clean. But the medical examiner had spelled out my worst fear. *Impact.* That was caused by me.

"Why don't you call a friend," my mom suggested, putting her hand on my back. "Kylie and Sarita left you voice mail messages here all day. You didn't lose your cell phone, did you?"

I squirmed. "Um. No, I didn't lose it."

"I drove by Kylie's earlier and saw the Fingernail outside. I bet she's home now if—"

"Oh, no! Kylie!" I looked at my watch. "I have to go. I'm missing Beth's birthday!"

KYLIE OPENED the door. And scowled. "Nice. You missed it," she said. "Rob and I are cleaning up. Mom's spent. She's lying down."

"Kylie. I'm so, so, so, so sorry. I was volunteering at this bike shop, and—"

"You lost the time at a *bike* shop?" Kylie shook her head. "Wow. Again with the bikes. I hope you win the Tour de France someday, for all the time you've spent on this sport."

I handed her a bouquet of wildflowers I'd picked from my mom's garden on the way over. "These are for your mom." They suddenly looked pathetic, wilting.

Kylie took them. "They're crawling with aphids." She handed them back to me.

"I'm sorry. My mom's sworn off plant sprays and she's trying integrated pest management. The aphids won't hurt anything. Can I come in and say hi to her?"

She angled her body to block the door. "She's resting now. Maybe another time."

"Right." I sighed. "Was is it a good party anyway? Did she have fun?"

"Oh, yeah. It was a real hootenanny."

"Kylie. I'm *sorry.* Like I said, I was at this bike shop. Get this. I talked to this girl mechanic named Mari, who I'd met at Chain Reaction. Turns out she knew Juan Carlos, and he volunteered in their bike shop a lot. And then I had to go to Harvard Square and have my phone—"

Kylie held up a hand. "Stop. Okay? Just. Stop."

"Stop what?"

"Obsessing about this dead cyclist!"

"He's not just some dead cyclist. I knew the guy."

"Barely."

"We talked. More than a few times. He was always really nice to me."

"But you weren't, like, friends. Or anything bigger. Right?"

I hesitated. "Right."

She reached out and touched the gold chain. "You're still wearing this thing?"

"It's a connection to him."

Kylie shook her head. "You've gone too far. You're taking all the energy you put into Jake and transferring it to this guy. A *dead* guy. Which is the ultimate in not available."

"You don't know anything about it."

"I can see what you can't see. What good are friends if we can't keep each other on track? I don't think what you're doing is healthy. Somebody has to say it. Look. You have every opportunity to have a great summer. You have two healthy parents. I know your dad has that heart thing, and he just turned sixty. But he's here. You're not locked into taking care of someone who's sick. You don't have to drive anyone to chemo, or cook meals, or clean up those meals once they've been puked up all over the floor."

I shook my head in amazement. "Kylie. I'm sorry. I didn't realize things were so bad, or that you and your brother had to do all that."

Kylie shrugged. "It is what it is. Anyway. You have real freedom, Tessa. You could be doing something great."

I bristled at that. "What's not great about volunteering for a bike drive? That's what I did today. And I was feeling pretty good about it, until I came over here."

"Volunteering there isn't the whole story, and you know it. You're spinning your wheels, hanging around this bike shop, chasing somebody's ghost. You're trying to solve his problems, which have nothing to do with you. And I'm worried about this Darwin guy. He's harassing you, and he's got the wrong person. It's a mistaken identity case! Call the police. Let them deal." Retching and coughing sounds erupted from somewhere inside the house. "Besides." Kylie's voice softened. "Juan Carlos is dead. He doesn't need you. *I* need you."

I nodded. "I know. I'm sorry. I know I haven't really been there for you, through all this. I'm going to try harder. I promise. But I wish you could support me, too." I turned to go before she could see my face. I wished Kylie could understand how it wasn't so easy to just call the cops. And how important this stolen bike was to me—not only because finding it would get Darwin off my back. My path *was* linked to Juan Carlos's path. I'd swerved right into it.

21

THE NEXT morning I got up early to help my mom with those graduation proofs. I couldn't stop thinking about the real proof I needed to be looking at. Proof of Juan Carlos's stolen spare bike. Or at least a solid lead. Having to work for my mom all day today was a huge setback. But that was the deal my parents had offered. Start paying off the Chain Reaction debt today, and I could go back to Compass Bikes tomorrow. Tomorrow: the day Darwin needed me to deliver the bike. Or else.

I started to twist my hair into the old sideways braid. Then I shook it out, brushed it, and let it hang straight over both shoulders. I slipped on a blue cardigan to cover up my arm bandage and put on a little makeup. I stepped back from the mirror. Not so bad.

I beat my mom to the studio. I paused in the doorway, turning on the lights, illuminating all those photos of happy children and parents on the walls. It made me sick to my stomach to think Darwin was capable of destroying all this with the push of a button, the click of a mouse, sending a fake incriminating photo and a complaint to the local police. Even if nothing could be proved—because of course she didn't do anything—the complaint alone would bring her down. People trusted her with their children. Nobody would go to a family portrait studio that had a hint of scandal, just like most sponsors wouldn't back cycling teams that had any suspicion of drugs.

I didn't have much time to myself before my mom came to work. I went behind the screen she used to separate an area for portrait sittings. I set up my video camera on a tripod, then sat down opposite it, on a stool against a plain black screen. I hit RECORD using the remote control. I'd memorized the introduction I wrote out last night. The words came easily now.

"Hi! Welcome to Volunteen, my brand-new vlog about young adults who are making a difference. I'm Tessa Taylor, and I'll be your guide as we journey into all kinds of communities and meet some truly inspiring people. We'll learn what's at the heart of their volunteer work, whom it benefits, and how you, too, can get involved. Our first episode will take us to Cambridge, Massachusetts, and a unique shop called Compass Bikes, right near MIT. 'Taking You Places' is their slogan. And they aren't kidding. A shipping container filled with four hundred donated bikes, and countless bike parts and gear, will be heading to Ecuador tomorrow. I'll be helping them out, and giving you the inside story about this awesome project. Along the way you'll learn about a cyclist with a vision. Juan Carlos Macias-Léon, of Quito, Ecuador. Join us for the journey."

My mom was standing in the doorway.

I hit the STOP button with the video camera's remote.

She clapped softly. "You look beautiful, honey. And you sound great."

"Is it okay? I'm going to upload it right now."

"It's good," my mom said. "But do you really think it's on the same level as *KidVision*? Are your viewers going to find your vlog online, with all the other stuff that's out there?"

I sighed. "I don't want to repeat *KidVision*. I'm trying something different now."

"Your dad and I were thinking we could have a meeting with Kristen . . ."

"I don't want to go back to *KidVision*, Mom. I want to be able to talk about whatever I want. To come up with my own ideas and write my own questions."

My mom stood for a moment longer, looking at me, then took a seat on a stool opposite me. "I think I understand why you want to do this vlog."

"You do?"

"Sure. Being your own boss? That's freedom. That's why I like my job so much. Most days anyway. I think the six-month-old I photographed yesterday afternoon was calling all the shots." She laughed wryly. "Anyway. I knew when I was about your age that I wanted to do my own thing. Watching you do this vlog—wow. It brings it all back."

"Wait—you knew since you were my age you wanted to take pictures of kids?"

She looked down. "No. I came into that later. What I really wanted to do? When I was your age, and into my twenties? I wanted to be out in the field. Working for human rights organizations, as a photographer."

I stared at her. "I thought you loved taking pictures of kids."

"I've *come* to love it. It has its rewards. It's steady work—people seem to keep having babies. And it's great to think I'm preserving memories for generations." She gazed at a wall of framed baby and toddler portraits. "But to this day, for every well-off family's kids I photograph, all those cuties in their little J.Crew outfits, I can't help thinking of very different kids, all over the world, or even in our own city, who don't have heirloom photographs. Or expensive clothes. Or even basic comforts. Those are the kids I thought I'd take pictures of. It's their images I see when I look at that wall, like negative images. Ghosts. The photos not taken. They haunt me."

I let this sink in for a moment. I'd never seen this side of my mom, this sepia tinge of regret. "How would taking pictures of needy kids change anything?" I asked.

"Because pictures are powerful. I thought I could be the kind of photographer who uses images to inspire change. But that wasn't the path I took."

"Why not?"

"I don't know. Fear, maybe?"

"What were you scared of?"

"Let's see." My mom counted on her fingers. "Risk? Success? The unknown? Everything." She let out a long breath. "Yeah, everything. Here's a story. About being afraid. When I was twenty-seven, *Newsweek* gave me my big break. I had money to go to Juárez, Mexico, with a journalist and take pictures of border town kids."

"What happened?"

"I lasted three days. I got a terrible case of Montezuma's revenge. *And* roving gangs of young men followed me around when I did manage to crawl out of my hotel room for an hour. Then one of them stole my camera bag. I lost my Nikon, my lenses, everything. The journalist I was partnering with was furious. He demanded they send someone down to replace me. Which they were only too happy to do."

"Oh my God, Mom. You never said anything about all this." I glanced at the photo of the slums on a hill. "Wait. Did you take that picture? In Mexico?"

"I did." She smiled. "I've always liked that image. I keep it up to remind myself that there are other people and things to document. It gives me some perspective."

"And the Mexican blanket—was that from the trip, too?"

"Yes." She laughed wryly. "My one souvenir. I wrapped myself in it like an enchilada the whole time I was in that hotel room. I keep it to remind myself I went there. Otherwise it would feel like some distant dream. But it was real. As real as it gets."

The morning sunlight shifted through the window, lighting up my mom's face, softening her features. I saw her in a new light, too. It was freaky that she had had other dreams and ambitions I never knew about. Freaky, but kind of cool. "Why didn't you go back there and try again?" I asked her.

"It's water under the bridge. I did consider it, once. Even before your dad. I thought I'd do portraiture for a while until I got up my nerve to try again, or to face *Newsweek* and grovel for a second chance."

"But you didn't?"

"No. I met your dad and spent some years working in retail, in camera shops, just to help pay the bills while he was still working for Greenpeace. Then we had you, and suddenly running off to war zones or refugee camps didn't sound so appealing." My mom looked at me. "I guess what I'm trying to say, Tessa, is that I was scared. I let one negative experience define my entire career. I took the easier road. Even though, looking back at that brief stint in Mexico, what I remember most is how *alive* I felt. Being scared, being sick, that was all part of the experience."

"So let *me* have an experience," I pleaded. "I want to make some of my own decisions. Even if they're not the best ones."

My mom looked at me, searchingly. "You know what I see? My talented daughter putting herself out there in the world. How many kids get to be on TV?"

I shrugged. "I had nothing to do with it. Dad got me the job."

"He had a connection, yes, and he knew some media experience would give you a leg up for a reporting career. But you wouldn't have held that job for so long if you weren't talented. Am I right?"

"I guess."

"And now, look how you're branching out. Volunteering at a bike shop, when I've never even known you to hold a screwdriver! Starting a vlog! Tessa, I don't want to see you take unethical risks, like that charity ride business. That was totally wrong."

I looked down, bracing myself for a fresh lecture.

"But I guess what I'm trying to say, Tessa, is I see your point. We've taught you to be extra cautious. Maybe too cautious. You should know how to rise to a challenge."

I held my breath. Where was she going with this?.

"You know something?" she went on. "I'm glad to see you trying new things. I don't want you to be someone who does everything to please other people. I don't want you to be some character. I want you to be a person of character."

"So . . . can I go to Compass Bikes today *and* tomorrow, to help out and to film?"

My mom smiled and handed me my video camera case. "Pack it up. I'll give you a ride."

22

ALL MORNING at Compass Bikes, I interviewed mechanics and salespeople. Remembering one of Bianca Slade's tips about getting sources to relax and to trust you, I started out with simple questions about what bikes they liked best and how they got into cycling. Eventually I worked my way around to asking about their connection to Juan Carlos. I got great stories about Juan Carlos's quiet sense of humor, his patience, and his burning motivation to help his country—especially Ecuadorian kids.

A portrait of a saint emerged. The guy had no dirt in his history. No one could even tell me how he'd gotten that scar on his neck. Some said they'd never even noticed it. Had he hung out much with non-cyclists? Shady characters? No, just his teammates, people said. Most often, he came into the shop on his own, worked a shift with the kids, and left. A condition of his visa was enrollment in school, so between classes at Newton North, online study, working out, and training, he didn't have much spare time for friends. "The poor guy had no life. No free time for doing just normal teen guy stuff," one older salesclerk said with a sigh.

Occasionally, she added, he talked about his best friend and fellow racer el Ratón back home in Ecuador. "He was hoping to help his friend come to the U.S. and race here," she said, showing me a printout of an Ecuadorian newspaper article that had been pinned up on the growing shrine. The article, dated from before Juan Carlos came to the United States last year, was about the two promising young cyclists in Quito, the Mouse and the Condor. A photo showed both of them atop a hill, holding bikes up above their heads like conquering heroes.

I also asked those who'd gone to Chain Reaction if they'd seen Juan Carlos before the ride. Nobody had. They'd all been busy manning the Compass Bikes booth in the staging area.

On my morning break, I worked up the courage to talk to Gage. After all, he'd been at Chain Reaction all that morning, too, and might have noticed something. He might even know about the stolen bike.

"That's impossible," Gage said when I asked him if he knew anything about the stolen bike. "If Juan Carlos's spare bike got stolen, it would have made the news."

He was right. I'd been checking news websites and cycling forums regularly, and there'd been no mention of a missing bike. I sighed. Why did every path I went down have to be a dead end?

I had no leads. I'd be giving Darwin nothing tomorrow. Would I have to go to the ghost bike shrine empty-handed, so at least these guys wouldn't show up at my house? My nerves felt frayed. My heart raced. There had to be some nugget of information I could dig up about that bike, some bone to throw Darwin so that he would leave me alone.

On my lunch break, I borrowed a staff member's laptop and took it to a picnic table outside. I went to the Chain Reaction website, scanning desperately for any sort of lead, any possible new mention of a reported bike theft. As soon as I got to the home page, a new icon popped up, showing a camera. The link promised newly uploaded photos from the race and the recreational ride. Maybe a photographer had caught something. Like my mom had said, images could be powerful. I just had to find the right one.

I clicked through a slideshow of approximately one million pre-ride pictures, paying extra-close attention to pictures with trees in the background. No shadowy characters emerged.

I read on the site that a photographer had been stationed on the side of the road at mile ten, taking pictures of everyone. I scrolled through thumbnail after thumbnail. Hundreds of mile-ten portraits. After a while I forgot I was looking for possible bike thieves. I wanted to see the look on Jake's face. Maybe it would betray his guilt. Or regret at having ditched me.

But even after clicking through the whole gallery, I found no mile-ten portrait of Jake.

That didn't make sense. The photography checkpoint was at a narrow stretch of road where the riders were forced to ride single file. There were concrete barriers on either side; there was no way he could have skirted that camera. Jake had texted that he'd made it all the way to mile twenty, to the first official water stop, before realizing I wasn't behind him.

How could he have made it through mile ten but escaped the photographer's lens?

Had he really made it as far as he said he did? Or had he lied to me? And why?

23

LATER THAT afternoon, while still puzzling over the missing mile-ten picture of Jake, I caught up with Mari. She was alone, finally, in a corner of the mechanics' shop, with a bike on a repair stand, cleaning a chain. She seemed hypnotized as she cranked the pedals around to run the chain through the degreasing solvent, which smelled strongly of oranges.

"Hey," I said. "I want to thank you."

"For what?" She picked up something that looked like a toothbrush. Solvent spattered as she scrubbed the derailleur.

"For letting me volunteer here and film my vlog. And for not completely hating me."

She shrugged. "It was Gage's idea to let you work and film here."

"Oh. Right." I looked down.

Her face softened. "But I don't hate you, Dora. I respect what you're doing. Juan Carlos would respect it, too. He wanted more people to know about Vuelta, and about Ecuador." She gave the pedals a few more spins. The solvent dripping into a bucket below went from milky orange to black. Mari looked around, then said, in a hushed voice, "So what's up with this rumor you're spreading? About Juan Carlos's missing spare bike? I've heard you asking questions all morning, about what people saw at Chain Reaction."

I hesitated. I wanted to trust her. But not knowing where Darwin's eyes and ears were spooked me. What if someone was planted here in the bike shop, and heard me talking about him? Darwin would immediately make good on his threats. And I didn't want Mari to get on their radar, either. So now was not the time to tell her the whole story about that spare bike. If Darwin connected Mari to me, she could be harassed, too.

"I heard his spare bike could be missing," I said, trying to sound casual. "So I thought I'd see what I could find out, while I'm interviewing people about him."

Mari gave me a long look. "Where are you hearing about this missing bike?"

"Online. Cycling forums."

She folded her arms across her chest. "That's not true. I read them all. Nobody's mentioned a missing bike."

I looked around. Gage was busy with a customer. Everyone else around us was busy with bikes. I spun a chain through the degreaser so the sound would mask my words. "Okay. I saw it," I confessed in a low voice. "His spare bike. With the white handlebars. When I cut through the woods with Jake."

Mari pressed her lips together and stared at me, intently.

"I passed it in some bushes, near the walking trail," I explained, deliberately skipping the whole Darwin chapter. "And when I went back to the woods the next day to look for it, it was gone."

"So why didn't you report the bike on Sunday, at the race?" Mari demanded.

"Because I was bandit riding. Because I might incriminate myself and Jake, being near it. And because I have no proof of what I saw."

Gage loomed behind us. "Keeping busy, girls? I have lots to do if you're running out of work."

"We're fine," said Mari. She took the bike off the stand, put another one its place, and attached the chain cleaner to it. She spun the pedals, almost violently, until Gage, apparently satisfied, went into his office.

"I don't get why you're so mad at me. I'm just asking a few questions," I said.

"I'm not mad. Not at you anyway." Mari sighed. "They're closing the crash scene investigation tomorrow. That's what pisses me off."

"Closing the investigation?" That meant I was out of the woods, so to speak. No helmet camera or witness had come forward to finger me. I wasn't going to be questioned.

But what was Mari hoping an investigation would turn up? If she thought I was at fault in some way, due to my bandit riding, she could have reported *me* by now. And she hadn't.

I followed Mari's lead, hoisting another bike onto a stand. She set me up with another chain degreasing kit, and continued talking in a low voice as we both turned pedals.

"It's just completely lame," Mari said. "This whole half-assed investigation. The Cabot Police Department doesn't care about cyclists."

"What makes you say that?"

"Cabot has the worst statistics for bike accidents on their roads. They're going to call this another accident and be done with it. It doesn't help that Juan Carlos is from another country. They're not going to put any money into figuring out what happened. And now the truth about why Juan Carlos went down is going to be buried with him."

I reached out to her bike and stopped her pedals. "Wait. What do you mean, 'the truth about why he went down'*?* Why would you say that? What are you hoping they'll find?"

"The truth about the bike he crashed on."

I pictured the recurring image from the news: the badly mangled frame, broken into two pieces. Dirt streaks on green-taped handlebars.

"Everyone talks about this 'tragic accident,'" Mari went on, her brows furrowed. "Tragic? Yes. Accident? Not so much. I'm not convinced anyway."

My thoughts whirled. Was Mari suggesting Juan Carlos might have died on the route because of a mechanical issue? Or *foul play*? If he had—*if* he had—I was not completely responsible for his crash or his death. "Why aren't you convinced? Tell me your reasons."

"Some rider snapped a picture of the bike on the ground, right after Juan Carlos got loaded into the ambulance. I can show you," she added, watching Gage leave his office. "Follow me," she whispered, as Gage went to help a salesclerk with some problem at the register.

Mari led me to Gage's office and sat me down at the computer. The window was open to a website called Sports Xplor. The screen image was mostly black, with white and yellow text.

I noticed a list of major pro cycling events running down the screen and what looked like weird dancing fruit beneath each event. Tour de France, Giro d'Italia, Vuelta a España, USA Pro Cycling Challenge, Pan-American Cycling Tour. When I read that last event title, a sob caught in my throat. Juan Carlos was going home in a body bag, not on a bike. Not with his teammates to compete in his homecoming tour.

"Should we be in here?" I asked.

"It's fine. He lets me use his computer when I need to. This'll just take a second anyway."

Mari opened a new window, went to a cycling forum, and pulled up a photo a user had posted. It showed Juan Carlos's bike, split apart in two places on the frame: at the top, near the seat, and on the lower bar. Twisted metal threads made me think of guts spilling out.

"Wow. It almost looks like it exploded," I said.

"That's what carbon fiber does when it fails. Gage says these bikes are death machines and everyday riders shouldn't be on them. He won't even sell pure carbon fiber bikes here."

I thought back to Bianca Slade's interview with Chris Fitch. Cadence made carbon fiber bikes for high-end consumers and for racing teams, and one consumer model had had a safety issue. It sounded like there'd been a recall.

"If carbon's so dangerous, why do all the pro teams ride carbon fiber?" I asked.

"It's ultralight. It's fast," said Mari. "Racers go through bikes so quickly, they're usually replaced before problems show up. And they don't train on full carbon. But the way Gage explains it, these frames are mortal, and carbon fiber can have cancer."

"Cancer? It's a bike!"

"The carbon can be really vulnerable to damage, but you usually can't tell by looking," Mari explained. "Not like aluminum, which will bulge or bend if there's a problem and at least give you some warning. Here, check this out." Mari rummaged through a box under Gage's desk and pulled up a one-foot hunk of a bike frame. "See? The tube looks solid, but it's soup inside. Little threads. The resin splinters easily. If anything compromises the integrity of the frame—a hit to it at the right angle, or some defect—those fibers will just blow apart in a crash."

I took it from her, inspecting it. I couldn't believe something so light and delicate would hold up a person. At high speeds, too. "What's this collection of broken stuff for?"

"We've had bikes in here that people have run into a guardrail, or dropped off the back of their car," said Mari. "Customer thought it seemed fine, and then they hit a pothole. The whole frame can fail if it's been weakened. Gage collects these pieces to help educate customers who are determined to ride all-carbon bikes." She took the carbon tube fragment from me and tossed it back in the bin.

"Maybe that's what happened to Juan Carlos's bike in the crash," I suggested. "Maybe he hurt his bike before and didn't even know it."

"I thought of that, too," said Mari. "But the team had brand-new bikes from Cadence. The Chain Reaction race was their maiden voyage, a test run on them before the PAC tour. Most racers don't crash from catastrophic carbon failures. Regular people do because they don't take care of their bikes right, or they use them too long."

"What about product failure? Could Juan Carlos have been riding a defective bike?"

"Probably not. Racing bikes are ruthlessly inspected both in and out of the factory, and by the team mechanic before they go out on a race. Anyway, I've studied this crash picture for days. It doesn't seem right. At a relatively low speed, under thirty, his bike shouldn't have completely blown out like that. If I could only see the damage myself, I could get a better idea."

"So what's your theory?"

She hesitated. "I think somebody didn't want him to finish that race."

I squeezed the arms of the desk chair as I let Mari's words sink in. For days I'd been totally focused on the bike theft. That was important to figure out because Darwin was demanding I hand over that bike. But I hadn't been thinking about the bike that *crashed*, or the possibility that there might have been two separate bike crimes. A theft *and* a sabotage.

And if Mari's sabotage theory were right? This was *huge*. It meant I wasn't to blame for his death. Although it didn't bring Juan Carlos back, I could live with myself.

But who would do something so awful? And why? "We have to see that damaged bike from the crash," I said, standing up fast. "We have to get over to the Cabot Police station."

"It's with Dylan Holcomb," Mari said. "The police didn't keep the bike because it was just an accident, not involving a car. Dylan stores all the bikes at a bike school he runs on the side."

I followed her out of Gage's office, back to the bikes we were cleaning. "How do you know that?"

"Gage called over there yesterday, wanting to see the busted frame, and Dylan was really rude. He said the damage was consistent with what you'd find in an accident. End of story."

"If you found evidence that it was tampered with, would that be a game-changer?"

"Well, yeah," said Mari. "If there were signs of foul play, the police would have to keep the investigation open. Because then it's not just a bike accident. Then we're talking homicide."

Murder.

Unlike the bike theft situation, where I was implicated, the possibility of sabotage had to get reported to the police. And Darwin couldn't be mad about that, since it was a whole separate issue. I started pacing, thinking out loud. "So we could take the frame to the police and—"

"Whoa. Slow down, Dora," said Mari. "This isn't a TV show. You can't just make a three-step plan and have a happy ending in thirty minutes. First of all, we can't take the frame. It belongs to the team. And I'm sure Dylan Holcomb wants to keep that busted bike under the radar."

"Why?"

"Because if there are questions about its performance, he's

going to have some explaining to do. Those team bikes are his responsibility."

Dylan Holcomb. The new team mechanic had had unobstructed access to both Juan Carlos's main bike and spare bike. Could he be a suspect in either of the bike crimes?

I didn't know enough about him. It didn't seem like he could be working for Darwin, or else Darwin would have gone straight to Dylan to find Juan Carlos's spare bike. He wouldn't be bothering me. And I couldn't imagine a motive for the team mechanic to harm the star cyclist.

Still, even if Dylan had nothing to do with either theft or sabotage, it was his responsibility to safeguard the bikes. "We have to talk to Dylan," I said, my voice rising with excitement. "Maybe he knows more than he's letting on. And you have to look at that bike from the crash."

"When? Team Cadence-EcuaBar leaves for Colombia to start the Pan-American Cycling Tour on Friday."

"Tomorrow, then?" I still had a day to get Darwin a lead.

"No, tomorrow's the container load here. I'll be busy with that all day. Then I'm leaving for Ecuador on Saturday."

"So we have to go talk to Dylan today. How soon can you get out of here?"

24

IN THE neighborhood of Jamaica Plain, Mari parked in front of a bodega around the corner from Dylan Holcomb's bike school. We didn't want to park too close to the school. The Compass Bikes van Mari had borrowed would surely make Dylan suspicious of why we were visiting him.

Mari turned off the ignition but made no move to open her door. "I'm not so sure about this," she said. "Dylan's seen me before, at the bike shop. He might think we're up to something, poking around here and asking questions. He'd probably think someone put us up to it."

"But we've come this far," I reasoned. "This is our big chance to get some answers about how Juan Carlos died and how his spare bike got stolen."

"Maybe. But this is a storage facility, not a museum," said Mari. "Dylan doesn't have to show me anything. What am I supposed to say? 'Hey, I'd love to see Juan Carlos's busted bike? And by the way, can I take a really close look at it to make sure you're not lying?'"

"I see your point. But I can find a way to get Dylan outside. When he's out, you run in and look for the bike frame." I took my video camera out of the case. "Put this in your pocket."

"Sounds ambitious, Dora," said Mari, though she slid the camera into the wide front pocket of her gray hoodie.

I frowned. "Hey. Stop calling me that. Look, you cared about Juan Carlos, right?"

"Of course I did. I do."

"Me too. So let's find out what really happened to him. Okay? Are you with me on this?"

She gave me a long look. "You know, I can fix bikes. That's what I'm really good at. I don't know if I can fix what happened to Juan Carlos. You know, figure out this puzzle, about how he went down. But you're on this path to finding some answers. You feel confident about this? About looking around on our own?"

"Yes," I said, trying not to let my voice waver. "I'm confident that crashed bike will tell you something, and I'm confident I can get you in there to see it. I'm a good talker."

Mari looked at me a moment longer, her long lashes blinking slowly. She bit her lip. "Okay, then. I'm on your ride. Let's get in there and see what we can find out."

We hurried down the street and came to a white building with an auto body shop sign out front. A sculpture garden took up much of the parking lot. The sculptures were made out of rusting bicycle parts. Frames were welded together to look like stems and leaves, sprouting wheels for blossoms. Handlebars, fenders, wheel spokes, and other bike parts were bent into shapes, transformed into animals, dancers, robots, and bugs.

I left Mari in the sculpture garden and jogged around to the side of the building, where a handmade sign was tacked to a purple door:

Open Road School of Bicycling
(& Sculpture Garden/Gallery)

Find your balance—on a bike!

Free spiritual advice. Cheap tea.

Open by appointment and at whim.

Peace!

The sign might as well have read WELCOME TO CRAZYTOWN. Team Cadence-EcuaBar was rolling in money, compared to most cycling teams. Preston Lane was rich from his energy bars and his family trust fund. Cadence was a high-end bike manufacturer. Between Preston Lane and Chris Fitch, the team should have been flush with cash. So why was *this* the new guy they'd hired to keep the team's bikes safe? How was he an improvement over the über-professional Gage Weston?

I went inside. More bike sculptures, animals, were displayed on shelves and plant stands. The walls were filled with a gallery of framed photos of international cycling legends and photos of Team Cadence-EcuaBar. I stepped closer to one of the pictures. It was a computer printout, tacked to a bulletin board instead of matted and framed like the others. It was the photo I'd witnessed being taken just before Chain Reaction. The one with Preston Lane and Chris Fitch.

The one with no Juan Carlos.

I stared at that picture, as if willing Juan Carlos into the shot. So it was true. He'd never made it there after we talked. Where, then, had he gone?

"You like them?"

A woman with messy black hair and bright blue bangs came in from another room; as the door closed behind her I could see a room filled with Cadence bikes, spare tires, and other gear.

I started. Dylan's website and Twitter feed had made the place seem like a one-man operation. I hadn't expected this woman.

Now I had to get *two* people out of the building so Mari could come in and inspect the damaged bike frame.

Then I realized where I'd seen this woman before. The blue bangs. The thick, black, men's-style glasses sliding down her long nose. The heavily tattooed legs. This was the photographer who'd been working with the team right before the race.

"The sculptures," she prompted. "Do you like them?"

"Um. Yeah. They're great."

She smiled. "Thanks. Everything's for sale. Great gifts for the cyclist in your life. I love sculpting people's spirit animals. What's yours?"

"Actually, I'm looking for Dylan."

"He's teaching right now." She pointed out a different window.

"He teaches? I thought he just owned this place."

"He doesn't teach as much these days, because he's busy with another job. But he still takes on students when he can. Boston's an expensive city. We're finding out the hard way since we moved here. Nothing like Oregon, that's for sure. We do what we can to get by."

Odd. Again I wondered about Preston Lane and Chris Fitch. With their combined resources, and all these fancy new bikes, couldn't they pay their mechanic enough so he didn't have to moonlight?

I looked out the window. At a school parking lot across the street, a guy—Dylan, I presumed—jogged after a boy on a bike. The boy, swathed in all kinds of padding and a bright yellow helmet, was hesitantly pedaling, then slamming his brakes. Dylan wore baggy shorts, a black T-shirt, and a baseball cap backward, and tattoos twining around his arms and legs.

"Dyl's four o'clock lesson canceled," the woman said. "And those two out there are wrapping up soon. Do you want the slot?"

I looked at the class rates posted on a wall sign. Thirty dollars would buy me a half-hour lesson. Worth it? Totally. This was the perfect way to question Dylan, under cover, so he might feel free to talk. I'd play the role of a curious student. I handed over the cash.

"Great. I'm Amber, by the way." The woman shook my hand. "You are . . . ?"

"Tessa."

"What's your level, Tessa?"

"My level?"

"Are you an out-of-practice intermediate? A lapsed learner? A semi-beginner? A total newbie? If you're a newbie, we can loan you knee pads, elbow pads, anything you need."

"Oh. Um, newbie, I guess. Would you mind introducing me to him? I'm a little nervous."

"Sure. Not a problem."

As Amber went off to gather my gear, I glanced outside at Mari, who was lurking in the sculpture garden, watching Dylan's lesson across the street. I telepathically signaled to her to give me just five more minutes before she burst in here. I hoped she got the psychic message.

25

SIX MINUTES later I was waddling over to the school parking lot with Amber, pushing a clunky upright bike with straight handlebars, a low seat, and padded pedals. I wore elbow and knee pads, hip pads, padded gloves, and a round helmet that seemed better suited for spelunking. All I needed was a mouth guard, goggles, and earplugs to complete the Total Newbie look. But at least all the padding would cover my bandages and prevent Amber and Dylan from asking tough questions about why I happened to have them.

Mari, hiding behind a robot bike sculpture, gaped at me as I passed. I gave her a thumbs-up sign and mouthed "Go," pointing to the door that Amber had left wide-open.

Dylan's current student was practicing in slow, wobbly circles. Dylan jogged over to meet me, and Amber introduced us. He held out his hand for me to shake. As he grinned, various face piercings moved: an eyebrow ring, a stud in his chin, black metal disks in each earlobe.

"Wayne here was going to practice on his own a few minutes more, but he's had a lot of time. We can get started," said Dylan.

"Oh, let him practice a little longer. I don't mind," I said.

"I'll watch Wayne," said Amber. "It's the end of the day. There's no one in the gallery."

That's what you think. I glanced at the building. Mari was in there somewhere.

I gave Wayne a big thumbs-up, remembering how much Juan Carlos liked working with kids. "Go, Wayne!" I cheered as the kid wobbled by.

The boy looked up in terror and crashed. His face crumpled. He burst into tears.

Once Wayne was up and running again, with Amber's help, Dylan returned to my side.

"I always like to see where we're starting from," he said. "Any bike experience?"

"Nope," I lied. "I got through my entire childhood without learning to ride. I blame my parents. I was raised on TV."

Dylan laughed, not getting my double meaning. Good. He didn't know who I was.

"You wouldn't be the first. Lots of people are late bloomers. No problem! We'll just have to start at the very start. Good a place as any."

Dylan explained the basics of balancing on a bike and showed me how to get on. He held the bike steady while I pretended to find my balance. I felt sick for a moment, remembering my attempt to mount my Bianchi back in my driveway at home. This bike's seat was so low, and the frame so sturdy, I wasn't as afraid. Then again, I wasn't really a novice.

"I think you're ready to try gliding," he said, "just to get your balance while moving. No pedals yet. We're going to use this slight downhill grade. Think of gravity as your friend. Now glide along, lifting your feet up for as long as you can. Squeeze the brakes or put your feet back down if you really need to. Try to go in a basically straight direction. Think you can follow this line?" He pointed to a yellow line down the center of the basketball court.

I pushed off with my feet and glided, my feet splayed out on either side and not touching the pedals, ready to catch me. Fear surged again—then ebbed again. It actually felt okay to be on a bike again, moving slowly. Then again, there was no one right by me to crash into. Or kill.

"Hey! You're a natural!" Dylan exclaimed, jogging beside me. "Look at you go!"

I wobbled a little to look more convincing. I put my feet on the ground on either side of the bike and pretended to mop sweat off my brow. "Whew. I need a moment."

"Sure thing. Collect yourself." He grinned. "So. What made you want to learn to ride?"

"Oh, I've been watching some bike racing. And following Team Cadence-EcuaBar."

"That's my team!" He puffed out his chest. "I'm their mechanic. You're lucky you caught me here today. My teaching hours are really erratic these days since that's my main gig."

"Sounds like a fun job."

"Oh, yeah. It's been awesome for me and Amber." He pointed to the woman, who was jogging alongside Wayne now. "She got a gig as the official team photographer. We were lucky. It's hard for married couples to get jobs together. Best part is we get to travel with the team. We're headed to South America on Friday. Even though . . ." His eyes welled up.

"El Cóndor, right? I heard," I said.

He sighed. "Great guy. Supertalented. He was going to change the whole image of pro cycling. If anyone could have conquered the Pyrenees in the Tour de France without EPO doses, without blood transfusions, without all the funny stuff, it would have been Juan Carlos." He cleared his throat and coughed, the way guys do when they're trying not to cry. "Okay, break's over. Ready to glide?"

I resumed gliding, with Dylan loping beside me. Dylan seemed truly broken up about Juan Carlos. And he seemed like a careful and thorough guy, despite the appearance of this bike school. He paid such close attention to the way I sat on the seat, how I gripped the handlebar—his eyes didn't miss a thing.

"What made him crash so badly?" I asked Dylan.

"It's still under investigation."

"Any theories? What does the team think about all of this?"

Dylan hesitated. "Well. Just between you and me? Basically, some of the team managers want to blame Cadence Bikes and file a defective product claim. I sure hope they don't."

"What's wrong with that?"

"We need Cadence as a co-title sponsor. So we need to show the public that Cadence bikes are safe and reliable, not just fast."

"Are they?" I asked, all Bianca Slade now. I even had the head tilt and the pursed lips down. The only problem was my head tilt sort of threw off my glide.

"They're the best bike on the market these days," Dylan said. "And if we start accusing them of a faulty product—even questioning them—Chris Fitch will freak."

"Why's that?"

"When people see a champion win on a nice bike, they want to buy that bike, too. Lance Armstrong did it for Trek. Sales shot sky-high after he won the Tour de France on a Trek. And the funny thing is, he didn't even ride a real Trek the whole time!"

"He didn't?"

"Nope." He grinned. "It was painted to look like one, to satisfy his sponsor. But Lance had his own opinions about what he wanted to ride."

I could see why some people on the team weren't eager to get that crashed bike properly inspected and pursue the faulty product angle. But if someone had sabotaged Juan Carlos's main bike—if the crash wasn't due to a factory error—that was a whole different story. Chris Fitch, as well as Preston, would surely want to explore that. And wouldn't sabotage make Cadence look even *less* to blame for what happened? It certainly made *me* feel less to blame.

"Here's an idea," I said as Dylan had me walk the bike to the start of the yellow line and glide again. "Could someone have messed with el Cóndor's bike before the ride?"

"Sabotaged it?" Dylan frowned. "Absolutely not. I did a post-crash inspection, and I would have caught that. Besides, that would mean someone accessed his bike before the race. And that's impossible."

"Are you sure? Was there anyone unusual hanging out around your trailer?"

"The usual rubberneckers. I didn't pay much attention. Before a race, my total focus is my job. Getting those bikes ready, and safe, and distributed to the riders."

"So you were with the bikes the whole time?" I watched his face carefully, then fought to catch my balance again as the bike veered toward his feet.

"Of course," he said, straightening out my handlebars and front wheel. "I'm in charge of the bikes and the safety of all our pro and junior riders. I take that very seriously. My job is on the line, and I need this job. More than you know," he added almost under his breath.

"You don't think someone could have gotten into the team trailer at any point?"

"No."

"You never left the trailer before the event started?"

"No. Well, once." He frowned. "I went out to use a restroom. But I locked the trailer up. I *did*," he added, as if trying to convince himself more than me. "Yes. I'm sure I did. I'm almost a hundred percent sure that I did." His voice faltered, and he looked down.

Again I glanced at his bike school. The door was wide-open. Mari was in there now. Security just did not seem to be top-of-mind for this guy.

"Did Juan Carlos have any enemies?" I asked next. "Other cyclists? Someone who might have found a way into the trailer while it was locked?"

"Not a chance. The guy worked so hard. Everyone respected that. The only rival I ever knew him to have was this kid from the junior team, who ended up getting the boot, for drugs. But that loser's long gone. Whoa, steady there," he added, reaching an arm out as I wobbled at the mention of Jake. "Now if you feel like you might go over, let yourself do that. It's okay. Sometimes it's good to know what it feels like to fall. I mean, everyone does at some point. Might as well get it over with. You dust yourself off and get back in the saddle, right?" He winked. "That's the free spiritual advice part of the lesson. I learned that in rehab last year."

Rehab. This was a person looking for a new road in life. He did need this job. I couldn't believe he'd do something willingly that would put it in jeopardy. And he obviously had huge respect for Juan Carlos.

I faked a few false starts, then pedaled very slowly as I thought about all Dylan had said. He didn't seem like the saboteur at all. But what about the other bike crime, the stolen spare bike?

"I heard a rumor that Juan Carlos's spare bike went missing for the race," I ventured, choosing my next words carefully. "Maybe stolen. Is that true?"

"That's ridiculous. All the bikes are accounted for. I just went through the inventory this morning because I'm going to be packing them up for our flights to Bogotá, as soon as this lesson is over."

Was he being honest about the inventory being intact? Or covering up his lapse in attention? Preston Lane had a heart, but he was a businessman. He had no trouble firing people. If he thought Dylan had been careless and let two bikes be stolen and rigged, Dylan would be out of work.

Dylan narrowed his eyes. "Where'd you hear this weird rumor anyway?"

"Um, I—"

"Hey, Dylan! I'm finished!" Wayne called out. He looked at me. "Hey, I know you. You're Tessa Taylor."

"Should I know you, too?" Dylan asked, looking at me intently.

"You don't know her? She's, like, famous," said Wayne. "She's the host of this show called *KidVision*. But the website said the show was canceled. My mom said it was because she cheated on a charity ride last weekend and she doesn't set a good example."

Dylan glared. "I don't know what you're trying to pull here, but the joke is over. So's the lesson. I'm not going to wind up on some TV show talking about this."

Amber marched up to me, a stern look on her face, and held out her hands for my helmet.

"Here's your thirty dollars back," said Dylan, slapping three tens into my hand. "I don't take money from liars. Now get the hell out of my bike school."

26

BACK IN the Compass Bikes van, Mari cued up the bike frame inspection she'd filmed. Meanwhile, I was still shaking from my blown cover.

"Good thing you found the bike so fast," I said after I'd explained what had happened with Dylan and me.

"I was so scared I wouldn't," Mari admitted. "I had to go through three rooms. It was like Goldilocks and the Three Bears. From Hell. The first room had a bunch of beater bikes stored for classes. The second room was a storeroom for Team Cadence-EcuaBar stuff. Lots of bike boxes for airplane shipping. And Juan Carlos's bike was there, by the way. The spare with the white handlebars."

"What?" I exclaimed. "The spare bike was there? But—that's not possible!"

"I saw it," she insisted. "Every rider had three wall hooks for their bikes. One for their trainer, one for the main bike, one for the spare. The space for Juan Carlos's main bike was empty, which makes sense because it's busted from the crash. But the spare? It's here." She showed me a picture she'd taken. A sign on the wall said J. MACIAS. Below it hung a basic black training bike. The next set of hooks, where his green-handled bike should have been hanging, was empty. And below those hooks hung his spare—a bike with white bars—just like the one I'd seen in the woods.

"Are you okay?" Mari asked, looking at me curiously. "This is good news, right? It means his spare bike wasn't stolen. Dylan wasn't lying to you."

"If there's a spare, that means Darwin—" I stopped myself from saying more, suddenly remembering I hadn't told Mari everything about that morning in the woods.

"Who?"

"Never mind," I said, shaking my head in disbelief. I felt dizzy.

So the spare bike wasn't missing now. That meant someone had returned it to its rightful place, maybe Dylan himself. Or maybe Juan Carlos had gotten my text message in time, picked up the bike, and brought it back to the trailer, and that's why he got a late start for the race. Problem solved!

I couldn't steal it and deliver it to Darwin tomorrow, but I could tell Darwin where to find that bike when he texted me again. Then he'd leave me alone.

But something didn't make sense: Why didn't Darwin just come and ransack this place in the first place? Why not start with the obvious choice, the team mechanic—why go after me?

"Are you watching?" Mari moved on to the third room she'd filmed. "This must be that woman's workshop for those bike sculptures. It was filled with bike stuff. Parts, broken bits, frames, wheels, you name it. Juan Carlos's broken bike frame was in there. I found it on a table. I filmed my inspection. Tessa, this totally looks like a sabotage case. There, on either side of the downtube, right behind the fork, are two weak spots. Like bruises on an apple." Her gloved fingers, in the video, pointed out the two spots.

"Would a crash have caused those?"

"No. Too symmetrical. And it's not where the crash impact was."

"I don't get it. What does this prove?"

"Within the bruised areas—I'm zooming in now—there are two small slits. See?"

"I can see. Barely." The slits were so small I'd never have noticed if Mari hadn't pointed them out.

"That's not accident damage. Someone weakened the structure of the tube first by hitting it with something. A ball-peen hammer would do the trick. After the bruising, someone could have used a razor to cut the carbon fiber threads inside. Those two things would compromise the integrity of the frame."

"English, please?"

"If the frame was weakened in that key place, it would fall apart at even the slightest impact. I'm sure Juan Carlos wouldn't have made it the whole hundred miles without it falling apart."

I felt a surge of emotion I hadn't felt in ages. *Relief.* If Juan Carlos hadn't crashed as a direct result of my paceline pullout, he could have gone down anywhere else on the route. At any time. Yes, I'd still played a role in all this by causing a crash he reacted to. But his crash also could have been triggered by a pothole, a stray rock, a rogue patch of sand. And his catastrophic bike failure was the result of the sabotage. This was concrete evidence that I was not entirely to blame.

Then I slumped in my seat. Was Dylan lying to me when he said the bike couldn't have been sabotaged? Had he played a role in this crime? Or was he really a flaky guy who wasn't about to admit he might have accidentally given someone access to Juan Carlos's bikes in the trailer?

"There's more," said Mari. "Now I'm showing the rear brake. See my finger turning it? It had been loosened. Just a little, but just enough."

I sat forward. "Enough for what?" I asked, though I already had an idea of where she was going with this. My fingers tightened around the seat belt, as if bracing myself for a new crash.

"If someone looking at bike damage was concentrating on the front of the bike, where the impact was, they might not even notice this. But the brake was loosened enough so that the cable would slip if the rider pulled the brake fast. That's what Juan Carlos must have done. That probably put even more stress on the bike and flipped him over the handlebars."

"Oh my God," I breathed. "Someone wanted him hurt at Chain Reaction."

"Or killed," Mari added grimly.

"But if you really want to take someone out, a gun's more of a guarantee, right?"

"Sabotage is a good way to kill from afar," said Mari. "Less chance of getting caught, especially if it looks like an accidental death."

"So who would do something like this? Who would know how?"

"Someone who knows about bike engineering."

"A mechanic."

Mari sighed. "God, I hate to think that. We're in the business of making bikes safe, not turning them into lethal weapons. But *maybe* Dylan? He'd have the skill, and access to the bike."

"I thought of that. But he has no motive," I objected. "You should have heard him raving about Juan Carlos. How about Gage Weston?"

Mari looked horrified. "Are you kidding? Mr. Safety? Mr. Follows-All-the-Rules?"

"Maybe he wanted to get back at team management for firing him," I suggested.

"He wouldn't do it like that," said Mari. "He understood why he got canned."

"Why?"

"Because he's not just an anti-carbon guy. He's an *outspoken* anti-carbon guy. He's on a bunch of cycling forums under the name CarbonHater. Preston needed to bring in Cadence as a sponsor, and Gage was too controversial. Bad for publicity. So he got the ax. But he's not bitter. He felt ready to move on, he told me. Plus, it was his idea to speed up the container drop with the bikes, in honor of Juan Carlos. Gage totally admired the guy. There's no way he was the saboteur." She thought a moment, twisting a lock of hair around one finger. "What about a teammate?"

"Dylan swore he didn't have any enemies. Everyone respected him."

"A former teammate?" She gave me a long look. "Your boyfriend?"

"He's not my boyfriend anymore. And I don't know."

"I heard they were rivals on the junior team."

"They were." Did Jake hate Juan Carlos enough to hurt him? Or *kill* him? It was hard to believe I would have missed those signs. Though Jake had made threatening remarks to Juan Carlos before, and punched him in the stomach. An image flashed into my mind: that poison ivy rash on Jake's ankle. It potentially linked him to the place where Juan Carlos's spare bike had been hidden. Now I had to wonder if Jake could be both thief and saboteur: a bike thief for hire, working for Darwin, *and* a saboteur, out for revenge on his rival.

While Mari put the camera back in the case, I turned this idea over and over in my mind. Jake had decent basic mechanic skills. He knew the team's trailer and maybe had a key. He could have sabotaged Juan Carlos's main bike on his way back from getting the water bottles, while Dylan had stepped away for a few minutes. Then he could have taken the spare bike and hidden it in the woods. A double crime: sabotage and theft.

Jake had said he knew bikes got stolen all the time, and he

knew so much about fences. Maybe Darwin had approached Jake before. They could have had a scheme to sell that spare bike. But then Juan Carlos could have found the spare bike there—thanks to my timely text message—and foiled Darwin's plan to retrieve it. Juan Carlos himself could have brought his spare bike back to the trailer and never reported it missing. That would explain why he was late for the race—and why a spare bike with white handlebars was hanging in Dylan's storeroom at this moment.

But Jake, a saboteur? Even if all the dots connected and led to him for both crimes, the idea of Jake as a killer was too horrible to accept. Could I really have gone out with a thief and a murderer all these months, and not had the slightest idea about some sinister plan he was hatching?

Strains of Latin music drifted from the bodega. People came in and out with shopping bags. One woman carried a box fairly bursting with ripe mangoes, and that weird thing Darwin had said in the woods came back to me in a rush.

Mangoes are best at this time of year.

Darwin. He'd be resurfacing soon. But now I had a solution to that problem. As soon as he texted me, I'd tell him to check out the Open Road School of Bicycling. He could be Dylan's problem now. Besides, what did it really matter now if Darwin got his hands on that bike? Juan Carlos wouldn't be riding it again.

I had a more important thing to worry about now: finding the bike saboteur. If Juan Carlos died because of foul play—and not entirely from my poor decisions—the killer had to be found. And I really hoped that killer wasn't Jake.

Realizing Mari had been quiet for some time, I turned to look at her—and saw she was crying, quietly, her face buried in her hands. "Mari? What's wrong?" I asked softly.

She wiped her tears with one hand and sniffed. "It just hit me.

I think it was seeing that bike. Juan Carlos was alive just three days ago, and now he's . . . not. His family has no money. Preston Lane is arranging to ship the body back, and the thought of el Cóndor flying alone, dead, it's just so—" Her voice broke, and tears sprang to my eyes, too. I'd gone to a lot of dark places in my imagination these past few days, but nowhere as dark as that.

"God. I miss him so much," said Mari. "He was my friend, you know?"

"Were you two—going out?" I asked cautiously.

"No. I don't know." She sighed. "It was complicated."

"Ah." I fought off a surge of jealousy, remembering the touch of Juan Carlos's hand on mine, the brush of his fingers on my neck as he clasped the necklace around it.

"We had so much in common," Mari went on. "I have family roots in Ecuador; he's from there. We both love bikes—he raced; I fixed—I thought it was maybe meant to be. But he wasn't in a good space for a relationship, he told me. I respected that, you know?"

I swallowed hard. "He wanted to tell me something," I said. "I saw him before the race. We were supposed to meet up afterward. But we never got to. Any idea what that could be about?"

She gave me a strange look. "No idea. Sorry."

"He never mentioned me to you?"

"No. Never." Mari abruptly turned the key in the ignition, and the van started up with a roar.

"Okay." I looked away as she backed out of the parking space, so she wouldn't see my face twist into disappointment. I couldn't tell Mari what I'd thought—or hoped—Juan Carlos might have said to me after the race. Some confession of long pent-up feelings. Was it so crazy to think that he might? He did have a way of showing up whenever Jake and I hit a rough patch, and saying just the right thing. I guess that had led me to think there might have been something between us, if we were both free to explore that.

Like this one time, last fall. Jake and I were supposed to go to a Shady Pines school dance. With my friends. Jake had refused, last minute. He went into Old Man Mode—tired from training, saving energy for a time trial. He couldn't waste his legs, he said.

"Are you seventeen or seventy?" I'd asked. "Can't you come to one thing of mine?"

You come to so many races. I think you must be a very nice girlfriend, Juan Carlos said to me before a circuit race that weekend. *Jake, he is a lucky guy.*

But if Juan Carlos had never mentioned me to his friend Mari, and if they were a borderline item, whatever he wanted to talk to me about that day probably wasn't so personal.

Plus, he'd asked if I had a laptop, I suddenly remembered. Why? There was nothing romantic about a computer.

"I don't know what he wanted to tell you," Mari said as we drove through Jamaica Plain's narrow streets. "But I know what he'd have wanted you to do."

"What's that?"

"Come to Ecuador. With me."

"Yeah, right."

"I'm serious! Volunteer for Vuelta. Film it for your vlog. Maybe we can't solve the mystery of his death, but we can help the cause he cared about so much. Help his dream live on."

I considered this. I'd always wanted to travel. With no *KidVision* taping season, and no boyfriend, I had time on my hands. And my mom had given me that whole speech about taking healthy risks. Maybe they could be persuaded to let me go. "How'd you sell your parents on this?" I asked Mari.

She shrugged. "I didn't ask them. I *told* them. I'm eighteen. I'm going to MIT in the fall for mechanical engineering. These are my last weeks of freedom. They couldn't stop me if they tried."

"They're not worried about where you'll stay?"

"Nah. I have an older cousin who lives in Quito, and her parents—my aunt and uncle—live in the city of Cuenca. I'm going to stay in my cousin's apartment. Only, just between you and me? My cousin has a boyfriend in another town, and she's barely at home. The place will be practically mine!" Her eyes danced. "You should totally come."

"I don't know, Mari. My parents—"

"Tessa. You *have* to go. The Pan-American Cycling Tour is going to put Latin American cycling on the map. Quito is the place to *be*. You could do such an exciting series for your vlog about all this"

I indulged in a fantasy for a few seconds. Merengue music. *Empanadas*. Cute Ecuadorian boys. Someone teaching me to salsa. Me in that red halter dress.

"Besides," she said, "Juan Carlos always wanted more publicity for Vuelta. He wanted people in the U.S. to know about it, so they'd donate money. If you could get your TV station interested, that would be so amazing."

I flinched. Yeah, right. Like Kristen or anyone at GBCN would want me to crawl back and pitch an idea for a new show.

"Ask your parents," she urged. "What's the worst that can happen?"

"Fine, I'll ask," I said. "But I can't promise anything."

"You have to start somewhere, right?" Mari smiled. Then she looked worried. "Hey, what should we do with our video? I told Gage I was borrowing the van for an errand. I'm not sure how thrilled he'll be if he finds out we broke into the Team Cadence-EcuaBar storage site and did this inspection."

"We didn't break in. Amber left the door open," I reminded her.

"You know what I mean. We're on murky ground here."

"Let's bypass Gage and take it straight to the police."

"Even if we were trying to do something good, find this proof, we were breaking the law. Trespassing." Mari slapped the top of the steering wheel. "Why didn't we think of that before? What if Dylan decided to press charges against us? For trespassing?"

"I have another idea." I smiled. "Bianca Slade."

"The *Watchdog* lady? With the freaky striped hair?" Mari shuddered. "She's spooky."

"She's not spooky. She's *efficient*," I countered. "She's tough."

"Oh, yeah, you work with her at GBCN, right? You know her?"

"I met her at a holiday party once." For one minute, where she signed that 8×10 glossy photo of herself before breezing past me to talk to some station executives. "But I could give it a shot," I added quickly, as Mari looked disappointed "I think she's the link we need to launch this investigation. She gets police interested in potential cases after she airs them. And she was already asking Chris Fitch some questions about bike safety on TV the other day. I bet she'll be all over this story if she thinks there's a problem with Juan Carlos's bike."

"But the police will have to ask how she got the video," Mari reminded me.

I remembered Bianca's blog post. The Qualities of Good Investigative Reporters #7: Being Trustworthy. *Investigative journalists protect their sources.* "She won't expose us. I'm positive."

"All right," Mari agreed. "Let's send it. Today."

27

THE NEXT day passed in a blur. I spent it all at Compass Bikes, helping to load up a shipping container on a flatbed truck parked behind the bike shop. I alternated loading with filming and interviewing, and got some footage for the vlog.

At 4:00, Gage jangled a cowbell. "Everyone! Outside!" he called.

I followed the other fifteen or so volunteers out back to view the huge white box, now packed floor to ceiling with bikes and bike parts.

Mari was in it, stacking the last of some boxes in front of the rows of tightly stacked bike frames. Her face glistened with sweat. She beamed at the small crowd. "We're on schedule! You guys rock!"

A cheer rose up from the crowd. High fives were slapped all around. People clapped me on the shoulder, too, and said things like, "Hey, Tessa, nice work!"

Holding my video camera, rotating and trying to capture the moment, I smiled. I *glowed.* It felt great to be part of this group and this project.

Plus, Bianca Slade had called me at home yesterday morning to ask some follow-up questions about the video I'd emailed her. She said she found this case intriguing, and promised to get a bike forensics expert and a camera crew over to Dylan's bike school right away.

Every time I thought about Bianca's plan, I found myself grinning. If Bianca and her team successfully got a look at the bike and ran a story on it, getting the police involved as a result, Mari and I would have helped launch a criminal investigation into Juan Carlos's murder. That was something I could be proud of. A huge step in setting things right.

As for Darwin? I could finally breathe easier. I'd checked my phone before going to Compass Bikes that morning, eager for a text this time. I couldn't wait to tell him the bike was at Dylan's place, and get him off my back once and for all. I even had a screen shot from Mari's video that I was planning to send him as proof.

Sure enough, a text was waiting for me. The fact that Darwin was a talented enough hacker to bust through the new antiviral software didn't surprise me. The content of the text did.

NEVER MIND, WE FOUND IT YESTERDAY.

I stared at the words. He'd found it? Had he followed Mari and me to Dylan's bike school? I texted back to ask him where it had turned up, curious what kind of information he might volunteer. But he didn't respond. Seconds later, our brief exchange was completely wiped out, as always.

I kept picturing Darwin going into Dylan's place. Would he just barge in and grab the bike off the wall? Or send someone else for it? Would he threaten Dylan and Amber and make them hand it over? Throughout the morning, I tried to reassure myself that it wasn't my problem anymore. Darwin wouldn't be bothering me about that spare bike again. And gradually, as the container load work got busier, my mind drifted away from all that. All I could focus on were bikes and bike parts and lifting and carrying and getting that shipping container packed as tightly as possible.

"See you in Quito!" Mari said to the bikes, as she hopped out of the container.

"Yes, see you in Quito!" said a familiar voice behind us.

I turned to look. Preston Lane. And with him? Chris Fitch of Cadence Bikes.

Everyone made a path for the two men as they walked to the shipping container. Gage introduced them to everyone. I heard him mutter to Preston, "Hey, man, thanks for coming by. I thought you were still in Vegas."

"Whirlwind trip," said Preston. "Besides, this is our guy's legacy, right here. I wouldn't miss this moment for the world."

Chris clapped him on the back and nodded, somberly. Then he turned to the crowd of bike shop staff and volunteers. He made a broad gesture, as if addressing a kingdom. "When Preston and I heard you were rushing this shipment, in honor of Juan Carlos, we both wanted to come by and thank you personally for helping his vision to live on. This is an outstanding bike shop—even if you don't carry Cadence bikes. Yet." He winked at Gage, who raised an eyebrow. "Seriously, though. I have a lot of respect for what you do here. It's a boost to the team's morale to know Juan Carlos's project is moving forward."

"Yeah, guys, this is awesome," Preston chimed in. His voice sounded enthusiastic but his eyes looked glazed, as if he hadn't slept. "Vuelta was a cause dear to Juan Carlos's heart. These bikes will help so many people. You should feel very proud of yourselves today. Awesome job." Then he thumped the steel side of the shipping container with his fist. "And I look forward to the honor of opening this bad boy myself there." He grinned, and people applauded again.

While the other volunteers filed inside for pizza, and the Compass Bikes staff thronged around Chris Fitch to hear the bike company CEO talk about their newest frames, I caught up with Preston, who was edging toward the door as if trying to escape undetected, and finishing up a call on his cell phone. I lingered a few feet away to wait until he was done.

"What?" he said into the phone. "No, no, no. Nothing back door about it. The ice crackdown forced us to move in a different direction, that's all. We'll write up a blow-by-blow for you, and allay any concerns you might have, okay?"

I rolled my eyes. *Ice crackdown. A blow-by-blow.* This was the kind of business lingo Sarita loved to learn, but I thought it sounded ridiculous, like some kind of made-up language.

I stepped right up to him as soon as he ended his call. "Excuse me. Mr. Lane?"

"Yes?" He squinted at me.

"I don't know if you remember me? I'm a Shady Pines student. And the host—well, the former host—of *KidVision*. I interviewed you for our show last year?"

"Oh? Yes! Of course! Tessa Taylor, right? Aren't you Jake Collier's girlfriend?"

"I am. I mean, was." I winced at the mention of Jake. How weird that my school world and my boyfriend world intersected at Preston Lane.

"Oh, I'm sorry to hear that. How's life at Shady Pines?" His eyes flicked toward the door.

"Closed. It's summer."

"Oh. Right." He glanced at his watch, a Rolex. An odd choice for a bleeding-heart liberal guy, even if he was from old money. Other than pricey sporting equipment and athletic wear, he wasn't into showy status items.

"Um. Do you . . . have a second?" I ventured. After all my reassurances to Kylie that Preston Lane was no one to fear, my heart was suddenly racing. I didn't know what I wanted to say. I just sensed, in this moment, that he was a strong connection to Juan Carlos. He'd brought him here, legally sponsored him, even let him live in his home until Juan Carlos turned eighteen and moved in with some teammates. I wanted to feel that connection. Maybe get a sound bite or something for the video. Yes! He'd be great to have on Volunteen, talking about what this project had meant to Juan Carlos. Only—crap. I'd left my camera outside on the ground, with my backpack.

"I'm sorry." Preston sidestepped me, glancing at Chris, who extracted himself from the crowd of mechanics and started heading toward the door. "We have a meeting we're already late for. Please forgive me. But good to see you again. Stay awesome, okay?"

Stay awesome. He'd ended our *KidVision* interview with those same words last year. He'd sounded cool then. Now, for some reason, he seemed sort of pathetic..

I watched him leave with Chris. Chris shook hands with Gage. Preston didn't. The door banged closed behind him. Preston seemed so different from the upbeat guy who'd spoken at our assembly—and so different from the shaken, sad man who'd been interviewed at Mass General four days ago. It felt like a strong weather system had breezed in and out of Compass Bikes. And it left me cold.

I WENT back outside to get my backpack but paused behind the big white box. Each corrugated steel door had double sets of metal bars running up and down, with latches going across them. Each latch had a heavy padlock. I walked around to the side. The truck's engine rumbled while the driver sat in the cab, talking on a cell phone and going over paperwork.

But the door latches weren't yet pulled. I wanted to see the bikes one more time and get a really good shot of them for the vlog, without all the people. I went around back again and pulled a door open. I peered into the darkness of the container. The bikes were packed in so snugly. Some were flattened, and some were completely stripped; the bikes that had broken parts had to be taken down to the frames. They all fit in like a massive puzzle.

I took my video camera out of my backpack and turned it on. I panned across all the frames, secretly hoping for one last look at my green-and-white Bianchi. Mari had checked it out and said it was safe to ride. They'd fixed it and loaded it in whole. Who would be its next rider?

I climbed into the back of the container to film a little closer. I pushed into the second row of bikes to get a better angle. One area looked like some of the tightly packed bikes had slipped, about four or five rows back. If the bikes loosened more during transport, they could get damaged. I wondered if I should get Gage or Mari and tell them there was some kind of packing problem in that row.

Then I lost some of my light. I turned around.

A shape now filled the doorway.

I crouched down, not wanting to be seen. I was only filming for my vlog, but I didn't want Gage or any of the staff to think I was up to something. Paranoid.

The silhouette of a girl with a model's figure filled the open doorway. She wore a Compass Bikes T-shirt and cutoff shorts. She looked like any of the volunteers I'd worked with today, but none of them in particular. I squinted, trying to make out her face, half in shadows.

She stepped closer, bringing her face—and her bouncy red hair—into a ray of sunlight that pushed through the open door.

Another figure climbed up onto the back of the container, standing beside her. A tall skinny guy whose back was stooped, wearing his hair in a ponytail, with a courier bag slung across his chest.

I froze. I'd seen them before. In EcuaBar volunteer outfits, passing out samples at Chain Reaction. They had to be part of Darwin's network of "eyes and ears"!

The two of them peered into the container, as if scanning the bikes. The girl took a few pictures with her cell phone camera. I blinked at the flashes.

"I told you, it's good to go," the guy muttered. "I got it in just fine. Now let's get out of here."

Then they both jumped off the back of the container.

SLAM. The door closed.

SCREECH. The metal bar outside the door slid across the latch.

"Hey!" I shouted. "Hey, wait! I'm in here! Let me out!"

CLICK. CLICK. CLICK. The tumblers in the padlocks turned.

I squeezed out of the tangle of bikes I'd wedged myself into, and made my way to that space by the doors. I banged on the doors. "I'm trapped! Let me out!" I cried at the top of my lungs.

Then I was thrown against the doors as the truck went into reverse.

28

A SHARP series of beeps let the outside world know the trailer was moving backward. It didn't do a thing to let the outside world know that *I* was trapped inside with four hundred bikes bound for latitude zero.

The truck turned, then turned again. Leaving the bike shop behind.

I scrambled in my pockets for my phone. No phone. I swore, remembering it was in my backpack, and my backpack was on the ground, where I'd left it before jumping into the back of this box.

The bikes were lashed together in rows and stacks. Wheels and spare parts were lashed to the container walls. Still, everything jiggled and rattled in an unsettling way as the truck picked up speed. I found an empty two-foot-square patch of floor where I could crouch and hopefully avoid injury as the truck merged onto the highway. A handlebar poked the back of my neck. A bike pedal pushed into my ribs. The container was sealed. No light leaked in at all.

I tried to focus on positives but could find only one: I was still breathing.

Think, Tessa, think. Obviously this truck was not driving the container all the way to South America. Shipping containers went on ships. Where did the shipping containers leave from? The Port of

Boston. A loading dock. Back at Compass Bikes, I'd seen *MassPort* on the bill of lading, the customs document itemizing all the contents of a shipping container. *Four hundred bikes. Twenty boxes of parts. Forty-two tires. One very freaked-out seventeen-year-old girl.*

The idea of going to the Port of Boston brought me cold comfort. I did not love the idea of being in a steel box, lifted in a crane, and plunked down onto a barge and then an ocean freighter. How long could someone breathe in this thing? Sometimes illegal immigrants stowed away in containers and made it across the ocean. I'd once heard a news story about a cat who'd lived sixteen days in one, with no food or water. And another story about a Bangladeshi port worker who'd crawled into one for a nap. He had survived nine days when he got locked in; they pulled him out dehydrated and delirious, barely alive.

Bangladeshi man: nine days. Cat: sixteen. How long was this container's journey? I tried to recall the shipping information I'd seen on the bill of lading. The ship was due at Ecuador's Port of Guayaquil on July 16.

That was in twenty-two days.

THE TRUCK slowed and descended a ramp. We were leaving the highway. A few minutes later it stopped, and the engine turned off.

I unfolded myself from my crouching position between bikes and stiffly rose to a standing position. I immediately started yelling again, kicking the walls and the door.

Nobody came to my aid. I guessed the truck driver had gotten right out of his cab and gone somewhere right away. If this was a drop-off, his job was done.

I needed to get some kind of light to see if I could find an emergency handle or knob.

I found a cardboard box with bike parts to my left. I opened one on top. My hands scrabbled around in it, sensing various types of tools. I prayed for a flashlight, a penlight, any light at all. I was about to give up when my fingers closed around a familiar object. A bicycle light, for riding at night. LED. It had to be battery-powered. I found a switch and flicked it on.

A soft white light glowed. I breathed out. "Thank you." I scanned the walls and doors, looking for an emergency release of some sort. An alarm button. Nothing. I looked for a crack where I might push out a piece of paper with a note. No cracks. This box was tight as a tomb.

I started to feel dizzy. I would have given anything for Kylie and Sarita to drive up in the Fingernail right now and rescue me. I wanted them to take a crowbar to that door. My only hope was that Mari or someone at the bike shop would notice my backpack on the ground behind the bike shop and guess that I'd hopped into the shipping container and gotten locked inside.

Had I been locked in accidentally, though? Or deliberately, by Darwin's crew? Had that redheaded girl and the ponytail guy seen me before closing the doors? I couldn't be sure.

But it didn't make sense that they would lock me inside. There was no need for revenge. Darwin had already found the bike he was looking for, and I hadn't ratted him out.

I took a break from yelling and pounding on walls to inspect my prison. Holding up my LED light, I surveyed the tangle of bikes four rows back, where it seemed like incorrectly packed bike frames had come loose and slipped. Suddenly I spotted something that made me almost drop my light.

A black, green, and white frame was wedged in between a bunch of hybrids and urban cruisers. Its drop handlebars gleamed white.

What?

I lowered the light to look at the rest of the frame, and now saw this bike was at a different angle from the others in the row, and it hadn't been flattened like the surrounding frames. It had been deliberately wedged in between the others, as if it had been stuck in after the row was packed. I sucked in my breath as I read *Cadence* in flourishing script, running along the downtube. And, beneath the tube, I could just make out the decal.

J. MACIAS.

29

I LEANED against the cold wall of the shipping container and just stared at that bike. Dizziness and nausea rolled over me in waves. I was five feet away from Juan Carlos's stolen spare bike. Maybe this had been Darwin's plan all along: to smuggle the stolen bike out of the country, camouflaged in this shipping container full of donated bikes. This ring of thieves could be selling to a black-market buyer in Ecuador. If they had stolen it from Dylan's, they could have snuck it in here, while we were all inside the bike shop. I could have overheard them checking to be sure that bike was safely on board.

I needed a closer look. The LED light had a clip, which I fastened to the strap of my tank top. I started moving bikes, frames, wheels, and handlebars to get to Juan Carlos's spare bike. The only way to inch out the bike was to move other things one by one, enough so I could extract it and move it toward the doors. It was like playing a game of Tetris. From hell.

Sweat dripped into my eyes and soaked my shirt. My scraped fingers stung and bled. I kept lifting, shifting, nudging those bikes until I had my hands on those handlebars at last.

I had to find some way to alert people that I was trapped inside. And then I had to get this bike out of here. If there was any chance Jake was linked to the bike theft and the sabotage, maybe this bike would tell the truth. Maybe it still had his fingerprints on it.

I was almost at a point where I could pull and scooch it out from the stack. I managed to move it about two inches. A loud crash interrupted me. Something heavy struck my head, and I went down, falling against a stack of bikes.

I looked up, rubbing my throbbing temple. I inspected my hand in the light of the LED that had fallen and was now out of my reach. At least I wasn't bleeding. A rack of bike wheels had slipped from the wall rack and one of them must have clipped me. Juan Carlos's spare bike was now buried again.

Suddenly I heard running footsteps outside.

"Over here! It was coming from inside this one!" a woman shouted.

I found a horn on a kid's bike near me and pumped the rubber bulb, letting it squawk repeatedly to signal my location.

I heard scraping and clanking sounds at the doors, and then the doors swung wide-open, flooding the container with light. Sweet light.

I jumped out of the container, gasping for breath. And stared into the unsmiling faces of the truck driver, a U.S. Customs official . . . and the two people I'd seen just before the door slammed closed. I couldn't take my eyes off Darwin's spies, even as the truck driver stepped right in front of me and glowered. What were these two doing here?

"What the hell were you doing back there?" the driver demanded. "Is this some prank?"

"No! I was filming for a show I'm doing, and I thought since the door was still open, you weren't going yet. Then I found a stole—"

The redheaded girl glared at me. She made a sharp motion with her hand. *No. Don't.*

"You're lucky your friends were on the ball and called the dispatcher," the driver said. "You could have had a serious problem, young lady."

The girl smiled sweetly and handed me my backpack. "You left this on the ground, and I got worried, so I had the dispatcher tell the driver to check for you at the dock. Your phone's inside," she purred. "It was buzzing like crazy. I'm sure you missed a lot of messages."

I glared back and snatched it. "Thanks."

"So this is the volunteer who got locked in? Problem solved?" asked the customs official.

"Sorry about all that," the driver apologized. He glared at me. "Teenage hijinks. Clowning around a shipping container? I guess they thought that was funny. But I have daughters. Believe me, this is tame compared to the crap they put me through. I'll lock up, and these kids can be on their way."

"I'll just need to check inside," said the customs official. "Security. You understand."

"Be my guest. It's just a load of bikes and bike parts. I have the bill of lading right here."

As the customs official and the driver stepped into the back of the container, shining flashlights, I turned to the guy and the girl. "I've seen you before. Who the hell are you?" I demanded.

The two of them looked at each other, then beckoned for me to follow.

I hesitated. If they tried to hurt me, my cries would be heard. This was my chance to get information. I had to go with them.

They led me behind another shipping container, an orange rusty one, a few yards away.

"I am called Pizarro," said the ponytail guy. He leaned against the orange shipping container, his thumbs hooked into his tight jeans pockets. He seemed like a college student, a mix of casual and intense, scruffy and composed. His T-shirt said THAT'S FUNNY, IT WORKED ON MY MACHINE. His eyes glittered as he slowly chewed a piece of gum and looked me up and down.

"And I'm Balboa," said the girl. "I know, right? Sucky name." She made a face. "I'm new to the organization, so I get the bottom of the barrel on the aliases."

I glared at them. "So you work for Darwin."

"We do," said Balboa, a note of pride in her voice.

"Did you guys lock me in that shipping container?"

"No," scoffed Pizarro. "We didn't see you when we closed the doors."

"Thank God I saw your backpack," Balboa added. "You were so helpful yesterday, leading us right to the bike."

Leading them right to the bike. Great. So they *had* somehow tailed us to Dylan's place.

"But I didn't expect you to join the bike and go along for the ride," Balboa went on. "You almost screwed everything up."

I ignored her insult. "Explain to me why there is a stolen bike on that container. Where is it going?"

A smug smile traveled across Balboa's face. "To Ecuador, of course. Why else would it be in that shipping container?"

"This bike's not going to Vuelta, though," I said, narrowing my eyes. "You have someone else expecting it."

Balboa started to answer, but Pizarro cleared his throat.

"Sorry. That's classified." Balboa looked down.

"So your buyer is there?" I guessed. "What's that bike worth, anyway?"

"A lot more, now," said Balboa, and Pizarro shot her a look. Again she looked down. I sensed that she was willing to talk, but Pizarro was in control.

A chill ran through me. Was Balboa suggesting Darwin would

make an even bigger profit on the black market, now that Juan Carlos was dead?

I took a step forward. My jaw clenched so hard it hurt. Just yesterday I'd convinced myself it didn't matter where the stolen bike ended up; it was his other bike, the sabotaged bike, that could tell the story of Juan Carlos's death. A murder. But now I was filled with hate for Darwin and for these two idiots standing before me who sought to capitalize on Juan Carlos's death. "There's a customs official in the container right now. I could show him the bike and tell him it's stolen. I know where you wedged it in."

"But you won't." Pizarro smiled, reached into his courier bag, and showed me a knife. The blade glinted in a shaft of sunlight.

I gasped and stepped back.

"And Darwin's got the bike where he wants it," said Balboa. "He says he'll leave you and your family alone now, and there won't be any more scandalous articles posted about you, unless you decide to squeal."

I froze. "Scandalous articles about me?"

"Yeah. Online. Like the one I wrote and posted for *Daily Commonwealth Online News*."

"You?" The earth tilted. "You posted that?" So the Team Maureen woman hadn't recorded me or taken my picture or written a word of that. It was all this crazy girl. "Why would you guys do that to me? I lost my job because of that article!"

"Because," said Balboa, "you lied about where the bike was in the woods. You misdirected Darwin. He lost valuable time there, and someone else intervened. That article was to teach you a lesson about lying, and about what he was capable of doing to you. Anyway, not bad for my first foray into journalism, was it? I was an English major, before I dropped out of college."

"I hate you," I said. And I did. That bike could tell a story.

If the saboteur—maybe Jake, maybe someone else—had anything to do with that spare bike, it could have fingerprints or DNA that could put police on the right trail. And these criminals were going to make that trail to justice turn cold.

She shrugged. "I'm just doing my job. Look, you seem like a really nice person. I'm going to give you some advice. Don't mention the bike in that box. To anyone. There's something inside it that needs to get safely to Ecuador."

"What's inside it?" My heart pounded. Whatever it was, it couldn't be legal. And that customs official was in the container now! I cast a longing look in that direction.

"Hey. She doesn't need to know all that," Pizarro snapped at Balboa.

Balboa looked stung. Her confident smile fell. Then she turned back to me. "Fine. Just know that Darwin can destroy your mom's business in an instant. He wasn't kidding about that. He could spread dirt about your dad, too, and take him down. If you care about your parents, remember that. Because we can do worse. Much worse."

I shivered. What could possibly be worse than what she'd just described?

Pizarro stroked the blade of his knife with one finger. Then he came right up to me, in three long strides. The knife blade glinted between his fingers.

My breath came in short, sharp bursts.

"It's actually a good thing we found you here," he said. "Because the bike's not the only thing we've been looking for. Why don't you just hand it over?"

"What? Hand what over?"

"The information."

"What?"

"The valuable information that you were entrusted with."

Pizarro scowled, his thick brows knitting together. "Don't play innocent, and don't waste our time."

"But I don't have anything!" Tears of frustration burned at my eyes. "I don't know who you guys are, or who you think I am, or what you think I have!" *Valuable information.* About what?

"You knew el Cóndor," Pizarro hissed, taking one more step toward me. "You were one of the last people to speak to him. We saw you. You must have it, or at least know something about it."

I flattened myself against the cold steel of the orange shipping container. The corrugated siding dug into my shoulder blade. I had a metallic taste in my mouth. I'd bit the inside of my mouth so hard it was bleeding. "I don't. I swear. The only *information* he gave me was his phone number!"

"Pizarro," said Balboa softly. "Maybe she really doesn't have it."

"Of course she has it," Pizarro growled. "The intel was solid. She just needs a stronger incentive to give up what she knows. Or has." He took another step forward, bringing the knife blade two inches from my throat.

Balboa pulled him back. "Hey! That's not how we—"

The container doors of my former prison slammed shut.

"Look around the corner," Pizarro commanded me. "Tell me what they're doing."

I peered around the corner of the orange shipping container and saw the customs official and the truck driver closing up the white container with the bikes.

"All right. Looks good to go," the customs official announced.

I took a deep breath. "There's a bunch of policemen coming this way," I lied, hoping that might protect me. "Looks like about six of them. And a news camera."

I turned to see the looks on their faces. But Pizarro and Balboa were already gone.

30

THE NEXT day, I sat on the porch swing at home eating ice cream while my parents, inside, debated my fate. I had pleaded my case for going to Ecuador as best I could over dinner. I'd made some pretty good arguments, thanks to Sarita's intense coaching the day before. Like how doing volunteer work for a good cause, and filming it on my Volunteen vlog, would help my public image. I would gain international work experience. My Spanish would get a boost. It was a great opportunity to take a risk, so I wouldn't have regrets someday, like my mom did.

My biggest reason, though, I kept for myself: I had to see that stolen spare bike unloaded in Ecuador and find out what was inside it. Possibilities kept swirling in my mind. I'd actually gone online the night before and researched things that got smuggled in bikes. Among the items that came up: drugs, small weapons, stolen jewels. Using new, state-of-the-art X-ray equipment, K-9 units and other screening measures, immigration and customs officials had detected all kinds of contraband in bike handlebars and bike tubes at international airports.

It sounded like Darwin and his team could be involved in something like that. Using a bike to transport something illegal. Maybe on a shipping container, hidden among four hundred bikes, it would elude scrutiny at borders. Those bikes weren't going to be taken out individually and screened. But why would people want to use Juan Carlos's bike to smuggle anything? And had Juan Carlos had any idea about this?

I was way too scared to report the bike. For one thing, I was sure Darwin would find out somehow. Second, what was I supposed to say? I tried writing out possibilities, rehearsing the call I'd make to the Boston Police, but everything sounded lame. *Hi! I'd like to report a stolen bike that I neglected to report a few days ago, which I think might have something illegal inside it, inside a shipping container that I got locked into. Have a nice day!* No way. The police would either not take me seriously, or I'd be incriminating myself for failing to report all this in the first place.

But if I could get to that bike first, as a Vuelta volunteer at the container unload in Quito, I could take it apart to check it out. I could "accidentally" find whatever contraband it was smuggling. Then I could hand it over to the police in Ecuador, safely out of Darwin's range. The Ecuadorian police could contact the FBI, or U.S. Marshals, or whoever handled international crimes. And then those authorities could determine if the bike theft and the bike sabotage were actually linked.

I couldn't tell my parents this plan. I hadn't told Kylie and Sarita, either. I hadn't even told Mari, when she emailed me her contact info in Quito. I was too scared of Darwin's eyes and ears. I couldn't put my friends at risk. All I had to do was intercept that bike before the "buyer" got it, and get it on the path to justice.

Hearing a tire on gravel, I squinted into the darkness. Someone was riding up the driveway on a bike. Someone wearing a black T-shirt and cargo shorts, and no helmet. As our porch motion-detector lights clicked on, my suspicion was confirmed.

"You shouldn't be here," I said as Jake pulled up to the porch and dismounted.

"I've been trying to call and text you all day," he complained. "You never answer your phone."

"It's broken."

"This won't take long. I need you to come talk to the Cabot Police with me. Tomorrow."

My breath caught in my throat. "The police? Why?" I felt dizzy. I had a pretty good idea of why he was talking to them.

"The news isn't public, but it will be," he said. "Juan Carlos's death is a homicide case."

My eyes widened. I hadn't expected Bianca to have come through so fast.

"You mean you didn't see the news?" Jake shoved his hands in his pockets. "So I guess that reporter you're in love with, Bianca Slade? She went to see the Team Cadence-EcuaBar mechanic. She was doing a consumer report on the dangers of carbon fiber. Somehow she wrangled her way in to have a look at the busted bike frame, from the crash, and she had an undercover forensics expert from MIT with her."

"And?"

"The guy found signs of sabotage on the bike Juan Carlos crashed on. Front tube and rear brake both showed signs of tampering. They tipped off the Cabot Police. Now there's a detective on the case, and guess who got called in for questioning?"

I gripped the porch swing chain tighter. It was one thing to develop a theory that Jake could have been involved in all this. It was another thing to confront it head-on, to hear him saying these words—and to think that I might have been right. I might have been dating a thief and a killer for almost a year, and not known it.

"How'd you become a suspect?" I asked, my mouth dry.

"I'm a person of interest, for now," he said. "They found my biking glove. It must have fallen out of my saddle bag. Right near the Team EcuaBar bike trailer."

I narrowed my eyes. "What were you doing near their trailer?"

"Taking a shortcut. So I could get back to you quicker. Of course, that was when I had no idea you'd sneak off to hang out with Juan Carlos."

"I didn't sneak off to hang out with Juan Carlos. I told you, I moved to get away from TV cameras. But none of that even matters now. Juan Carlos is dead." I glared at him.

"I know you suspected me of taking the guy's bike. Don't tell me you think I'm a murderer now."

I continued to stare at him, searching for some fleeting expression that might reveal the truth.

His expression was skepticism, which turned into doubt, then shock. "Oh, God. You do. You actually think I rigged el Cóndor's bike. To kill him."

"I don't know what to think, Jake. Now I know you were near the trailer, and you never told me that. How'd they know the glove was yours anyway?"

"My name was on it. It was part of a pair I used to race in. All our clothes and gear were labeled. Tessa." His eyes were wild. No. Scared. "I didn't want him to get hurt. I wanted him to go back to his home country. Or evaporate or something, once he started coming on to you."

"Coming on to me?"

"You know what I mean. Every time I turned my back, he'd show up and talk to you. And he used to ask me, all the time, how things were going with us. It was like he was prowling around a house looking for cracks, for some place to get in."

I shook my head in amazement. I never knew all that. Was Jake telling the truth?

"It drove me crazy," Jake went on. "Yeah, I was pissed. But I didn't want him to get hurt or to die. I swear, I didn't do anything to him. And I'm going to have a hell of a time convincing the police about that."

"Why?"

He sat at the opposite end of the swing and grabbed the other chain.

"Okay." He looked down. "There's something I never told you. The doping allegations? It wasn't my bag they found those drugs and syringes in. They were in Juan Carlos's bag."

Now my jaw dropped. "Juan Carlos was doping?"

"No. He was clean. I planted the stuff. Okay? I did it."

"No!"

"I did it," he repeated. "And I was stupid enough to get caught. A surveillance camera at the gym where the team worked out showed me going into the locker room with a bag. Later they found my fingerprints on it. Now I'm on the record as someone who tried to get Juan Carlos kicked off the team. So I'm sure, on paper, I look capable of bike sabotage. Someone could look at this as a great act of vengeance."

I looked away so he wouldn't see my eyes glistening. I wanted to throw up. Or cry. Or scream. Or all of those things at once. All those weeks, months, I'd been the supportive girlfriend, standing up for him—even to my own parents—were based on a lie. He'd tried to sabotage Juan Carlos's racing career, and then lied to me about it. All this time, I'd been defending a liar.

"God, Jake." I shook my head. "Why did you do it? I mean, if you'd gotten away with it, he would have been deported." If Jake could sink this low, could he be capable of worse? Like bike sabotage . . . like murder? I moved two more inches away. I glanced at Jake's hands in his pockets. Who was this person beside me now?

"He'd taken my place. There wasn't room for two champions on the team."

"But Juan Carlos could have lost his whole racing career," I argued. "What else would he do? His family doesn't have much money. Cycling was his big ticket out. At least you had other options. You had college. Going pro would have been a great perk, but you didn't have to." I frowned. "Where'd you get the drugs and the syringes?"

"It's not important. Everyone knows someone. The point is, I was stupid, okay? I got caught, and now it's on my record. I was so embarrassed. I didn't want to tell you the whole story. I thought I'd lose cycling, and my scholarship, and then I'd lose you."

I looked away to hide my tears. "It's too late. I don't love you anymore. I can't hold you together or fix whatever's broken in you. And I can't love a liar."

Jake's hopeful expression curdled into a scowl. "Ah. Miss Honesty. The girl who lied to her parents about us. And who lied to me about her cozy little chats with Juan Carlos. In Harvard Square. At Chain Reaction. Where else? How often? I'd be the last to know." Jake stood up. "You know, you have this holier-than-thou perception of yourself as an incredibly honest person. You've confused yourself with your *KidVision* persona, which, by the way, was manufactured for you. The real Tessa Taylor? She's as capable of deceit as the rest of us. None of us are perfect. We all lie or cover things up when it suits our needs. You're no exception."

His words stung. I hated to admit he could be right. I'd told so many half-truths since Chain Reaction—even since Jake's doping scandal—while trying to do the right thing. Maybe my idea of myself as an honest person was the biggest lie of all.

Still, I'd spent the past two weeks dreaming up ways to do good, to be a person of integrity, and he was making me feel like all those blog comments about my bandit riding episode were right. That I was a liar, a cheater, a fake. This was what I hated about Jake. How he always made me crash.

He sat down again, closer, and the swing lurched crazily. I grabbed the chain to steady it.

His eyes were pleading. Desperate. "I need a solid alibi. I have to prove I didn't go into the Team EcuaBar trailer that morning. I need a witness to support me. Come see this detective with me tomorrow. Tell them you were with me every moment that morning, until we got separated on the ride."

"We did not 'get separated.' You *dropped* me. And we were not together every moment that morning."

"Hey, you were out of my sight, too," said Jake. "You feel like talking to a detective about why you tampered with evidence at a crime scene? Why you didn't report a stolen bike right away?"

Now I stood up. "You wouldn't let me report it! You said not to call the police!"

"Tessa. Listen to me. If I have to fight a legal battle, all because of a goddamn glove, it will kill my mother. It'll suck up the last of my college savings on lawyers. I'll lose any chance I have of getting to UMass in the fall. Please. I am begging. It's the last thing I'll ever ask of you. We both say we were never apart, not for one second, before the ride started. Deal?"

Could I trust him to have my back? Could I defend him again? Only if I was certain he wasn't at fault. I now believed Darwin *was* running a high-end bike theft operation, and Jake could have been uninvolved in all that. But I had no proof to offer to send the cops after Darwin. And bike theft now looked petty compared to the bigger bike crime. Sabotage. *Murder.* Jake didn't look good. The timing. The dropped glove. The know-how. The motive.

"You're being honest? Explain this." I stared him down. "I looked through all the photos on the Chain Reaction website. Every rider got their picture taken at mile ten. You couldn't miss the camera. But *you're* not pictured, and you told me you got to mile twenty. Why is that? And don't tell me it's because you're so fast you were a blur."

He looked down. "You're right. I never made it to mile ten," he admitted. "Or even to mile five. I went around the bend and cut back into the woods."

"You went back into the woods? What for?"

"To check out that bike you'd found. I had to see it for myself."

"And did you?"

"No. It was gone. I didn't see that guy you mentioned, either."

"Aviator sunglasses? Buzzed hair? Thick neck? You swear you never saw him?"

"I swear. But I believed you did. And I've had my suspicions that Juan Carlos was up to something for a while now. That's what I went back to prove."

"What would he have been up to? Doping?"

"Maybe. I've studied his racing videos online. He's had some really significant breakaways ever since he went pro."

"He doesn't win every race. I've looked at his stats."

"That could be strategic," Jake insisted. "People started smelling a rat about Lance Armstrong because he won too much. If a coach or someone was behind a doping scheme now, they'd want to make sure the wins were spread out. Only the most important races or stages. Anyway, something was definitely up."

"Why do you say that?"

"He came back from his off-season training in Ecuador in February, and he was like a different rider at spring training camp the next month. People said it was because he'd been training in the mountains."

"Right. He had more red blood cells and lung capacity. The altitude gave him an edge." I could hear the hopeful note in my voice. I did not want to think of Juan Carlos as a cheater, as a doper.

"It wasn't just that," Jake said. "He'd changed. All through the spring, he stopped doing interviews. At pre-season team meetings, he was really serious and quiet. He wouldn't speak up. So I started paying attention. It seemed like he had something to hide. But I also didn't think it was drugs."

"But if he wasn't doping, how would he be cheating?" I asked.

"I thought he might be doing some kind of bike-switching scheme. Having people swap out his bike, after inspection, for one that's not approved. One with modifications. Maybe even a motor in the seat tube."

"A motor?" I laughed. "Come on."

"It sounds crazy, but believe me, it's possible. It's called mechanized doping. With enough money sunk into developing a product, and with a willing team of accomplices, a pro could get away with it. I thought if I could find any proof, I could take it to the cycling board. When you said his spare bike was hidden in there—and a guy was there—I felt like it had to be a cheating scheme with a swapped-out bike. Catching him in the act was more important to me than finishing the ride—or taking care of you. And I'm sorry." He sighed. "I guess I just lost myself that day. And now I've lost you."

"So why did you lie to me again, and tell me you made it to mile twenty? You didn't."

"Because I didn't find the bike in the woods. Or the guy you mentioned. And I felt like a total idiot. It seemed easier to say I'd made it to the checkpoint. Now I see that was wrong. Look, I'm telling you I'm sorry. For everything. What more do you want from me?"

"Right." More lies, more explanations, more apologies. I'd had enough. I stood up. "I think you should just tell all this to the police. I can't help you."

"I can't. My word counts for nothing with cops. So I'm just

going to tell them I was riding with you. The whole time. Please, Tessa. Come back me up. I swear it's the last thing I'll ask from you." He took a step toward me. I turned, backed away, and crashed into the swing.

Jake reached for me. He bent low, and I felt his breath on my cheek.

I swatted at him. "No! Get away from me!"

"Jesus! I'm just trying to help you up, Tessa. Why are you acting all—"

The front door flew open. "Tessa?" said my dad, as Jake and I both sprang apart from each other. "All right. Get the hell out!" he shouted at Jake. "You are not a welcome visitor!"

"Okay, okay! I was just leaving." Jake scrambled to get on his bike.

My mom joined Dad in the doorway, and together they watched him ride off.

"Your mother and I had reached a decision," said my dad. "We were going to let you go to South America next year, after graduation. But now?" He glared at Jake's departing figure, then gave my mom a long look. She nodded. Firmly. "We've changed our mind," my dad said.

My heart sunk.

"We think some perspective in another country, and some time away from that loser, would do you a whole world of good."

PART 2

latitude zero

ECUADOR

31

I GAZED out at the darkening sky and the jagged peaks of the Andes. As the plane began its descent, soft yellow-gold lights winked through thick clouds. Then trickles of lights, and then streams spilled down from the sides of mountains, pooling into a valley. Quito, Ecuador's capitol city. My home for the next three weeks. As we soared over el Cóndor's homeland, I imagined an Inca sun god had scattered gold across velvety hills.

I rested my forehead against the window. Somewhere, among those lights, my host family waited for me. I'd wanted to stay with Mari in her cousin's apartment, but my parents had laid down the law. "That girl is eighteen," my dad had said. "You're not. Homestay or nothing."

I hadn't argued. I was grateful they'd let me go at all. They'd gifted me credit-card flier miles and paid the Vuelta program fee. That's how desperate they were to get me away from Jake. Not to mention the unfolding criminal investigation into Juan Carlos's murder.

Now Juan Carlos's death was officially considered foul play, and Jake's future was on the line.

After Jake's unannounced visit, I'd had to confess to my parents that Jake was a person of interest in a homicide case. They freaked out. Then they took action. It turned out my dad knew a detective in the Cabot PD. He took me there personally the next day to tell Detective Lauren Grant about the morning of Chain Reaction, especially the two brief periods of time when I couldn't account for Jake's whereabouts. I knew they'd use this information against him in his questioning. But I turned my heart into steel. Jake had deceived me since April. I owed him nothing.

Once I got started talking, I'd wanted to tell Detective Grant even more. About Darwin's threatening texts. About Pizarro threatening me at knifepoint, demanding "information." About Juan Carlos's stolen spare bike and its secret contents, now en route to latitude zero. I couldn't shake the feeling that the spare bike and its contents had some link to the saboteur of the main bike, or would help to explain the reason behind Juan Carlos's death. Two bike crimes against the same person, at the same event, had to be connected somehow.

Yet when Detective Grant had said, "Anything else you want to tell us today, Tessa?" I'd gone silent. I remembered Balboa's warnings about what else Darwin might do to destroy my family and me online. Who knew what other dirt Darwin had dug up—or could make up?

Still, every day that the investigation focused on Jake brought detectives one step closer to me, I was sure. That dropped glove didn't look good for Jake. At all. Police were looking into Jake and Juan Carlos's history of rivalry on the junior team, just as Jake had feared. In a *Boston Globe* article about the case, a reporter described the whole doping scandal and Jake's possible motives for vengeance.

"Only a matter of time before reporters come sniffing around here," my dad had muttered, flinging that newspaper straight into recycling.

Then, about a week later, a startling new development emerged.

A ball peen hammer and razor—the tools Mari had said were

likely used for the bike sabotage—had been found on the Team Cadence-EcuaBar trailer floor. Forensics tests showed the razor had paint flecks matching the paint on Juan Carlos's spare bike. And the fingerprints found all over the tools? Not Jake's.

Dylan Holcomb's.

That was not so surprising. They were, after all, his tools—as Dylan explained tirelessly in news interviews. Dylan also insisted he hadn't seen any signs of sabotage upon his inspection. Then he changed his story. He admitted that upon his post-race inspection, he'd noticed indications of sabotage, but he'd been afraid to report it for fear of losing his job. He'd left the trailer for a few minutes on a bathroom break, and hadn't double-checked the lock. That lapse had given the saboteur a small window of time in which to enter the trailer and do the job.

With a shifting story line, no other fingerprints but his on the tools, and no alibi, Dylan had replaced Jake as the prime suspect. While he was being questioned, Dylan wasn't allowed to leave the country. He couldn't even go on the Pan-American Cycling Tour with the team. I was relieved the focus was off Jake. But I felt bad for Dylan. Maybe he was a flake about security, but he just didn't seem capable of hurting Juan Carlos.

That shipping container unloading date couldn't come fast enough. If the smuggled spare bike contained evidence to help get the right person into custody—even fingerprints or a strand of hair from the thief—Dylan could be a free man.

The pilot interrupted my thoughts, announcing that we'd be landing soon. From my backpack, I took out a printed copy of my host family's introductory email and family photo. I studied the printout of the Ruiz family's smiling faces.

My pretty host mom, Lucia Ruiz, looked to be in her early forties. With her sharp suit, sleek updo, and perfect makeup, she had the polished look of a news anchor, but her letter said she was a stay-at-home mom. My host dad, Hugo, was an economist. He wore delicate wire glasses that made him look intellectual, and he had an athletic build. They both looked way younger than my own parents. Fifteen-year-old Amparo had a heart-shaped face and long, dark hair, brushed straight and glossy. The letter mentioned (twice) that she was the second runner-up for Miss Teen Quito. She posed with careful posture, as if balancing an invisible tiara on her head. Andreas, my twelve-year-old host brother, had long, tousled hair that hung in his eyes and wore a soccer uniform. He held my host poodle, Peludo.

I reread the letter. They were "so exciting" to have me come as a "last-minute replace" for someone who'd had to cancel. They would "eagerly to meet me at airport on 12 Julio." My room "was preparation and waited for me." They had "many exciting actividades planning."

I hoped they weren't planning too many *actividades*. I had plenty of *actividades* of my own planned. Like volunteering for Vuelta, and doing interviews for my vlog. Like finding out why Juan Carlos's spare bike was supposed to end up in Quito, and getting my hands on it in the hopes it would help unravel the mystery of Juan Carlos's death.

The plane bucked from turbulence. The woman next to me clutched her armrests and murmured prayers in Spanish. As we were pushed through the cloud cover, the lights of Quito rose up to greet us.

Wheels skidded onto the tarmac, and the passengers burst into applause.

32

IN THE airport, I confronted only stress and chaos. Sputtering white fluorescent lights. Endless lines at customs. Tired babies shrieked and wailed, ignored by exhausted mothers. Dazed tourists fumbled with fanny packs. Recorded announcements in Spanish and English, at regular intervals, urged travelers to hold on to bags, and not to carry anything on behalf of a stranger.

I couldn't wait to get out of that scene and find my host family. For the first time, it hit me: this was serious travel. I'd been to eco-resorts—Costa Rica, Aruba—and on a school band trip to Montreal. Always with parents or chaperones. Now I had to do all my own navigating.

After finally clearing customs, I went to a restroom to splash water on my face. Scraping my tangled hair into a ponytail, I made a face at my reflection. Everyone around me wore full makeup, cute outfits. Elaborate footwear—lots of high heels—peeked out from under the stalls. I wore a pair of old Chuck Taylors and a hopelessly wrinkled T-shirt. I'd spilled tomato juice on my jeans. I probably wasn't going to make the most stunning first impression on the Ruiz family.

Leaving the secure area of the airport, I passed through a long metal tunnel, like a cage. People were pressed up against the other side of it, calling out to family and friends. Boys my age—and some older men—stared as I passed through. Some whistled or clicked their tongues. Others murmured catcalls.

"¡Qué guapa!"

"¡Qué rica, la gringa!"

I wanted to run or hide my face. But I thought of my mom, younger, cowering in a hotel room, afraid to go out in the streets in Juárez, Mexico. I wouldn't be like that. And this was Quito, a cosmopolitan city. I turned my skin to steel, imagining words and stares glancing off.

Then I realized, as the men called to some other girl walking behind me, that nobody here knew who I was. In Quito, I wasn't Tessa Taylor, the fallen star of *KidVision*. I wasn't "Jake's girl." And I definitely wasn't an overgrown Dora the Explorer. I was just some gringa to whistle at. Just a person walking by.

That thought was incredibly freeing.

I made three loops around the waiting area at the airport. I scanned the crowds of travelers reuniting with loved ones, businesspeople meeting associates. Everyone got whisked away in taxis and waiting cars. I kept my eyes out for a sign with my name. I passed lots of people holding signs for strangers they were meeting. Not one of them said "Tessa Taylor."

Had the Ruizes forgotten me?

I rummaged for their letter in my pack. I hadn't brought my cell phone to Quito—my parents cheaped out on the international roaming charges, which was fine by me. I didn't need Darwin staying in touch.

I could probably find a pay phone—I'd read on an Ecuador travel site that pay phones could still be found at some stores and Internet cafés. But the letter wasn't in my pack. With a groan, I realized it must have fallen out on the plane, probably during that turbulence, which had knocked my pack over. I wished I could call Mari—she'd know what to do—but she had no cell phone in Quito either, and her cousin had no landline—too expensive,

Mari had explained when I asked. It was almost eight p.m. on a Friday evening, and the Vuelta offices would be closed by now. None of the taxi drivers looked like people I really wanted to jump into a car with. The drivers stood with arms crossed, or paced back and forth, or lit up cigarettes, looking hungrily in my direction.

I sat down on a curb, zipped up my hoodie, and rubbed my arms to keep warm. So much for summer. It was cold here up in the Andes Mountains. The tropical paradise part of Ecuador, and the steamy jungles and cloud forests promised by the brochures, must be far away.

I looked up, as if for a map in the stars. I blinked back tears. And caught my breath. Oh my God. Those stars! Diamonds flung on black velvet. I wanted to reach out and grab them.

The airport crowds began to thin out. A boy approached me, holding a sign.

"Excuse me? This is you?" The sign had my name on it, misspelled: TERESA TYLER.

The voice jolted me. The accent, the pitch, the musical lilt—it sounded so much like Juan Carlos! I scrambled to my feet, half expecting to see him.

It was not Juan Carlos standing there, of course, but a different guy. He was tall—probably over six feet—with milky-brown skin, light brown, curly hair, and deep blue eyes that made me think of those pictures of earth shot from space. He wore dark wash jeans, a pale blue polo shirt, and a brown leather jacket. He didn't look like anyone in the Ruiz family photo. He also seemed around my age—too old to be my host brother. Good-looking, I couldn't help noticing, but smiling eagerly, in a way that made me cautious.

"Who are you?" I held my backpack tight.

"Santiago Jaramillo," he replied with a warm smile. As if I

was supposed to know who he was. *"¡Bienvenidos a Ecuador!"* He leaned forward—or lunged. I thought of Pizarro with his knife and turned my head at the last second.

Santiago's nose bashed my ear.

I backed away, crashing into a garbage can.

"Oof," said Santiago, rubbing his finely arched nose. "Sorry. Here in Ecuador, we greet each other with *besos*. In the United States, you are accustomed to handshakes, I think? Okay, then. We can shake hands." He grinned and extended his right hand. "We start over. Yes? *Mucho gusto*."

I shook his hand, still wary. "I wasn't expecting you."

"Yes, I can understand the confusion." He laughed. "I wasn't expecting me, either. I was at my home, studying for my TOEFL."

"Your what?"

"Test of English as a Foreign Language. A very important exam for study in the United States. But then the Ruiz family called to my father. They said they could not get to the airport."

"Wait—who's your father?"

"Wilson Jaramillo. The director of Vuelta?"

Of course. *Jaramillo*. That's why his name sounded familiar. But I'd just talked to Wilson on the phone the other day, and he hadn't mentioned a son.

"He sent me to get you," Santiago went on. "There is a road problem. Our house is closer to the airport, and I am an excellent driver. I know all the back roads here."

Wilson hadn't mentioned road problems, either.

"The main road, it is blocked," Santiago explained. "A protest has closed down the Pan-American Highway."

"Who's protesting what?"

"*Los indígenas*, Ecuador's native population. They are protesting our president's decision to open more rain forest land for multinational oil companies and to make roads to the pipelines."

I'd seen something about that on an EcuaBar wrapper. EcuaBar donated part of its proceeds to combat rain forest deforestation in Ecuador's Amazon Basin. And Preston Lane had mentioned something about this issue in his commencement speech. "Should I be worried?" I asked.

He made a dismissive gesture. "It is mostly an inconvenient. Ready to go?"

I still felt unsure about trusting him. Being harassed by thugs and lied to by your boyfriend will do that to you. Your inner compass goes off-kilter, your instinct a spinning arrow.

"Do you know Mari Vargas?" If he had anything to do with Vuelta, he should know her.

He shook his head.

"She's a Vuelta volunteer. A friend of mine. She got here about two weeks ago."

"The TOEFL prep has been taking all my time. I have not met the new volunteers yet."

He could be telling the truth. Still, I'd feel better if I could get in touch with my host family. "Can you call Mr. and Mrs. Ruiz? I had to leave my cell phone at home."

"Of course." He patted his jacket pockets, then his jeans pockets. Then he shrugged, with an apologetic smile and empty hands displayed. "*Ay*. I left it in my car. Shall we walk?"

"Is it far?"

"Not far." He pointed in a vague direction. He might have pointed to a distant star.

I glanced at the taxi queue again. Not appealing. He offered to carry my suitcase and backpack, but I shook my head. Gripping my suitcase handle tightly, I followed him around the corner to his car, a white Nissan Pathfinder.

Santiago opened the door and reached in for his cell phone.

I stood a few feet away, ready to bolt.

Santiago spoke to someone on the phone in Spanish. I could hear a man on the other end. The two of them laughed about something before Santiago passed the phone to me.

My host father spoke in a mix of Spanish and English, slowly apologizing for the confusion. He sounded warm. Fatherly. I clutched the phone with two hands, grateful for the kind reassurances, suddenly aching for my own dad.

My host mother talked, too. There was food and a comfortable bed awaiting. I heard yipping in the background. Peludo the poodle.

That dog sealed the deal. The dog existed. The Ruizes were legitimate. Santiago must be who he said he was. I was going "home." I slid into the passenger seat and closed the door.

Then I noticed a figure under a streetlight about ten yards away. A tall, thin guy with a ponytail. He turned toward Santiago's car. Under the streetlight's glare I saw dark eyes glinting beneath one dark eyebrow.

I gasped and sank low in my seat.

Pizarro? No. No way. Balboa had promised me that Darwin would leave me alone, now that the spare bike was heading to Quito. He wouldn't go back on his word, would he? Were they monitoring me for some other reason? Maybe this was just someone who looked like Pizarro.

I stole another glance out the window.

Damn. It *was* him! He looked right at me and *beckoned.* I slid down in the seat again.

"You are not well?" Santiago cast me a worried look.

"Not so much," I mumbled, feeling dizzy. I poked my head up and looked again.

I saw a black Honda Civic. Headlights winked on. Pizarro got in the passenger side. I saw a shape in the backseat, a mass of hair, glinting red beneath the streetlight. Balboa!

And the driver of the car? Darwin. I could see his broad shoulders, his thick neck, through the open window. He was still wearing aviator shades, even though the sun had set.

Come here, he mouthed, looking right at me.

I hunched low in my seat, breathing hard, my heart pounding. All three of those creeps were here in Quito. Together. They hadn't been on my flight—I'm sure I would have noticed them—so they must have arrived before me. Maybe that's why I hadn't gotten a text from Darwin in five days. How had they figured out I was coming here? And, more important, why did they care? I clearly had nothing to do with that bike! Did they still think I had some kind of "valuable information"? Or were they onto my plan of intercepting that bike—and its secret contents—in the shipping container, and here to make sure that I didn't?

I turned to Santiago. "You look like someone who loves to drive fast," I told him, even though he didn't look like that at all. He looked exactly like the kind of guy who'd be studying for a TOEFL exam at home on a Friday night.

Santiago grinned. "I do like to drive fast. How did you guess?"

He cranked up the radio—a maniacal merengue song with blaring trumpets and a rhythm the pace of a heart attack. He put the car into gear and laid rubber. A Virgin Mary picture swung wildly from the rearview mirror.

I looked at the picture, then reached up and held tight to Juan Carlos's necklace. If Darwin had it in for me, I'd need all the protection and backup I could get.

33

SANTIAGO'S EYES slid toward me as he finally slowed down for a stoplight. "Forgive me for what is a personal question. But you are anxious about something. Yes?"

"Anxious? I'm not anxious. What makes you think I'm anxious? No. I'm excited to meet my host family! Let's go, *muy, muy rápidamente*!" I looked back as the light turned green and Santiago accelerated again. Those headlights stuck close behind us. "Are we taking this road the whole way?"

"No. At some point, soon, we will need to turn onto smaller roads."

I didn't love the idea of being on a network of small, dark roads, with a car of thieves behind us. What did they want with me now? Their damn stolen bike was already on the way, due to arrive in just one week. "Let's stay on this nice wide road with the traffic."

"But the blockade is coming up."

"There must be some way around it. Or can you just bust through it?"

Santiago turned off the radio and looked at me. "Please tell me what is going on," he said. "Is there some kind of trouble? If I am driving you, and if you are asking me to break a law, I must to know why."

"I'm being followed," I confessed. "There are two guys and a girl in the car behind us. They were looking at me in the parking lot."

Santiago gaped at me. "*¿En serio?* Why they are following *you*?"

I didn't want my story to get back to his dad. I might get kicked out of Vuelta before I began if I looked like a magnet for criminals. "They must think I'm someone else," I said. I remembered the announcements that had kept blaring in customs, about holding on to your bags. "They seemed pretty interested in my, um, backpack."

Santiago blew out a long breath. "*Chuta.* I am really worrying now."

"Why?"

"Drug trafficking is a big problem at this airport recently. Foreigners have been targeted by dealers working for cartels. Especially young people with backpacks. They can be hired as carriers, or even used as *mulas*—mules—without even knowing about it."

"Carriers? Mules? For what?" I sat up straighter.

"Drugs, maybe, or money from deals. Sometimes a mule can hide this in someone's bag. Then the bag is carried to the next mule, or to some location. If these people were looking at your backpack? Believe me, you do not want them approaching to you."

I sucked in my breath. Drug dealers! Maybe that's what Darwin and his group were!

I recalled the State Department website my parents had made me read back in Boston, with all the travel advisories. While Ecuador was considered one of the safer, more politically stable South American countries compared to its neighbors, it had its share of drug cartels. I hoped Darwin was just a fence for a high-end bike-theft ring. But now, thinking of my knifepoint encounter with Pizarro, and the fact that all three of those people had tracked me at the airport, everything was pointing to drug dealing, not just a bike theft. Maybe the "valuable information" Pizarro had asked for was contact information for someone involved in some drug deal. Maybe someone Juan Carlos had known! But would the bike be filled with drugs? That didn't make sense. Drugs came *out of* Latin America, not into it. Cash from drug deals seemed more likely. I wondered how much cash would fit into a bike handlebar. Or into a seat, or a hollowed-out frame.

Any way I looked at it, it seemed likely that Darwin and his crew were connected in some way to drug cartel activities in Ecuador. Maybe the bike contained drug money.

And Juan Carlos? How did he fit into this darkening picture? I thought of Juan Carlos's jagged scar. Painful as it was to consider, he could have had a secret life, or a past, that no one ever suspected. Something he'd tried to leave behind when he left Ecuador. Shadows to race away from.

I wiped my hands on my pants, suddenly aware of how much I was sweating. I'd seen Quentin Tarantino movies. Drug dealers were seriously scary people. People got killed over deals gone bad.

Could Darwin be the person behind Juan Carlos's death? If so, could he have framed Dylan or Jake for the bike sabotage? And if Juan Carlos had information related to drug deals, and that information was now missing, maybe Darwin would do anything to find it. Like chasing a teenage girl who seemed like she knew something, all the way to the equator.

I swallowed hard. I glanced behind me again, at those blinding headlights so close to us now.

"The road will divide soon with a detour for avoiding the blockade," said Santiago. "We must lose these people. There is only one thing to do. Is your seat belt on?"

"Yes, but why—"

"¡Vámonos!"

"Oh my God!" I cried out as the car lurched forward.

Santiago sped up until the lights behind us were distant dots. Approaching an exit ramp, where cars in front of us turned left, for the detour, he stayed the course instead.

I looked behind. No headlights. Thank God. "That was amazing! You ditched them!"

"Ditched? This word I do not know."

"You got them off our trail. Sent them packing. Cut them loose." I smiled.

Santiago smiled, too. "I hope these idioms appear on my TOEFL." Then he looked worried. "But we still have the blockade ahead. They will probably tell us to turn back."

I rolled down my window. An acrid smell filled my nostrils, making me cough. The air was thick and hot. Logs, tree branches, and plastic barrels were heaped together across the width of the road. Piles of tires were burning bright. Flames flickered orange, licking the night sky.

Through the smoke haze, I could see men, some with long braids, wearing ponchos and felt hats, pacing in front of the blockade. Some raised their fists as we approached. Not in solidarity. In anger. Other men, and some women—some with babies lashed to their backs—shouted at armed soldiers in front of a jeep.

I suddenly longed for a bicycle. If we had bikes, we could ditch the car. Be free of this scene. And completely throw Darwin and his crew off our trail.

"Could this thing get violent?" I asked as a soldier brandished a rifle at a small crowd.

"Mostly these protests are peaceful," said Santiago, slowing down. "They try to make the roads inconvenient for travel. Sometimes they can shut down Quito for days."

“Days?” I thought of the shipping container, which had to be trucked from the Port of Guayaquil on the coast, over the mountains and into Quito.

Santiago made a vague gesture. “Days, maybe weeks. And sometimes, yes, protests can become violent. A match can strike, and then we have riots.”

Fabulous. I’d been in Ecuador for less than two hours and landed in a sandwich of angry protestors on one side, possible drug cartel enforcers on the other. Spin the wheel, take your chance!

A man in gray camouflage waved a rifle in our direction.

“He is a military man,” said Santiago. “He is wanting us to turn around and go back.”

But Santiago kept the car rolling forward. Near the military guy, he stopped and rolled down his window.

Their Spanish was rapid-fire, but I got the gist of the conversation. Military Man yelled at Santiago for ignoring the detour signs. Santiago apologized. He explained we were being pursued by robbers, and we’d stayed on the highway to escape them. He reached into his pocket and handed Military Man a twenty-dollar bill. The guy pocketed it and pointed to a hill off to our right. He explained something in Spanish. The next thing I knew, Santiago was throwing the Pathfinder into reverse.

I gripped my seat belt. “Are you going through the blockade?”

“No. Off the road. This man has shown to me a place I can safely drive. There I can connect with another road into Quito. He will offer us protection if we do it fast.”

About a football field’s length back from the blockade, Santiago turned the car to the right. And floored it.

My teeth clacked as the wheels left the pavement. My stomach churned, and my mind flashed back to the last off-road ride I’d taken: with Jake, at Chain Reaction, on bikes.

Yet as the car wheels churned on the grassy road shoulder, and the car rumbled over bumpy terrain, I didn't feel as scared this time.

Santiago leaned his head back on the headrest and flexed his fingers on the wheel. "*¡Que raro!* I cannot believe only one hour ago, I have been studying *verbos* for the TOEFL exam. Now I am driving a—what do you call it?—a getahead vehicle." He flashed me a grin. "I admit. That was fun. I hope these people will now forget they ever saw you. This is a big city. You will not be troubled."

I wasn't so sure, but I smiled back. "You went above and beyond. Thank you. And it's a *getaway* vehicle. Let me pay you back for the bribe." I reached for my backpack.

"No. I cannot accept payment. *Tranquila.* Sit back and relax. We will be at the Ruiz house in no time."

Santiago turned the merengue music up loud. We merged with light traffic on a quiet road, smooth asphalt thrummed beneath our wheels, and the gold lights of Quito beckoned.

34

THE RUIZ family greeted me with hugs and *besos.* My host sister, Amparo, gave me a huge white stuffed bear with a red heart necklace, in case I missed my family and needed something to hug. Andreas gave me Ecuadorian magazines "for practicing in Spanish." I thanked him, trying to ignore the fact that Juan Carlos was on the cover of almost all of them, with teasers for stories about *la tragedia ciclista.* Hugo carried my suitcase and backpack to the room I would share with Amparo. Lucia served me a late dinner: steak with eggs cooked over it, and a heaping plate of *papas fritas.* Peludo the poodle covered my arms and face with sloppy licks.

I was beyond tired. And sleep should have come easily. For the moment anyway, I was safe. The Ruiz house was tucked away in a maze of hilly streets, all lined with elegant homes—fresh white paint, red tile roofs, gracious arched brown doorways. The homes, including the Ruiz *casa,* were also heavily barricaded: ringed by cement walls iced with glass shards.

The Ruiz house was further guarded by a man in a booth at the gate. He wore a beret, fatigues, and a semiautomatic weapon slung across his chest. After Santiago had pulled up at the curb, we'd had to pass by that booth. As the guard tipped his beret and murmured, "*Buenas noches, señorita,*" I'd actually felt grateful for that gun. Especially now that I was thinking Darwin and those guys were involved with international drug trafficking—and with Juan Carlos's murder.

Not so long ago, when I couldn't sleep, I used to lie in my bed back home and let my thoughts drift to Jake. I'd replay our good times—like biking out to Cabot Pond on hot summer nights and swimming to the far edge to kiss—and more—beneath a willow tree, whose gracious branches offered a private room. Sometimes, when things weren't good with Jake, my thoughts would drift to Juan Carlos instead. To our halting conversations in Spanish, to the slow spread of his smile, to the way he said to me once, almost wistfully, "Jake, he is lucky to have a girlfriend like you." I'd replayed that memory so much I'd almost worn it out.

But now, lying between crisp pink sheets in Amparo's spare bed, my thoughts veered away from both of them . . . to Santiago. He had risen to the occasion, driving that "getahead vehicle" like a pro—and he didn't even know me! He'd also given me his cell number before he left. "If you need anything, call," he said to me before he left. "And I will see you on Monday?"

"Monday?"

"At Vuelta. I'm working for my dad at the headquarters, part-time, for my summer job."

"You're working at Vuelta, too? Doing what?"

"Updating their website. So if you need to have another high-speed chase or something, I am your guy. *Chao!*" He waved—no attempt at a *beso* this time, as he rubbed his nose and winked.

"Chao," I replied, remembering, with a pang, that *chao* was the last word Juan Carlos and I had exchanged.

I tossed and turned, trying to plump up my flat pillow. I took off Juan Carlos's crucifix and set it on the nightstand so it wouldn't dig into my skin. I still couldn't sleep. Amparo's snores were fearsome. And now the airport chase haunted me. All the emotions I'd fought to quell on that ride came flooding in.

Darwin and his cohorts had wanted to talk to me. They'd made no effort to hide. Only after I ignored them did Darwin press the pedal to the metal. Maybe I should have just talked to them in the parking lot and asked them directly what was going on, instead of having to wonder. By ignoring them, I'd pissed them off.

Anyway, how did they know to find me in Quito? And at the airport? Aside from my host family and the Vuelta office, no one had my itinerary. Except Mari.

I sat bolt upright in bed. *Mari.* We'd exchanged a few emails in the past two weeks. One had my flight times and my host family's address. Maybe Darwin had somehow intercepted our emails. Or maybe one of Darwin's spies had gotten information out of her, about when I was coming. I had to know who she'd talked to lately—and if she was okay.

I grabbed my laptop from my backpack and turned it on. I padded softly through the house, trying to find an Internet signal, until I came to the open-air patio in the middle of the house.

This patio was the best part of the Ruiz house: a secret square, protected from the streets, surrounded by the walls of adjacent rooms. In addition to the washing machine and clothesline, it contained a large collection of potted plants, some with elaborate vines creeping up the wall and some with strange, bulbous fruits. And above: nothing but sky. Just those brilliant stars, so close they seemed like I could reach out and grab them.

I found a blanket folded up on the washing machine, drew it around my shoulders for warmth, and breathed in the rich scent of dirt and flowers. Then I sat cross-legged on the cool tile and fired off a note to her. She'd been quiet on email, not responding to my last few messages. I hoped she'd reply to this one. I kept it simple.

> Arrived. In Quito. We have to talk. You might be in danger.
>
> When & where can we meet up tomorrow?

I sent it and waited for what I hoped would be an almost instant response. No response came. It was almost midnight. I hoped she was having some party at her cousin's hip bachelorette pad. Dancing. Living *la vida loca*. Safe.

I sent quick emails to my parents, and to Kylie and Sarita, letting them all know I'd safely arrived. I kept those emails breezy and brief. I couldn't alarm anyone. I wished Kylie extra good luck on her Lane Scholarship interview.

I checked my inbox again. Still nothing from Mari.

To distract myself from compulsive email checking, I surfed to the Team Cadence-EcuaBar website and looked up the latest stats on the Pan-American Cycling Tour. I learned that without its star rider at the helm, it had won two circuit events and some time trial events in Bogotá, but placed fourth in the Bogotá one-day classic, with the favorite Ecuadorian team—Equipo Diablo—taking a solid first. Cadence-EcuaBar was suffering without its star climber. In Venezuela this week, the team was now doing a weeklong stage race, La Vuelta a Venezuela, and performing somewhat better, the strongest North American team in the tour—but three strong riders from Ecuador's Equipo Diablo were surpassing them at every leg of the race.

Thinking of that Ecuadorian team made me think of their soon-to-debut rider. El Ratón. My quick search on him led to an interview posted a month ago on an Ecuadorian TV station's website. A local reporter asked him how his friend Juan Carlos got started in racing.

El Ratón hesitated, his brows furrowed. "Juan Carlos?" he asked.

"Yes. You are good friends."

If el Ratón was at all annoyed that the interview was more about his friend, he didn't show it. He nodded and launched into the story, in Spanish, as if he'd told it a hundred times before. "

"One day an American businessman—Preston Lane, of EcuaBar—noticed Juan Carlos competing in an urban downhill race, and he got him into the Vuelta Youth Racing Club. He believed Juan Carlos had what it takes for road racing. And he was right. A few years later, with many prizes under his belt, Juan Carlos was recruited for the EcuaBar junior development team. And he spent very little time there before he went pro. He's an inspiration to us all now, about what is possible if we push ourselves, and if someone believes in our talents."

"How did that feel, seeing your friend go off to the United States to start a racing career?" asked the reporter. "After all, you used to ride together."

"We did ride together. Since we were nine years old," said el Ratón with a smile. "We grew up in the same south Quito neighborhood. Juan Carlos and I found abandoned bike frames in parks, or around the city, and we learned to put them together. We learned about bikes and improved. Then we spent all our time in the mountains, riding. When we were fourteen, we started racing urban downhill. But are you asking me if I was jealous of my friend, for all his opportunities?"

"It would be natural, wouldn't it?" said the reporter.

El Ratón chuckled and shook his head. "He is like my brother.

We are from the same place. His success is my success. Jealous? Me? Never."

I wondered if that were really true. I had flashes of envy when Sarita got higher grades than me, or won academic awards that I didn't. I also wondered what this urban downhill thing was. I'd never heard of a specific downhill racing event for cycling, let alone an urban one, but maybe that was some specialized term here. A background in downhill racing could explain why Juan Carlos was fearless on hills. So why did he end up fatally crashing on a descent? It just wasn't fair.

I checked my email again. Nothing from Mari. I snapped my laptop closed. If I didn't hear back from Mari first thing tomorrow morning, I'd go to her apartment. There had to be some reason she'd ignored my last few emails. I really hoped she was okay.

I headed back to Amparo's room, then realized I'd opened the door to a different bedroom off the open-air patio, not the door to the hall. This room was hardly bigger than a walk-in closet. It had a green shag rug and a twin bed in one corner. Beside the bed was a nightstand with a phone and a lamp; the lamp had plastic figures of Mary, Joseph, and the baby Jesus affixed to the base. A small shuttered window faced the courtyard.

I sat on the bed. Then lay down. Aside from the faint smell of damp earth—like a basement that had flooded once—the room was cozy. And, like the patio, it felt safe. No windows to the outside world.

I pulled the scratchy wool blanket up around me and drifted off to sleep.

I dreamed of Juan Carlos. He was riding the ghost bike. He wore an all-white cycling outfit, matching the white frame, the white handlebars, the white wheels. Turning his head to look back at me, he flashed me his most dazzling smile. "Tessa Taylor!" he called to me. "Can you catch up?"

I was cranking along on an old beater bike. The downtube was rusted. Wheels squeaked and pedals jammed. I looked down and saw I had training wheels, one of them coming loose. "I'm trying!" I called back. "Hey! Come back!"

But he didn't come back, and I couldn't catch up, and the distance between us yawned. Only once did he look back at me. When he did, his face was covered in blood.

35

"¡AY, PELUDO! *¿Qué hicistes? ¿Pipi aquí? ¿Qué bestia!"*

I awakened to Lucia Ruiz's shrill voice. I rubbed my eyes and opened the shutters. I peered out into the open-air patio, now awash in sunlight. Lucia was berating the poodle, who had just peed all over the floor and was now munching on that white stuffed bear Amparo had given me. Lucia yanked the bear from the dog's jaws and muttered something, in Spanish, about how the crazy dog was always chewing everything in sight.

Amparo rushed in, dodging the puddle. *"¡Tessa no está aquí!"*

For a moment I enjoyed the drama as she explained to her mom—and then to Hugo and Andreas, who came into the courtyard—that I wasn't in bed. It was almost like being a ghost.

When I realized the Ruizes were seriously freaking out, though, I burst out of the room.

"Buenos días," I said shyly, suddenly aware that I was the only one not yet fully dressed. They were all staring at my right arm. The bandage was off, but a big angry scab—a memento of Chain Reaction—remained.

Since I was still holding the blanket I'd found on the patio last night, I covered my arm with it, and my thin nightgown, and explained how I'd wound up in that bedroom by taking a wrong turn on a nighttime walk through the house.

Everyone laughed, and Hugo told me it was the room of their former maid.

"We haven't found a replacement as good as her," Lucia added. "This is why the house is not so clean. I apologize."

Not clean? It was spotless! I took a step backward and looked at this family, especially Amparo, through new eyes. These people had had a live-in maid. Their life seemed so different from that of the people by the blockade we'd passed by last night.

"I like the room," I admitted. "Could I stay in here?"

"This room?" Lucia's eyebrows shot up. "*Ay, no, mi hija*. This room is not so comfortable, not for you. Besides, Amparo would be lonesome."

Amparo looked hurt. "My room—*our* room—is so much nicer than this one, Tessa."

"Of course. I'm sorry, I didn't mean to sound ungrateful. Your room is great."

She beamed. "Thanks. I have to show you all my photo albums, and my pageant trophies. Will you help me with a speech? I have to write a new one for Miss Tierra Ecuador."

"Who's she?"

"Not a *she.* A *what.* It's the Miss Earth Ecuador pageant." Amparo's eyes lit up as she spoke. "This contest, it combines beauty with awareness of environmental concerns. I thought because you worked in television, you would be the perfect person to help me. Maybe today?"

"I'd love to help." I smiled back, suddenly aching for Kylie and Sarita—and panicking, in the next moment, about getting to Mari. "But today I have to see my friend from back home. She's working with Vuelta, too."

"Another day, we would love to include her," said Lucia. "But it is Saturday, and Hugo is not working, so we have our *actividades familiares* already planned."

Family activities. I managed a weak smile. I was seventeen. Couldn't I have any say in my schedule? I hadn't felt so programmed since kindergarten.

After breakfast, I checked email again. Nothing new except a note from my mom. *(We're so proud of you! Work hard, wear sunscreen, have fun!)* I'd just have to get the Ruizes to route our *actividades* through Mari's neighborhood and make an excuse to go see her.

I pulled out the map from my Vuelta welcome packet and located the address of her cousin's apartment, in a neighborhood called La Mariscal, more commonly known as La Zona. That was easy enough to remember.

LATER THAT morning, Hugo backed the car down the driveway with the whole family and me inside. He stopped at the booth by the gate and introduced me to Paolo, the day shift guard.

"Buenos días, señorita," he said with a friendly grin, touching his beret and displaying silver-capped teeth with his smile.

"So the guards will just let me in if I knock at the booth?" I asked my host parents as we continued down the driveway.

"Let you in? Of course. But from where?"

"I thought after our sightseeing you could drop me off at my friend Mari's place. I can find my way back here."

"Mari. This is the girl who lives alone? In an apartment?"

"Yeah. Her cousin's place. It's in some area called La Zona—"

"La Zona!" Amparo exclaimed, clapping her hands together. "*Mami*, I want to go with Tessa. Can I?"

"Absolutely not. It's a nightclub scene."

"Sounds fun," I said. My mind flashed to my red sundress, folded neatly in my suitcase. Sarita had taken me shopping in Harvard Square the day before I traveled. She'd ordered me to buy the dress and find a hot guy to dance with. "One salsa," she'd commanded. "To shake Jake out of your head. And Juan Carlos, too, while you're at it."

"It is not fun," Lucia said sharply. "It's the most dangerous section of Quito. It's full of gringo tourists—sorry," she added to me. "Not like you. People who are out looking for trouble."

"But I'm seventeen," I reminded them. "My parents let me go to some dicey areas in Boston. I think with some common sense I'll be fine. Besides, it can't be that bad if Mari is staying there." I sounded confident, but I quaked inside. If La Zona was really such a hotbed for criminals, wouldn't that be where Darwin and his crew were most likely to hang out?

Lucia jabbed a bobby pin into her sleek bun. "This is the problem in your country," she said. "Too many kids are raising themselves. Parents are not conveying good values. In my opinion, this is why your country has so much violence."

I glanced out the window behind us as we drove away. Paolo tipped his beret at me and continued polishing his gun.

36

I SAW most of Quito that day through the tinted window of the car. Insulated. We drove around the modern section, with its sleek hotels and office buildings, its plazas with fountains and red poinsettia trees, growing wild and unpruned, like little explosions of Christmas. Rogue palm trees sprouted up in plazas and boulevards, hardy in the mountain air, and reminders that the Amazon Basin—the jungle—wasn't so far away after all. I loved the wild, random, sprawling feel. Boston and Cambridge seemed so planned, so pruned, in comparison. I wished I could just run outside and get lost in the maze of streets here.

But I was safest with the Ruiz family, in the car. The whole time, I kept one eye on the sights and one eye peeled for Darwin, Pizarro, and Balboa. I even picked up a disguise at a crafts fair we visited: a white blouse with embroidery from an *indígena*, which I immediately slipped on over my T-shirt. A wool shoulder bag with llamas marching across it and a wool hat with ear flaps completed the full-on Ecuadorian tourist look. I tucked my hair up inside it, and pulled the hat low over my head.

"Are you cold?" Lucia guessed with a sympathetic smile. "They call this the City of Eternal Spring, but tourists are surprised by the altitude. The mornings can be quite chilly."

"A little. We are pretty high up, aren't we? The air feels so thin."

Hugo pressed two bottles of water into my hands and slipped another one into my new Ecuadorian tote bag. "Drink plenty of this," he advised. "Altitude sickness can sneak up on you these first few days. You must be on the alert for it."

I opened a bottle and drank, wishing altitude sickness wasn't the only thing I had to be on the alert for.

Leaving the crafts market, I tried to be a dutiful host daughter and admire the sights they were pointing out. I had to admit, Quito was stunning in its rough beauty. The hills that embraced the city were the lushest green. The clouds hung low, as if dropped from the sky. The buildings rose unevenly and were painted in an array of colors, a mix of concrete, stucco, and glass. High on a hill overlooking the historic district stood a metal statue of a woman that reminded me of the Statue of Liberty. But this statue had a halo and angel wings. She held up one arm in a graceful gesture, as if blessing the entire city at her feet.

"That's el Panecillo," said Amparo, pointing to the statue. "Or the Virgin of Quito. She is our city's madonna."

"She is made of seven thousand pieces of aluminum," Andreas chimed in.

"Wow, it's gorgeous." A far cry from Amber's bike sculptures. "I bet the view's amazing from that hill." I startled as a black Honda Civic drove by. I shielded my eyes from it and gazed into the distance. "Can you walk up?" *Can we go there now?* Someone was parking the Honda Civic. It looked just like the car Darwin had driven away from the airport. I pulled my hat lower.

"Yes," said Andreas.

"No," said my host parents at the same time. "There have been muggings at El Panecillo," Lucia added. "It isn't safe to hike there. But she is beautiful from afar, isn't she?"

A family of four got of the car and went to a *ceviche* restaurant. Not Darwin. I breathed easier. But I kept looking behind me and all around me, like someone in a bicycle race, expecting Darwin or Pizarro or Balboa to pop up anytime, anyplace.

BY LUNCHTIME, all the clouds had burned off, revealing the rolling green hills that embraced the city and the snowcapped volcanoes beyond. Everyone was hungry. I found a restaurant on a map that was right by La Zona, but Hugo and Lucia had other plans: a ritzy café on Amazonas near the financial district. In the complete opposite direction.

From our table by the window, Hugo pointed to the highest hill. "That is Guagua Pichincha, our resident volcano," he said. "And there. Our jewel." He pointed to a far-off mountain that reminded me of an ice-cream cone. "Cotopaxi."

I barely looked. Instead, as Hugo and Lucia lectured me about Ecuadorian natural attractions and geology, I stared out the window at a bus stop.

A big poster advertised the Pan-American Cycling Tour, coming to Quito in just five days. It wasn't a true photograph, but more like some kind of enhanced graphic, or computer-generated art. Gorgeous. The picture showed a peloton of cyclists: the Ecuadorian team, dressed in red, yellow, and blue—thundering down a cobblestoned street. They rode beautiful, fire-red bikes, with the brand-name Diablo spelled out on the frames. They all had intense looks on their faces. Like any cycling team. I gazed at it. I'd forgotten how much cycling inspired me.

From where I sat, I could just make out the text on the poster. Equipo Diablo headed a list of twenty other teams in the PAC Tour—up-and-coming teams from the United States, Latin America, and Europe. Team Cadence-EcuaBar was right beneath them. But Equipo Diablo was spelled out large. It jolted me, seeing Team Cadence-EcuaBar so diminished, and not the headline act. But Equipo Diablo was the home favorite here.

My gaze shifted to a poster beside it, which was equally stunning. This one advertised the city's weeklong cycling expo. The guy featured in this picture—a real photo, not an artistic rendering—wore a red jumpsuit and a red motorcycle helmet. But he was on a bike. He and that bike were flying down a long stone staircase, both wheels off the road, cobblestones beneath. So this must be urban downhill racing. I shivered. It looked terrifying, just from the picture.

Then I saw, in blazing letters below the soaring bike:

¡Venga a ver el último viaje del Ratón!

El Ratón? I inched close to the window and looked closely at the photo. It was hard to see the face with that helmet on. But that had to be Juan Carlos's best friend. How many well-known cyclists named el Ratón could there be?

And why was this his *last* ride?

The Ruizes, having figured out I wasn't listening, followed my gaze to the posters.

"Ah! El Ratón! He is famous!" said Andreas.

"Why do they call him 'the mouse'?" I asked him.

"Because he is small and quick and impossible to catch. He is the best downhill racer in Quito. But he has been training for road racing. This is why he appears in both posters."

I squinted at the first poster. Sure enough, the cyclist leading the Equipo Diablo peloton was el Ratón. Even though the image was artistically enhanced, it was the same guy I'd seen with Juan Carlos, in photos, and in the TV interview I'd watched online last night. He had high cheekbones and a distinctive cleft chin. Though he wasn't the cycling poster boy that Juan Carlos had been—I couldn't picture his face on a billboard—he had rugged good looks, like Quito itself. The kind of face you'd look at twice and find something in to admire.

Something else didn't make sense. "If he's in this downhill cycling expo in a few days, but Equipo Diablo is in Venezuela right now, how can he race both events?" I asked Andreas, since he seemed to know the most about cycling.

"El Ratón is ending his downhill career this week," Andreas explained. "The five-day stage race in Quito this weekend marks his debut with Equipo Diablo."

"It seems a little optimistic, don't you think? Putting him in front of the peloton when he's never ridden with the team before?"

"Oh, but he's very good," said Hugo. "Andreas and I have been following his career. El Ratón has trained with the Vuelta racing club for two years. Cycling team scouts from Ecuador, Colombia, even *los Estados Unidos*, have been saying he is *el próximo!*"

"The next what?"

"The next el Cóndor."

Lucia made a dismissive gesture that made her bracelets jangle. "He is good but not the best. It is strange to me that he got this position so suddenly, when other cyclists have worked longer for the honor. Then again, it's not really about talent, is it? I think they put him in that picture only because of the media."

I sat forward. "What's the media here saying about el Ratón?"

"There was a lot of, what is the word, hype?" said Lucia. "Because el Cóndor was coming home for the PAC Tour."

"The big race between two best friends, on rival teams, was going to be the biggest sporting event Ecuador has seen since Jefferson Pérez won the Olympic gold," said Hugo.

I understood how the media could shape a story. That wasn't necessarily bad. Especially if it got more people interested in watching a sport like pro cycling.

"Who'd they want to win? El Cóndor or el Ratón?" I asked.

"El Ratón, of course," said Andreas.

"El Cóndor," said Amparo at the same time. "No. Not everyone here supports el Ratón," Amparo corrected. "I wanted el Cóndor to win."

"Only because he is *muy caliente*," teased Andreas. He kissed the air.

Amparo swatted his arm. "That is not why. And Mami wanted el Cóndor to win, too."

I looked at Lucia. "Really? How come?"

Lucia pursed her lips, thinking for a moment. She chose her words with care. "He is—he was—a brave young man," she said. "Brave to go to another country, so young. Very hardworking, too. I felt he represented us Ecuadorians, and he gave us a sense of pride and possibility. We do not have so many sports heroes here. And this downhill racing business"—she made that dismissive gesture again—"it is an exciting sport. But road racing can take an Ecuadorian athlete to Colombia, to the U.S., to Europe . . . to the biggest races in the world."

Hugo shrugged. "In your country, and in Europe," he said, "the sport is about the characters, the big personalities. In Ecuador, cycling has been more about teams than individuals. This is changing now. I think because of the success Juan Carlos has had in your country. Here, we used to be happy if any team placed well in an international event. It was good for our country, psychologically. Now, though, people are interested in these two big names, in individuals. The Great Bird versus the Mouse. Even betting on their racing results." He shook his head. "Before Juan Carlos died, all this talk of the PAC Tour homecoming—it was a circus."

Lucia clapped her hands together. "Enough talk about this bicycle tragedy. It is too sad for lunchtime conversation. Let us talk of happy things. Tessa, what do you think of Ecuadorian food so far?"

Lucia proceeded to explain the various dishes. Then Hugo pointed out some banks as we continued eating. The Ruizes kept wanting me to look up, up, up—at the sky, at the statues, at the buildings, the hills. But my eyes kept drifting down, to images of very different lives.

Across from the bus stop outside, I saw women, maybe my mother's age, almost bent double as they lugged burlap sacks of potatoes, cabbages, even whole dead chickens. I saw men and women in ragged ponchos setting up pyramids of produce to sell—in the median of the street—while their babies toddled toward the street and cars brushed by within inches. I saw lottery ticket hawkers, men carrying huge bags of soccer balls, umbrellas, and pink toilet paper rolls, all for sale.

And I saw children. Everywhere, children in need of baths, hairbrushes, meals. They picked lice out of one another's hair while sitting on the sidewalk. They chased businessmen with shoeshine kits, crying out, *"¡Señor! ¿Limpianos?"* They came into the restaurant to sell red roses and gum, calling *"¡Compre! ¡Compre!"* and weary waiters shooed them away. Meanwhile, all these well-off Ecuadorians and foreign tourists chatted away, oblivious. The Ruizes, too.

What had Juan Carlos's life been like here? Where had he fit in? What life was he pedaling away from when he took his chances and joined an American team?

I'd heard he was from humble origins, his father a glass factory worker. Would Juan Carlos have done anything to get away from the hardscrabble life here in Quito?

Like get involved with a drug cartel? Or fail in a desperate attempt to break away from one? What had Juan Carlos kept close to his chest, besides that crucifix necklace?

"*HOLA*. SANTIAGO? It's me. Tessa." I spoke in a hushed voice on the phone that evening, on the extension in the ex-maid's room. I needed a moment of privacy—hard to find—and a break from looking at Amparo's fourteen pageant photo albums. I also desperately needed help. I'd never made it to Mari's neighborhood; the Ruizes whisked me from one *actividad* to another all day, and were adamant about steering clear of La Zona.

"Tessa!" Santiago exclaimed, sounding pleased. *"¿Qué tal?"*

"Not much. Am I interrupting you from anything?" I asked.

"I have just been studying the present perfect progressive tense," Santiago said, speaking slowly and precisely. "How is it? I have been using it correctly?"

"*Perfecto*. And I'm sorry to interrupt your studying, but—"

"It is a happy interruption. It is nice to hear your voice. I have been thinking about you."

I smiled into the phone, surprised at the warm feeling his words brought to me. I'd felt cold, almost numb, since Chain Reaction. My small reaction to Santiago's compliment reminded me that somewhere inside me, I still had emotions. I still lived. "Really?" I said, almost shyly.

"Present perfect progressive tense. How did I do?"

I hesitated, then managed to laugh. I didn't know why I'd assumed that his words carried some deeper meaning. Santiago was just a friendly guy. Just practicing his *verbos*. He was probably the least mysterious person I'd met in recent weeks.

"I have a huge favor to ask you," I went on. "Can you help me to contact my friend Mari? I can't reach her, and I'm getting worried."

"I do not know this Mari," said Santiago. "You are sure she is with Vuelta?"

"I'm positive. Please, can you check? Her full name is Marisol Vargas."

"I will ask to my father right now how you can reach her. *Momentito.*"

I heard faint conversation in Spanish. Then Santiago returned.

"My father says she is here in Quito. She arrived on schedule."

I let out a long breath. So she was here in the city.

"She worked at Vuelta for one or two days only, my father says. Then she had some kind of health problem, she said. *Migraña.*"

"Migraine?" I guessed.

"Yes, yes. She has migraines. She left a message for my father on the phone. She has not been in to the office for more than one week. Someone else is teaching her classes, but the students, they have been asking for Mari. My father says our receptionist came by to check on her and to bring her soup. Mari said her cousin is taking care of her, but she cannot say when she will return to work."

Cradling the phone, I lay back on the bed, trying to process this unexpected development. Mari had missed over a week of work? Could migraines be so bad they'd make her skip out on the job she'd traveled thousands of miles to work at? She'd never mentioned chronic migraines to me. Something felt deeply wrong.

"Tessa? You are still there?" Santiago asked.

"Uh, yeah. Still here." I blew out a long breath to counter my rising panic. Darwin could have figured out Mari had a personal connection to Juan Carlos. A connection much stronger than mine. She'd be way more likely than me to have something they wanted. Maybe they were harassing her now. Maybe they'd even done something to her! Pizarro's knife flashed into my mind.

"Tessa? I have videos of my dance routine. Are you coming?" Amparo called out to me.

"Momentito!" I called back to Amparo. "I need to see my friend Mari tomorrow morning," I said to Santiago, talking fast. "But

my host family won't let me go to La Zona. Can you take me there? Please. I hate to bother you. I know you're studying for the TOEFL. But it's an urgent situation. I have to see her in person."

"*Bueno.* I can think of some way. I will liberate you at nine. Be ready!"

37

THE NEXT morning, true to his word, Santiago showed up right at nine. If there was such a thing as Latin American time, as Chris Fitch had said, it was me who was on it, not Santiago. I was barely out of the shower. Santiago chatted with Lucia in the living room, while I hastily dressed.

Jake used to show up late all the time, I remembered, using his sense of precision timing only for his road races. But then his whole face would light up when he saw me, and he'd wrap his arms around me, enfolding me into his world, and none of that would matter.

I ran a comb through my half-dried hair, vigorously, as if to rake out all thoughts of Jake. I hadn't come to the middle of the world to brood over him.

Amparo's mirror was adorned with pageant photos of herself, and snapshots of her and her friends. All of them looking like models or *telenovela* stars. I made a face at my face. I set down the brush and tucked all my damp hair up in the woolen cap with the ear flaps. Dorky, yes, but I was going out in the city with spies on the loose. This was disguise time. *Not* a date. And I didn't want to be intercepted by Darwin and his crew on the way to Mari's.

"So where are you two going?" I heard Lucia ask Santiago, in Spanish.

"I forgot about a Vuelta activity scheduled today," said Santiago, also in Spanish. "I am taking some volunteers up to El Panecillo."

I closed my eyes for a moment, listening to him speak his native language. It was like hearing Juan Carlos again—the words, the cadence, even the laugh, a kind of sly chuckle. I could almost pretend I was hearing Juan Carlos. But Santiago's voice was deeper. Different.

Lucia made a clucking sound. "Walking up there is not safe. There have been robberies."

"It is no problem this time of day. There will be a group of us," Santiago assured her. "And I will drive to the top." He went on to describe the group excursion so beautifully—the views we would enjoy, the lunch afterward in the Old Town—I started to wish I was going.

His description worked its magic. Lucia let me go.

Amparo flounced on the couch next to her brother, who was playing a handheld video game. The sound of tiny bullets ricocheted in staccato bursts.

"You'll still help me with my pageant speech this afternoon, right?" Amparo asked me.

"I will. I promise," I said, wincing as I remembered making similar vague promises to Kylie. Why did I always manage to let people down when I was trying to do the right thing?

"YOU LOOK different," Santiago said as I slid into the passenger seat of the Pathfinder. "Your outfit, maybe. You are cold?"

"A little." I was wearing yesterday's full Ecuadorian tourist disguise again, including the hat. I'd also added another layer between me and Darwin's "eyes and ears": big rhinestone-studded sunglasses, obvious knockoffs ("Lucci" brand), borrowed from Amparo.

Santiago stared at the sunglasses in surprise. I could see why.

The low-hanging clouds and haze lingered, as if the neighborhood, and the city and the hills beyond, had all been draped in gauze. "The sun's brighter in Ecuador even with the cloud cover, thanks to the hole in the ozone," I said. "Anyway, thanks for springing me."

Lucia's concerned face appeared at the living room window.

"There she is again. Watching," I said

"This is strange for you?"

"Are you kidding? It's deeply strange! I'm used to going out at home whenever I want."

"Some families in Ecuador are more careful with their girls," Santiago admitted as he backed the car out of the driveway. "I am not saying this is right, but this is common. And she has concern because we are the same age, you are a boy, I am a girl," he said. "I mean, *I* am a boy. *You* are a girl." His cheeks reddened.

I smiled to myself.

I waved at Lucia, who waved back but still looked worried. My driving with some boy? Santiago should be the least of her worries. I was on the radar of spies, who might also be drug dealers, and who could resurface anywhere, anytime.

She shouldn't worry about me and Santiago together anyway. I stole a glance at him. He was absolutely not my type. So different from Jake and Juan Carlos. A what-you-see-is-what-you-get type. Santiago didn't seem to have a lot of stories.

He slammed on the brakes to avoid plowing into the day guard, Paolo, who was running toward the car, waving his hands. He rapped on my window. I rolled it down.

"Buenos días, señorita. Disculpe." He handed me a folded piece of paper. "This arrived for you. It was taped to the gate when I arrived this morning."

"Did you see who left it?" I asked in Spanish.

"No, I have seen nobody since I began my shift," he replied. "Perhaps someone came by in the night. I will ask Victor if he saw a car or a person stop."

"Gracias, Paolo. *Muy amable."*

"De nada, señorita. Que tengas un buen día."

There was no stamp. No address. Just my name scrawled on the front in block letters.

"Maybe it is from your friend? From Mari?" Santiago suggested as he drove.

"Maybe." I had a sinking feeling, though, that someone else had dropped by last night.

I tore the envelope open. It was a computer printout of a note, in all caps.

WE HAVE AN ASSIGNMENT FOR YOU.

OPPORTUNITY FOR LUCRATIVE PAY.

TIME IS OF THE ESSENCE. ACT NOW!

USE A PAY PHONE TO CALL THE NUMBER BELOW.

A phone number, with the area code for Quito, followed.

Shaking, I folded up the note and stuffed it deep in my jeans pocket.

Darwin and his crew. At least now I had some idea of why they were after me here. To get me to do some assignment. If they were part of a drug cartel, did they want to hire me as some backpacking mule, ferrying money or drugs across borders? And if so, why me? This country was full of backpackers and students, many of them desperate for money and willing to work. Maybe Darwin had something else in mind for me.

I had no intention of calling that number.

And yet. I fished the paper out of my jeans pocket and read it again. I could be a step closer to finding out who killed Juan Carlos, and how that stolen spare bike might be connected to the bike sabotage, if I called this number and just talked to Darwin. Bianca Slade wouldn't ignore a hot lead like this.

But first I had to talk to Mari. I had to find out why she wasn't answering my emails and if anyone from Darwin's group might have gotten to her—either because they thought she might have information, too, or because they thought they could get to me through her.

"So this note, it was from your friend?" Santiago asked, casting me a look of concern as I folded up the paper and repocketed it. Small lines appeared in his smooth-skinned forehead.

"Um, yeah," I lied. "She said to come by her apartment today."

"Ah." An awkward silence fell. I was pretty sure he knew I was lying; my story made no sense. But I appreciated that he didn't ask more questions.

"So. What do you do at home?" he asked. "For fun?"

The question startled me. It sounded like a foreign language, even though he spoke in English. "Fun?" I rolled the word around in my mouth. Fun. Had I had fun before Chain Reaction? Before Juan Carlos died? Before scary people followed me around and chased me out of international airports and left me strange notes in the night? Maybe I had. It seemed long ago.

I'd had fun with Kylie and Sarita. I suddenly, desperately, missed them. Especially Kylie, who hadn't gone on the pre-trip shopping spree with Sarita and me, just wished me safe travels in a short, curt email. So on the way to La Zona, I talked about my friends. Lattes in the Fingernail. Our favorite ice-cream place, near Cabot.

Answering Santiago's questions about my friends and Shady Pines made the ride fly by. He then told me he had one year left in the polytechnic high school in Quito, and hoped to study engineering at a university in the United States. But that's all I had time to get out of him, because suddenly we were in La Zona.

Santiago parked on a side street. I peered out the window, thinking I'd witness drug deals in alleys, or hear gunshots ring out.

But I didn't see anything scary as I got out of the car. The buildings were warm and inviting, all pastel and white stucco. Red geraniums spilled out of window boxes. There were night-clubs, yes—all closed—including one called Salsoteca Mundial, with thick red drapes covering all the windows, that looked more intriguing than seedy. I saw lively cafés with plastic tables and Latin music spilling out into the street. Waitresses serving fresh-squeezed juices in tall glasses. Backpackers poring over maps and guidebooks. Art galleries. Boutiques.

"I don't get what Lucia was so worried about," I said when Santiago got out of the car.

"In the night, it is different," he explained. "Tourists attract thieves. And many over-the-table business deals have taken place in these clubs and cafés."

"Don't you mean under-the-table?"

"Yes, yes, that is the expression." He flashed me a sheepish smile. "But relax. These deals take place mostly after dark. And you are not a target for such things."

That's what you think. Darwin's note crinkled in my jeans pocket every time I moved my leg.

"After you," said Santiago, gesturing for me to pass in front of him to the crosswalk.

"Aren't you taking volunteers up to El Panecillo?"

"I made that up. I was trying to get you out of the house. I thought the Ruizes would let you go on a group activity. But if you would like to go to El Panecillo, we can go there, yes. In fact, why don't you invite your friend, if she is home and if she is all right?" Santiago suggested. "We can all go together. Maybe she needs a break from this problem she is having."

Oh, no. I liked Santiago. But I couldn't bring him along to talk to Mari. He couldn't know what I had gotten mixed up in. I started walking toward a yellow-painted building that matched the address she'd emailed me.

"Not today, thanks. Another time. That'd be great." I knew I sounded brusque, even cold. The look on his face said it all. But I had to find Mari.

"Wait! You do not know if she is at home." Santiago jogged after me. "At least let me make sure you get inside. It is our custom here to not leave people in the street."

Something softened inside me. I knew how it felt to be left at the side of a road. Santiago was offering me an alternative. But I couldn't put Santiago in harm's way, or jeopardize my position at Vuelta.

"I really need to go alone," I said. "It's . . . complicated. If she's out, I'll wait for her here."

He gave me a long look. I couldn't meet his gaze. *"Bueno,"* he said, shrugging and shoving his hands into his jeans pockets. "I will get a coffee and pick you up here, by the door. How much time do you need? One hour?"

I thought fast. If Darwin showed up here—if I were walking into some trap he'd set up—it would be good to have that get-ahead vehicle and a capable driver on hand. "That'd be great. In fact, if you wouldn't mind waiting here at the car, that would be awesome."

"But—"

"Thanks a million. You're the best. *Chao!*" I winced at the forced cheer in my voice. And I felt his eyes on my back as I hurried to Mari's place, alone.

38

MARI'S COUSIN'S apartment was in a dirty, lemon-colored building. A small restaurant with plastic chairs and tables took up the first floor. A woman sloshed buckets of water over the tiles out front. Rivulets of brown water rolled toward my feet.

No armed guards manned this building. I ran up a dingy staircase to the third-floor apartment, passing closed doors that concealed crises. An alarm clock beeping. A cat in heat, yowling. A woman crying, a man shouting—real life or a *telenovela*? I couldn't be sure.

I came to *apartmento cinco*, which was quiet. The number five hung crookedly on the apartment door, which was covered by a wrought-iron gate. I pressed the buzzer beside it. Then I pressed it again. Finally I saw movement at a peephole, then heard fumbling with locks inside. Lots of locks. The door opened a couple of inches. And, finally, Mari peered out. She sucked in her breath. "Tessa?" she whispered. "Oh my God. You're here."

Looking at her through the iron gate, it almost seemed like she was in prison. She seemed thinner. Tired. Her unbrushed hair hung loose around her face, more of a shaggy mop than her usual sleek bob or ponytail. I peered past her, trying to see if there were other people in there with her. Like Darwin, Pizarro, and Balboa. All I could see was a body on the floor of the room, behind her, lying, limbs splayed, beneath a blanket.

A body! I jumped back and prepared to bolt.

Then the body stirred. It was somebody sleeping.

Mari looked down the hall behind me, both ways. "Are you here alone?" she whispered.

"Yeah. But why—"

"Shh." She fumbled with two more locks on the iron gate.

The last lock sprang free, and Mari ushered me inside. Then she closed the door and locked everything up again. Six locks. "My roommates are sleeping. They were out late partying last night," she said with an apologetic look at the body under the blanket. Two bodies, I now saw, a guy and a girl, their limbs and long hair all entwined in a way that made me think, strangely, of worms.

"Where's your cousin?" I asked.

"In Riobamba. With her boyfriend. She practically lives there now. She just keeps this apartment in case her parents visit. Then she kicks everyone out to the youth hostel for a night."

"Are you okay? Are you really having migraines?"

Mari bit a nail and looked down. "No."

"Wilson said you only showed up at Vuelta for two shifts. And you haven't replied to my emails for days." I could feel my voice rising with panic, but I couldn't stop. "I got followed out of the airport. By people who knew Juan Carlos. Has anyone been talking to you? Asking you weird questions?"

She stared at me, fear in her eyes. Then she nodded, and glanced at the sleeping roommates. "There's a balcony off my room where we can talk. Follow me."

I stepped over piles of clothes, plastic shopping bags, paperback novels and Ecuador guidebooks, and empty SuperChicken containers. The place smelled of rotting fruit and greasy food. Mold crept up one wall. The living room was furnished with cast-off furniture and cardboard boxes. The whole place just seemed . . . sad.

"So who lives here, besides you?" I asked.

"Jim and Liz back there, whose faces you almost stepped on? They're backpackers," said Mari. "Sandy and Susannah are the two girls who have my cousin's room when she's away. They're ESL teachers and part-time Vuelta volunteers. Oh, and there's an older woman who comes in and out sometimes—she has the couch."

"Wait. You have *five* roommates?" Suddenly life at the Ruiz house didn't seem so bad. These guys were living like mice here. "And this is your room?" I looked around in disbelief.

Mari had led me around a tall bookshelf off the kitchen. It separated her sleeping quarters from the rest of the apartment. There was a thin mattress and a sleeping bag on the floor, and a suitcase, opened. A tool kit with bike tools. A copy of a book called *The Saddest Pleasure*. That was all.

"This isn't a room, Mari. It's a partition!" A large bug ambled across the white tile floor. "Really? Is this healthy?"

"It's cheap," Mari said, lifting her chin. "I'm not earning a salary here, remember? I didn't want a homestay. I wanted to show my family I could live on my own, so they'd let me live away from home when I start at MIT. And you can't beat the location. I can walk or bike easily to Vuelta from here."

"But you're not walking or biking to Vuelta," I reminded her. "You're not there at all. What are you doing all day?"

"Reading a lot." She gestured toward some books. They were well-thumbed through, with bookmarks, too. "Come outside. I don't want my roommates to hear anything and worry. They think I'm just having some trouble with migraines. It's easier to let them think that."

"Easier than what?" I asked.

"The truth."

I followed her out onto the balcony, where we sat on cracked plastic chairs that looked like they'd been swiped from the restaurant below. The emerging sun heated up the blue and white tiles beneath our feet. I removed Amparo's sunglasses and the woolen cap with ear flaps. I shook my hair loose.

Mari offered me a bottle of warm Inca Kola. "Juan Carlos's favorite," said Mari, clinking her bottle against mine. *"¡Salud!"*

"Salud." I took a sip of the sickly sweet yellow beverage.

"What's with the outfit?" she asked, observing my ensemble and the hat I'd laid on the table. "You look like a crafts market explosion."

"First tell me what's with all the locks on your door?"

She sighed and rubbed her forehead. For a moment, she looked like she did have a migraine. "We were robbed soon after I got here."

"Robbed!"

"Well, the only thing they took was my laptop. But that sucked, since I needed that for college, and nobody else's computer got stolen. Plus, the place got ransacked. They went through everything."

I almost knocked over my Inca Kola.

Her laptop had been stolen! Mari and I had emailed each other about what to pack—and my flight itinerary. That must be how they knew when I'd be at the airport. It would be easy for Darwin to pull out that information from her computer.

"Did you report this?"

"I called the police," Mari confirmed. "And they filed a report. But"—she shrugged—"they made it pretty clear they're not going to pursue a breaking and entering case, especially here in La Zona, where this kind of thing goes on all the time. I could tell they thought I was just some stupid tourist who brought a fancy laptop to a bad neighborhood. They probably thought I deserved it."

"Did the police have any ideas of who did it?"

"They suspect a gang looking for drugs. Or cash. They told me to change the locks. So I blew through most of my summer travel money on that. I'd wanted to get a temporary cell phone, even a landline, but I went nearly broke on the locksmith." She chewed what was left of her fingernail. "And I don't want to ask my parents for money. I can't."

"I can see why you'd change the locks. That's so scary! What do your roommates think?"

"They think I'm being paranoid. Lightning can't strike twice and all that. Everyone here has been mugged or hassled at one time or another. They think I'm taking it to an extreme, and so I've stopped explaining."

"But why wouldn't you go to Vuelta?" I persisted. "At least there you'd be around people all day. You're like under house arrest here."

Mari drew her legs up onto the chair and hugged her knees. "Honestly? I don't like to go out," she whispered. "I'm being followed."

39

I STARED at Mari, who was now shivering in her plastic chair as if she were cold to the bone. I, too, felt cold. Numb. With fear. "Followed?" I repeated. My suspicions were right. Mari was on Darwin's radar.

"Oh, great. You think I'm paranoid, too."

"No. I don't. Who's following you?"

"Some skinny dude with a ponytail," she said. "I started noticing him a few days after I got here. Like, wherever I was, there *he* was."

Pizarro. The one with the knife. Oh, no. Though Darwin was a phone hacker, and Balboa a hack writer, I had the sense that Pizarro wouldn't mind using a real weapon to hack at someone who didn't comply. He'd been quick to flash that silver at me that day at the Port of Boston.

"When I left my afternoon bike mechanics class at Vuelta?" said Mari. "He'd be across the street, or at a kiosk or something, pretending to shop or eat or talk on his phone, but watching me. I could feel it. Or I'd go to a café or a restaurant with the other volunteers, and he'd show up, sit by himself in a corner, and eat. Then I was biking home from work one evening, alone, and he came up behind me. On a bike. He called out to me in Spanish. He said he needed some information, and could I come and talk to him? Well, no way was I going to do that. I figured he was trying to lure me over, so he could mug me or something. Playing 'lost tourist' or something, even though his accent was clearly from here."

Information. He'd asked her for information, too. "What'd you do next?"

"Rode away. Fast. I managed to ditch him. I haven't seen him since. But there's a girl who follows me, too. A redhead. Big hair. Not much older than us."

That had to be Balboa.

"She came into Vuelta twice, poking around, looking at the used bike section, it seems, but really looking at me, into my classroom when I'm teaching," said Mari. "She didn't buy anything, and when someone asked if they could help her, she left. Then last Sunday, I rode in the *ciclopaseo*, and—"

"What's the *ciclopaseo*? A race?"

"No, it's this community event every Sunday, where they close the whole street of Amazonas for bikes. It goes all the way from north Quito to the Old Town. It's super fun. I mean, it's fun if you're not being stalked. Anyway, she was on that ride. Tessa, I swear, this girl chased me! She tried to run me off the road and make me steer into traffic! A bus almost hit me. I've never had such a close call."

I could imagine Balboa doing something like that. She'd seemed keyed up, on edge, when we talked at the shipyard. Was there any chance Balboa could have orchestrated Juan Carlos's crash? Could she have been the one who rigged his bike?

I quickly tried to recall everything she'd told me. She'd said she was a new recruit to Darwin's group. Maybe in addition to the suckiest alias, she also got the suckiest job. Going in for the kill.

Now I didn't know which of these three guys I should fear most.

"What'd you do then?" I asked Mari, sitting on the edge of my broken chair.

"I managed to get the bike off the main drag. I ducked into a crafts market, and hid behind a display of hammocks. I lost her. But I'm pretty sure some other people were working with her. I saw four guys—Ecuadorians—following on bikes, not far behind." She let out a long breath. "So I told the police people were following me, and that maybe they were the same people who broke into this place and stole my laptop. They wrote down my descriptions."

"Can they do anything?"

"Not without proof, they said. So I just filled out a bunch of paperwork no one will ever read. This one detective I keep talking to, he just thinks I'm crazy. He even asked me if I was on medication! So I've been lying low, hoping they'll think I've left the city."

"Mari. Listen to me." I set down my bottle of Inca Kola, hard, on the plastic table. "I know who these people are."

She leaned forward. "You do?"

"Yes. And they're not giving up. They've been tailing me, too." I told her, finally, everything, going all the way back to the discovery of Juan Carlos's spare bike in the woods. She listened, mouth open, barely blinking.

"And you said they all have weird code names?"

"Darwin, Pizarro, Balboa. I'd file that under 'weird.'"

"Charles Darwin did his natural selection theory research in Ecuador's Galápagos Islands. Francisco Pizarro and Vasco Nuñez de Balboa were South American explorers."

I groaned. Any good investigative reporter would have Googled those names right away. If I'd done that, I'd have realized the names all connected to this region, and that Ecuador would not offer any escape.

Mari buried her face in her hands. "Oh my God. I wish I'd never touched that bike!"

"Touched what bike?"

"Juan Carlos's bike. The one in the woods."

My heart pounded. *I'd* touched that bike. And so had she? When? "I think you'd better explain that," I said.

A loud knock at the door interrupted us. Mari and I exchanged terrified looks.

We heard one of her roommates—Jim or Liz or both, still entwined—shuffle to the door and answer it. And then a guy's voice, in accented English: "Sorry to disturb you. I just brought something for Tessa and Mari. If they are busy talking, it's no problem, maybe I can just leave this bag for them here?"

Santiago. He'd come up. Even after he told me he'd just meet me at the car in an hour. An hour had not yet passed. Was this normal Ecuadorian courtesy? Or stalkery?

"Who the hell is that?" Mari asked, eyeing the balcony railing as if she might leap over.

"Santiago. Wilson's son. He drove me here. He's cool. But I told him not to—"

"I think Mari's outside on the balcony," one of the roommates was saying. "Go right on in. Her room's just behind that bookshelf."

And then Santiago was approaching our window, grinning sheepishly, holding out a paper bag and two paper cups, steam swirling up from them.

"They're not really lattes," he said. "Just Nescafé with a lot of hot milk. And here are some fresh-baked rolls from the *tienda* downstairs. I know you're catching up. So I guess I should be going." He looked at me uncertainly, making no move toward the door.

I heard Mari's stomach grumble appreciatively. I could smell the bread through that paper bag. And I warmed, pushing aside my worry that he was checking up on me like Jake sometimes did. Santiago had actually *listened* to me in the car, as I talked about my friends and our latte tradition. He probably thought Mari and I had the same tradition. He'd gone out of his way to make me feel at home, to find a link between that world and this one. Jake had never gone out of his way like that, to make my friends and me comfortable. Maybe that's the kind of guy I wanted to find next time around.

But Mari still owed me some information. So I thanked Santiago for the refreshments and looked at the door, hoping he'd get the hint. "I'll see you outside. I won't be long," I said.

But Mari whispered something to me about "Ecuadorian hospitality" and led him out to the balcony. Santiago eased his long limbs out the window and folded himself into a third plastic chair while Mari divided the rolls. He didn't make one judgmental remark about Mari's humble living conditions. From the questions he asked, he seemed genuinely interested in how we knew each other through Compass Bikes.

"It was my idea to get Tessa on board with the Vuelta bike donation project," Mari concluded, after giving a mercifully brief account of how we'd first met. "We both wanted to honor Juan Carlos by helping to finish this project."

Santiago's mouth turned down at the corners. "I still cannot believe he died in that terrible way," he said. "His own team mechanic!"

"Did you ever meet Juan Carlos?" Mari asked him. "Since your dad runs Vuelta?"

Points for Mari. Here I was, the aspiring investigative journalist, and it hadn't even occurred to me to ask Santiago that question.

"Once or twice, yes," Santiago said. "He seemed like a really good person. And his death hit our country hard. Ecuadorians had high hopes for him, to help put Ecuadorian cycling in a map."

"On the map," Mari and I corrected, in unison.

When we were done eating, Santiago proposed a sightseeing trip up to El Panecillo next weekend. But Mari said, "Hey, what about now? And we can bring Jim and Liz, too, now that they're finally awake." She stood up so quickly that I suspected her enthusiasm was all manufactured. She wanted to avoid my questions.

"We are so not done talking," I whispered to Mari in the stairwell as we all followed Santiago out to his car. "You were starting to tell me about Juan Carlos's bike in the woods! Darwin's trying to get in touch with me, too. I need to know everything you know about what he's hiding and what he's been up to here, so I can figure out some kind of game plan."

She looked scared. Then she nodded. "Okay, okay. I'll tell you everything when we get there. There's a place at the base of the statue where we can talk privately."

Santiago drove to the Old Town, down bumpy cobblestone streets. While New Quito was all gleaming and colorful buildings, a hodgepodge of modern architecture, Old Quito was a step back in time. Grand white colonial buildings rose ahead of us. On either side of us, pastel-painted buildings were squished together like layers of wedding cake. Santiago pointed out sights along the way—a grand plaza, a famous cathedral, old art galleries—and then he ascended a hill. At the top, he parallel parked behind a few other cars and a tourist bus. As we all walked toward the statue, and Santiago talked about the Quito School of Art and the inspiration for the statue, I barely heard a word. Mari had seen—no, touched—that bike! Had *she* been the original thief? Or the one who'd foiled Darwin's plan?

At the base of the statue, while Jim and Liz bought some overpriced magnets from a souvenir stand—and Mari and Santiago helped them to negotiate the price down in Spanish—I took a close look at the statue. Up close, I saw its surface wasn't smooth at all, but a rough patchwork of aluminum pieces. The Virgin of Quito stood atop a globe with unexpected grace, given the heaviness of her materials. She seemed to be almost dancing on it. Stars adorned her halo. And then, with a start, I realized she held in one hand a long chain, which was attached to a serpent.

She seemed free, but she was tethered. Burdened, almost, by that chain. As was I. I played with Juan Carlos's necklace. It felt heavier than ever. I had to figure out for sure if Darwin and his group had killed him, and what they wanted with Mari and me. His crew could resurface anytime. His eyes and ears could be here. I looked behind us. Another tourist bus had arrived and was emptying itself of passengers, who were armed with cameras and guidebooks.

All five of us started walking around the statue's pedestal, but as Santiago went into tour-guide mode, I grabbed Mari's long sleeve and held her back. A strong breeze gusted. "You lied to me. I mentioned the stolen bike in the woods. Twice. Why didn't you tell me you knew about that?"

Mari had looked happy a moment ago, helping Jim and Liz to buy souvenirs, but now her face fell. She nodded and beckoned for me to follow her a few yards away, around the corner from the shop. The breeze blew more briskly there, and an Ecuadorian flag flapped loudly, obscuring our words from anyone who might listen. It also smelled of urine, and there was litter all over the ground.

"I've wanted to tell you the whole story," she began. "I've hated walking around with this secret. But I also wanted to protect Juan Carlos."

"Protect him? From what? Or from who?"

"From cheating allegations."

"Cheating!" I thought of Jake's theory about motorized bikes and other enhancements.

Mari sighed. "Okay. Before Chain Reaction started, I was parked in the Compass Bikes van at the edge of the staging area," she said. "That's when I saw Juan Carlos, riding his bike down Great Marsh Road."

"Right. But you told me you *didn't* see him that morning!"

"I know. I didn't know if I could trust you. You didn't tell me everything, either, you know. You could be a little more understanding."

"Point taken. Go on."

She took a deep breath and continued, closing her eyes as she spoke, as if conjuring up the scene. "Juan Carlos rode fast. He looked behind him a few times, like he thought someone might be chasing him. I thought he was just warming up. And racers do that. They look behind them."

"I know." Jake used to joke he was paranoid that way, glancing behind him even while strolling at the mall or waiting in line at the movies. Looking behind him was how he'd seen me and Juan Carlos talking at the café in Harvard Square that day, while he happened to pass by.

"But then Juan Carlos rode into the woods," said Mari. "He stayed in there for about five minutes. And then he walked out. With no bike! He stood under some trees, like he was hiding."

"Praying," I said. "He always prayed before races, when he was on the junior team."

"Oh? I didn't know that," said Mari. "Anyway, I was about to run over and ask him if everything was okay," Mari continued. "Then Gage drove up with cases of water for the van, so I had to work. But I saw you and Juan Carlos talking. Juan Carlos ran off. Your friend Jake came along. Then the two of you went into the woods. And you didn't come out. Now I'm thinking, this is messed up. I thought you guys were up to something."

I reached out to the statue base to steady myself. I felt dizzy, maybe from altitude. I wished I'd brought a bottle of water. Or maybe the realization that I had been observed with Juan Carlos before the race—by both Mari and Balboa—was making my head spin. "What would we be up to?" I asked.

"Helping Juan Carlos to cheat."

"No way! We would never!"

"Well, I know that now. But that was my thought at the time."

"So that's why you were asking me about my friend in the black jersey, when you helped me after the crash. You were wondering where Jake had gone."

"Yeah. I thought he was helping Juan Carlos pull off some cheating scam. The only thing that didn't fit the equation was you, an obviously less experienced rider. And once I scooped you off the road and talked to you more, I realized you were just a bandit with her boyfriend. You seemed so clueless. I didn't think you'd be capable of helping him cheat."

"Thanks. I guess. But . . . you really thought Juan Carlos was cheating?"

"He wouldn't be the first pro to do it."

"How would he cheat?"

"Stash an unapproved bike in the woods until after the pre-race bike inspections were over. Then pretend to have a mechanical failure, pull over, and have someone swap his regulation bike for a tricked-out one, with enhancements. He'd need an accomplice. Like your old buddy Jake. That's what I thought anyway."

"Jake wasn't an accomplice. He suspected Juan Carlos of cheating, too." I shook my head. Picturing Juan Carlos as a cheater was almost as hard as imagining him caught up in shady business with a drug cartel. "But why would he even consider cheating? He was an amazing rider."

"He was," Mari agreed. "But he felt tons of pressure ever since Cadence came on board. Chris Fitch was really on his case about needing to win."

"Juan Carlos *had* wins," I pointed out. "Have you seen his race stats this season? He was on a streak."

"He needed *big* wins," said Mari. "Record-breaking times. Juan Carlos told me, the day before the race, that Chris wanted world champions riding on Cadence brand bikes."

"Why?"

"Because people love to buy what champions ride. Look what Lance did for Trek."

"Dylan said something about that."

"Sure. That's what consumers want. The bicycles of champions. I hear it all the time at the shop."

"So Juan Carlos was supposed to do well at Chain Reaction, to kick off the Cadence-EcuaBar partnership?" I guessed, remembering the team photo, the unfurled banner.

"That's what Juan Carlos told me."

I sank into a nearby chair. I'd known el Cóndor, the character. Not Juan Carlos, the person. He'd made everything look so effortless, but clearly it wasn't that way. He had pressure, too, to fit other people's expectations. To exceed them, even.

"Chris was so mean about Juan Carlos, when he didn't show for the photo shoot," I recalled out loud. "It seemed like he didn't like Juan Carlos, or care if he missed the team photo. Wait. Mari!" I suddenly remembered Chris's TV interview with Bianca Slade. "Chris Fitch's brother died. *In a bike crash.* Don't you think it's a little weird that the CEO of Cadence knows two people who died in bike crashes?"

Mari tipped her head, considering this. "It is a pretty big

coincidence. But you don't really suspect Chris as the bike saboteur, do you? He wouldn't kill his star cyclist—someone he was making money off of—in a public place. On a bike that his company manufactured. That doesn't make any sense."

"No. I guess you're right." I scratched the back of my neck and let my gaze drift to the statue's aluminum patchwork, while I tried to piece all this new information together. So far, Darwin was the more likely missing link between the bike theft and Juan Carlos's death. For a moment I'd let myself hope that I wasn't being stalked by a murderer on the loose. That hope was fading fast. I glanced behind us again. The tourists from the bus were approaching now. I talked faster, in case "eyes and ears" were among those tourists. "So what happened? You found the bike in the woods. Did it seem enhanced in any way?" I thought of Jake's motor-in-the-seat-tube idea. "Heavier, maybe?"

"Heavier? No, I don't think so. And everything looked regulation on the outside. I didn't get a chance to take stuff apart, though, because then I heard voices."

"You must have heard Darwin and me talking. After he chased me down the path."

"I'm sure I did. But at the time, I just thought I'd stumbled into a cheating scam, and I didn't want Juan Carlos to get into trouble. I grabbed that bike and ran like hell. Then I stashed it in the back of the Compass Bikes van."

I held my breath. So Mari was the one who'd foiled Darwin's plans! While Darwin was threatening me in the woods, Mari had found Juan Carlos's spare bike. And all the time Darwin was searching the woods, based on the information he'd gotten from me, Mari had been putting that bike in her van. And then I'd ridden in that same van, with his bike—and whatever was in it—smuggled in the back.

"Where did you take the bike?" I demanded. "Did you return it to Dylan? Is that why it was at the Open Road school?"

"Not quite." She shoved her hands in her jeans pockets and sighed. "I went looking for Juan Carlos. To tell him I'd taken his bike back, and to talk him out of cheating. But there wasn't enough time, and no one could find him. The race started without him. And then . . ." She looked down. "He joined the recreational ride and tried to catch his team. But he didn't get far. And there I was with this bike on my hands."

"So then you turned it over to Dylan?"

"No. I thought about it. But I couldn't."

"How come?"

"All these TV people were hovering around the team trailer. I didn't want him to look bad. I did not want cheating to be his lasting legacy. Not when all those kids looked up to him. So I hid his bike in the Compass Bikes basement, under a bunch of tarps, thinking I'd just return the bike to Juan Carlos when I saw him next. When he recovered"—she kicked a piece of litter on the ground—"which he didn't."

Santiago, Jim, and Liz jogged back in our direction. "Are you two coming?" Santiago called to us. "There is an entrance to the observation deck. We can climb up inside the statue."

I waved them forward. "Go ahead! We'll catch up in a sec!"

"Bueno," said Santiago. He looked at us—at me, it seemed—for just a moment longer, the wind ruffling his wavy hair and lighting it up almost gold. Then he turned to follow Liz and Jim, who had disappeared into the statue.

"He's really nice," said Mari, watching them go. She elbowed me and gave me a sly grin. "See, didn't I tell you another guy always comes along?"

I ignored her comment, in no mood to dish about Santiago. "Here's what I don't get," I said, pacing back and forth. "Juan

Carlos's spare bike, the one I saw in the woods, was in Dylan's storage room, hanging on the wall. You even filmed it. How did it get back there if you didn't take it?"

"No idea," Mari admitted. "It confused the hell out of me when I saw the bike there, but I didn't think I could tell you why. Back at Compass Bikes that same afternoon, I checked, and the bike *I'd* taken was still under the tarps in the basement. So whatever bike I saw hanging at Dylan's had to be an extra bike—maybe Juan Carlos had more bikes than his teammates—or it didn't even belong to Juan Carlos. Then, Friday morning? When I went back to work to pick up my last paycheck? I thought I'd take the bike back to Dylan, and tell him what I'd done. But I looked in the basement and it was gone."

"Because it was put into the shipping container!" I exclaimed, remembering what Balboa had told me. "The girl spy, Balboa. And the other guy, Pizarro. They snuck it on the day we did the load, either when we were busy and didn't see them, or when we all went inside." Then I frowned. "But wait a second. How would they have known to look for it at Compass Bikes? I thought they picked up the bike from Dylan's storage room."

"Did they say that's where they got it?" Mari asked.

I thought a moment, mentally replaying texts and conversations. I shook my head. "Darwin said they'd found it, but he didn't say where. I assumed he got it from Dylan's because he found it the same day we went there. Then Balboa said I'd led them right to the bike, so I assumed they'd followed us there." Then I groaned. "My stupid cell phone. Darwin was tracking me on it. I was near Compass Bikes, with my phone turned on, on Wednesday. They probably followed my trail of electronic crumbs and poked around the shop until they found the bike you hid in the basement. Then I bet they took advantage of the container load the next day to get it shipped under the radar.

This is all my fault. I should never have turned my phone on near the shop."

Mari patted my arm. "It's *not* your fault. I bet they would have come by the shop eventually to check it out, knowing Juan Carlos volunteered there. But let's think about what this all means. The spare bike I saw at Dylan's place, hanging under Juan Carlos's name? That couldn't have been the bike they were looking for. It must not have really been Juan Carlos's spare, because I had that in the basement right up until the container load. I bet it was someone else's spare, just as a place holder. You know? Maybe Dylan was trying to make it look like he didn't screw up and give someone a chance to break into the team trailer."

I nodded excitedly. "You could be right! Dylan didn't want to lose his job. He loved that job, and he needed the money. He wouldn't want to risk an inspection of all the team bikes. That's why I don't think he's the killer. I think Dylan was framed by Darwin."

"Or Dylan could have been paid off to help in some way, if he needed money so badly," Mari suggested. "I could see him being bribed to look the other way. Maybe to leave the team trailer unlocked to let the saboteur in."

"He might not have known what was going to happen," I added. "Maybe that's why he felt so broken up about what happened to Juan Carlos. I mean, the guy was practically crying."

"So if Dylan's not the real killer, who is?"

I thought for a moment. "Darwin has to be involved," I said. "And the bike that's in the shipping container might help us to understand the why and the how, especially since Balboa started to tell me that something was inside it. That's possible, right?"

"Sure," said Mari. "But what do you think it is?"

"Money from drug deals? Could you fit a lot of cash in the handlebars or the tubes?"

"It's possible," said Mari. "The carbon fiber could be hollowed out. And the cash could be rolled up small."

"Well, if Juan Carlos was trying to take or hide a bike stuffed with cash, and not following some kind of order, that could explain why someone wanted him dead," I said. "I know one thing for sure, though. We have to get to that bike before Darwin does. Once he moves it to its final destination, wherever that is, it'll be lost for good."

"You're right. But we won't see that bike for five more days," said Mari. "Maybe more, if the protestors block the highway from the coast. I wish we could figure out what kind of information Darwin is looking for. Maybe that would be enough to take to the chief of police here, or to the U.S. consulate or something. And then we could get authorities to intercept the bike—and Darwin—at the container unload."

The note from Darwin crinkled in my pocket. "I have an idea—" I ventured. Santiago's voice, calling to us, interrupted me.

"Mari! Tessa!" he shouted. Jim and Liz were waving to us from the observation deck. "The view is amazing. Come up!"

Glancing at the rapidly approaching throng of tourists—or possible spies—I winced at the sound of my name being shouted. I figured now was a good time to vanish, so I muttered, "I'll tell you later." Mari went into the statue ahead of me, scampering up the narrow staircase. I was about to follow when I felt a hand on my shoulder.

I turned to find a girl with a Panama hat, sunglasses, and flaming red hair. She handed me an envelope, then turned and ran off, weaving through the growing crowd of tourists.

40

STILL AT the base of the statue, I tore open the envelope. Inside was a bad printout, unevenly inked. An invitation.

BAILA BAILA BAILA!!
DANCE PARTY HAPPENING SOON!!!
PARTY LIKE YOUR LIFE DEPENDS ON IT!
CALL THE NUMBER BELOW TO RSVP AND RECEIVE DETAILS OF TIME AND PLACE

The invitation was decorated with bad clip art—outlines of people dancing—and a phone number was typed at the bottom.

I pulled out the note from the Ruizes' gate this morning.

The phone number was the same.

So this was Darwin's new cover. Sending old-fashioned notes to me on paper, since I wasn't using my cell phone here. And email was probably too traceable, too risky.

This communiqué looked, at first glance, like an invitation to an underground party. I'd gotten something like this before in Boston, walking down Newbury Street, and also in New York City. Back then I was flattered that someone thought I was hip enough to invite. Now I was just creeped out. Because of course there was no dance party. This was a not-so-veiled threat.

Clutching the invitation, I ran after Balboa. She was easy to spot with that Panama hat, white with a black band, and her long red hair. Her hip, nightclub-style outfit also marked her: tight black jeans and a close-fitting black T-shirt with rhinestones, beneath her leather jacket. She was the opposite of undercover, standing out in this fanny-pack-wearing crowd. As if daring herself to get caught. Yet she *was* undercover at the same time, I suddenly realized, posing as someone trolling for hip young tourists, soliciting underground partiers.

"Hey!" I shouted as she headed toward a taxi queue. "I need to talk to you!"

She glanced back, then ran faster.

I knew Balboa had a scary side. She had run Mari into the street on that bike ride, and possibly helped to orchestrate Juan Carlos's death, too. But I doubted she had a gun or a knife tucked into those skin-tight jeans. She probably wouldn't attack me with her bare hands, at least not out here in the open. And she was close to my age. Potentially approachable. If I could convince her that Mari and I knew nothing and had nothing, maybe I could get her to talk. And get answers.

I was within four feet of her when she whirled around. "Get away from me," she hissed. "I'm just here delivering a message. I'm not supposed to interact."

"Did you guys take my friend Mari's laptop? And follow her around?" I demanded.

I took her tight-lipped glare as a yes, and I fired off more questions. "What are you looking for? Why are you after Mari now? And me?"

"You'll have to talk to Darwin. Call that number."

I glanced at the paper. *Party like your life depends on it!*

She turned and ran again, back toward the street. I chased her, heart pounding. "Hey! I'm not done with you! Did *you* kill

Juan Carlos?" I called after her. "Did *you* run him off the road so he'd crash on a sabotaged bike?"

"No!" she called back over her shoulder. "Are you kidding? That's way out of my job description. I'm in communications!"

I caught up with her and grabbed her arm. "Then start communicating. Did *Darwin* kill Juan Carlos? Or Pizarro? Or some other creep in your shady spy operation?"

"No. No one in our group killed him. I swear. Let go of my arm!"

She tried to wrench it free. I held tighter.

"Does Darwin know who did it? Did he have anything to do with it?"

"I can't talk to you! I already got in trouble for talking to you at the shipyard."

"You seemed happy enough to talk to me then."

"I felt sorry for you, okay? You weren't supposed to go poking around in there and get yourself locked in. You almost screwed everything up. Your dying in there would have been a disaster. Now leave me alone. You're compromising my mission!"

"I will not leave you alone. Tell me about this 'mission.' What do you know about how Juan Carlos died? And what is up with that bike in the shipping container? We know you're trying to smuggle something into the country that customs can't find out about. Is it money? How much? And where is it going? If you're going to follow me around and pass me these little notes, I have a right to know."

Her head snapped to the right. "Help! Help!" she shouted toward a newly arriving group of tourists, hikers, coming up a path a few yards away. "I'm being mugged!"

I let go of her arm, fast. Balboa fled and jumped into a yellow taxi parked by the curb. The taxi sped away, rubber streaking the pavement.

I swore under my breath. I'd blown it. I'd watched Bianca

Slade enough to know that badgering or intimidating the source was not the way to get information. I should have eased my way in, warmed her up, gained her trust.

Two men from the tourist group jogged over to me. "What's going on?" one man asked, in a German accent. "I'm going to call the police!"

"No, please don't!" I protested as he pulled out a phone. "She's my sister. We were just having an argument. She was being dramatic."

The men looked at me with suspicion, then at each other. "Okay," said the German reluctantly, pocketing the phone.

"You should be careful," said the other man, more kindly. "There have been muggings up here lately. And worse. Our hotel concierge warned us about this. El Panecillo is no place for girls to come alone."

I raced back to the statue. Darwin was the missing link between the crimes. There was now no doubt in my mind. Even if he didn't kill Juan Carlos directly, he had to know who did. He'd likely been the one to arrange it.

Mari greeted me at the observation deck of the statue, wide-eyed and worried. "I was about to go look for you!" she whispered. "I saw a taxi peel out of here. I thought you'd been kidnapped!"

Keeping my voice low while Santiago talked to Jim and Liz, I told her about Balboa, and showed her the "invitation." "I'm going to find a pay phone after we leave here, and call him," I said. "I'm not going to let him chase us all over the city like this. I want to find out what he wants."

"Tessa, you can't!" she protested.

"I have to meet with him," I insisted. "But I'm going to videotape our conversation. If I can get some kind of confession from him about how he's connected to Juan Carlos's death and the bike theft, I'm going straight to the embassy."

She shook her head. "It's way too dangerous, Tessa. You're getting in over your head. Police do this kind of work."

"And how far have you gotten with the police here?" I countered.

She had no response.

"Exactly. Look, I'll be okay. I do interviews all the time. That's how I'm thinking of this meeting. Just an informational interview."

SANTIAGO DROPPED off Mari, Jim, and Liz, and then headed back to the Ruiz house. "That was fun," he said. "Or at least I thought so. You and your friend seemed worried. I am not so sure you were having fun."

"No, we had fun, too," I said absently, scanning the stores that we passed for any sign that one had a pay phone. Then I saw a sign in the door of a convenience store. *Teléfono públicó.* I was already unbuckling my seat belt. "Would you mind stopping at the store on the corner?"

He pulled over. When he started to get out of the car with me—Ecuadorian manners again—I held up a hand. "I'll just be a moment. I need to get some . . . personal products."

"Ah. Of course." Reddening, he sat back down and closed the car door.

I ran in and asked the old woman manning the tired-looking *tienda* if I could make a call. I handed her some coins, and she put the receiver of an antique-looking rotary-dial phone in my hand, I felt her staring at me while I dialed the number on the "party invitation."

Turning my back to the woman, I walked to the other end of the counter, stretching the coiled phone cord as long as I could. I stood by a shelf filled with bins of delicious-smelling gold-brown rolls and bread loaves.

While the phone rang, I felt something tugging at my shirt. I looked down and saw two small boys standing there, staring at me with dirt-streaked faces that seemed hardened beyond their years. *"¿Señorita? ¿Limpieza?"* asked one of them, pointing at my shoes.

A shoe shine? Were they kidding? I was wearing sandals. Maybe they just wanted money. I dug in my pocket for some coins, gave them to the children, and pointed to the bread bins.

But the woman at the counter shooed them away before they could buy any bread, and I couldn't run after the kids because another woman's voice was talking in my ear.

"¿Hola? ¿Quién habla?" She cleared her throat. *"¿Hola?"*

It wasn't Darwin. Maybe this was some kind of secretary I had to go through first. "Um, my name's Tessa. I got an invitation," I finally said, in Spanish. "I'm calling about a dance party."

There was a pause, and then a different person came on the phone. "Tessa Taylor?"

Of course it was Darwin. His voice was harsh and raspy, just like I remembered. Remembering our brief, scary encounter in the woods—the last time we'd spoken in person—I almost hung up.

Instead I channeled my inner Bianca Slade, and continued. "I'm willing to meet with you, but only if you'll quit following my friend Mari. She came here to volunteer, not to be stalked and harassed. You leave her alone, or we don't talk."

He laughed. "You have a knack for negotiation. You're a lawyer's kid, all right. I admire that. All right. But this meeting is serious. If you fail to show, our deal's out the window, and all of my previous warnings apply. Remember those warnings?"

I clutched the receiver with both hands. I remembered them all too well.

"I can spread more dirt about you online, and destroy your

mom's business in an instant," he reminded me. "I can ruin your dad, while I'm at it—I know the defense in the case he's working on now would be very interested to hear about his radical activist past. Including allegations of links to cold cases involving arson. I can make that happen."

My whole body went cold. My dad needed his job. And I couldn't imagine him holding up well under the stress of such horrible, career-killing false accusations. I pictured the calendar in our kitchen, the boxes darkening with doctors' appointments. "Leave my dad out of this!" I burst out. "Don't you dare make up a story about him!"

The woman minding the cash register looked over at me.

"Then you'd better do what I say," said Darwin. "Oh, and about your friend Mari? Let's just say, among other things, her college financial aid package hangs in the balance. One anonymous tip from my organization about her work as a drug mule, and all her federal support will be gone. Felons don't get financial aid. In other words, Tessa, you'd better follow through, and you'd better not sing out. *¿Comprendes?*"

My grip tightened on the phone receiver. "*Comprendo.* I got it." The ground seemed to buck and sway beneath my feet. There was no limit to the ideas this creep could think up.

"Now listen carefully. I am going to give you an address. Write it down. I'll see you at six P.M. tomorrow. A man will ask you about mangoes. You'll tell him they're best at this time of year, and he'll let you in."

I shivered. The mango code. I'd guessed right. It was used to identify personal contacts, people in their ring.

"And Tessa," Darwin finished, "make sure you come alone. Or else."

41

THE NEXT morning, as Hugo drove me to Vuelta for my first day as a volunteer, my stomach roiled. Maybe it was from the bag of *chicharrón* that I'd bought from that corner store. *Chicharrón* had looked, at a glance, like potato chips, but they actually turned out to be fried pork rinds—I'd eaten half the bag last night before noticing the strange wiry hairs poking up in some.

Or maybe I was just terrified of my impending meeting with Darwin.

Hugo talked on and on about the protests and how the new president was handling them, but I barely heard a word. All I could think about was how I would get to that address from Darwin by six in the evening, and how I would explain to the Ruizes why I would be late for dinner. I didn't yet have an excuse, except maybe playing the parasite card. I could say I was too sick to take the bus back to the house.

"You are lost in thought," said Hugo in a kind voice that reminded me, achingly, of my own dad. "I see I am not captivating you with this political talk. Maybe like Amparo you would rather talk about something else? Friends? Music? Play the radio if you like. Be comfortable."

"No, I am interested in politics. I'm sorry. I do have a lot on my mind."

"*Pobrecita*. You must be nervous. Your first day on the job!"

I was nervous, all right, but it was because of my planned sting operation. Maybe Mari was right, and I was getting in over my head. But I saw no other options. It didn't help that I couldn't trust all the police here. And without proof of anything, how could the embassy help? Or even Hugo Ruiz, who had government connections? That's why I had to get Darwin recorded, on a device that he couldn't hack into.

AFTER WISHING me luck, Hugo let me out at the Vuelta office. I stood at the gate for a moment, clutching the gallon of water he'd insisted I take. With the heavy plastic container slipping in my hands, I watched him drive off, and fought the urge to chase after his car. I looked around at my new surroundings. The office was up a hill from a shopping mall, on a quiet, mostly residential street. It was an impeccable modern building, painted lime green, inviting—except for the imposing bars on all the windows.

Those bars everywhere—a constant reminder that I was never entirely safe.

Inside, I waved at Mari, who was already in one of the classrooms with a group of six attentive women. She looked happy, laying out tool kits at workstations. I was glad I'd at least bought her some time by agreeing to meet with Darwin.

For the first time, the full reach of Darwin's power hit me. Hard. And I seethed. He'd made me hide out in my house and give up my cell phone. He'd made Mari miss more than a week of work. Who knows how many other people he'd cyberbullied, stalked, harassed, and threatened. These were serious crimes. It wasn't fair that we lived in fear and hid out, while he and his cohorts ran around freely.

It also wasn't fair that Darwin had *something* to do with Juan

Carlos's death and he didn't have to pay. Maybe Juan Carlos had been involved in a drug smuggling ring, but no one deserved to die like he did. Darwin and anyone he worked with had to be apprehended. Unless the investigation back home led authorities to Darwin's trail, I was the only one now who could make that happen.

Sylvia, the receptionist, had me fill out some forms for new volunteers. While she was on the phone, I took a moment to check my email from her computer. I found messages from my parents, and a new note from Kylie.

Kylie! I went straight to her message. Finally, she was reaching out again. Maybe she'd decided to forgive me for "ghost-chasing," as she'd put it, in Ecuador.

> Hi Tessa! (Or "Qué tal," I should say!)
>
> I hope everything's good down at latitude zero. Have you seen the equator yet?
>
> I've heard the toilets flush the opposite way at the middle of the world. Is it true?
>
> Anyway, here I am writing about toilets flushing, but I have amazing news!!
>
> Had my interview with Preston Lane the other day. OMG. It ROCKED.
>
> He asked all the questions we brainstormed, and a few more we hadn't, but I was warmed up by then and I think I gave good answers. And I thought of him in spandex like you said to, and it totally

worked. I wasn't nervous at all. If anything he seemed a little nervous! Kind of distracted, like you said.

I know he's off to Ecuador for that bike race thing in a couple of days. I'm hoping he'll make a decision about the scholarship before he goes. I'm not sure how much longer my mom can stave off the tuition bills for senior year. My dad says he's tapped out, since he's just doing contract work these days and I don't think he can cover it all either. Anyway, cross your fingers, send good karma, light a candle, do anything you can!!!

I grinned like crazy. *Go girl.* I knew Kylie could do it. I typed a quick and gushy congratulations note to her. The moment I sent it, Sylvia got off the phone and ushered me into the bike shop section of Vuelta.

Sylvia introduced me to a few other volunteers, and then to Wilson Jaramillo, Santiago's dad, who was helping a volunteer named Emma, from Ireland, fix a punctured bike tire.

Like Santiago, Wilson was tall and lean, and dressed simply and conservatively. Like his son, too, he was friendly, in a calm way. He asked a few questions about how my homestay was going, and then got down to business, handing me a piece of paper with an address.

"Your first assignment," he said. "Three classes at this location."

"Teaching?" I stared at the address in horror. "There must be some mistake. I said on my application that I was interested in working in communications and publicity."

"We do have some publicity and marketing you can help with," said Wilson. "But right now, our most urgent need is covering these classes. Another volunteer had to return to the U.S. for a medical emergency, and these students are in desperate need of a teacher."

"But I've never taught cycling," I protested, trying to hand back the paper.

He pressed the address into my hand. "It is not a problem. The girls are not absolute beginners. They just need practice, tips, and confidence. If you can ride a bike, you can teach! Now here. You may borrow this bike." He took a clunky hybrid bike off a stand and wheeled it over to me. "This is much faster, I think, than taking the trolley across town."

My face burning, I took the bike and I walked it out of the shop. In the hallway toward the front entrance, I passed the open door to Mari's classroom.

Seeing me, Mari left a student's side and ran to meet me, still wielding an Allen wrench. "Well?" she asked. "Did you call Darwin yesterday?"

"I did. I called him. We spoke."

"And? You have to tell me. We're a team, right? We're in this thing together."

I hesitated. After all our confessions yesterday, I hated to hold anything back from Mari. I totally trusted her now. And we'd been a great team, getting the evidence about the sabotaged bike and leaking it to Bianca Slade. But just like with cycling, maybe there were times to work together and times to break away. I didn't want to put Mari at more risk. And Darwin had specifically told me to come alone. If I told Mari about our meeting, she'd insist on coming, too.

"He, um, couldn't really say much at the time," she said. "He got interrupted. I'm supposed to call him again this evening."

"Oh." Her face fell. "So we're not any closer to finding out what he wants."

"But you're safe for now." I tried to sound cheerful, to bolster her spirits. And mine. "I said I'd only talk to him if he left you alone. And he will." I bit my lip, hating the fact that I was lying again. But what else could I do to keep her safe? I couldn't handle any more people getting hurt.

"Thanks. I hope you're right. I've really missed teaching." She glanced back at her students with a wistful smile. "I should get back to work. Where are you off to now?"

I showed her the address Wilson had written down.

"Oh, cool. That's a woman's shelter." She grinned. "You're going to work with women and kids who've left domestic abuse situations. That's awesome. Bikes save lives, remember? You're totally empowering them."

I returned her smile and felt a notch better. This was the kind of work I'd wanted to do to make up for my past bad decisions.

If only I didn't have this new phobia of bike riding.

Mari looked at my hybrid bike and laughed. "I see Wilson gave you Gertrude to ride. That's what we call this clunker. But she's a good ride on uneven roads," she added, patting her handlebars affectionately. "She'll get you where you need to go."

I managed a weak smile. "I was actually planning to take the bus or the trolley."

"At rush hour? No way. This bike's better. And Wilson likes to promote bike advocacy by having volunteers ride as much as they can. Good luck!" She turned to go back to her class, and then paused. She looked at me carefully. "Are you okay?"

"I'm just a little spooked about riding to this job, I guess, after Chain Reaction."

"Really?"

I shrugged, embarrassed. "I haven't managed to get on a bike again. It's one reason I donated my Bianchi. I figured my cycling days were over."

Mari shook her head in amazement. "You can do this, Tessa. Haven't you ever heard that if you learn to ride a bike, you never forget?"

"I should go," I said, "or I'll be late."

I walked the bike out of the Vuelta building. I turned and saw Wilson, Sylvia, Santiago, and a couple of volunteers watching at the window. They waved at me. I waved back, then walked the bike down the hill, and around the corner, until I came to Avenida Amazonas. I held out my arm, and a taxi pulled over.

42

"¿AQUÍ, SEÑORITA?" the driver asked me ten minutes later.

I checked the address and looked at the sagging two-story building, the unpainted cinder blocks. Steel bars, like strange uncut hairs, sprouted from a third floor that had never been completed, and faded laundry was strung up between them. The windows wept rust like tears.

The address matched the building, so this had to be the place. *La Casa para Mujeres Abandonadas.* The House of Abandoned Women. There was probably no sign on the door because it was a shelter. These women did not want to be found.

Maybe this was a good place for me to hang out. I didn't really want to be found, either.

I paid the driver and took Gertrude the Bike out of his trunk. I made my way toward the house, tripping over the crumbling sidewalk. The smell of urine and diesel fumes made me cough. A mangy dog gave me a cold look and slunk away. A girl who looked my age, or younger, nursed a baby on that top floor, by the laundry.

A group of about eight children, young girls and boys, ran up to me from behind the house. They tugged on my shirt and backpack. *"¡La gringa! ¡La gringa!"* they chanted. I froze, smiling helplessly. One of them touched my hand. Another ripped my Shady Pines pin off my backpack.

I wanted to open my backpack and give them everything in it. I didn't have much, just four EcuaBars, slightly smashed, that had been in the bottom of my backpack since Boston. I broke them in half and handed them out, and the kids devoured them.

Watching them eat, I thought of the ghost children that haunted my mother. The lives that had gone unremarked, unrecorded. While the kids ate, I took out my video camera. I turned it on and watched them through the lens for a moment, my finger hovering over the RECORD button.

Then I lowered the camera, slowly, and turned it off. Maybe not everyone's moment had to be filmed. This moment wasn't my story to tell.

The nursing girl on the top floor called down to me in Spanish. "You are the new bike teacher? From Vuelta?"

"I am."

"Everyone is ready for the lesson. Come to the back of the house."

I walked my bike behind the building, the children following close. I came to a concrete patio—cracked and crumbling, so different from the oasis within the Ruizes' house. An assortment of beater bikes were propped against a cinder-block wall. They were the ultimate in castoffs—they made Gertrude look like a supermodel. I sifted through them, taking stock. Basic three-gears. One ten-speed from about forty years ago—my dad still had one like it in our garage. A couple of low-end hybrids. A bike that looked to be a counterfeit—snazzy, like a Trek bike, but it said "Trel" instead, and the chain was choked up with black gunk. A Barbie bike with a sagging, dirty basket and crumpled streamers in the handlebars.

Across from the bikes, my eight students waited. All girls from about age seven to nineteen. Two were pregnant, including the one who'd come down from the roof. One girl, who looked about fourteen, was barefoot.

"Zapatos," I said pointing at her feet. "First rule. Everyone rides with shoes." I repeated this in Spanish, remembering that I wasn't likely to find fluent English speakers here.

The barefoot girl shook her head and displayed empty hands.

I looked at her a moment longer. Her long black sideways braid, slung over one shoulder, reminded me a little of the way I'd worn my hair not so long ago.

I kicked off my Chuck Taylors and handed them to her. She grinned and slipped them on.

"Helmets? Do we have helmets?" I didn't know the word in Spanish, so I pantomimed.

All the girls laughed.

"Okay. I see I'm a comedian today. No helmets. So the third rule is no falling."

That got another laugh.

"Everyone choose a bike," I instructed in Spanish. Maybe I could direct them to go up and down the street, and I wouldn't have to do any actual riding.

They looked confused at first, then slowly chose bikes and stood beside them.

"Well? What are we waiting for?"

"We do not know how to ride," said one girl.

"We have never ridden these bikes," another said.

"You didn't have another teacher before?"

"We were supposed to, but she never came," said a third.

"Right." I stared at them, chewing my lip. Wilson had oversold this class to me. This was the Total Newbie group, with me, a Total Newbie teacher. The least qualified person in the world for this job. What could I possibly teach these girls?

But they stood there, watching me with eager and expectant

faces. One of them started stretching out, and another jumped an imaginary rope to limber up. They were raring to go.

I thought back to the Open Road school. What had Dylan and Amber done? Dylan had been so encouraging and supportive with that kid. Amber had been so patient. They'd also had lots of padding.

An hour later, the girls—with makeshift pads from blankets lashed to their arms—were working on gliding across the patio, which had a very slight incline like the playground where Dylan had "taught" me to glide. I drew a line with chalk, and I recalled Dylan's words to me as he'd coached me on a simple glide. "Find your balance," I told each girl that I coaxed along the line. "That's all we're doing today. Balance, and try to stay on the line."

Some girls were hesitant at first. Then they tried and got bolder. The girl borrowing my Chuck Taylors—Rosio was her name—fell and bawled her head off. Then she got on again, and everyone cheered. Even the tired-looking women, watching us from windows, applauded as the girls experienced, one by one, some success. One of the moms even came out to try it herself.

Another wave of students came over, and some of them had clearly had lessons before. They wanted to work on starting and stopping, using the pedals. Not gliding.

"Can you show us?" the smallest girl asked shyly, pushing the Barbie bike toward me.

I shook my head. "Sorry. I have a bad knee today."

They all looked disappointed.

I felt disappointed, too. But shoving off, using the pedals, and maneuvering around people and things, scared the crap out of me. Just imagining myself doing those things brought Chain Reaction rushing back in an instant.

All morning long, it took all my powers of concentration to keep the girls safe on the bikes, to teach them anything I knew using words and chalk diagrams on the asphalt instead of demonstrating. Dylan's strategies worked, though. He'd had a lot of tricks up his sleeve, as a teacher. Did he have tricks up his sleeve as a mechanic, too? The more I remembered my meeting with Dylan, the less likely it seemed that he could have committed such a horrible crime, that he would have wanted a cyclist to get hurt or to die. Anyone working with bikes, as a mechanic, teacher, or coach, had to be acutely aware of safety issues. More and more I felt that Dylan, unsuspecting, had been set up to take the fall for Juan Carlos's death.

"See you tomorrow?" they said hopefully when the lesson was over.

"Hasta mañana," I confirmed. "I will be here tomorrow. Count on it."

I hoped that after meeting with Darwin I would still have a *mañana*.

After my classes were done, and Rosio had reluctantly returned my shoes, I pushed my loaner bike back toward the main street. I tried to hail a taxi. None stopped, but a pink bus, belching exhaust, finally pulled over where I stood. I saw on the sign it was going to Mariana de Jesus, the street that Vuelta was on.

I hauled my bike up the steps and paid the fare.

The driver shook his head at me and pointed at the bike, then at the crowded seats and aisle behind him. "Please. I'm sorry. I have to take this on," I said in Spanish. "It's an emergency."

The driver sighed and shrugged. *"Bueno. Venga."*

Passengers glared at me as I pushed the bike down the aisle. I apologized to everyone I passed. My face burned. This loaner bike might have been more than most of these passengers could afford. Who was I to barge onto the bus like this and demand to take up space?

I finally found a spare seat near the back and, holding the

bike upright, settled in for the bumpy ride. Music blared. A child wailed. A man ate a piece of corn on a stick. A suspicious substance that might have been vomit oozed slowly down the aisle. I moved my foot. I fought a wave of tears. I was here all because I was too scared to ride my bike in traffic, among people.

The woman next to me smiled at me kindly, and something melted inside me. I couldn't help smiling back. At the next stop, a trio of musicians hopped on and sang some kind of ballad. The blend of pan flutes, guitar, and vocals stirred something in my soul. As the music-filled bus pushed on through the crowded streets, I began to feel better.

This was life. Not perfect. Not comfortable. Just pulsing, fragrant, sticky life. A normal life, for so many people. My mom had faced hardship in Mexico but gave up when life there seemed too hard to handle. I would not make the same choice. I was going to face life in any form. Head-on.

The girls at La Casa and I lived such different lives. All the opportunities I'd been handed—a TV job, a private school education, enriching extracurriculars—I'd taken for granted, even complained about! My parents overscheduling me? I thought of Rosio—and her young mom, a soft-spoken woman who'd appeared, like a shadow, in a black-and-white maid's uniform to watch her daughter ride before heading off to work. Being "overscheduled" had a whole new meaning suddenly.

But on the bikes these girls and I were not so different. We were all working on finding our balance and making our way down a road. And the girls' eagerness to learn, their risk-taking, had taken my breath away. They were every bit as amazing as the kids I'd met on *KidVision*. Maybe normal life could be amazing, too.

The bus jerked to a stop. I fell into the aisle, on top of my bike.

I righted the bike and sat back down. I strained to see out the window where all the other passengers were looking.

A roadblock and protestors were in our way a few yards up ahead. We were stuck behind a row of cars and a *triciclo* with a trailer of ice cream. The smoke from the tires, on top of the bus's exhaust fumes, leaked into the bus and made my eyes burn.

The driver swore and tried to turn, but traffic blocked him in on all sides. The driver got off. The musicians and the passengers followed.

I waited a moment longer, but it seemed the bus was being abandoned, and so I got off, too, even though I had no idea where we were—somewhere between the old and new towns.

I pushed my bike through the crowds. Walking it on the sidewalk was cumbersome. I was getting jostled on all sides. I moved the bike out to the street. I got on. I pedaled a few yards, swerved to avoid a broken bottle, hit a bump on the uneven pavement . . . and promptly tipped over, Gertrude clattering loudly on the uneven pavement.

43

I RETURNED to the Vuelta headquarters sweaty. Dejected. Defeated. So much for my dream of an empowering ride back to the office. All I had to show for my effort was a ripped knee on my jeans, a skinned palm, and badly jangled nerves.

I wheeled Gertrude into the shop and snuck her back into the rack. I gave the back tire a swift kick, for good measure. I wasn't getting on that thing again. Then I looked around the office and the bike shop. Maybe I could do some interviews with volunteers and take my mind off my impending meeting with Darwin.

The shop was eerily quiet, though. There was just one other volunteer at work—a twentysomething Australian guy, whom everyone seemed to call "Aussie Guy." He was signing out rental mountain bikes to a couple of German tourists.

I knocked on Wilson's office door, to ask if he wanted me to get started on my next assignment. When he didn't answer, I pushed open the door a little.

Santiago was at the computer. He looked up and smiled—though less warmly than before, I couldn't help noticing. "Where is everyone?" I asked.

"The staff and volunteers, they are all at lunch. We can join them at the café. I was waiting for your return, to bring you. How was La Casa?"

"The girls weren't as experienced as I thought they'd be, but they made good progress."

"¡Súper bien!" Santiago smiled and looked genuinely happy. "You must be a natural teacher." Then his gaze drifted back to his computer, and his face grew serious. "Actually I am sure your teaching skills must to come from your television show."

I froze. *KidVision.* I hadn't talked to him about my show. Had Mari mentioned that to him? When they were in the statue together yesterday?

"I looked you up online. Here you are."

I went over to his side of the desk. Sure enough, he'd found the *KidVision* site with the archived shows. A video was paused on an image of me, age thirteen, helping a first-grade classroom harvest cucumbers at a community urban garden. Me, with braces, a bad haircut, a goofy smile, and skinny legs—my "chicken legs" phase, Kylie and Sarita used to tease me. Oh my God.

"You are a famous person," he said, raising one eyebrow. "I had no idea." I couldn't tell from his face or his voice if this was a good thing or not.

"Oh, I'm not famous," I said. "Really. I'm not."

If he'd looked me up, what else had he seen? The awful blog "article" Balboa had posted about my bandit riding? The recording she'd made of my conversation with Gage? All the commentators who'd publicly taken me down? It was up there, forever.

"This show, I like it very much," said Santiago. "It is good practice for me, for the listening portion of my TOEFL exam." He clicked a link. "This I liked. Cycling for Change."

And suddenly there was Jake's face filling up the screen, as he talked about the junior Team EcuaBar's community outreach programs: "Yeah, sure, it feels great to give back. To show the world that not all cyclists are doped-up hammerheads. A lot of us are all about the sport. That's what we want to show the kids."

I held my breath, listening to him. He came across as eager. And sincere. My thoughts about his character kept taking switch-back turns. First I'd thought he was a huge booster for cycling and community service, not to mention an exciting boyfriend. But then he'd tried to frame a teammate for doping. But then it turned out he had doubled back to check out that bike I'd found in the woods, and he'd been right that something weird was up with Juan Carlos. He wasn't the guy for me, but that didn't mean he was guilty of any crime here. Or that he was a bad person. He was someone who'd made some bad decisions. I knew something about that myself.

I hoped I'd find out something soon from Darwin that would help to clear Jake's name as well as Dylan's. Jake was already paying, as he should, for trying to frame Juan Carlos for doping. He didn't deserve to be dragged through the media as a person of interest in a homicide case.

I was relieved when the clip of Jake ended—I didn't like the feeling that my Ecuador and my Boston worlds were colliding here, in this office. But then that clip with Juan Carlos came on, and I sat forward to watch. "Turn it up," I whispered to Santiago, and he did.

"Bicycles are one solution for to turn around problems like pollution and poverty," Juan Carlos explained. "One meaning of Vuelta means 'to turn,' and that is what we are doing. More cyclists means less dependence on the cars. Less gas and oil. This is something we are very concerned about in my country, in these days."

"That's fascinating," I said to Juan Carlos in the interview. "So how are bicycle *racers*, as opposed to regular, everyday cyclists, helping to turn things around in your country?"

"Bike racing can show to kids a career path. A way out of their circumstances. It can give them opportunities for prize moneys, for scholarships to study, for travel, for lots of things. This is why Preston Lane started the Vuelta Youth Racing Club. To invest money in young racers."

Santiago tipped back in his chair and looked at me, twirling a pen between two fingers. "So did you know Juan Carlos well?"

"I told you I interviewed him for my show." What was he getting at? Why did he keep looking at me as though he didn't believe me?

He stopped the video clip. "The first guy—he is your *novio*?"

"My what?"

"Your *novio*. Boyfriend."

I stared at him. He meant Jake. I wanted to pretend I'd never known Jake. But I couldn't look into Santiago's clear blue eyes and lie again. "He was, once. Not anymore."

"And Juan Carlos? You were with him or not?"

"No!" Where was he getting these ideas? Had he read my thoughts, my past, on my face, as we watched the videos together?

He shrugged. "Well. I must to close the office and take you to the café to join the others for lunch."

"I can grab a sandwich later. I'm not hungry." And I wasn't. I suddenly just wanted to hide somewhere and prepare, mentally, for my meeting with Darwin. Just as Juan Carlos had needed his five minutes of prayer and peace before racing, I now craved something like that for myself.

"I know you are a hard worker," Santiago said with a small frown. "But here in Ecuador, we take the time and we stop to eat lunch. We will go join our friends and take the break, yes?"

"Yes. Okay." I sighed.

"Momentito."

As soon as he ducked into the bathroom, I rushed to his computer and looked at the other windows he had opened. One had html code; he was updating the Vuelta website with information about Pan-American Cycling Tour events this week.

One was an article in *El Comercio*, Quito's main newspaper, about how EcuaBars and Cadence bikes were both selling like crazy worldwide since the cyclist's crash. People had become fascinated with Juan Carlos, and how his promising career and his life were cut short by a member of his own team, the mechanic. People interviewed for the article said they wanted to buy these products to support the companies that had nurtured this great talent. Or they felt closer to him, eating the product he endorsed or riding the same brand of bike.

I frowned at a picture of Chris Fitch and Preston Lane cutting the ribbon at the start of a new bike path opening in Boston. They looked happy, smiling. I wasn't sure when the picture was taken, but it made me wonder. Could *marketing* be a motive for murder? Was Juan Carlos worth more to them dead than alive?

No. Impossible. He had to be worth more alive, as a money-maker for both companies. Besides, if either businessman was behind his death, they'd have to be linked to Darwin, too, and that was inconceivable. Talk about coming from totally different worlds.

Another window was open to a mostly black screen, with dancing fruit, and a list of different teams, in English, organized by sports. *Sports Xplor!* it said at the top. I'd seen that website before, in Gage's office. Once again, it caught my eye because it looked so strange. It resembled an ad in a pop-up window, with simple graphics, basic design. I saw a list of cycling teams, and I realized that's what this must be. Some kind of ad.

I clicked on the icon for the next open window, and that one freaked me out.

It was the article about my bandit ride, with the audio clip of my "confession." Just as I'd feared, Santiago had found that, with a simple search of my name.

The toilet flushed. I quickly closed those windows.

Was Santiago doing some sleuthing of his own about Juan Carlos? Or about *me*?

44

AFTER LUNCH, Wilson put me on an office project with Emma, the Irish volunteer—a relief after the stress of teaching at La Casa. A relief, then a bore . . . then a panic. We had to stuff hundreds of envelopes with letters soliciting donations. Wilson and the team were starting a big campaign to expand their youth outreach and programs.

"I don't see why these all have to go out tomorrow," I grumbled, glancing at the clock and the darkening sky. Sunsets flared up like a candle and blew out just as fast in Quito, I'd already noticed. And the sky was especially dark, as storm clouds roiled down from the surrounding hills. The first patters of rain spit against the windows. I glanced at a wall clock, and panic seized me. I had less than an hour until my meeting with Darwin. I had to get out of this place. Why had we all lingered for nearly two hours over lunch? We could have finished this project by four!

"He said they had to go out immediately because it's Quito's Bicycle Week and the homecoming event of the PAC Tour," said Emma. "Everyone here will have bikes on the brain. They might be more likely to donate some cash."

More like everyone had Juan Carlos on the brain, I thought. The newsstands were full of magazines with his face splashed all over them. And Juan Carlos was a figurehead of Vuelta. I could see why Wilson was trying to capitalize on all the hype. Still,

Juan Carlos's face staring out at me from all those covers was a constant reminder that I was failing in my mission.

I pushed my chair back from the table. "I have to get out of here," I mumbled. I felt bad leaving her with a mountain of paper to finish, but if I didn't get to that meeting, Darwin was going to start his online trail of destruction, his digital bulldozing of my family's lives.

Emma stood up, too, and followed me out of the back office. "Are you sick? You look really pale."

"Yeah. Not so good. Stomach stuff. Sorry I can't finish. Tell Wilson—"

But I ran smack into Wilson as I opened the door to the building. "I was just coming to get you two!" he said. "The surprise is coming!" Behind him I saw Santiago, Sylvia, and the seven other volunteers, including Mari, standing on the sidewalk.

Suddenly I heard something that sounded like a middle school marching band. Some kind of parade. A tinny brass section, a crashing bass. An *oompa-oompa* beat. And then a bus turned the corner and pulled up by the curb, and all the volunteers, including Mari, burst into cheers and applause.

It was the wildest bus I'd ever seen: antique-looking, with wooden sides, painted bright yellow and green. An eight-piece band sat on the rooftop, continuing to play their *oompa* song. The bus was open air, no windows, with benches for seats. Inside were shiny streamers and bunches of colorful balloons.

The Vuelta staff and volunteers started chanting, *"¡Chiva! ¡Chiva!"* and filed onto the bus.

Santiago raised his eyebrows when he saw me, but he didn't smile as wide as he had yesterday morning when he picked me up at the Ruizes' house. Something was definitely up with him.

Maybe I'd pushed him away. He'd been so friendly from the start, and I'd been aloof and preoccupied. But I couldn't make up for it now. I had only twenty minutes to go until my face-to-face meeting with a possible murderer!

"My father rented a *chiva.* A party bus," he explained.

"Looks fun," I said. "I wish I could come." And I did wish that, powerfully.

"What?" Santiago grinned. "But you are coming. Everyone is invited. It is for the volunteers."

"But I have to—"

"¡Oye, señorita! ¡Venga!" the driver insisted, ushering me on with an impatient gesture.

"¡Venga, Tessa*! ¡Venga!"* everyone on board shouted at me, in unison.

I hopped on and took the seat in front of Mari, who was sitting by Aussie Guy. Santiago slid onto the bench beside me. "How could you even think about missing this?" he asked, with a broad gesture, as the band thundered on above our heads. Symbols crashed, trumpets blared, and the drum banged on and on. "This is a classic Ecuadorian experience!"

I could feel a headache coming on fast.

A woman passed around whistles, party blowers, and little cups of Inca Kola, and away we went, shuddering and lurching into the evening, the song growing more frenzied at every turn.

I turned to look at Mari as everyone started blowing their whistles and party blowers. "Where's this bus going?"

"Nowhere," she said, playfully shaking a plastic castanet at me. "Why?" Then her eyes widened. "Darwin. Did you call him yet?"

"No. I have to get off this thing. And what do you mean the bus is going nowhere? Everything has to go somewhere."

"Not this bus. *Chivas* just drive around. Why don't you use Santiago's phone?"

"But I don't need to call—" It took me a moment to realize what she was talking about. Mari thought I needed to call Darwin; she had no idea I was actually meeting with him. "Um, I mean, Darwin said use a pay phone only. I guess that way it's harder to trace him."

"I bet you're right. Let's keep our eyes out for a public phone sign."

The bus careened around corners, and more Inca Kola cups were passed down the aisle. I took some and immediately spit it out. It was Inca Kola mixed with fire. "Rum," said Aussie Guy, his eyes dancing at me as he downed his cup of the concoction in one shot. "Have another go. The second sip's always better."

Santiago laughed at the face I made on my second sip. "I do not like this drink, either," he said quietly. "I can take your cup. You do not have to drink this."

As Santiago reached across my lap to take my drink away, I noticed the hint of stubble on his face, and the long upward curve of his eyelashes. I warmed at his kindness, disposing of my drink when no one else was looking so I wouldn't be embarrassed.

There were other guys out there. My life didn't have to vacillate between the two poles of Jake and Juan Carlos. Maybe I'd meet someone when all this was over, and feel things again. Like love.

Santiago signaled to the *chiva* assistant, or whatever she was. She took our empty cups and, with a gracious smile, flung them outside.

My eyes widened at the blatant recycling violation, and Santiago threw up his hands in frustration. "We are sitting on gold here, with this beautiful country, but people still are throwing their trash in the streets." He looked closely at me. "Something is troubling you. Is it the cups? You are a big recycler. I know from your TV show," he added.

"Ah. Right."

"I like very much your show. But it seems you are not a host any longer?"

I looked at my lap. "Kind of a long story."

As the bus slowed, Mari poked me in the back, and then pointed to a hotel with a sign advertising a pay phone inside. *"Call Darwin,"* she mouthed, making a phone gesture with her hand.

"Maybe you can tell me the story sometime? I am curious," said Santiago.

The bus lurched forward again.

"Maybe." I gazed at the hotel we passed, and the canyon of office buildings around us, as the rollicking bus barreled down another side street. From my wool tote bag I showed him the address Darwin had given me. "Do you know where this place is?"

"Juan León Mera Street . . . that's in La Zona."

"La Zona!"

"Yes. Not so far from Mari's apartment. And about three blocks from here. The driver is passing by there on the way to the Old Town." Santiago took a closer look at the paper. "Is this place someone's home? Or a club?"

"A club." That was the easiest answer. And I hoped it was correct. I didn't want to be in somebody's apartment, with Darwin, completely alone. I chilled. Why hadn't I even thought to ask Darwin what kind of place we were meeting in?

Santiago gave a short laugh. "I thought at first you were different. But maybe you are a typical *gringa* after all? Here to find an *aventura*?"

I stared at him, my face hot. "What do you mean?"

He looked down, his cheeks reddening. "Nothing. Never mind. I did not mean to sound in that way." Then his eyes met mine again. Not angry, just direct. "But maybe you could just tell me why you're really here?"

Aussie Guy interrupted us, tapping Santiago on the shoulder to ask him something about an Ecuadorian drinking song. I leaned over the back of my seat and talked into Mari's ear.

"I'm getting off here."

"No, Tessa! I don't think it's a good idea after all. Not here, anyway. "

"I saw a sign for a pay phone," I lied. "Cover for me, okay? Tell Wilson and everyone I got sick again and went to your place. It's just a few blocks away."

Before she could protest again, and as the driver slowed for a red light, I slipped off the bench and jumped off the *chiva*.

I tripped and landed on my knees but quickly scrambled to my feet, unhurt.

I ran down the street as fast as I could. Footsteps slapped the wet pavement behind me as the light rain turned steady. I turned and saw whose they were.

"What are you doing?" I said to Mari. "Are you crazy? Who's covering for me if you're here?"

"You're not just calling Darwin from a pay phone, are you? Something's up. I know it."

"Fine. I'm meeting him. At this address."

She snatched the paper. "No way are you going in there to meet him alone."

Fat, heavy drops, splatted on the sidewalk with fury now. While people ran for cover under restaurant awnings and in doorways, Mari and I stood there and glared at each other.

"This is *not* just your problem, Tessa," Mari said, her voice breaking. "It's mine, too. I should have inspected Juan Carlos's damn bike more carefully while I had the chance. I had a gut feeling the bike wasn't right, and I never followed through and took the whole thing apart. If I'd done it, we might have found out what was inside it before it left the country."

"But two weeks ago, what would you have taken the bike apart for? To look for enhancements?"

"Maybe. Or drugs."

"So you were thinking about drugs, too? Before I mentioned it?"

She nodded. "My aunt works for the TSA at Logan Airport. She saw a bike come through once, from Mexico, stuffed with bags of white powder. I didn't want to go there in my head, you know? To think that about Juan Carlos. And I'm sick of stereotypes about drugs and Latin America. But I have to face reality. That might be what's going on here."

"But why would they be bringing drugs into Ecuador? Don't they travel the other way?"

"Right. So maybe it's cash, and maybe it's not in the handlebars. I've been thinking a lot about this," said Mari. "Carbon fiber can be hollowed out. You saw it for yourself. The whole frame could be stuffed to the gills."

I swallowed hard. "Santiago told me there was a lot of stuff going on here lately with young people working as drug and money mules. Maybe that's what Juan Carlos was doing." He traveled internationally. With a bike. A bike that could conceal contraband. Like drugs coming into the U.S. or drug money flowing back out. Had Juan Carlos been helping Darwin's group at one point as a mule? What if he had screwed up, or deliberately turned against them, making them mad enough to kill him? The bike stashed in the woods, and the "information" these guys were looking for—none of this made Juan Carlos look good.

"Look. I want to get to the bottom of this as much as you do," Mari said, softer now. "If my friend was involved with a drug cartel, I want to know why."

"I get that. But Darwin specifically told me to come alone," I explained. "If I break my word, and bring someone, he'll spread dirt about me and my parents online. He's already set up someone to frame my mom for harassment, and he'll go after my dad, too."

Mari glared at me a moment longer, then blew out a long breath. "Fine," she said. "But I'm not going anywhere. I'll wait across the street."

We hurried down the street, following the numbers until we came to the address of the meeting place. Salsoteca Mundial.

Mari whistled under her breath. "Oh, no," she said. "Not this place."

"What's wrong with it? It looked okay during the day. Seems like a real nightclub."

The nightclub pulsed with salsa music, and a line was forming out the door even though it was early in the evening.

"At night?" Mari shook her head. "It's a place where money gets laundered and all kinds of shady business deals take place. It's been written up in the paper, and the Vuelta staff told us to avoid it." She gave me a long look. "If you're not out in thirty minutes, I'm coming in to find you."

As I left Mari and approached the line at the door, I checked to make sure Juan Carlos's necklace was safely tucked beneath my shirt and my cotton scarf. I also buttoned my sweater up tight. This seemed like the perfect place and time to have someone run by and grab jewelry off my neck, if they happened to see a flash of gold. Even if the necklace wasn't real gold, I didn't need to look like any more of a target than I already was.

While Mari lurked in the doorway of the SuperChicken across the street, a heavy-set bald man in a cream suit and a Panama hat—a bouncer, I guessed—came up to me and whispered in my ear, in English, with breath that reeked of cigar smoke, "What do you know about mangoes?"

"Mangoes are best at this time of year?"

The bouncer lifted a velvet rope, ushering me underneath. My heart racing, I pushed open the heavy wood door to the club, then parted the thick red velvet drapes in the foyer.

The mango code had worked.

And after this meeting? I was never going to eat another mango as long as I lived.

Once inside, I immediately ducked into a restroom, and into a stall, to avoid the restroom attendant's curious stare. I quickly set up my video camera inside my woven wool bag from the crafts market. I pulled apart some of the threads on the outside of a pocket to make a small hole. Then I nestled the camera lens right up against it. I stuffed wads of stiff, pink toilet paper around the camera in the pocket, to keep it in position, and zipped the pocket tight. I almost laughed, thinking of the projects and inventions I'd demonstrated step-by-step on *KidVision*. I'd come a long way from pizza box furniture.

Back in the nightclub entryway, I scanned faces in what little light there was. Where was Darwin? Would he be alone? With a gang? Couples were shimmying and sliding around the dance floor in exotic salsa moves. I couldn't imagine Darwin dancing. Small round tables, filling up with spectators, surrounded them. Nobody looked like him.

Then Pizarro swooped in, seemingly out of nowhere, and took me firmly by the arm. "Right this way, *señorita*," he said, maneuvering me through the crowds.

"Ouch. You're hurting my arm," I complained.

Pizarro only squeezed tighter. "You're a flight risk. And we all have a job to do. Mine is to deliver you to my boss, and make sure you're coming alone." His face was carefully arranged in a pleasant expression, as he nodded or waved at people he knew—mostly bouncers, burly men posted around the club. But his voice was acid. He brought me to the farthest corner of the club, where five archways were cut into the brick walls, each one covered with red curtains. He made eye contact with one of the bouncers nearby. "Know that we have many friends here. Some of them work for the police. I suggest doing everything Darwin tells you to do." He brought me to an archway, pulled back a curtain, and pushed me inside toward a table. The heavy fabric swished closed behind me, and I was with Darwin, alone.

45

IT TOOK my eyes a moment to adjust to the dim light. Votive candles in red glass cups were all that lit this alcove. Darwin, seated at a wooden table, motioned for me to sit opposite him on a bench.

In front of him was popcorn in a little dish, and a short ceramic mug with some kind of steaming hot beverage, which he sipped. The scent drifted my way. Hot red wine. But when it sloshed in the cup as he set it down, it made me think of blood.

There was also a bottle of Inca Kola on the table, which he slid toward me. I refused it. For all I knew, he'd laced it.

Other than sitting under a blood-red lamp, alone in a salsa club, Darwin looked not unlike a tourist himself. A young businessman passing through town, maybe looking to have a good time. In his black pants and striped polo shirt, he looked almost as straightlaced as Santiago, at first glance. But he still wore aviator sunglasses, as he had that day in the woods. In the lenses, the reflected light of the votive candles flickered.

"So." A slow, crooked grin spread across Darwin's face. "You're quite the globe-trotting teen. So far from home."

I thought I might faint or throw up. I did not want to be in here, where nobody could see us or hear us.

But I was so close to catching Juan Carlos's possible killer! I positioned my tote bag in front of my chest and hoped the camera would pick up at least the sound. The drapes muted the music from the club a little, yet music still leaked in.

"What's this meeting all about?" I asked, speaking loudly so the audio on my camera would pick up.

He tossed a handful of popcorn into his mouth, chewed it, and leaned forward. "Information," he said, drawing out the word. "Missing information, that is." He fell silent but kept on looking at me. Despite the candlelight dancing in his lenses, and the heat in the club, his gaze made ice run through my veins.

"For someone interested in information, you don't give very much of it."

Darwin chuckled, though I didn't see what could possibly be funny. "I've got a problem on my hands, Tessa Taylor," he said. "A certain individual stole classified information from someone in the organization that I represent."

An organization! It hadn't even crossed my mind that Darwin could be part of a larger chain of command, that he might be working for somebody else. "What organization?" I demanded. I was so excited to finally get information from Darwin that I actually forgot to be nervous. I angled my tote bag upward, praying I'd catch his words and maybe his face on film. This was it. The grand confession! I braced myself for the words to come.

"I'm giving information on a need-to-know basis," he snapped. "You don't need to know the specifics. But the stolen data got put on a flash drive, which we've been attempting to locate. If the data is leaked, it will cost the organization millions of dollars, irrevocable reputation damage, and a possible prison sentence for my client of up to twenty years if the feds were to come after him. This is something, I assure you, he does not deserve. It's a situation that can too easily blow up over a simple misunderstanding." He leaned forward again, and the reflected candle flames leaped in his shades. "I'm an information specialist, Tessa. Data is my business. But you might think of me more as a plumber. I am doing whatever I can to stop the leak."

A prison sentence was at stake? Millions of dollars? This had to involve drugs, and serious drug money. But now it sounded like Juan Carlos was trying to expose someone for buying or selling drugs, not participate in that business himself. He was trying to be a whistle-blower. A hero. A warm feeling slowly replaced the ice that had filled my veins.

"So Juan Carlos took your client's data?" I asked, shifting the tote bag with the camera even closer. I had to get all this recorded.

"Ding ding ding!" Darwin pantomimed ringing a bell. "You win the sweepstakes! Yes. Juan Carlos should have stuck to the cycling path, but he rashly stole a flash drive belonging to my client, containing backup data from his personal computer. In doing so, he veered into my territory, and set off a whole chain of events with very serious consequences."

I leaned forward to pick up Darwin's every word, his breath, even the upward curl of his lip. "So is that why you killed him?"

Darwin looked startled. Then he laughed. "You think I killed him? You seriously crack me up. I can see why you were so popular on TV and why you already have four hundred followers on your new vlog. You're very entertaining. Look. I told you, I deal in information. I kill reputations, not people. I don't like blood on my hands. It's not my thing. I didn't knock your friend off his bike. If anything, his stupid accident made my work harder."

"Was it someone else you work with, then?" I tried to hold my gaze steady. "You know, don't you, who rigged his bike?"

He barked a laugh.

"It wasn't Dylan Holcomb, was it?"

He gave me a long look and drummed his fingers on the table.

"No," he said slowly. "That moron of a mechanic was useful as a portal, though."

"What do you mean, a portal?"

"He was willing to leave the trailer unattended long enough to let someone in. For a modest fee."

"You paid him off to leave the trailer? Did he know why?"

Darwin smirked. "Dylan's not exactly the brightest bulb. He didn't have a clue. But money talks, so he didn't ask. Just as I predicted."

"Then call the police and tell them that!" I burst out. "Tell them who Dylan *did* let in!" I narrowed my eyes. "Who did Dylan let into the trailer when he left it unlocked?"

He waggled a finger at me, as if I were a misbehaving child. "You're changing the meeting agenda. I don't like that. I'm here to talk about that missing flash drive. I'm not a murderer. Not even from afar."

"And I don't have a flash drive," I retorted. "Just like I didn't have that bike you were looking for."

"You led us directly to the bike. In the bike shop where Juan Carlos worked as a volunteer."

"I didn't even know it was there!" I spluttered. I wanted to explode. "Come on. You've cyberstalked me, you hacked my phone, and you had Balboa post crap about me online, and all for no reason! Why are you coming after me now?"

Darwin shifted in his seat and folded his arms across his broad chest. "It has come to my attention that you were perhaps not as aware of the bike and its whereabouts as we once thought," he said. "I understand now that another party may have had a hand in the bike's removal. In fact, we're grateful that you unwittingly led us to the bike shop, where our field agents could comb the premises and eventually locate the bike. So I'm no longer interested in your connection, or lack thereof, to the bike."

"So what's this all about? Why follow me to the middle of the world to keep bothering me?"

"Information. Connections."

"What?"

Darwin scrutinized me a moment longer before continuing. "My organization has received intelligence that Juan Carlos planned to leak my client's stolen information to the media. He planned to expose the person in question at Chain Reaction, which was crawling with cameras and reporters. We figured out you, of all people, were his media contact. A kid. What are the odds?"

I gripped the edge of the table. So that must be what Juan Carlos had wanted to talk to me about so urgently after the award ceremony! The information he stole! It all made sense now. He'd wanted to confide in me, or use my connections to GBCN. Not to confess his secret love for me or whatever. That was why he asked me if I had a laptop. If he had a flash drive on him at Chain Reaction, he could have shown me these incriminating files right then and there, and I could have brought them to someone at GBCN.

Although why did he have to do this in person? Why not simply email information, as I'd mailed the bike inspection video to Bianca Slade?

"You look surprised," said Darwin said with a smirk.

"How'd you know for sure I was the media contact?" I demanded.

"It's a fascinating chain of events, actually," said Darwin. "Juan Carlos had called a friend here in Ecuador, the day before the race. We intercepted the call and learned that he planned a leak at the event. Then two of our agents, embedded at Chain Reaction, saw Juan Carlos ride off toward the woods and then come out of the woods. With no bike. Those same agents saw you and Juan Carlos talking shortly after. They witnessed other suspicious behavior, like transferring a phone between you and ducking behind a tree with him. Then once I learned who you were and that you worked at GBCN," Darwin continued, "we simply connected the dots."

I was shaking, badly. I put my hands beneath the table so Darwin wouldn't see. Now I could see how the trail led to me. If Juan Carlos hadn't been killed, he would have told me everything. I didn't know what made me madder: Darwin's wild assumptions about me, or the missed opportunity to talk to Juan Carlos and prevent this whole mess in the first place.

"You connected the dots? No," I said. "You jumped to conclusions. The only information Juan Carlos gave me was his phone number. And I went to tell him about a team photo shoot he was missing. Not to get 'information.'"

"But you knew Juan Carlos," Darwin insisted. "You'd seen the bike in the woods. You'd filmed it on your phone. And you worked in the media. You were a loose cannon. We had to get you off the air and away from your immediate media connections."

I sucked in my breath. "Is that why Balboa posted that article? And is she the one who filmed me in the medical tent and posted that photo and audio file?"

"You are correct. That was also our insurance policy. You know what we can do if you don't cooperate with us. Now, can you look me in the face and tell me you don't have the flash drive?" Darwin lowered his shades, and I saw his eyes. Or eye.

One eye was missing. The skin around the sewn-up socket was mottled and scarred, as though he'd been burned. His other eye was blue and intense, piercing through me, unblinking.

I shuddered, but I held his gaze. "What happened to you?"

"Hockey injury. Long story. When you're a mother someday, don't let your kids play that sport. It's dangerous. I've avoided sports ever since. It's why I turned to computers. Safer that way. If you know your way around them." His upper lip curled. "So you see, if I'm squeamish about contact sports, how could I be Juan Carlos's killer? I operate at arm's length, or farther, as much as I possibly can, in all my business dealings."

I forced myself to stare at his face, including his hideous eye socket. "I do not have a flash drive," I said slowly and clearly. "He didn't give it to me."

Darwin regarded me a moment longer, then slid his glasses back up his nose. "I believe you," he said. "But I also believe you can help us find it."

"But where was Juan Carlos after he talked to me? Why didn't he make it to the starting point on time? Did your little spies happen to see where he went? There's a lot of people who'd like to know."

"Persistent interviewer, aren't you? I can see how you're in the school of Bianca Slade. That must be why you put her on the path to a criminal investigation."

I shuddered. So he knew about that.

"You see, you're entirely too interested in Juan Carlos to be completely innocent of involvement," said Darwin. "Now I'll tell you an amusing story. Right before the race, my field agents grabbed Juan Carlos."

"Balboa and Pizarro," I guessed, picturing them in their EcuaBar volunteer outfits.

"That's right. We had a van stationed nearby. They held him there. They demanded he hand over the flash drive that he'd been planning to leak to the media at Chain Reaction. They also asked who else had this information. Had he made copies of the drive? Sent it to the cloud? We had to know, and determine the risk."

I pictured Pizarro and that gleaming knife, held against Juan

Carlos's neck, in a van, while his junior teammates and Preston Lane and Chris Fitch looked for him in the staging area, not suspecting a thing.

"And?" I prompted, feeling sick.

"And finally, he buckled under pressure thanks to my skilled interrogators. He confessed that he'd already given the drive to a media contact. Though he wouldn't name names, at least we had a lead. Then we asked him where his spare bike had gone, because it contained something else he'd swiped from our organization."

"Money?"

"You're an A+ student, Tessa Taylor." Darwin clapped his hands together. "He took a pretty tidy sum of money that did not belong to him. One of my field agents had intelligence about his plan to turn that cash in to the authorities at Chain Reaction, where we were supposed to pick up a payment. Again, my young interrogators got him to confess he'd hidden the bike in the woods until he could safely bring it to a media contact and a police officer immediately after the race. He told them he'd placed his bike with our cash in the woods near a spray-painted rock. When my source gave me that lead, I immediately went off to find it. I found the rock but no bike. I looked all around. I smelled a rat. I figured he'd deliberately misled us. And then"—he smiled slowly—"I saw you. Little Red Riding Hood. Too conveniently traipsing through the woods, exactly where you didn't belong."

The puzzle pieces of the Chain Reaction morning finally snapped in place. So when Juan Carlos had talked to me on Great Marsh Road, Balboa—lurking across the street—must have shown up in time to see us talking. She must have alerted Pizarro. They accosted him on his way to the photo shoot, and that's why he never got there. If Juan Carlos had been held up in a van, being interrogated at knifepoint about the missing flash drive and a cash-stuffed bike, he wouldn't have been ready to start the race with his team, and his teammates wouldn't have seen him. That's why he started the race so late. And Darwin was probably talking to Balboa and Pizarro when I overheard him talking on a cell. But Juan Carlos must have misdirected them to buy himself some time. Because that bike was definitely not by some spray-painted rock when I'd found it.

"So Juan Carlos eventually got out of that van, right?" I guessed. "I know he picked up his main bike from Dylan at some point. Then he tried to catch up with his team."

A muscle twitched at his temple. "Yes, he overpowered my agents. For a small guy, he was pretty strong. He managed to wrestle Pizarro, knock a knife out of his hand, rush the door, and get out. But now I've said enough. You now have all the relevant information you need to consider our assignment. Our generous offer, I might call it."

"Your assignment?"

"Finally. We're getting down to business." Darwin smiled. "Marisol Vargas is a person of interest to us. We understand you are friends. We have learned of her connection to Juan Carlos at Compass Bikes. From correspondence we have intercepted between Juan Carlos and his good friend here in Quito, we believe Mari has the flash drive now. We also believe that she may have been entrusted with additional confidential information concerning my client."

I almost wanted to laugh. "Maybe you should write spy novels," I said. "You're really good at coming up with theories based on circumstantial evidence. And yes, I'm a lawyer's daughter and I know what that means."

"It's not circumstantial evidence. Juan Carlos told his friend that he and Mari spoke at length before Chain Reaction, and that he habitually confided in her."

"Look. Mari doesn't have a flash drive, either. Or any other information." The more I spoke, the braver I felt. "You're totally wrong about us. We're just students! Kids!"

"Ah, but kids can be very savvy in the business of information," said Darwin. "And that's where you come in." He reached beneath the table and pulled out a stack of cash. Crisp hundred-dollar bills rubber-banded together. He ran his thumb across the short end of it and made the bills flutter, like a fat deck of cards. Then he shoved it toward me.

I recoiled. I didn't want to touch this guy's filthy money.

"Here's the job," he said. "I need you as an inside operative. A deeply undercover agent. You'll get further with her than we will because she trusts you. She likes you. Find out where the flash drive is, and what else Juan Carlos might have confided in her. We need to know what she knows. You'll report your findings to us daily, giving us fresh leads, calling the number you used before. Cool cash, under the table, and all you have to do is what you're already so good at. Talking. Listening. Reporting."

"No."

He tilted his head. "You confuse me. I thought you wanted to be an investigator. *KidVision* was child's play. A small step up from Barney. This job is closer to your intended line of work than that show ever was."

"This isn't reporting. It's spying!"

"Are they really so different?" asked Darwin. "Bianca Slade went undercover, as did you, to dig up information."

"I'm not a spy. And Mari's my friend. You couldn't pay me to do this."

"Really?" He inched the cash back toward me. "But teens just love working for us."

That jolted me. "Wait. *Teens* work for you? Doing what?"

"Mostly they move money around for us."

"They work for you as money mules?"

"Something like that. For smaller jobs, since cash smuggling has become so risky lately. Some have other assignments. Over half our staff right now is young people under twenty-five. We're an international organization, so we use backpackers, study abroad students. Transient types."

My eyes widened. "And none of them have ratted you out?"

"We hire well. They're desperate for cash, and they're too scared to squeal. Usually they've got something they need to protect. Secrets of their own. See, it all comes back to information. Who needs a gun when you can find out or make up anything about people, and make it public, forever?"

My God. Darwin was taking advantage of young people in desperate situations. How low could this guy get?

"Come on. What teen doesn't want a wardrobe refresher? Or her very own car?"

"Not me."

"Ah. That's right. You're different. Let's see. Maybe you could use some cash to reimburse your parents for covering your little bandit riding snafu? Making a Chain Reaction donation? Helping a dear friend finish her senior year at Shady Pines?"

Oh my God. How did he know all that stuff?

My phone. Of course. He'd hacked into it. He'd probably pulled or read all my texts with Kylie and Sarita.

"And if I refuse?"

He smiled his biggest smile yet. "We'll tell the world your secret."

"My secret?"

"That you killed Juan Carlos."

I dropped my tote bag. I was shaking so bad I could hardly pick it up. I didn't know if the camera was okay.

"We have helmet camera footage of you pulling out of a

paceline. We can fabricate some key eyewitnesses to talk about how you purposefully veered into his path on a ride you didn't belong on."

"You wouldn't."

"What could stop me?"

Rage surged in me. This guy was pure evil.

But the only way out of this meeting was to tell him I'd take the job. Then I'd run to the nearest police station with this camera, and let them deal with Darwin, while the trail to him was still hot. Smoking hot. I'd get them after Darwin before he even left this club.

"Fine." I scowled. "I'll do it."

"Good girl." He peeled off some bills from the stack and put the rest in a briefcase. "Consider this an advance. Time is of the essence. With all the media coming for the PAC finale, that's a prime time for a leak, especially from someone who's so inclined to finish projects that Juan Carlos started. You need to begin immediately. I look forward to your first communiqué."

The red drapes parted, and Pizarro appeared, ready to usher me out.

46

PIZARRO STEERED me by the arm again, toward the door. I had no idea how much time had passed in the alcove. Pizarro put both hands on me and maneuvered me through the crowds.

At the corner of the dance floor, Pizarro suddenly spun me around. The next thing I knew, we were whirling right into the crowd of salsa dancers. Swaying elbows and hips jabbed me from all sides. A woman with a spike heel stepped on my foot, then shot me a dirty look, as if it were my fault.

"Stop! Stop! I don't want to dance!" I cried out, stumbling.

In the kaleidoscope of spinning dancers and lights, I caught Pizarro's evil leer. *"¿No quieres bailar? ¿Pero, porque?"* he murmured into my ear.

Then I was being pushed off the dance floor and toward the door, and the bouncer in the cream suit and Panama hat shoved me into the street, into a downpour.

I looked down and my wool bag—with the camera, with all my evidence—was gone.

I ran across the street, gasping for breath, and found Mari, still waiting, with a terrified look on her face. "Twenty-eight minutes! I was about to go in to find you. What happened?"

"Darwin told me all kinds of crazy stuff. Enough to convict him of multiple crimes."

"Like killing Juan Carlos?"

"Not that. Though I think he knows who did it. But he said a lot of other stuff." I briefed her on our meeting, including the fact that Dylan was almost certainly innocent. And I told her about the job he'd offered me.

"Spying on me?" she burst out. "God! I want to go in there right now and kick him in the balls!"

A group of nightclub hoppers passing by stared at her curiously.

Mari ignored them. "He's using you—*paying* you—to get to me? Based on an overheard phone conversation that makes them think I have information? That's insane." She turned and ran down the street, back toward the club.

I jogged after her and pulled on the hood of her lightweight jacket to stop her. "Mari. Are you really going in there with all those undercover bouncers and spies to give Darwin a good talking-to? *That's* insane."

She spun around, eyes blazing. "So let's take that camera to the police right now!"

I displayed empty hands. "We can't. Pizarro took my bag. With the camera! And some of the police here work with this group. Pizarro told me himself. Oh, God." I leaned against the side of SuperChicken, feeling like I'd bonked on a long bike ride. "I don't have any proof." I took a shuddery breath. Tears burned my eyes. "I tried so hard. We've come so far. I just wanted to make everything right! I blew it. I failed."

"Hey." Mari put her hands on my shoulder. "You didn't fail. You can't talk like that. A lot of people would have gotten off this crazy ride a long time ago. You've gone farther than anyone else would. Farther than I would, that's for sure."

"Really?"

"Let's call the police anyway," said Mari. "Let's just tell them what went on in there, describe Darwin, and explain he's connected to a murder case back in Boston."

"There's no point." I glanced at the club. "What are we going to say? Some scary guys swiped my tote bag? Happens all the time in La Zona, right? Forget it." I slid down the wall and slumped on the sidewalk. I hugged my knees to my chest. "It's all over. Darwin's going to wreck all our lives. Especially now that he knows I tried to smuggle a camera into our meeting. There's nothing we can do."

"Stop it," said Mari. "There's always a way out. Come on." She yanked me to my feet. "Where's that relentlessly, annoyingly positive girl who used to host *KidVision*?"

"Long gone," I said morosely. "Lost."

"Then I'm taking over your job. I think we can solve this problem. But first we have to get you out of here. Maybe we can catch the *chiva* on its way back."

We ran all the way to the street corner where we'd jumped off the bus and listened intently for *chiva* music over the sounds of passing cars through the puddles. No *chiva* materialized out of the mist.

"I just want to go home," I said, burying my face in my hands.

"To your host family?"

"No. *Home.*"

"Well, that's not happening, so get over yourself. Let's get you back to the Ruiz house. Let's find someone with a cell phone we can borrow and call Santiago."

"His number's in my tote bag. Which is missing, remember?" Surely at some point Santiago had noticed both Mari and I had vanished. If he'd had any suspicion I was a sneaky person, or dishonest, that must be confirmed in his mind by now. I didn't want to go back to Vuelta to wait for the *chiva* and get a ride home. I didn't think I could look Santiago in the eye right now. He'd been so helpful, so up front with me, and all I'd done was use him for rides and scheme about how to get away from him.

"I'll just take a taxi," I said, raising one arm. "I have two dollars in my pocket. That should get me there. Or close."

"I'm going with you."

"You want to sleep over?"

"I don't know. I was thinking I'd just make sure you got there. But now that you mention it? Maybe. Do you think your host family would let me?" Mari looked embarrassed.

"I'm sure they would. They're really nice."

She gave a short nod and looked away. "It's funny. I came here just wanting some freedom. But being around a family actually sounds sort of okay right now. Just for a night," she added quickly. "Just to get a good night's sleep."

"Of course."

We turned to go, rounded a corner, and almost bumped into Santiago, who was jogging toward us. "What happened to you two? Did you fall off the *chiva* or something?"

It almost sounded funny, the whole idea of it, but Santiago wasn't joking. He wasn't smiling at all.

47

WE ALL stood blinking at each other under a streetlight, like stunned moths, and finally Mari spoke.

"It's not what you think," she said to Santiago. "Tessa got sick, and I wanted to help."

"Really? I thought you ditched the *chiva* party. And our group," said Santiago, looking at me more than Mari. "We have volunteers who do this sometimes. They jump off the bus in La Zona and run off to a nightclub. I didn't think you would do that. But when we realized you two were missing, my father asked me to go back and find you. I've been in every club for four blocks."

Santiago didn't seem angry in the way Jake used to get angry. His voice didn't turn into acid. He wasn't playing mind games. He was just legitimately bewildered. If I were in his shoes, and were responsible for the safety of foreign volunteers, I'd feel the same way.

"I'm so sorry," I said. "We should have told someone we needed to go. And we did go to a nightclub. But it's not what you think. It was for a meeting. I can explain."

"Can you explain this, too?" Santiago held up a small black box, about the size of a pack of cards. "I found this attached beneath my car earlier today."

"What is that?" Mari said, reaching for it. "A garage door opener?"

"No. A GPS tracker," he said. "It attaches by magnet." He showed her.

"A GPS tracker!" I grabbed the device from Mari and inspected it. It didn't look like anything special. "You mean this could tell someone where your car is?"

"That's high-tech spy gadget stuff!" Mari exclaimed.

"No, it's not," said Santiago. "You can buy them online for three hundred dollars or less. Sometimes people buy them to track a grandparent who has dementia, or a cheating lover, or a teenage driver."

"You're a teenage driver," Mari reminded him. "Maybe your parents put it there."

"They would never," said Santiago. "My mother does not drive a car. My sisters do not yet drive. My father takes his bike almost everywhere. I am the family chauffeur. My family, they would not even know what this thing is."

That lie Mari told about my getting sick was possibly about to come true. I felt seriously nauseated as the meaning of that gadget hit me. "The airport," I said slowly. "They put it on at the airport. Darwin and his crew. They watched me go to your car, and one of them probably put it on there when you were calling my host family."

Mari's eyes widened. "That's how Balboa found us at El Panecillo yesterday!" she exclaimed. "I was wondering about that. Santiago drove us there. Now it all makes sense."

"And that's how they found the Ruiz house. Santiago had driven me there. So they knew where to leave me a note."

"Wait—who came to the Ruiz house and put that note on the gate? I thought you said that was from Mari?" said Santiago. "What is all this you are saying?"

I rubbed my forehead and looked away, unable to meet his gaze. All my efforts to protect Santiago, to avoid dragging another nice person into this mess, had been useless. He was now a target of this spy ring, too. Literally. And now I looked like a liar on top of everything else.

"Let's go back to Mari's place so she can pack," I finally said. "We'll explain everything there."

"But first?" Mari took the tracking device, with its blinking green light, and affixed it to a parked taxi cab with nobody in it. "There," she said, with a grim expression. "Let them chase after that for a while. That should keep them busy."

Back at Mari's empty apartment, while Mari stuffed a change of clothes in a bag, Santiago and I sat in the kitchen, amid the piles of take-out food containers and rotting fruit. I was glad Mari would be taking a break from this place. The air felt rank and toxic. I swatted at fruit flies and told Santiago everything, going all the way back to Chain Reaction.

"So we weren't behind Juan Carlos's death, in case you were wondering," I concluded.

"Yeah, we're not international fugitives or anything like that," Mari called out from behind the partition. I could hear her opening and closing drawers.

"And we helped launch the criminal investigation, by finding the sabotaged bike frame," I added.

"I didn't think you were fugitives," said Santiago. "But I've been following the case in the news. I had to wonder when you were both acting *misteriosas*, since both of you had a personal connection to el Cóndor. Now I understand. *Chuta.*" He had been twirling a pencil around in his fingers while he listened, and suddenly it snapped in two, he'd been gripping it so hard. "You are having a serious problem."

"Now do you believe me? That I'm not just here for clubbing adventures?"

"I do. I believe you." Santiago held my gaze. "You do not wish to go to the police with this?"

"No way," I said. "Darwin's got plants in the police force."

"I agree. There are problems with our police right now, and it is too big a risk," Santiago said. "If people are desperate for cash, they can be persuaded to do all kinds of things."

Or paid to look the other way. Even the military officer at the protest the night I arrived had been easily bribed; Santiago had slipped him a twenty to let us around the blockade. Is that how Darwin's note on Saturday night had arrived at the Ruizes' gate? Had Victor, the night guard, been paid to ignore it?

"The consulate," I said, thinking out loud. "I saw on the State Department website that there's a hotline you can call to report crimes."

"They'll contact the local police anyway," said Santiago. "The embassy does not have jurisdiction."

"Then I'll go straight to the top. Who's the U.S. ambassador?" Excited by my new plan, I stood up and started pacing, thinking out loud. "I'm sure he's in touch with FBI field agents or customs people. They can go after Darwin and then find the links back to Juan Carlos's murder."

Mari popped her head around the side of the bookshelf partition. "His name is Michael Carver. I thought of that already, and I even called to try to get an appointment," she said. "But he's on vacation, in Venezuela this week, watching the PAC Tour. Turns out he's a big cycling fan. He won't be back until the PAC Tour comes to Quito in a couple of days."

My hopes for a speedy resolution shattered.

"But the ambassador knows Preston Lane," Santiago added. "I am sure when he returns he will be willing to talk with us if we tell him that you know Preston personally."

"Wait, how does the ambassador know Preston Lane?" I asked.

"Ambassador Carver knows all the foreigners who do a lot of business with Ecuador," Santiago replied. "The EcuaBar cacao farms are all based in El Oriente, and Preston Lane gives to many charities and nonprofits here. Such as Vuelta. Have you seen the picture of them with my father, in my father's office?"

I shook my head.

"Preston Lane got the ambassador interested in cycling. This is why the ambassador is away now. But I wish you had told me of this spy situation earlier," Santiago said to me quietly when Mari went back to her packing. "I am more than a getahead vehicle. I am deeply interested in what happened to Juan Carlos."

I winced at the mention of how I'd used him for his wheels. "I know. I'm sorry. I didn't mean to keep relying on you to take me places. But why are you so interested?"

"Why?" He looked surprised. "For the same reason everyone in Ecuador is interested. One of our heroes has fallen. But I have a special interest as well. Juan Carlos helped Vuelta become visible internationally. And Preston Lane has donated large sums of money to Vuelta. Now, with his star rider gone, we don't expect donations to continue for long. My father is worried he will go back to struggling to keep the organization continuing. He wants to use Juan Carlos's name to help as long as he can, but if there is something wrong about his death, it is something we need to know."

I gave him a long look. "What's wrong about Juan Carlos's death, Santiago, is that Juan Carlos is dead."

"I know."

"But I'm at the end of the road after tonight. There's nothing more I can do."

Mari emerged from her makeshift bedroom lugging an overstuffed duffel bag. Clearly more than a day's change of clothes.

"I thought you were only staying one night," I said.

"I am. Do you think they'd let me do some laundry at the house?"

"Of course. Got Juan Carlos's flash drive in there, too?" I made a feeble attempt at a joke.

"No! Tessa!"

"Sorry. Just doing my job. Now I can call Darwin tomorrow and report our revealing conversation. I'm sure he'll faint from shock."

Santiago had been tipping back in a chair, but suddenly he brought all legs down with a crash. "There are two choices here, I think," he said. "We look for the information Juan Carlos stole. Or we look for the person he stole it from, the person Darwin is trying to protect. The first choice seems easier, and less dangerous. They are looking for one single flash drive. But don't you think Juan Carlos was smart enough to make extra copies of the information? Or send it to somebody else? Darwin said Juan Carlos talked to a friend in Ecuador. That was before Mari arrived."

"So if Juan Carlos didn't give it to Mari, who else could have it?" I asked.

Mari sank into a kitchen chair. "His best friend. El Ratón. Why didn't we think of that before?"

"Yes!" Santiago thumped the table so hard in his excitement that a pile of take-out containers slid onto the floor. "Why aren't Darwin and his spies bothering that guy?"

"Maybe they are," I said slowly, as a new realization dawned on me. "Darwin said he'd intercepted correspondence between Juan Carlos and a friend here, and that's how he got the idea Mari might have this information. The local friend? I bet you anything it's el Ratón."

Mari sat up straighter. "I bet you're right. And since el Ratón was Juan Carlos's best friend, he's probably sitting on his friend's information, doing all he can to protect him."

"We must find him at the urban downhill race tomorrow," said Santiago. "We'll ask him if Juan Carlos sent him any files, and tell him to give us a copy. I'm sure he'll want to help us finish his best friend's mission."

"But even if we get a copy of the information from el Ratón, we can't just hand it over to Darwin," Mari pointed out. "Right? Otherwise he wins! That's not what Juan Carlos would want."

"Right," agreed Santiago. "So we need to find out what kind of information Juan Carlos was trying to leak. Then, if we agree with his cause, we can finish his work and leak it ourselves. We can give it to the U.S. ambassador when he returns to Quito. If he has hard evidence, the chief of police in Quito will have to take this seriously, as well as the immigration and customs enforcement officials."

"That bike coming in the container's important, too," Mari added. "If the flash drive is so important to Darwin, it might explain where the cash in the bike came from, and link Darwin and whoever Darwin's client is to Juan Carlos's murder. I'm sure there was some reason Juan Carlos was trying to expose both the cash and the flash drive to the media at the same time. We need to follow through on his plan. We need to get both the flash drive and the bike into the U.S. ambassador's hands. Together."

I nodded eagerly. Even though everything we talked about sounded scary, it felt good to have a plan again, to be out of that place of despair. "Juan Carlos was looking for a media person to expose something. But I think we should show it to the authorities who can actually prosecute. Darwin's crimes—cyberstalking, physical stalking, smuggling, maybe murder—these are international crimes. We have to make sure the ambassador is at the container unload on Friday."

"I can send him a special invitation from Vuelta and tell him it's an important cultural exchange," Santiago promised.

"And don't forget, Preston Lane will be at the unloading, too," Mari added. "I think he'll be very interested to see what comes out of that shipping container in four days and what it might show about his top cyclist's death."

Outside, Santiago hailed a taxi, and we all rode back to the Vuelta office to pick up his car. Santiago sat between Mari and me. My head turned to look at Salsoteca Mundial as we passed. There was a longer line at the door now, and the bouncer in the cream suit was gone.

"Too bad Darwin picked that as his hangout," said Mari, following my gaze. "I always thought it looked like a fun place to dance. Is it?" she asked, turning to Santiago.

"What? Oh. I wouldn't know," he said, looking embarrassed.

"You've never been there?" said Mari.

"No." He gave a half smile and scratched his head. "Actually? I do not dance."

"What? Why? I thought all Latin guys danced," said Mari in a teasing voice.

"All but me," he admitted. "I think I have the honor of being the worst dancer in all of Ecuador. Maybe all of South America."

I had a fleeting thought of my red sundress still folded up in my suitcase. In the next moment, I packed that thought away. There would be no dancing for me on this trip—my surreal spin with Pizarro did not count. And I definitely would not be practicing any hot dance moves with Santiago. I felt a twinge of disappointment. Then I packed up that feeling, too.

48

AFTER SANTIAGO dropped us off at the Ruiz house, Mari was instantly welcomed into their home. Amparo and Andreas wanted to hear all about the *chiva*—how it was before we both got sick and had to rush into a café restroom to throw up.

Street vendor food. That was the story the three of us had concocted to explain our disappearance, and to explain why Santiago was bringing us both home.

I hated the idea of lying to the Ruizes—again—but I didn't know what else to do. They were parents. They'd worry. They'd call my mom and dad. Confessing the truth to the Ruizes would only put them at risk and get me in trouble. I might even get sent back home. Then I'd really feel like a failure. Filming for my vlog was now impossible—I'd never see my camera again. Buying a new one, in Quito, was out of the question; my parents had me on a tight budget of spending money, and after all they'd done for me, I didn't dare ask for anything more. Yet I didn't want to lose the chance to solve the mystery of Juan Carlos's death—the one good thing I could still manage to do here. I had to finish this race.

After making us tea, Hugo and Lucia spoke in Spanish with Mari, asking about her cousin and her family's roots in Ecuador. Even Peludo the poodle snuggled up against her, wriggling excitedly. I felt invisible, and exhausted from speaking so much

Spanish. No one seemed to notice when I slunk off to Amparo's room to get ready for bed. They were too busy howling with laughter over Mari's funny stories about Compass Bikes, bonding with the homestay daughter of their dreams.

As laughter floated in from the living room, I went with my laptop to the patio, where the Internet signal seemed strongest, and checked my email. I found another note from Kylie. The subject line was a series of exclamation points.

> Amazing news—I got the Lane Scholarship!!!!!!
>
> Preston Lane actually called me into his office this afternoon to give me the good news personally!
>
> So fast—can you believe it?? He just wrote out a check right then and there and handed it to me.
>
> Senior year is PAID FOR. We're graduating together!!!
>
> Funny thing I thought I'd pass on to you—when he wrote the check, I saw a pamphlet on his desk. For Gamblers Anonymous. It's a group like Alcoholics Anonymous, I think, for people with gambling addiction. I think he saw me notice it and got embarrassed because he moved a Wall Street Journal over it, like to cover it up. Hard to picture someone like him wasting money on gambling—and maybe the pamphlet wasn't even for him. But if it is, do you think it's okay to take the scholarship money? I suddenly got scared that the check might not go through. Ha. Paranoid. I know. Never mind.

> Sarita and I are going out to celebrate! We miss you! Hope you're living it up down there! PS—Sarita wants to know if you've worn The Dress yet???

I couldn't stop smiling. Out of today's many failures, it was great to hear of one success. I wrote back right away to congratulate Kylie. At the same time, I felt strange twinges inside me, like the minor keys on a keyboard. I'd seen kids my age at La Casa with no shoes, or going out to do hard labor instead of going to school, or taking care of babies. I'd seen kids in the street, barely six years old, approaching strangers to shine their shoes. I wanted the best for my friend, of course, and I was thrilled that she'd stay at Shady Pines now. But part of me kept thinking: *How much does it matter?* Just going to public school in our city was a privileged opportunity.

I reread the stuff Kylie had written about the gambling pamphlet. That was so strange. Preston Lane seemed like the last person on earth to have a gambling addiction. He was too careful, too into conservation of resources to waste his money on casinos. Not to mention too busy running his company and the bike team, giving motivational talks, and supporting various good causes. That pamphlet had to be for somebody else, maybe a troubled employee.

Or did it? There was that trip to Vegas the week Juan Carlos had died.

A thought tapped at me, like a scratch on a window screen. Any chance Preston was the person Juan Carlos stole data from? The person Darwin was trying to protect?

I actually laughed out loud. Preston was too protective of his reputation, his company, and his money to risk it all on dealing. And he'd been one of the people to discover Juan

Carlos and help develop him as an athlete. He wouldn't want to kill him off.

But thinking of Preston made me think of his "proud pedal partner." *Chris Fitch.*

I'd dismissed Chris as a suspect before, but he kept haunting me. A lot of questions surrounded him.

I went to the Cadence Bikes website and studied Chris Fitch's picture. He was so not a cyclist type—which was strange for someone who owned a bike company. Those guys were usually former racers, or at least avid cyclists. Someone like Preston Lane seemed more likely to run a business like Cadence.

Next I read Chris's bio. He'd run various sporting equipment companies over the years, and other businesses, too. His brother, a former Olympic athlete, had started Cadence Bikes years ago. When his brother died three years ago in a car crash—a hit-and-run on a routine training route near his home on Boston's North Shore—Chris Fitch took over the company "To honor his legacy," as he put it. "And to keep producing top-notch racing and recreational bikes that my brother would be proud to ride."

They were beautiful bikes. All their models were streamlined and elegant, in classy color combinations. I clicked through the entire gallery. Yet Juan Carlos hadn't wanted to race on a Cadence. And when I searched "Cadence" and "failure," the words I'd heard in Bianca's Slade's interview, I got taken to complaints on bike review sites. Photos of split bike frames. A press release about a product recall from two years ago. Was Juan Carlos concerned about safety? Was there something about faulty products on that flash drive? But if so, what did that have to do with a wad of cash stuffed in a bike?

I reached for my notebook and, as Mari and the Ruiz family

started singing in Spanish in the other room—with Hugo on guitar—I wrote out fresh questions.

1. Chris Fitch had a reputation to protect. His company already suffered from bad publicity. Joining up with the squeaky-clean Team EcuaBar could help turn that around. If champions rode those bikes to victory, consumers would have more confidence in them.
2. Did Juan Carlos find information on Chris's computer that could make his company look bad? Is the "leak" about more bad bikes?
3. Mari said Chris put pressure on Juan Carlos for big wins. Did Chris arrange for Juan Carlos to cheat? Did the flash drive and the bike contain proof of that plan?
4. Could the money in the bike be the cash Chris Fitch was intending to pay to Darwin to keep a secret safe??

The more I thought about it, the darker Chris Fitch began to seem. Maybe Chris had information worth paying someone like Darwin to protect. Could Chris sabotage a bike to fail catastrophically? Sure. Juan Carlos had crashed on a Cadence, and Chris would know exactly where the bike could be vulnerable.

Chris had been near the team trailer, too, at the photo shoot. He could have gained access to the bikes when Dylan stepped out. Maybe something had been caught on film, even indirectly, to link Chris to Juan Carlos's sabotaged bike.

Amber. She must have taken lots of pre-race photos. Since

Dylan was innocent, according to Darwin, maybe I could lean on her for some help.

I looked up Amber online and got her bike sculpture and photography website. Using a new email account I created with a fake name—so Darwin couldn't track me—I dashed off a quick email to her. I told her who I was and apologized for going undercover at the Open Road school. Then I explained what I'd leaked so far to help launch the criminal investigation and that I had a good lead here, a chance to clear Dylan's name. I asked if she had any pictures of pre-race photos, like candid shots of the team, and if I might be able to see those. I hit SEND before I could chicken out. She probably would not reply. I hadn't exactly made a great first impression, lying to her at Open Road. But it was worth a shot.

I sat cross-legged on the cool tile floor, a blanket draped around me, while the washing machine rattled and churned, working on Mari's huge bag of laundry. I waited for Mari to come through the patio on her way to the former maid's room, where she was staying. I wanted to see what she thought of my new theory about Chris Fitch as a suspect. But the chatter in the living room showed no signs of letting up, so I gave up and went to bed. I lay awake for a long time, sliding Juan Carlos's crucifix along its chain, and thinking, thinking, thinking.

49

THE NEXT morning, I went to La Casa for my teaching shift with a heavy heart. I pushed Gertrude the Bike to the corner, dragging my feet, tripping over the broken sidewalk as I hailed a taxi. I threw the beater bike in the trunk of the cab that pulled up, without even looking behind me to see if any Vuelta volunteers were watching from the window. I didn't care. I had too much on my mind. Like the fact that I had to call in some kind of report to Darwin today, to make him think I was questioning Mari. And the fact that unless we got the information Juan Carlos was trying to leak, and the bike in the shipping container, we had no story to tell the authorities, because my camera was gone.

I mourned that video camera as much as the loss of Darwin's incriminating testimony. The camera hadn't been cheap. I'd paid for it all myself, from babysitting and birthday money. And now I couldn't even film stuff for Vuelta. During the taxi ride I concocted a whole story I could tell my parents. I was mugged—maybe a drive-by deal—and my bag with the camera was stolen. Knowing how important this vlog was for salvaging my reputation, maybe they would spring for another, or wire me money to buy one here. Then I erased the story in my mind. If my parents thought I'd been mugged, they'd probably freak out and make me come home. Besides, hadn't I already told enough lies?

At La Casa, I paid the driver, who got out and took the beater bike out of his trunk.

"Gracias," I said, and turned around to find six of the girls at La Casa staring at me.

"You pay a taxi to take your bicycle here?" Rosio asked in Spanish, a puzzled look on her face. "That's so expensive."

"Bad knee," I said, pointing at my right knee with a grimace. "I started to ride—that's why I have the bike with me—but I couldn't finish."

I lost myself in lessons for the next three hours, grateful for the happy distraction. Many of the girls were moving on to basic pedaling today, following the chalk line I now drew on the sidewalk. Some of them wobbled. Three fell. But not Rosio. Her eyes blazing, her jaw set, she never wavered on that line—or in her resolve to ride.

I admired that. Even if I couldn't hop on a bike as fearlessly as Rosio, I could muster up that same determination in seeking justice for Juan Carlos.

After class, Rosio walked me to the corner to wait with me while I hailed a cab. I complimented her on her quick progress. Her whole face lit up. "I like your classes," she said shyly, in Spanish. "You are a different kind of teacher. You don't show us everything. You expect us to figure out things for ourselves."

I looked away. *Because I'm covering up my fear of riding again,* I thought to myself. Suddenly self-conscious, I rummaged in my backpack and handed her a couple of EcuaBars I'd taken from the Vuelta vending machine. "Try eating one of these before the next class," I suggested, in Spanish. "I noticed you running out of energy near the end. This will help."

"EcuaBars!" she exclaimed in delight. "I love these."

"You've tried them?"

"My mother came home with a box of these once. She cleans rooms in Hotel d'Oro, the hotel where Señor Lane stays."

I stared at her. "Does your mom know him or something?"

"He gave these to her as part of a tip. He is a strange man, my mother says, but it does not matter to me. EcuaBars are the best."

"Why does your mom think he is strange?"

Rosio carefully opened an EcuaBar and nibbled a corner of chocolate. "One time, she came into his hotel room while he was in there. He forgot to hang up the privacy sign. She saw him taking apart a bike, on the floor of the hotel room. He yelled at her to get out, and frightened her. Later, he apologized and gave her a case of EcuaBars and an apology note."

I frowned. Preston always seemed laid-back. That kind of knee-jerk reaction, followed by an extravagant apology, sounded more like something that moody Jake would do. "What was he doing with the bike? What didn't he want your mom to see?"

"We don't know. My mother said it seemed he was taking things out of it," said Rosio.

"Taking things out of it? Are you sure? Like what?"

"My mother wasn't sure exactly what he was doing. She couldn't see well. And when she came back to clean the room later, nothing about it seemed unusual."

It sounded pretty unusual to me, given that we now knew there was cash hidden in Juan Carlos's bike. I said a hurried good-bye to Rosio and ran around the corner to hail the first taxi I saw.

I RAN into Mari's classroom as soon as I got back to the Vuelta office. "I have to talk to you," I whispered, ignoring the curious stares of her students.

We ducked out of the room, and I told her what Rosio had said.

"Preston Lane might have put money in his own bike!" I concluded.

Mari stared, then shook her head. "He was probably just fixing it. Juan Carlos said he went riding here every time he was in town. And just because there's some money in Juan Carlos's spare bike doesn't mean Preston has money in his. Besides, this is all circumstantial evidence. Rosio's mom didn't even see anything specific."

I admit, it stung that Mari didn't buy into my theory. "But why would he freak out on Rosio's mom like that? And then give her a gift? Don't you think he had something to hide?"

Mari shrugged. "Powerful men have a lot to hide. I just can't picture a wealthy guy like Preston running around with cash in a bike like some money mule. He has bank accounts and business operatives here, and I'm sure a big fat money belt when he travels. Maybe he had a woman in his room, someone he didn't want to be connected to publicly. Juan Carlos said he's a bit of a ladies' man." She grinned. "I bet Rosio's mom made up part of the story to explain all those EcuaBars to her daughter."

"Are you suggesting that Preston was hooking up with the hotel maid? Rosio's mom? And that's why he lavished her with EcuaBars?"

"Why not?"

I thought of Rosio's mother, so beautiful, with that long black hair and high cheekbones. Yes, why not? That theory made more sense than Preston hiding drug money in his own bike, and then taking it out in a fancy hotel room. Besides, Preston cared about Juan Carlos. He'd helped to launch his career. He'd arranged for him to develop as a cyclist and finish his education in the U.S. A cash payout to Darwin from Chris Fitch—somehow intercepted by Juan Carlos along with Chris's flash drive—still seemed like the likeliest theory of all.

"I've got to get back to class," Mari said, glancing at her students. "We can talk more at lunch. Lucia packed us some of those *higos con queso* she served us last night. Did I tell you she'll teach me her recipe, if I want to stay another night?"

"Do you?" I fought back a jealous wave. I'd gushed about the figs and cheese dish, too, but Lucia hadn't offered to teach me to cook it.

"Yeah, maybe. It is pretty comfortable there. Another night in a real house probably wouldn't kill me. I feel really safe there. You know?"

"Sure," I said as I turned to go. But the truth was, I didn't feel safe anywhere at all.

WILSON KEPT me busy with marketing outreach again all afternoon. I watched the clock on the wall with a sinking feeling, as the hours and then the minutes ticked by. Finally my appointed check-in time with Darwin rolled around, and I still didn't have a bogus story I could give him to make him think I was working for him. But I didn't dare not call him. I didn't want him to come looking for me. Jake had said I couldn't say words that weren't scripted for me. But I'd have to go way off script on this phone call. I'd have to totally wing it.

I left the office and walked to the small corner *tienda* with a pay phone down the street. The dance party flyer was creased and worn from being carried in my pocket and my sweaty palms, but I could still read the number. I dialed it now.

"I have been awaiting your call." Darwin's acid voice on the phone made my skin crawl. "You made a huge misstep at the dance club smuggling that video camera. I think you're due for another lesson about trying to mess with me."

"No, please don't. Please don't do anything to my parents."

"Then this is your chance to make up for it. I hope you have good news for me?"

I took a deep breath. "I've been talking to Mari. But I need more time. I can't just start interrogating her or I'll scare her off. Like you did. That's a big part of investigative journalism, you know. Getting your sources to trust you."

There was silence for a long moment, and the sound of Darwin breathing. I waited for him to explode at me.

"How much time are we talking?" he asked.

"I can't say for sure. At least a couple of days." I could feel my voice getting stronger. "But you know what? If I have to keep checking in with you like this, it's only going to take longer. I had to leave Mari to go make this call. I could have been finding out something right now, but no, I'm here on a pay phone, talking to you. You're right, I'm a good interviewer, and you hired me because you think I can get information out of Mari that you guys couldn't. But you have to let me do my job in my own way."

"Fine. I'll make you a deal," said Darwin. "I'll give you some space. But just for a couple of days. I'm expecting a check-in on Friday. That should be plenty of time to get your gabbing out of the way and find out what you need to find out. And that's final. No more negotiations."

"Great. Thanks. I won't let you down." I ended the call and let out a long breath. Friday. I'd bought myself a little more time and avoided the daily check-ins. I just hoped he'd keep his word and give me some space. I wanted him and his crew far from tomorrow's urban downhill race. I needed to be free to talk to el Ratón without eavesdropping spies.

50

THE NEXT day, Wednesday, Vuelta closed down early so that everyone could go see el Ratón's last urban downhill race. To my relief, Wilson suggested we not take bikes there, since the crowds of spectators would be too thick. So five of us piled into Santiago's Pathfinder, and the others took taxis. As Santiago sped down Amazonas toward Old Town, and some of the volunteers in the backseat placed bets on who would win, he turned to me with an encouraging smile. "Nervous?" he whispered.

"A little," I admitted. "I'm not sure about our plan. I mean, there's no guarantee el Ratón will want to speak with me." Santiago, Mari, and I had come up with an idea on an after-work stroll through a park yesterday. In my backpack, I now had Vuelta's own video camera, which Santiago had surprised me with after I came back from making that call to Darwin. Mari and I would pretend to interview el Ratón for a TV show back in the States. Our cover story to gain access to him from his handlers would give us a precious few minutes to find out what he knew about Juan Carlos's flash drive . . . and about who might have wanted Juan Carlos dead.

"Who wouldn't want to speak with you?" Santiago said. He sounded genuinely surprised that I would ask this question. He let his eyes rest on me a moment longer than he needed to, then looked back at the road ahead.

My face warmed. I looked away.

We came into the Old Town, and I gazed out the window. Pedestrians flattened themselves against the walls when the buses and cars, including ours, hurtled past them. We passed a grand plaza with a fountain, and beautiful churches that made me think of gold-studded jewelry boxes.

I wished I could just be a normal tourist. Or a normal Vuelta volunteer, talking about weekend exploits and adventures like Emma and Aussie Guy. Or even just a normal bike teacher. My classes the past two mornings at La Casa had gone great, especially this morning's class. Today Rosio had actually gone around the block all by herself. Even the smallest girl had managed to ride and pedal a few yards on the Barbie bike without my holding on to the seat.

Santiago found a parking spot on a side street. We got out and hurried to join the crowds of spectators who were swarming into the area.

Merengue music pulsed from speakers. Onlookers ate street vendor food and talked excitedly. The plaza was surrounded by cobblestoned streets and alleys and staircases marching up steep hills. Some of the staircases had boards stretched across them. Wooden planks extended from rooftop to rooftop, resembling makeshift bridges.

In the next instant, a cheer rose up from the crowd.

A downhill rider dressed in neon yellow came clattering down the hillside on a modified mountain bike with fat tires. He rode down the steps. Down stair railings. Across the planks. He bounced across rooftops, careened around corners, and squeezed through alleys between tall buildings. All at breakneck speed.

The cyclist zoomed right by us, hopping the bike over a fence, crossing a wooden plank suspended between buildings, and continuing down a stone staircase. “How did he do that?” I exclaimed, suddenly forgetting my entire mission.

“Exciting, isn’t it? Practice,” said Santiago, grinning. “Sometimes people start this when they’re kids, in the hill neighborhoods. The best of them get discovered. Like el Ratón.”

I shielded my eyes from the sun and scanned the surrounding hilly streets. “Is he up there somewhere? Where do we find him?” I whispered so Emma and Aussie Guy wouldn’t hear.

“I’ll take care of our friends,” Santiago said in a low voice. “You and Mari start walking up the hill. There is the starting gate.” He pointed. I could see a rider in a blue jumpsuit up there, adjusting a helmet. Awaiting his turn. “They race one at a time, not all together. It is a time trial race, like skiing. El Ratón is the big finish—all these people are here to see him—so he will go last. I’ll leave our friends in a few minutes and follow you partway, and keep the eye in.”

“Keep an eye out,” I corrected. “And thank you!”

“*De nada*. Good luck up there! I believe in you!” He gave me a thumbs-up sign and a grin so wide I noticed, for the first time, dimples.

I caught up to Mari, who had already started sprinting up the staircases on a side street.

“There he is,” she said, pointing to a small figure on top of the hill.

He looked just like he did in the poster, wearing a red jumpsuit and helmet. His handlers, a group of three men in identical red jackets, waved us away as we approached. “He will sign autographs at the bottom, after his descent,” one man explained to us in Spanish. “Right now, el Ratón needs to focus completely.”

“I’m with a TV show in the U.S.,” I explained, also in Spanish. “I would like to interview him, very briefly, before his ride.” I tipped my head and flashed him my most winning *KidVision* smile.

"Who is this?" he asked, frowning at Mari now.

"My assistant."

He studied both of us warily, then consulted with another handler standing nearby. Finally he nodded. "Okay. Five minutes only." He introduced us to el Ratón, who was standing with his back to us, doing some leg stretches. The handler then walked a few feet away to smoke a cigarette with his team.

"This show, it is real, yes?" el Ratón asked in halting English, looking uncertainly at the ten-year-old camcorder that Mari had slung over her shoulder. He sounded not nearly as fluent as Juan Carlos. He also sounded suspicious of us. Of me.

"Of course it is real," said Mari, in Spanish. She began fussing over me as if readying me for the camera, fluffing my hair and wiping an imaginary lipstick smear off my cheek.

"It's real," I echoed in English. *I'm just not on it anymore. I'm the one who's not real.*

I stared at el Ratón, taking in his narrow eyes, his long nose. He took off his helmet and scratched at his head. His large ears, I noticed, stuck out like a mouse's. I doubted I'd be seeing him on an EcuaBar billboard. But I stared at him, memorizing him, because he was a link to Juan Carlos. I could imagine these two talking, hanging out, riding bikes together in those lush green hills. I could imagine, for an instant, Juan Carlos alive.

I glanced at the handlers. They were all lighting up cigarettes now, talking among themselves. One of them looked vaguely familiar, but I couldn't place where I'd seen him. Maybe in something I'd seen about el Ratón or el Cóndor online. I didn't have time to waste figuring that out now.

"We knew your friend Juan Carlos," I said in a low voice to el Ratón.

"What?" He exclaimed. Then he narrowed his eyes at me. "What did you say your name was?"

"Tessa. Tessa Taylor, from *KidVision*. And this is Mari Vargas, from Compass Bikes."

El Ratón took a step back. "What is this about?" He glanced at his handlers, as if to signal to them to escort us away.

"No. Please don't. This is important," I said in Spanish. "Juan Carlos wanted to give me a flash drive a couple of weeks ago, after a race in Massachusetts. But I never got the flash drive. Now some scary people are looking for it. Did Juan Carlos ever email you some files? Or send you a flash drive in the mail?"

El Ratón looked startled. Then pained. "Juan Carlos was like my brother," he said, putting one hand to his heart. "I do not talk about this subject, his death. It is extremely difficult for me. I would like you to leave."

I froze. I hadn't expected that response. No one in all my five years at *KidVision* had ever reacted so negatively to me as an interviewer.

I wouldn't quit, though. "Isn't it more painful not knowing exactly why he died?" I said as he turned his back to us to resume his stretching exercises.

He stopped mid-stretch.

"If you can share any information, it will help us figure out what really happened at Chain Reaction," I persisted.

"Turn the camera off," he commanded.

Mari looked at me questioningly, and I nodded, remembering Bianca Slade's advice about protecting your sources. She sighed and did as he asked.

"Did he call you that morning and tell you I was the media contact he'd chosen?" I asked.

El Ratón hesitated. Without looking at me he nodded, barely, once.

"We need the information Juan Carlos was hoping to share with the media," I said, talking faster. "And we need it now. Did Juan Carlos send you a copy of anything? A hard copy or a digital file?"

"No, but he told me what the flash drive contained," said el Ratón. His eyes flicked to the handlers. "But this is not a safe situation here. Please. You must go. Immediately."

The handlers were walking toward us now, and the MC was announcing the next rider, now in position at the top of the hill. My eyes widened as I realized where I'd seen one of the handlers.

He was the bouncer at Salsoteca Mundial. The man in the Panama hat. He was wearing it now.

I could hardly breathe. Rage filled me. Darwin had promised to give me some space, but obviously he didn't trust me. I was so close to finding out what information Juan Carlos wanted to leak, and yet I was still being monitored.

Or maybe *el Ratón* was being monitored. My eyes flicked from the handler to the cyclist, noticing a look pass between them.

Mari nudged me and pulled me aside. "That guy in the Panama hat. He looks familiar. He was at the nightclub, right?" she whispered.

I nodded. "He works for Darwin."

"I'll go distract him," she muttered. "You talk."

"Mari, wait! No!"

Too late. Mari went sauntering up to the bouncer/handler in the Panama hat, with a twitch in her hips and a toss of her hair—totally unlike herself—and started talking to him. I couldn't hear what she was saying, but he looked both annoyed and confused.

"I need to know about that flash drive," I said to el Ratón. "I want to help your friend. What was he trying to expose?"

"I cannot tell you that." He raised his hands above his head and stretched out his shoulders.

"Why not?" I demanded.

He bent over in a forward stretch, touching his toes. "Because I cannot take the risk," he whispered on an exhale. "I told him not to do it, not to throw away his career because of this. Nothing is going to change because of what one guy on a bike happens to say. I wish that Juan Carlos had listened to me."

I touched my toes, too, so we'd be at the same level. "Please. We need your help. Some guys think Mari and I have the information, and we don't. And we think the information might help explain his death."

El Ratón stood up so fast I could feel a breeze. I stood up, too. When he faced me again, he looked fearful. "It is not safe for me to have this information," he whispered. "It is not safe for you to have it. It was not safe for Juan Carlos to have it, and you know what happened to him. Now go."

The handler from the nightclub brushed past Mari, striding toward me now and tapping his watch. "*¡Oye!* El Ratón is about to race. He needs to prepare himself mentally. This interview must end," he said brusquely.

"Thank you for interviewing me. Good-bye," el Ratón said curtly.

The handlers moved in close to separate us from el Ratón, and two of them escorted Mari and me back to the staircase that led down the hill. The man from the nightclub gave me a little push when we got to the staircase, throwing off my balance. I clutched the railing and caught myself from falling.

I wanted to scream. To punch and kick someone, or something. Why wasn't el Ratón talking? Why was he so quiet and sullen? Then I remembered one more thing I wanted to ask. I might never get another chance. Maybe he'd talk about this one thing that might shed light—or dark—on Juan Carlos's past. I broke free of the handler and jogged back to el Ratón.

"Hey. How'd Juan Carlos get that scar on his neck? Was he in a fight with someone?" I pictured Pizarro's gleaming knife, his razor-sharp smile. Maybe they'd had an encounter before.

I expected el Ratón to ignore me, but he turned around. "The scar? Window factory."

"Where his father works?"

He nodded. "Juan Carlos spent time there, when he was a boy after his mother died and there was nobody to watch him at home. One day a big windowpane fell off the factory line and broke right beside him. A shard of glass pierced his neck. It was years ago, but the hospital stitched it up badly, and he never got over that. I am sure if that happened in your country, the scar would be invisible by now." He smiled, wistful. "But I always told him the scar made him look tough. It is probably why people left him alone. They assumed he was a fighter, and not a guy you should mess with. For skinny bike-riding guys like us, a scar is not such a bad thing."

"Come to the U.S. embassy with us," I whispered. "Speak up. For the sake of your friend."

"I'm sorry," said el Ratón in a low voice. "I wish I could help. But I made my choice. My family depends on me."

His handlers closed in again—the nightclub bouncer guy casting me a look of disgust—and they led him away.

I made my choice. My family depends on me. What did he mean?

"Great job distracting Mr. Panama Hat. What did you talk to him about?" I asked Mari as we jogged down the hill to meet Santiago and the others.

Mari smiled mysteriously. "I just tried to act like a starstruck fan of el Ratón and asked him to set us up on a date."

"No way! That's so not you!"

She looked a little hurt. "I have some feminine wiles. They're just a little rusty."

"I'm sorry. Of course. What'd he say?"

"Nothing. I wouldn't let him get a word in. I just kept on talking so you could talk, until he swatted me aside like a fly. But at least it bought you some time, right?"

"It did. Thanks. I just wish el Ratón was as talkative as you were."

"Success?" Santiago whispered with an anxious look when we rejoined them at a lookout point halfway down the hill.

I shook my head. "El Ratón knows what Juan Carlos had on that flash drive," I informed both him and Mari. "Juan Carlos told him what it was all about. But el Ratón's not going to talk. He seems really scared of something."

"Or someone," Mari said darkly.

An MC speaking into a microphone introduced el Ratón, trilling the *r*, drawing the name out long.

El Ratón, a small red dot atop the hill, raised his arms in greeting.

Then he placed his hands on the handlebars and began his descent with a dazzling leap that sent his tires spinning. The sun caught the spokes and made them gleam.

The crowds cheered as el Ratón slipped into tight spaces. He darted. He dodged. He skittered and slid.

"A new victory for el Ratón! He has completed the course with record-breaking time on his death-defying descent!" the MC shouted in Spanish, as the crowd went wild. "We hope this is the start of many more victories to come, as he turns to road racing and leads Equipo Diablo!"

Loud merengue music pulsed through the speakers. The cloud went wild as el Ratón took a victory lap around the Plaza de la Independencia, pumping his fists in the air, then holding his arms up in a V as he pedaled, just like his friend Juan Carlos used to do.

Mari, Santiago, and I were the only people in the crowd not cheering or clapping. We watched his victory laps in morose silence. His victory was our failure. El Ratón wasn't talking about that flash drive, that was clear. Unless we found it ourselves, Darwin was going to start the wrecking ball on my family members' lives. And we'd never be able to finish Juan Carlos's job.

51

MARI STAYED another night with my host family, even though her laundry had finished. We all talked about the urban downhill race at dinner with them, marveling at el Ratón's record-breaking time and his heart-pumping, thrill-a-minute downhill ride. But when the conversation unexpectedly changed to religion, I shifted uncomfortably in my seat. The Ruizes were curious about my religious background—which was fairly nonexistent. We were talking in Spanish—part of the homestay experience, to improve my language skills—but it was exhausting to explain my school's Quaker values, and the history of the Quaker people, in another language.

"And yet you wear the crucifix," said Lucia, pointing at my chest. I'd taken off my usual necklace-concealing cotton scarf. "Surely this is not just for fashion?"

"Not just fashion," I admitted, my hand instinctively reaching up to cover the crucifix. "It was a gift. From a friend."

"Your boyfriend?" Amparo asked, wide-eyed and curious.

I felt Mari's eyes on me. "No," I said. "Just a friend."

As usual, the after-dinner Spanish went into warp speed. My head began to throb. I just wanted to crawl away. Besides, the Ruizes all seemed more interested in Mari and her family background, trying to understand where her various cousins had grown up in Ecuador and why they had moved to the States.

I retreated to the patio to brainstorm new fake reports to stave off Darwin. I'd just started listing some on my computer when Mari's figure suddenly appeared in the doorway, hands on her hips.

Her eyes traveled to just below my collarbone. "Tell me about that necklace," she said.

I looked down. The moonlight bathing the patio made the gold—or gold paint—on Juan Carlos's necklace gleam.

"I wear it all the time. I usually tuck it under a shirt or a scarf, here in Ecuador. Since it's gold. I don't want to be a target for muggers. Being a target for international spies is enough. Right?" I laughed.

Mari didn't. She knelt down beside me, frowning, and held the crucifix part in her hand. "Was this from Juan Carlos?" she demanded. "Did he give this to you?"

Her tone—a mix of hurt and angry—caught me off guard. "Uh, yeah. He did."

"When?"

"Right before the Chain Reaction race. He said to take care of it for him."

"Why didn't you tell me?"

"Honestly? I didn't see what it had to do with the case. I thought it was sentimental."

"It *was* sentimental. And it was supposed to be mine."

"What?"

"He tried to give this to me when he came to see me at the shop, the day before the race. I told him it always brought him luck, and I was afraid to take it. He said it wasn't the necklace he usually wears, it was new, and it was heavier than USA Cycling rules would allow. I told him to wear it anyway, that he needed all the help from God he could get at Chain Reaction."

"Look, I'm sorry he changed his mind. But he gave it to me, for safekeeping." And he'd guided me to stand behind a tree while he put it on me. As if he hadn't wanted to be seen.

As if he knew people were looking for him.

"Let me at least wear it tonight," said Mari, pulling at it a little.

"Ouch. You're pulling too hard."

SNAP.

"Oh my God," said Mari, as she looked down at the piece of the cross now separated from the rest of it, pinched between her thumb and forefinger, with a small black chip sticking out of the gold.

A flash drive.

52

THE MOMENTS dragged on as Mari and I sat in the moonlit patio in stunned silence, each of us staring at the piece of the cross we held. I had most of it—with the entire figure of Jesus—and Mari held the bottom quarter inch, the base with a USB port nested inside.

I heard a whooshing sound in my ears. The "valuable information" Juan Carlos wanted to leak had been right under my nose the whole time. Literally!

Darwin and his crew hadn't even noticed the necklace. Or if they had, they must not have figured out that the crucifix was actually an elaborate storage case for the flash drive.

"This has to be the data Darwin's looking for!" I exclaimed. "Juan Carlos must have wanted to show me what's on it after he finished the race. That's why he asked me if I had a laptop."

Mari handed me the drive. "Let's see what we've got here."

I plugged the drive into the USB port on my laptop.

A folder appeared, labeled BELIZE VACATION PICS.

Mari's face fell. "Vacation pictures?" She shook her head in disbelief. "Is that it? Must have been some vacation, if Juan Carlos had to carry those pictures around his neck. I can't think when he would have gone to Belize, though. I mean, there's no bike event there."

I kept staring at that label. "Juan Carlos didn't go to Belize,"

I said. "And Darwin said Juan Carlos stole his client's information. Whoever is in these vacation pictures should be Darwin's client."

"Oh, that's right!" Mari said.

"Unless, of course," I added, "these aren't really vacation pictures."

"What do you mean?"

"People can deliberately mislabel their files and folders. My dad does that for his clients."

"What are you waiting for? Open this up!" Mari urged.

I clicked on the folder.

I was right. There were no JPEGs, no photos. Just a list of files labeled SX CORRESPONDENCE BACKUP, and ranges of dates between March and May.

"SX correspondence? Is that what it sounds like?" said Mari, wide-eyed. "Do you think Juan Carlos was going to expose some kind of sex scandal? Not something about drugs?"

"I don't know." Cringing, I opened one dated from March, the first on the list.

Mari read over my shoulder. "This is to Gage!" she exclaimed.

> To: GageWeston@yazoo.com
> Subject: Moving On
>
> Gage,
>
> Just wanted to follow up on our discussion from last week. Thanks for taking the time to meet and to consider the offer. Sounds like you've made up your mind. It's too bad—I think you're missing out on the opportunity of a lifetime. You could secure

a good future for your wife and your kids. But it's your choice. I respect your decision. I wish you the best of luck with the bike shop. Thanks for all your hard work with the team. I'll have my agent personally deliver the cash for your severance pay, and for your discretion, which I'll appreciate in this matter for the protection of all involved.

Best,
Preston

Mari and I looked at each other. I clicked through a few more emails in that file to confirm my suspicion. They were backups of emails Preston had sent or received from various people—names I didn't recognize—about company meetings and promotional schedules.

"Preston Lane," Mari breathed. "You were starting to get suspicious about him the other day. With that bike in the hotel room stuff you heard about. I laughed it off, but now I think you were right. I don't know if he was hiding cash in his own bike—that still seems weird—but he's definitely hiding something."

I was trembling with excitement. Or fear. "I think Preston is Darwin's client!"

Mari nodded. "He has a reputation to protect."

"And he'd have the funds to hire someone like Darwin to protect him."

"And he probably had the means to pay someone to kill off his star cyclist," Mari added, "to stop Juan Carlos from exposing him, costing him millions of dollars, and landing him in prison for twenty years. Tessa. Do you think Preston Lane was involved with a drug cartel? He's such a socially conscious guy. It's so hard to imagine."

"Whatever he was up to, it had to be so bad that he'd kill his star cyclist—or have someone else do it—in order to stop Juan Carlos from spilling his secret."

We let that sink in for a moment. "So why was he emailing Gage Weston?" I wondered aloud.

Mari toggled back to the first email and reread it. "He's offering him severance pay in cash? That sounds fishy to me. When my mom lost her job a few years ago, she got severance pay, but they cut her a check. A company doesn't send a representative to give a laid-off employee a wad of cash."

"And the money's also for his 'discretion,'" I added, reading over her shoulder. "That almost sounds like hush money. Like being paid to keep a secret. Anyway, I thought you said Gage got fired because he spoke out about carbon fiber bikes and Cadence."

"That's what he told us mechanics at the shop," said Mari. "But this email makes it sound like he got approached about some kind of business deal and turned it down."

"Drugs are a business."

"So's sex." Mari pointed to the screen. "What's SX stand for, do you think? Sounds shady to me."

I frowned. "SX" did sound shady. But it also reminded me of something I'd seen lately, on Santiago's computer screen, and also on Gage Weston's back at Compass Bikes. That black screen with team names. *Sports Xplor.* Maybe that's what SX stood for! I typed "Sports Xplor" into a search engine, but all I got was a message that said the page could not be found.

I told Mari what I was looking for. "It was this weird black screen. With fruit on it. And team names. Cycling teams, in a list, and race dates, and stats. But now it's not coming up. Maybe it's defunct and they pulled it off the Internet."

"Or maybe it's a secret company," said Mari, who had resumed scrolling through March emails. "A side business for Preston. The fruit thing you mentioned makes me think of gambling."

Gambling. I suddenly remembered the email I'd gotten from Kylie. The Gamblers Anonymous pamphlet in Preston's office. I grabbed Mari's arm. "Could Preston Lane actually have a gambling problem?" I asked. "Maybe he was trying to get Gage, and others, into some kind of gambling scheme!"

Mari nodded. "I remember Juan Carlos saying something about Preston going to Vegas a lot. For meetings, but also to the casinos."

"And at the container load, when he came by Compass Bikes, I heard him say he'd just come back from Vegas," I added. I tried again, repeatedly, to get to the Sports Xplor website, even trying out different spellings in the search engine.

"Why do people kill other people, anyway?" Mari wondered aloud as I pounded the keyboard, desperate for some code or magic password that would get me back to that weird-looking website. "I mean, how far would he need to go to protect this secret?"

I shrugged. "Bianca Slade once said on her show, murders happen because of love, money, or secrets. I think Preston has got two out of three. A secret about how he spends his money."

"Yeah, but lots of people gamble, Tessa," said Mari. "It's not a crime to go to Vegas. And we don't know exactly what he was doing on those Vegas trips. We don't have hard evidence he was gambling. And so what if he was? He wouldn't face two decades in prison for that, or need to pay Darwin's group to protect him. There's got to be more to it. Let's see what else is in here."

I gave up on getting into Sports Xplor for now. We went back to the main folder and clicked on April. The first email in this folder was also from someone I knew of. Coach Tony Mancuso of Team EcuaBar.

To: Tony Mancuso@hotspot.com
Subject: SX link/password

Hey Tony—

We're fully operational! Here's the URL for the site, and this week's password. Just call the phone number on the site when you're ready to place your bet. Most of the big wins right now will be in the basketball games. Looking forward to getting the cycling up and running, and seeing numbers that rival the NBA bets!

https://sportsxplor.net/linkshare
Password: PAPAYAS

Good luck!
Preston

Mari gasped. "This means Preston Lane *is* a gambler—a secret sports gambler!" Mari exclaimed. "And the head coach of Team EcuaBar is, too! Sports Xplor must be a gambling website."

I clapped my hands to my mouth. More gears clicked into place in my mind. "Balboa. Pizarro. Those are names of explorers," I said. "They're in on it, too. And Darwin was sort of an explorer, too. Intellectually. He did research in Ecuador for his survival-of-the-fittest theory. Natural selection."

"Right. Those code names don't just connect them to South

America," said Mari. "They connect them to this organization. The names are all part of their operation."

"But sports gambling isn't illegal, is it?" I asked. "I know guys who play fantasy sports all the time. Online, even. You can do that when you're eighteen." A lot of Jake's friends had been into that, and Jake himself had won a cool sixty bucks on a fantasy baseball game, which went toward our prom expenses.

"That's *fantasy* sports. That's different," said Mari. "Fantasy sports are okay because they require a skill. Not chance. You have to create your ideal teams based on what you know about the individual players. My gambling addict uncle told me how all that works. Plus, people make private bets with their friends about sports teams, all the time. But we're talking about operating a sports betting scheme. That's illegal, except in a few places like Las Vegas."

"What about online sites? Like Sports Xplor?"

"There are lots of them," said Mari, "but they're based in other countries. And U.S. citizens technically can't place bets through them. It's a gray area."

"Other countries? Like maybe Ecuador?"

"Maybe," she said. "I'm sure there are rules about that here, too, but it's harder to track where money goes if the gambling ring is outside the U.S. Sometimes the servers and management are based in several different countries, I think. But what does he mean by 'getting the cycling up and running'? People don't bet on cycling. It's a niche sport."

"No, I think they *do* bet on cycling!" I said, remembering something else that had been on the Sports Xplor screen when I'd seen it before: a list of all the major pro and high-level amateur cycling events of the season. Different quantities of fruit followed each listed item. Almost like the star rating system for movies. "Maybe this is all part of Preston's famous entrepreneurial spirit." I clicked on the link in the email, and it took me to that black screen with the clip-art style fruit icons dancing and blinking.

Mari scrolled down the page, and I read over her shoulder.

WELCOME TO SPORTS XPLOR!

YOUR BEST CHOICE FOR THE ADVENTURE OF SPORTS BETTING!

WE ARE THE BIGGEST ONLINE BETTING SITE INTERNATIONALLY.

ADDING NEW SPORTS AND TEAMS EVERY WEEK.

DON'T BE THE ODD MAN OUT.
PAY TO PLAY, PLAY TO WIN!

PASSWORD:
_ _ _ _ _ _ _ _ _ _ _ _ _ _ _ ?

The question mark blinked urgently. I typed in *Papayas.*

Incorrect password.

I typed *mangoes.* Denied again.

Mari took over, typing every fruit we could think of, in both Spanish and English. *Tomatillos. Naranjas. Bananas. Borojo*—that last one was from Mari; I'd never heard of it before, though she swore it was a real fruit from Ecuador's Amazon Basin. *Borojo* got us nowhere, too. And then we got a warning message about too many incorrect password attempts.

"We're wasting time," said Mari. "We have enough information to incriminate Preston without needing to access the

Sports Xplor site. Let's see what else is on the drive."

My stomach churned as I clicked on the next item. Jake hadn't been who I thought he was. And now Preston, too, had this other, darker side. And his money funded good things! Like Vuelta. Like Shady Pines. Like the life-changing scholarship Kylie had gotten. All of that money seemed rotten now. It wasn't that gambling itself was so awful. What bugged me was that all of this was so secret. Layers of passwords. Layers of lies. Beneath his public persona, the real Preston Lane was a very different man.

The next email we pounced on, in the midst of more general business correspondence, was from Preston to Coach Tony Mancuso, again in April.

> Tony—the PAC Tour, our biggest event to date, will be here before we know it. Are you on board with the strategic plan? We need to start building the narrative now. I know you're concerned about potential impact on our home team, and it's hard to take some losses when we've been on such a streak. But most of the bets for the devil riders will come from Latin America. People love an underdog team, and our regional market research shows overwhelming support in that direction. Also, Tony, you can't just look at the race stats alone. Betting is about psychology too, and where statistics and emotions intersect.
>
> I understand it's discouraging to see our planned Chain Reaction loss, and the eventual series of PAC losses, but you have to reframe it as part of the larger story. A temporary setback. We'll come

back fighting at U.S. Nationals, when players here want their turn to cheer for the home team.

The big takeaway from last week's meeting in Vegas is that we need to be laying the groundwork now for the end-of-season comeback after the "setbacks" on the PAC Tour. Find out which U.S. cyclists and coaches are looking for cash and willing to deal in the second half of our season. Firestone-Panera has a couple of young rookies, I hear. Worth approaching them, see what their financial situation is and if they want in.

Excited for the new possibilities, and you should be too. This is only the starting line for the organization, you know. If this beta version proves successful, we're shifting operations to the Tour de France next year. The big time, Tony. Get ready for the ride of your life!

"Mari," I whispered. "What's he talking about?"

She kept reading, open-mouthed. "Tessa," she breathed. "Preston Lane isn't just gambling. He isn't just running a sports betting scheme. He's *fixing races*!"

53

IT TOOK me a minute to respond to Mari. I wasn't even sure if I'd heard her right. "Fixing races!" I exclaimed. "You mean, making certain riders or teams win and lose? Paying athletes and coaches?"

Mari glanced nervously at the door to the hallway and the rest of the Ruiz household. "Shh," she said. "We shouldn't talk here." She ushered me into the former maid's room. We sat on the bed, and she closed the door.

"My uncle—the one with the gambling problem?" said Mari. "He said sports bookies sometimes do that with major league sports teams. They get basketball teams to shave points off games and throw the odds, and that affects betting outcomes. Preston and the coach—I think they're doing the same thing with cycling teams. Paying off riders, buying and selling stage wins, tampering with time trials and race stats? That's illegal. It's called racketeering."

"Worth being locked up for twenty years?" I asked grimly. I opened a new window on my computer and ran a quick search on racketeering laws in Massachusetts. Sure enough, one of the penalties was two decades in the slammer.

Mari took the laptop from me and went back to the flash drive folder. We read through April and May, looking for names we recognized, and then we stumbled on one. The big one. An email exchange between Preston and Juan Carlos, which Preston had forwarded to Coach Mancuso. *This guy is trouble,* Preston had written before the forwarded email exchange.

To: ElCondor@ahoy.com
Subject: the offer

Juan Carlos,

I did not like how we ended our last conversation. Obviously you are very uncomfortable with the private conversation you overheard between me and Coach Mancuso. My offer still stands, and I think it will make you more comfortable. I'm offering you $10,000 cash for keeping quiet about that conversation. Sports Xplor is a confidential side business, still in a development phase, and I'd hate for some other entrepreneur to catch wind of it and beat us to the finish. You follow?

What you heard is top secret, Juan Carlos. Sports gambling isn't technically legal here—the U.S. government has not seen the light yet. Once they understand that it is a lucrative and harmless pursuit, the legislation will change. But until then, if I get called out for developing a system for cycling bets, I'm in serious trouble. The FBI will investigate anything associated with me, including this team, and then the whole team goes down together. You too. That would be the end of your racing career, and you could face deportation. Think about that before you make any hasty moves.

Finally, if you follow the racing strategy Coach Mancuso outlined for you and agree to throw the races we discussed, we will offer an additional $10,000 cash bonus.

To: Plane@sportsxplor.net
Subject: RE: the offer

Dear Preston,

I do not want your money. Your new business is bad for our team and for my country. You hide your profits there because you think no one will trace your money. But you're wrong. Ecuador is not a backwards place. This kind of sports gambling no is legal there. Eventually people will find you. And you cannot pay me any amount of monies to change my race results. I hope you to understand. Thank you.

Sincerely,
Juan Carlos

To: ElCondor@ahoy.com
Subject: RE: the offer

You don't want the money? Don't want to help your family? Fine. But if you talk to the media or the police, I will make sure you're off the team, and your racing days will be over in both the U.S. and Ecuador.

Here is my final offer. I will double the cash payout and offer you an EcuaBar sponsorship. I can get your face in every bike magazine in the country. On a billboard even. You can be the face of EcuaBar. That's worth more than any prize winnings or salary you're going to pull as a pro cyclist. You could change the lives of your entire family with what I'm offering you in exchange for your silence and your cooperation. Keep quiet, and follow the racing strategy Coach Mancuso has outlined for you beginning with the Chain Reaction race, and all of this can be yours.

Mari was actually crying, and I was coming close. I'd felt a surge of relief knowing that Juan Carlos wasn't doping or cheating. And then a slump of disappointment. He'd accepted the hush money and the sponsorship in the end. The billboard, the EcuaBar sponsorship—there was the proof. He'd changed his mind. Was Juan Carlos truly a good person, intent on blowing the whistle on his team owner's corrupt activities? Or was he a sellout, one of the vulnerable athletes Preston and Coach Mancuso seemed to be scouting?

"I don't see anything else in this file," I said, clicking out of the last document on the drive. "But I think we have enough to show the American ambassador that Preston Lane is up to no good. He's clearly helping to run this offshore gambling site and involved in a race-fixing scheme. Plus he had a clear motive for harming or killing Juan Carlos. Juan Carlos wasn't keeping up his end of the deal, even with the hush money and the sponsorship deal. He was going to come forward at Chain Reaction. Maybe Preston needed to silence him. Like, permanently."

"We have to call the police in Cabot right now. Or Bianca Slade. Or both!" said Mari. "Forget the bike in the shipping container. We don't even need that now!"

"No! We do need that bike," I insisted. "If the U.S. ambassador thinks highly of Preston Lane, then he's going to need really strong proof to turn him over to international law enforcement. Plus, that bike and the cash could help link Preston to Darwin."

"How?" asked Mari, frowning. "We don't know exactly where the cash came from. You told me Darwin said Juan Carlos stole it from 'the organization.' But did Juan Carlos steal it directly from Darwin? Or from Preston? And where is this money supposed to go? We have no proof that the bike links Preston to Darwin."

"I know we didn't see Darwin or his group come up in any of these emails," I said. "But we know they're connected. And we can't let Darwin get away with his crimes, either. We have to believe Juan Carlos had a strong reason for wanting to turn over the bike with this hidden money and the flash drive at the same time. Mari!" I sat up straighter. "Remember what Rosio said about her mom seeing Preston taking stuff out of his bike in that hotel room?"

"Yeah."

"What if it's *not* drug money? What if it's gambling profits?"

Mari's eyes lit up. "That's possible. According to ice, you can't bring more than ten thousand dollars into Ecuador. Maybe Darwin's helping him carry cash into the country, cash earned not from drug deals, like we first thought, but from the Sports Xplor business!"

"Wait—ice?"

"Immigrations and Customs Enforcement. I.C.E."

Something Preston had said once came back to me now. The fragment of a phone conversation I'd overhead at the Compass Bikes container load. *The ice crackdown.* My breath came fast. "Mari, is there some kind of crackdown by that organization about looking for cash smugglers?"

"Yes. Haven't you been following the news here?"

I shook my head. I was a news junkie at home, but here I'd been so focused on solving the mystery of Juan Carlos's death, and following the PAC tour, I hadn't tuned in to the major headlines.

"Cash smuggling into Ecuador has gotten worse lately, along with the drug mule problem," Mari explained.

I told her about the phrase Preston had used back at Compass Bikes. "He said something about moving in a different direction because of the I.C.E. crackdown," I concluded. "So maybe, before this crackdown, he used to move cash himself. Maybe he suddenly needed to go the extra mile to avoid customs, so he hired Darwin's group. He might have seen the container load as a golden opportunity to conceal this bike full of cash." I bit my lip. "I just don't get why the cash would be in *Juan Carlos's* bike. Who put it in there? Preston? Darwin? Or Juan Carlos?"

"I don't know. But this is huge, Tessa," said Mari. "We can't just sit on this information. Let's email Bianca Slade right now! She'll know what to do next."

I started typing Bianca's name in my email, then snatched my hands back from the keyboard.

"What is it?" asked Mari.

I shook my head. "I don't know if I can point the finger at Preston."

"Have you lost your mind?" Mari exploded. "How can you just keep quiet about this? This is a way bigger deal than bike theft or even drug dealing. We're talking racketeering. Cash smuggling. Money laundering. A major CEO bribing and blackmailing a young athlete. Possibly committing or hiring out a murder." She paused to let all this sink in. "This is your big chance to complete Juan Carlos's mission—the mission he wanted you to get involved with. If you don't share this information, you're basically betraying him."

I got up and started pacing the small room, feeling like a caged animal. There was no good option. "But if I do share it,

I'm betraying my friend Kylie," I said. "She just got awarded the Lane Scholarship at our school, to finance her senior year. And she deserves every penny. Her mom has cancer. She's taking an expensive experimental drug. If Preston Lane is hauled off to jail, Kylie won't get her money, and she'll have to go to public school senior year."

Mari rolled her eyes. "Oh, so sad!" She smirked. "Give me a break. I went to public school. Believe me, there are worse fates than graduating from Cambridge Rindge and Latin. Gee, I'm sorry she'll miss her cotillion or her debutante ball and the caviar in the cafeteria—"

"My school's nothing like that," I insisted. "It's not ritzy. It's always short on money, even with Preston Lane's regular infusions. Anyway, it doesn't matter if it's a rich school. That's where Kylie's gone to school since kindergarten, and it's where she wants to finish . . ."

My voice faltered. Mari was right. What was I saying? I couldn't possibly justify hanging on to Kylie's private school education if it meant covering up a racketeering operation . . . and a murder. Still, the thought of letting Kylie down, again, made me feel sick to my stomach.

If I didn't finish the work Juan Carlos had begun, Preston, Darwin, and this whole Sports Xplor organization would continue its shadowy business. My life would just go on. Kylie's scholarship wouldn't be at risk. What difference did it make?

A lot. I pictured the faces of kids I had interviewed over the years. Including Jake and Juan Carlos's teammates on the development team. Keeping quiet would let Preston go on corrupting sports and athletes, and letting a murderer go unpunished.

I'd just have to find a way to explain it to Kylie and hope that she'd understand.

I wrote Bianca a quick note explaining what we'd found, and

tried to attach the first file from the flash drive, but an error message popped up:

FILE TRANSFER DENIED.
USB COPY PROTECTED.

"Oh, no," said Mari. "It looks like this flash drive is locked or encrypted. To prevent leaks."

"Why would Juan Carlos do that?" I asked, trying now to copy the files to my hard drive. "He wanted to share the information, not lock it up, right?"

The error message showed up again, with a loud beep.

"If this is Preston's own backup drive," Mari reminded me, "I bet Preston had it protected—lots of executives do that to prevent data theft—and Juan Carlos took it."

"Why would Preston save emails on this flash drive, though?" I wondered out loud. "Some of this stuff looks like regular business, but a lot of it's really incriminating."

"To get it all off his hard drive and his email server," Mari guessed. "The cloud's not safe from hackers, either. A protected flash drive was probably a safer way to keep all his side business dealings separate from EcuaBar."

"And now I understand why Juan Carlos asked me at Chain Reaction if I had a laptop. He couldn't just copy the files to his own computer or flash drive and share them. Preston Lane had locked his backup drive."

"Right. So Juan Carlos had to give someone the actual, physical flash drive to share this information. Otherwise there was no way to leak it."

"But wait! Why wouldn't a screen shot of these emails work?"

"Good idea! Let's try." Mari leaned over me to press the commands on the keyboard. "We can email our screen shots to Bianca Slade, and to the Cabot Police, and they can take this information and run with it."

The screen shot Mari took of Preston's email to Coach Mancuso seemed successful—no error box showed up. But when we opened the screen shot file to check our result, all that showed up was a pixelated mess of garbled information. A message from Mars.

Mari tried again, and groaned. "That is one sophisticated USB lock," she said. "You can't even take a picture. Preston definitely didn't want this stuff getting into the wrong hands."

"Neither did Juan Carlos," I said, studying the pieces of the crucifix necklace and flash drive case. The two pieces fit together so snugly you could barely detect a seam. He must have spent some money on this. Not because it was gold—the gold was fake—but because it looked secure. I caressed the necklace. "I'm sure he wanted to keep this on him at all times until he found the right person to hand it over to."

"Right. You," Mari reminded me. "And now you have it. Just like he wanted. So what are you going to do?"

We exchanged a long look.

"Hand it over," I said. "First thing in the morning, we're going to the embassy office with this flash drive. The PAC Tour comes to Quito tomorrow. Didn't you tell me the ambassador was planning on attending? He must be back in town."

"And the bike?" Mari asked.

"We'll tell him it's coming Friday. And if he really enjoys a good cultural exchange program, he should come and check out our container unload."

"What about Bianca?" Mari looked at the screen, where our note to Bianca Slade awaited, along with a red X showing that our attachment was unsuccessful.

"We'll hold off," I decided. "There's no point in telling her about this without proof. There's nothing she can do from there. We'll get faster results delivering the flash drive to the ambassador here. Especially since Preston is coming this way."

BACK IN bed, I reassembled the necklace, with the flash drive nested inside, and laid it carefully on the nightstand. Then I picked it up and looked at it in the moonlight, letting the chain run through my fingers. It didn't seem as shiny as it had before, like Juan Carlos's spirit had flown out of it the moment it came apart. It was no longer a sentimental object, loaded with potential personal meaning or romantic implications. It was a storage case, containing a piece of electronic equipment.

I slipped it under my pillow.

Finally, I felt like a huge weight was lifting off my chest.

54

THE NEXT morning, Lucia greeted us with warm smiles, huge plates of breakfast, frothy glasses of fresh-squeezed *jugo de tomatillo*, and an exuberant exclamation: "It is *venticuatro de julio*!"

I stared at her as she plunked Ecuadorian flags on toothpicks into our breakfast rolls.

"Um, yay?" I said. "What's July twenty-fourth?"

Lucia frowned. "You do not know? There was no talk of this at Vuelta? It is *el natalicio del Libertador*!"

"The Liberator?" I echoed. That nickname sounded like another cyclist.

"Simón Bolivar. He helped to liberate Latin America from the Spanish Empire," Lucia explained. He is a very important figure. On this day we have a public holiday, parades in the street, celebrations."

Mari shot me a panicked look. "I'm sorry, Tessa," she whispered. "My cousin told me about this this holiday, and I totally forgot about it. This could really throw off our plan."

"If it's a public holiday, does that mean offices are closed?" I asked Lucia.

"Government offices, yes, and most businesses. Hugo will not be at work, so he will take you to the container unload this morning," Lucia explained as she stirred two short mugs of Nescafé.

I shook my head, struggling to keep up. "Today's Thursday. The container unload is tomorrow."

"No. It's today! Wilson called early this morning to say that it is arriving today, a day ahead of schedule, despite the protests," Lucia said, beaming. She handed Mari and me our coffee. "You must be at the Vuelta warehouse for the unload in one hour. Hugo will drive you right after breakfast. This means missing the circuit race for the PAC Tour, but I think this is more important, yes?"

Mari and I exchanged a look. "Santiago invited the ambassador to come to the container unload to see the bike tomorrow. Not today," I whispered to Mari when Lucia disappeared into the kitchen again. "He won't be at the container unload today. Or at the office—it'll be closed!"

"But he *will* be at the PAC circuit race," said Mari. "I guarantee. It's the first PAC Tour cycling event in Ecuador, and it's el Ratón's debut event with Equipo Diablo. The ambassador, as a cycling fan, wouldn't miss this for the world. And law enforcement will be a huge presence at the race. The ambassador should know which officers are trustworthy."

"Are you saying we're supposed to find the ambassador somewhere on the course?"

"It's a high-speed, two-mile course making a square through the business district," Mari explained. "The start and finish line are at the same place, since it's a circuit. That's where the grandstands are. El Parque Metropolitano. He'll be there, in VIP seating. We'll go there and give him the flash drive this morning."

"But how, if we have the container unload? We can't skip that."

"So we'll get the bike from the container and have Santiago drive us to the race as soon as we're done," said Mari. "We'll find the ambassador and give him both things at once."

"What about Preston?" I pointed out. "He said he'd be at the container unload."

"That was back when the container load wasn't scheduled for the same day as a race," Mari countered. "I'm sure Preston will be at the circuit race too, with the team. Tied up in team business. We can get the bike past him and to the ambassador. I'm telling you, this early arrival of the shipping container is the best thing that could have happened.

"But what if people see us loading a bike into Santiago's car? They might think we're stealing a donation!"

"Can you be just a little bit positive about this?" said Mari. "God, what's happened to you? We can get the bike into the car. If anyone asks, we'll just say we found a mechanical problem that wasn't caught back in Cambridge, and we're taking it back to Vuelta. No big deal. Hey." She lightly punched my arm. "Remember when you asked me to trust you? To go on your ride, when we went undercover at Dylan Holcomb's place?"

"Yeah."

"So now go on my ride. My plan will work. I'm sure of it."

Lucia returned with a basket of fruit. "Eat up, girls! You'll need your energy. Unloading those bikes will be a lot of work!"

I wanted to believe Mari. But I looked at the fruit, thinking of the Sports Xplor site, and suddenly felt sick.

AFTER BREAKFAST, while I waited for Mari to finish her shower, I checked my email, hoping something had come in from Amber.

It had. I called Mari over to read her note.

> **Hi Tessa,**
>
> **Yes, I do remember you. How could I forget the girl who came to our bike school to spy on my**

husband? And who got that Watchdog reporter to come sniffing around, which led to the police sniffing around, which led to my husband being accused of a heinous crime? I remember you all right. And I have to say, you're not exactly my favorite person right now. He's been through so much, finally getting his life back on track, and this false accusation is not what he needs.

But I appreciate that now you're trying to clear his name. I'm desperate to clear his name too. So desperate, I guess, that I decided to take your email seriously. I went through all the pre-race photos I took and found a few that looked odd. I have a bunch of Team EcuaBar riders goofing off by the trailer, like at any race, but something in the background made me look twice. I enlarged it and zoomed in on the suspicious area in the lower right corner. See the attached JPEGs.

I opened the picture file and made it full screen. Preston was removing a Cadence racing bike with white handlebars from the trunk of his Lexus SUV. The car was clearly his—the vanity plate said ECUABAR on it.

In the background of a second picture, taken moments later, Preston could be seen propping the bike against the side of his car, while talking to Coach Mancuso, who was also looking at the bike. In a third picture, the two men were doing something to the seat tube, it looked like. In the fourth photo, the men had moved to the back of the car, where they were looking in Preston's trunk. The fifth image showed Juan Carlos mounting that bike while Preston and Coach Mancuso talked. In the sixth photo, almost out of the picture frame, Juan Carlos was seen riding away. And in the seventh image, the coach and Preston were back on the side of the car, Preston's mouth wide open, aghast, and the coach making one of his wild, flailing hand gestures. If I could speed the pictures up like a movie, the sequence would show Juan Carlos taking off with a bike, surprising the team owner and coach who seemed to have other plans for it.

My heart pounded. The bike that I'd thought was Juan Carlos's spare when I saw it in the woods might not have been his at all! That would explain why Mari had seen Juan Carlos's spare bike on the wall at Dylan's place. Juan Carlos's spare bike had never been stolen. The bike was Preston Lane's. And the money stashed inside it had to connect Preston to the death of Juan Carlos.

I went back to Amber's email and read the end of her note.

> When I zeroed in on this sequence of background images, a narrative began to emerge. Maybe you can see it too. That bike didn't really belong to Juan Carlos. Yet. Dylan told me Preston had a new spare bike for Juan Carlos that he would give to Dylan to box up with the bikes going to the PAC Tour. That must have been the bike in the trunk. Dylan said he would want to check the fittings before he packed it, and run an inspection. Preston told him not to bother, just to pack it up the same day he got it. We both thought that sounded weird, but then Dylan said he never got the new spare bike from Preston, so he put it out of his mind. Now I'm going to show these pictures to the Cabot Police and see what they think. Clearly they

should be questioning Preston and Tony. Not our boyfriends.

Our boyfriends.

I'd stared at the word, not recognizing it for a moment. Maybe I'd been talking in Spanish so much, it seemed unfamiliar. But also the idea of Jake as my boyfriend now seemed so foreign to me. As did the idea that he was still a potential suspect. In my mind, I'd cleared him of suspicion. But until the truth about Preston and Darwin's group came out, Jake wasn't out of the woods. I wasn't, either.

LESS THAN an hour later, we were in Hugo's car, and he was driving us to a parking lot by a warehouse in a rundown area. "Why is this container delivery happening so far away?" he asked, frowning as we passed a busy long-distance bus terminal. He glanced at Amparo and Andreas. They had worn out their parents by pleading to come, and now sat in the back beside Mari.

"Because we've got nearly five hundred bikes coming, and we need a warehouse," Mari explained. "There isn't enough space to store them and organize them for distribution at the Vuelta headquarters. I'm sure it's safe. Equipo Diablo stores their equipment there."

Hugo pressed his lips together as we passed a row of shabby apartments. "Mm. I am not sure this is a good place for the children. I think my Lucia, she will not be so pleased."

"So don't tell her," Andreas suggested.

"*Papi.* Please. We're not babies," said Amparo, with an impatient toss of her ponytail. The front of her hair was secured with one of Mari's headbands, and instead of her usual frilly blouse or form-fitting T-shirt, she was wearing a Boston Red Sox T-shirt that Mari had given her. Andreas wore Mari's Bruins shirt.

"I don't see a shipping container or any bikes here," Hugo said. "Are you sure this is the right place?" He pulled into a parking lot in front of a huge concrete building, where a group of about fifteen Vuelta volunteers and staff had gathered. Someone had brought a radio, and merengue music was playing. Some of the volunteers were trying to teach Santiago how to dance. Aussie Guy and Emma were cavorting around him, trying to get him to twitch his hips and move his arms, and everyone was clapping and singing while he tried to duck away from them. It was like a party. People were getting their energy up to work fast, eager to empty the container as soon as possible and get over to the circuit race. I wished I felt free to join their party, to dance and to laugh. But Mari and I had a long road ahead of us still.

"The container *will* come," Mari assured Hugo. "And these are Vuelta volunteers." She pointed. "There's Wilson. Emma. The teachers. Aussie Guy. Oh, and Santiago. Honk, *Papi*!"

Papi. Already Mari was calling him dad.

Santiago looked embarrassed and sidled away from the dancers. He jogged toward our car to meet us.

While Mari introduced the Ruizes to some of the staff and volunteers, Santiago pulled me aside. "I called to the embassy hotline, but they told me the ambassador is at the race today, and there is no one in the office because of the national holiday. I cannot get him to come to this unload. So when the bike comes out of the container, we have to get it to the circuit race."

"Exactly. That and the flash drive," I said.

"The flash drive?"

"We found it last night."

"What? Where?"

I quickly told him what had happened, and showed him the

chain on my neck. Suddenly panic seized me. Had I snapped the flash drive back inside this morning, before I put the necklace on? I suddenly wasn't sure. What if the drive was still under my pillow?

I fumbled with the cross. "I just want to make sure it's there," I said.

"Here. Let me," said Santiago.

I held my breath as his fingers brushed my skin, sweeping the cross off my collarbone. His warm breath brushed my cheek as he bent closer to pop out the flash drive. An unexpected electric tingle ran through me.

He held the flash drive up to the light, inspected it, then nested it back into the cross and snapped the crucifix closed again. "Everything looks good," he said. "You are all set for delivery."

"Thanks." I smiled at him. Then I looked at him in wonder. "Why are you doing all this anyway, helping us out?" I asked him. "And please don't tell me it's an Ecuadorian custom to save girls from spies and help them bring murderers to justice. You're not just being polite."

He nodded. "Remember I told you, my father's business is affected by this matter?" he said in a low voice.

"Yeah."

"I found records of business transactions in my father's computer systems last night. Preston Lane has given big donations to Vuelta."

"Isn't that a good thing?"

"Not really. I discovered all the donations were in cash. Every six months, Preston Lane donates three thousand dollars."

My eyes widened. "That's a lot of money."

"It is. Especially in Ecuador, and especially for a charity. And I have heard he invests in other businesses here, too. The information you're telling me, it scares me." Santiago sighed. "Because if this money is from something corrupt like racketeering—even if it does good things—it could harm Vuelta."

"How so?"

"If Preston Lane has been laundering money here, it could damage the reputation of the youth racing club. And my father, too. He will look like a willing accomplice."

I suddenly remembered something I'd seen on Santiago's dad's computer screen the other day. The same black screen that I'd seen on Gage's computer at Compass Bikes. Sports Xplor. I asked him to explain that. "You weren't playing it, were you?"

"No," he insisted. "I found a cookie in the computer and wanted to find out what this was. I asked around, and some Vuelta employees and volunteers had heard about this gambling website. Some person came into the Vuelta shop and gave them flyers about betting for the PAC Tour. Equipo Diablo versus Team Cadence-EcuaBar. El Cóndor versus el Ratón."

"So people were really placing bets on those two cyclists? Before el Cóndor died?"

"Yes. Some of our staff looked into this because they were curious. Then some logged on and placed bets. Mostly on the Ecuadorian team. And even after el Cóndor died, the betting has continued."

"I've tried to get onto that site. I was locked out. How did Vuelta staffers get in to place bets?"

"The password was on the flyer. *Cacao*. It was supposed to be good for the duration of the PAC tour only."

Cacao. The cocoa bean. Of course! A fruit that Mari and I hadn't thought of last night, but should have, considering it was a key ingredient in EcuaBars. And the password had probably changed from *papayas*, the word mentioned in Preston's email to Gage back in April.

"Has anyone you know won anything on the PAC Tour so far?" I asked next.

"In the Colombian and Venezuelan events, yes, some people I know—Vuelta staff members, friends of my parents—they have made good profits on the Equipo Diablo riders. They wanted to bet even more money on them, for the big Quito races. Because of el Ratón."

"So locals were putting money down on the underdog team. Just like Preston had said in that email to Coach Mancuso!" It was all part of the "narrative" they were constructing to make Sports Xplor profit. They would boost the visibility of cycling in Ecuador, and give Team Cadence-EcuaBar a shot at redemption upon their return. That would lead to more wagers, more money. A cycle. More bettors, more viewers, more enthusiasts, more sponsors. Even with el Cóndor out of the picture, the machinery was in place to bring pro cycling into high-level sports betting, and to pay off cyclists—young athletes who really needed the money—in order to skew the results.

A low rumbling sound behind us interrupted our conversation.

"The truck is coming," said Santiago. "*Suerte*, Tessa. Good luck. We will need it."

55

THE TRUCK chugged up to the parking lot, towing the shipping container. A cheer rose up from the crowd. I reached into my backpack for the Vuelta video camera that Santiago had loaned me to interview el Ratón. If we couldn't get the official media here to get this recorded, *I* would be the media presence.

My view from behind the lens blurred as the truck turned into the lot and the container came into full view. My eyes welled with tears. The container looked like it had aged a hundred years since I'd seen it last. It was filthier than I remembered, and covered in scrapes and dents. If someone had said the thing had been dragged underwater by the ocean freighter, instead of loaded onto it, I would have believed it.

Thank God I'd gotten out. No one was going to open that thing and find my body inside.

The truck and trailer rumbled, closer, making the whole ground vibrate.

The container was ugly, yes. But it was also a thing of beauty. It contained the good intentions of countless people back home who wanted to give their bikes or parts to help strangers in a distant country. To help young girls in villages get to school.

And it contained the secret behind Juan Carlos's death. Soon, very soon, we'd be able to show that secret to the world.

The truck stopped, and the driver got out of the van. Wilson signed some forms on a clipboard. A black Ford Explorer drove up. And parked.

An Explorer. Crap. Was this Darwin himself? This seemed like something he'd drive.

The door opened. One leg emerged. Then Preston Lane stepped out.

I nudged Mari. "He's here. Just like he said he'd be. He isn't at the race."

Mari looked worried. "Okay. Slight revision of plan is in order." She let out a long breath and looked around. "There's nobody here to arrest him. We have to get his bike out of the container and not let him touch it. Why don't you talk to him, since you know him. If you can keep him talking, stall him, Santiago and I can go after the bike."

There was no time to discuss all the things that might go wrong. Preston Lane walked over to the driver and to Wilson. He shook Wilson's hand and said a few words to him, in English, thumping him on the back.

I walked up to Preston, while Wilson finished dealing with paperwork, and gave him my most winning *KidVision* smile. "Hey, there," I said. "Remember me? I'm doing a video about the container unload. Can you answer a few questions?"

"Maybe later. I'm afraid my time is limited," he said brusquely. He narrowed his eyes. "I heard you were here," he said in a low voice. Not friendly at all.

Of course he knew I was here. He and Darwin had to be in communication, working together to move money—or a money-filled bike—across international borders and to conceal Preston's secret business.

"I'm a Vuelta Volunteer," I said, forcing a grin. "I wanted to follow the shipping container and see how the story ended."

Something about holding a video camera in my hand made me bold. Bolder than I would have been standing there without it, and feeling the full force of his gaze, even as the warmth drained out of his face and he narrowed his eyes at me. "I'd prefer that you put the camera away," he snapped.

I feigned an innocent expression. "Oh? Why's that? Don't you want everyone to see how committed you are to this bike donation program? Think of all the bikes here going to communities in need. *All the bikes.*"

He glared at me. "You," he said, "need to learn a lesson about boundaries. None of this business concerns you."

"Señor Lane!" Wilson, smiling, approached him. "How wonderful to have you here. Will you please do us the honor of opening the doors?"

"My pleasure." He brushed past me and strode to the container.

Santiago and I exchanged panicked looks. Preston was getting ahead of us. If he was the first one inside the container, he could grab the bike as soon as he saw it. And take off.

The crowd around us applauded, and the Vuelta receptionist took photos of Preston standing by the container, holding up the key. Normally he'd enjoy the photo op, mugging for the cameras, but now his closed-mouthed grin and wild eyes looked almost maniacal to me.

"We must take our positions. Now," Santiago whispered to me. He beckoned to Mari, a few yards away. She came toward us, with Amparo, who'd linked her arm through Mari's in a sisterly gesture. I often saw women and girls in Quito walking arm and in arm like this, but now was not the time. I didn't want my host sister anywhere near this.

"Why don't you hang out with your family?" I suggested to

Amparo. A line of helpers was forming behind the container, as directed by a Vuelta staffer, and I pointed to Hugo and Andreas farther down the line, near the end.

Amparo squeezed Mari's arm and beamed at her. "Mari is family," Amparo said stubbornly. "And so are you. While you're visiting us, both of you are my sisters."

I heard the locks turn in the tumblers, even though traffic roared past on the highway and buses belched in the terminal nearby.

There was no time to lose. And maybe Amparo could be useful here. I handed my loaner camera to her, and instructed her to keep filming everything. No harm could come of that. Besides, I needed both my hands free to catch Juan Carlos's bike if it came my way. And if Preston did make a dive for the bike, at least we might catch that on film.

Preston struggled to slide the long metal bars on each door, and Santiago ran up to help him. Gutsy. Santiago had moved into a prime position to leap into that shipping container.

The moment the doors swung open, Preston lunged forward. But Santiago pushed him aside. He jumped up to the back of the shipping container. Mari and I got right up in front, further crowding out Preston. Santiago then began extracting the bikes and items closest to the doors and passing them to us. We passed them down the line of volunteers. Hands stretched out to receive and pass on each bike or component or box of parts. Six volunteers acted as runners, ferrying things into the warehouse.

Hugo had loosened his necktie and rolled up his sleeves. He laughed with Andreas as they fumbled to pass an armload of tires to each other. Amparo, meanwhile, stood a few yards away from it all, sweeping the camera up and down the chain of volunteers, then training it again on the back of the container, which Preston, scowling, still struggled to edge toward. Bikes and parts were flying out of there so fast, into volunteers' outstretched arms, that Preston could never get quite close enough to jump in.

Santiago passed a bike down to me. With a start, I realized what it was. My Bianchi. I clutched its familiar mint-green frame tightly, remembering those scrapes from my crash. It held so many memories, so many miles. I missed it. But I couldn't take back my donation.

I passed my Bianchi to Aussie Guy, and he sent it traveling on down the line.

"Excuse me," said Preston, elbowing people and pushing forward. "Can I get in there and help?"

"Help? Sure. Here you go. Catch." Santiago tossed him a cardboard box, almost knocking him over.

Preston staggered under its weight. "Jesus. What's in here?"

"Tools," said Santiago. "Do you mind running them over to the warehouse?"

"Unless they're too much for you?" I added to Preston. "We could find someone . . . younger, maybe?"

Preston, reddening, glared at me. "I can carry a box of tools," he said. "And I'm hardly the oldest person here." Huffing, he strode off to the warehouse, lugging the box.

Santiago grinned at me. "How'd you get rid of him so easily?" he asked.

I smiled mysteriously. "I had a little inside information," I said. "Preston's freaked out about getting older." Then my smile faded. "But we still have to hurry and get that bike out. He'll be back here soon enough."

"Can you see the Cadence bike? Are we getting close?"

I could just make out the white tape on the handlebars. "You're two rows away," I said.

"Jump in. And start digging."

I did, and Mari came in to help too. Contents had shifted in transit, and many of the bikes had capsized or become entangled. The two of us burrowed through bikes, extracting them—carefully at first, then less so—and handing them off to Santiago, who moved them on out to the volunteers.

"Preston's coming back from the warehouse," Santiago said over his shoulder as he picked up a children's bicycle trailer. "Are you close?"

My hands closed around one of the white handlebars. Mari's closed around the other. Together, we pulled.

"Hold on. It's stuck on another frame," said Mari, diving down to remove a pedal from the spoke of another bike's wheel. "Okay, pull."

I did. The bike gave way. "We got it!" I cried.

"Hurry!" Mari urged.

I rolled the bike toward the container door and handed it to Santiago. "Quick. Jump off and take it to your car before Preston comes out of the warehouse."

"No! Stop!" Mari exclaimed, as a Ford Explorer at the edge of the parking lot suddenly started up. The window lowered slightly. Santiago and I followed Mari's gaze. At the wheel was the guy in the Panama hat.

"Looks like Preston brought his own personal get-ahead vehicle," I murmured. "Crap. Now there's two people we have to worry about."

"Maybe more," said Mari, gesturing with her chin to two more identical cars, with tinted windows, parked on the opposite end of the lot. Right by Santiago's parked car.

As if to confirm Mari's guess, their engines roared to life.

56

"OH, NO!" Mari pulled at her hair. "Three cars with Preston's henchmen."

"And now Preston is coming back from the warehouse," said Santiago, pushing the Cadence bike over so it lay flat on the container floor.

Santiago passed armfuls of tires down to volunteers to keep the chain moving. I wiped sweat off my forehead and tried to keep breathing. "We've got to get this bike down to the circuit race along with the flash drive and give it to the ambassador! Preston knows I'm on to him, and I want both these things off my hands. Like, now."

"But we can't!" Mari protested. "Not with those Explorers flanking Santiago's car. We'll never get the bike in there without their intercepting it. They're totally in position to nab this bike from us."

"We have only one choice," Santiago said as he turned to pick up a box. "We must get this bike past Preston, past his friends in the Ford Explorers, and into the warehouse."

"And then what?" I demanded. "What good is the bike stuck in a warehouse?"

"There is a storage closet in the back," said Santiago. "You can turn the lock as you leave, and lock the bike inside there. Then run out to the street and take a taxi to the race. Give to the ambassador the flash drive and explain him what else we have found. Then he can come to the warehouse to see the bike himself."

"And you? You're going in the taxi too?" Mari asked him.

"No. I will stay and keep Preston busy while you two do this thing. And your host sister can help."

Santiago jumped out of the container and had a few words with Amparo, words Mari and I couldn't hear. "I don't like it," I said. "I don't think we should leave the bike once we have it. How do we know the Explorers crew won't find some way into the warehouse? Or that Amparo's safe?"

"We have to trust Santiago," Mari responded. "There's no more time. Here comes Mr. EcuaBar now."

Santiago immediately tossed Preston another heavy box, this one full of bicycle pumps. Preston started to hand the box back to Santiago, protesting, but Amparo trotted over to him, camera in hand. "What a wonderful thing you are doing for Vuelta! This will look great for Cadence Bikes publicity, Señor Lane," Amparo purred.

Preston immediately stood straighter and balanced the box in his arms. While Preston was occupied with Amparo, who seemed to have seized the opportunity to play interviewer and grill Preston about his involvement with Vuelta, Santiago ushered us out of the container. "Go!" he hissed, after quickly explaining where the storage closet was.

"All right. Let's do this," Mari muttered.

I leaped out of the container and Mari passed the Cadence bike down to me before jumping out too.

Santiago kept the human chain busy ferrying a fleet of kids' bikes down the line. Preston was trapped between the chain of volunteers and Amparo. Mari and I each held a handlebar of the Cadence bike and made a beeline for the warehouse.

Once inside, we headed straight for a far corner that was partitioned off to form a makeshift closet. The small space was filled with cleaning supplies. "What are you doing?" I asked as Mari suddenly knelt down. "Let's lock this thing up and get out of here!"

"Wait. While we're here, I just want to make sure this bike's really got contraband inside it," she said. "So we can be really specific about what we tell the ambassador. Amparo can't stop talking. Preston's tied up. We have time." She got busy, taking three tools from her jeans pocket. First she removed the seat post and looked inside. Then she pulled a bracket off the downtube. She put in her fingers and pulled out three tightly wadded-up bills. Hundred dollar bills. She peered inside the tube again, shook it, and whistled under her breath. "And there's a lot more where that came from," she said. "They're all crammed in there. This frame is totally stuffed."

I sucked in my breath. "Oh my God. It really is cash. So Preston *was* using Juan Carlos's bike to smuggle money into this country."

"And laundering it through Vuelta and other charities," Mari added, unfolding one of the bills. Then she turned to the bike and picked at the name decal. It unrolled easily. "This isn't even an official label," she said. "This is a home computer print job, on a sticker. The real decals are put on with heat transfer and they don't come off. Tessa." She looked at me. "We were right. This isn't even Juan Carlos's bike. Remember how I saw his spare bike on the wall at Dylan's place? I think Preston Lane labeled this bike with Juan Carlos's name so Juan Carlos would take the fall if anyone at customs found out what was inside. Juan Carlos would look like the cash smuggler, not Preston."

Relief, warm relief, flooded me. Juan Carlos was a good person at heart. I'd judged him well. And the cash in the bike was further proof that Jake had nothing to do with either of the bike crimes from the morning of Chain Reaction. I didn't love him, or even want to see him again, but at least his name would be cleared.

"There's tons more cash in here. But we can let someone else count it up." Mari quickly screwed the seat and the downtube bracket back on. "We have to get the bike and the flash drive down to the media circus at the starting line. The race is starting soon."

"I thought we were locking up the bike and just taking the flash drive."

Mari smirked and pointed at the lock on the doorknob. The latch could be turned, yes, to lock the door on the way out—but the doorknob itself was hanging off-kilter. "Seriously? This is hardly high-level security," she said. "If Preston comes in to the warehouse to look around, or the guys in the Ford Explorers, they could easily bust their way in. No way am I leaving this bike and the money here."

I turned and looked around. Mari was right. The closet was little more than a partition with a door. The walls of the partition could be scaled with a ladder, or even punched through with a heavy object.

"But how will we walk the bike out and get a taxi, without Preston's backup creeps following us?" I asked.

"Did you happen to see a box of used bike shoes and helmets? I packed it myself. That should have been one of the first things off the container."

"Yeah, I saw it by the door. Why? Why is this important right now?"

"Grab it. We need shoes for clip-ins."

I darted out into the main warehouse area and grabbed the box, wondering what this was all about. When I came back, Mari had Juan Carlos's bike and a Diablo bike that she had snagged from a rack just outside the partition. "Find two pairs of shoes that might fit us," she said.

"But I can't ride in—"

"Don't argue, Tessa. No time. If we bike the side streets and alleys, we can ditch the cars and make it down to the race. We can throw the cars off our trail, and leave them stuck in traffic."

We quickly exchanged our sneakers for bike shoes and strapped on helmets. My hands were shaking so badly I could hardly fasten my helmet. I thought of Rosio and the determined look on her face as she completed her maiden journey around the block the other day. If she could ride so fiercely, why couldn't I? I had to put Chain Reaction behind me and get back in that saddle.

But just as we grabbed the handlebars of the bikes—me with Juan Carlos's Cadence, Mari with the Diablo—we heard a man's voice. "Going for a little ride, are we? What fun."

In the makeshift doorway stood Preston Lane.

57

PRESTON CROSSED the floor to us in three steps. He put his hand firmly on the bike I was holding. "I believe that belongs to me."

I gripped the handlebar tighter. "You can't take this," I said. "We're finishing Juan Carlos's ride."

"Oh, really."

I held his gaze. "Yes. We have evidence that you're a consultant for an illegal sports gambling business."

He laughed, but then stopped when he saw I was serious.

"We know it's called Sports Xplor," I went on. "We know you and Coach Mancuso have been trying to fix races. I have media connections, I know where the flash drive is, I'm holding a bike full of cash you put in it, and I'm going to make sure this gets out. Just like Juan Carlos wanted it to."

"You know where the flash drive is?" His eyes lit up. "Where? Do you have it now?" He held out his hand.

"It's in a secure place," I said mysteriously. "With one of our own agents. Who will release the data to the media if anything happens to Mari and me."

He sneered at me. "You're quite the little investigator. I see you're getting a good education at Shady Pines. Glad my money is going toward fine minds like yours. Didn't I just award a scholarship to one of your classmates? You should think about that before you run to the cameras and the cops."

"Taking away my friend's scholarship won't change my mind. This is bigger than Kylie."

He glared. "I don't have time to play games. I have ways of silencing people. Now give me that bike."

"Silencing people? Oh, we know all about that," said Mari, glaring back at him. "You're a murderer. You killed Juan Carlos, didn't you?"

He laughed. "That's the craziest thing I've ever heard."

"No. It's not," said Mari. "You made sure those tools had Dylan's fingerprints on them, and you put them where the cops would find them when the investigation turned into a homicide case."

"And you bribed Dylan to leave the door to the trailer open, so you could get in there and do that sabotage job yourself," I jumped in. "And you're laundering money here in Ecuador, through charities like Vuelta. We found it in the bike. *Your* bike. This bike never belonged to Juan Carlos. You just put his name decal on it so he'd be blamed if customs took a closer look at the Team EcuaBar bikes it was originally going to be shipped with."

Preston flinched. Then he smiled, almost sheepishly. "Look. I'm a businessman. I'm willing to make a deal here just to get us out of this awkward situation. How much do you girls want?"

Mari and I exchanged a look. Money? I hadn't expected that response from Preston.

"I'll give you half of what's in that bike. You can split it between you." He sounded almost pleading. "That's about three thousand dollars for each of you."

For a moment I thought of presenting Kylie and her mom with a stack of cash. For medical bills. For that experimental drug.

In the next instant, I erased that thought. "We don't want your money," I said. "You're ruining cycling and your charities and EcuaBar, and even my school, with all this illegal money. It's corrupt. And people should know."

"Fine." Preston's smile curdled. "Then I'll have my team plant some drugs in your backpacks, make a phone call, and get you locked up in the Quito prison before the day is over. Did you know that Ecuador has one of the longest prison sentences for attempted drug smuggling? And that the criminal justice here is woefully inept? People rot in prison here for years, just awaiting a trial. And there's not a thing the U.S. Embassy can do for you except get you an English-speaking lawyer, whose hands will be tied, and who won't spring you or even move your case along."

I sucked in my breath. I had no doubt he could work with Darwin—or on his own—to do something like that.

"Tessa. I don't want to be locked up in an Ecuadorian prison," Mari whispered to me.

I didn't, either. But I couldn't stop the words that came next.

"Yeah, speaking of jail? Dylan doesn't deserve to go there," I said, surprised at the strength in my voice. "Neither does Jake Collier, or whoever else you set up to look connected to Juan Carlos's 'accident.'"

"You're a criminal," Mari added, lifting her chin. "We're going to make sure people know the truth. And we can still talk in prison." She linked her arm through mine. "You really want to frame us? Go ahead."

I nudged her. That was taking it maybe a little too far.

"We'll still tell everyone what you did," Mari went on. "We're going to talk and talk, until somebody listens. Starting now." She opened her mouth wide, as if to shout.

"Girls, girls," he said, holding out his hands in a gesture of peace. "Let's be reasonable. Let me explain myself before you do something regrettable. I did work with Sports Xplor. You're correct. I did ask Juan Carlos not to share classified information about the company's business plan."

"Asked him?" I spluttered. "You bribed him!"

"Business plan? You mean evil scheme," Mari added.

"You act like I'm this heinous individual," Preston protested. "I'm not. I'm an investor and a consultant. Sports Xplor will soon be above board. Because eventually—sooner than you think—our government will see the light, sports gambling will be legal in our country, and Sports Xplor will be in prime position to profit from the sports gambling craze. Not only that, I'm helping the cycling industry."

I raised an eyebrow.

"It's true," he insisted. "Bringing cycling into sports betting is making cycling visible again. Exciting again. If people invest financially in a sport, they invest emotionally, too. It all comes around. Sports betting helps cycling. I'm turning around the whole industry."

"With racketeering? Money laundering? Race fixing?" I shook my head. "That's mafia stuff. Not philanthropy."

"I believed the gains outweighed the risks in this case. Although the race fixing . . ." He sighed and leaned against the doorframe, in a casual pose that deliberately blocked our exit. "Honestly? That was my colleagues' plan, not mine. I was starting to have mixed feelings, and planned to pull out. I was just going to fix the Chain Reaction race result as an experiment, and then argue it wouldn't work long-term. Then I would buy myself out."

"But you didn't," I corrected him. "You were going to take this race fixing scheme, if it worked, all the way to the Tour de France next year. We read the emails."

"Yes. But you have to understand how intoxicating it all became," said Preston. He attempted the affable grin he used at his Shady Hill keynote speech—only now it looked more like a grimace. "Bets were pouring in for the PAC Tour. There was so much drama with the two 'rival' cyclists, and the organization wouldn't let me stop. They put me up to making Juan Carlos an offer to throw his result at Chain Reaction, as a test run, and then at certain legs of the PAC tour. But Juan Carlos refused to do it. He was intent on leaking our information."

"How did you know that for sure?" Mari asked.

"He told me he'd overheard conversations between Coach Mancuso and me about Sports Xplor, as well as our plans to ship cash in a Cadence bike mixed in with the team bikes. If I didn't stop him from leaking that, we'd never be able to launch our scheme. Let alone participate in the PAC tour."

"So you threw him in a van?" I asked, remembering Darwin's story the other night.

"There was no *throwing* involved. Your language is very dramatic."

"What would you call it?"

"When our agents intercepted him, they *contained* him in a van, where they could reason with him away from the public eye. But he burst out, overpowering our agents, and threatening to expose Sports Xplor and my involvement in it."

Talk about dramatic language. "That's not all he was going to expose," I said, looking at the cash-stuffed bike. "There's a whole other component to your plan."

"International shipping," Preston said in a smooth voice. "There are many methods. This happened to be one of them, to avoid paying unnecessary duties and taxes."

"It's not international shipping. It's international smuggling," Mari corrected. "And because Juan Carlos was going to expose your involvement in all of this stuff, you rigged his bike to fail."

Preston ran his hands through his hair. "I admit, I got scared," he said, "I'm human. Okay? What can I say? Humans get scared."

My skin crawled. He reminded me so much of Jake in that moment, Jake at his worst. Backpedaling. Explaining. Playing the emotional card.

"Look, this issue between me and Juan Carlos goes back months," he said. "It's personal. I knew Juan Carlos had overheard some key conversations between me and Coach Mancuso. He lived in my house. When I realized his English was getting good, fast—and that he was using my home computer for some of his homework—I took all my Sports Xplor data off it, for safety. I put it on a protected flash drive and kept it in my briefcase. But he wouldn't give up pestering me about my international shipping methods for cash. He just wouldn't leave it alone. When I came to Quito for business in February, Juan Carlos was training here, and he made a bold move. He came to my hotel room—he found some way to get in with the help of a maid there—and he caught me taking cash out of a bike I had packed."

That must have been Rosio's mom. So she'd been paid off with EcuaBars, for her silence. But Juan Carlos had been offered more. Much more. And if he'd stumbled on this cash-smuggling secret back in February, that could explain why Jake thought Juan Carlos acted differently after training in Quito off-season. "You paid him hush money," I prompted. "A lot."

"Which he didn't take. At least, not right away," said Preston. "But the trust between us was gone after he caught on to my shipping plan. I couldn't have him under my roof anymore. I'd caught him in my office, looking around, more than once. So I paid for him to leave my house and live with some older teammates.

"The day before Chain Reaction, my flash drive with the Sport Xplor data went missing," Preston continued. "We had a team meeting, to get to know Chris Fitch, and I must have left my briefcase open just long enough for Juan Carlos to have a look. I had to leave the room to take a call, and he must have found a way to look around. When I looked for my flash drive that night, it was gone. And at the race the next morning, when I saw Juan Carlos ride off on my Cadence bike—the bike I'd intended Dylan to pack up with the other team bikes—I knew that was when he planned to leak the information. And suddenly everything was at stake." He made an open-armed, almost pleading gesture. "Everything I've worked for. Girls, put yourself in my shoes for a moment. How would you feel? I had to stop him. I didn't see another way out."

"So you rigged Juan Carlos's main bike. Yourself," I said. "You weakened the tube with a hammer and a razor so the carbon fibers would fail. And you rigged the rear brakes for extra insurance."

Preston heaved a long breath. "I didn't think it would kill him. Just put him out for the season. To teach him the power of keeping his end of the deal and listening to his managers. I know it may sound incredible to you, but honestly? I thought it would do him a favor."

"Some favor," muttered Mari. "Broken bones? Brain injury? Paralysis? Death? There was no good outcome."

"Please. Hear me out," said Preston. "I knew Sports Xplor had crossed a line when they moved into race fixing. I thought of exposing them myself. But if Sports Xplor were prosecuted, I'd be implicated. And what good am I to anyone, especially to Juan Carlos, in jail? What good is my money if it all goes to legal fees? No good at all. But if Juan Carlos were injured in an accident, just a little, just enough to be out of the racing scene, I thought I could get the Sports Xplor guys off my back."

"You couldn't bribe the star rider if the star rider couldn't ride," Mari said. "I get it."

Preston nodded. "Right. That would get me off the hook with Sports Xplor, for the race fixing. Then I figured I could set up Juan Carlos with some other team when he recovered, and not drag him into this mess. I planned to take some of the business profits to Ecuador for the last time, pay off the people that I needed to pay off there, and be done with the whole organization. And that's exactly what I will do." He reached for the bike.

"Why use the shipping container?" I asked, snatching the bike away and backing up with it. "You've been taking money here in your own bike, on your own business trips."

"I have," he admitted. "Customs has never bothered me or looked closely at the bikes. I know people in high places. And everyone knows I travel with bikes. But then this I.C.E. crackdown on border security got in the way. My friends couldn't guarantee they'd help me, like they used to. I needed a safer way to move cash here. That's why I feel so grateful to you girls."

"Grateful? To us?" Mari looked skeptical.

"One of you got the bike to Compass Bikes. One of you led Darwin to the bike shop with the GPS on your phone. And since the container load was in full swing when my agents showed up there, and the bike was already on the premises, I got this genius idea. Use the container load as a way to avoid customs inspection and move the cash."

"But your genius plan didn't work so well, did it," I said. "You don't have the bike in your hands, or the money, or your flash drive. And your star cyclist is gone."

He looked down and played with his watchband—a simple leather band, not the gleaming Rolex I'd seen before. "You are right. The sabotage part of the plan worked too well. Juan Carlos is gone. And I'll be paying for that for the rest of my life." He looked at me, eyes glistening. "I don't need jail time to think about what I've done. I'll carry this burden around every day. In my heart."

I watched him carefully. He seemed sincerely regretful now. More like the guy I'd seen on TV right after the crash, distraught and wild-eyed at Mass General Hospital. But did sincerity and regret make up for the loss of a human life?

A part of me truly did sympathize. I'd made bad decisions, too, and tried to pull out too late. Like that paceline at Chain Reaction. But my deceptions and bad decisions were nowhere on the scale of what Preston Lane had done. And if he was anything like Jake, his remorseful moment would soon pass. "There's help for people with problems like yours, you know," I ventured. "Gambling is an addiction problem."

"Gamblers Anonymous. I know. I started to work with them," he said. "And I told Sports Xplor I was done consulting for them, done fixing races. But I'd signed contracts. My hands were tied. And I'd already invested so much of my own money in the business. I could lose it all if I didn't follow through and at least complete the PAC Tour plan." He held out his hand toward the bike. "You're a person of conscience, Tessa," he said. "And integrity. I know your type. We went to the same school. Somewhere, deep down, we're not so different, are we? Help me out. Help me get out of this situation and turn my life around, and I'll make sure the Sports Xplor agents never bother you girls again."

"No," I said.

"No?" he repeated. "Is that your final answer?"

"It is. I can't let the wrong people take the fall for your bad decisions."

"Tessa! Now!" Mari shouted at me, grabbing her bike. And she rushed for the door.

I followed, yanking the bike out of Preston's hands. Preston ran after us through the warehouse, to the door. Our cleats clattered on the cement floor, and Preston's business loafers slapped close behind.

"Is there a problem here?" Wilson asked, staring at us in confusion as Mari and I burst out of the building.

Mari slammed the door shut, and we both threw all our weight against it to hold it tight.

"Yes! Call the Embassy! Tell them Juan Carlos's murderer is in here!" Mari shouted. Santiago ran up to us with the key and turned the lock tight, locking Preston Lane inside the warehouse.

"I don't understand what this is all about," Wilson said. "Santiago? What is going on?"

"Preston Lane is extremely dangerous," I said. "And he's not alone. Those people in the Ford Explorers over there? They are working with him. They're part of a sports gambling and racketeering ring. And he's laundering the profits here in Ecuador. Some of them through Vuelta."

Wilson pressed one hand to his chest. "Gambling! Money washing? What is all this you are telling me?"

"Sports Xplor, *Papi*," said Santiago. "We'll explain more later. But Preston Lane is part of it. Trust me. He's in the inner circle."

Mari hopped on the Diablo bike and pedaled to the edge of the parking lot. I followed, trotting on foot, pushing Juan Carlos's cash-stuffed bike. "Tessa! What are you doing?" called Mari. "You have to ride the bike!"

"Ride the bike. Yeah. Okay. I can do that."

"Hurry! You can do this!"

"Right. Okay. I can do this." I tried to coach myself, to urge myself on. My throat was dry. My breath came fast.

Mari looked right and left, and all over the lot, to find the easy way out. "I think we can turn a sharp right and get out on the other side of this lot. That will take us to Avenida Colón, and it's almost all downhill to the starting line from there." She flung one leg over the Diablo bike and prepared to push off.

"Downhill?" I couldn't even get my leg over the frame of Juan Carlos's Cadence. "What if this bike falls apart? The frame is totally compromised. I'm riding on cash, not carbon."

"Avoid potholes and rocks. Find the smoothest road you can. And listen to the bike. If you hear any weird creaking sounds, get off."

"Right. *Weird* creaking sounds. As opposed to the perfectly normal ones?" I muttered.

"Ready?" Mari said. "Let's roll."

Just before I turned, I caught the shocked and dismayed looks on the faces of Hugo and the Ruiz kids, who probably thought we were thieves. But there was no time now to explain.

"Go faster!" Mari urged me as one of the Ford Explorers backed out of its parking space.

We exited the lot and headed down the street.

I looked down at my churning pedals. My legs, strong and healthy. My tires skimming over the pavement. And I grinned. I was riding again!

In the distance I could see a swath of green amid the buildings. El Parque Metropolitano. The starting line for the race.

I prayed that our bikes would hold up. Did I hear creaking sounds? I couldn't even tell, as traffic was whooshing by us. I followed Mari off the sidewalk, which was cracked and bumpy, and into the smoother street. I felt the heat of the cars on my legs.

A traffic light at a busy intersection forced us to stop abruptly. A moped purred behind us. And then I choked. Everything went dim around me as something—a hand—grabbed my throat, and then yanked the necklace off of it. I heard something snap and prayed it wasn't a bone.

No. It was the chain.

The light turned green, and the moped driver zoomed off, clutching the gold necklace. As the driver turned the corner to a side street, and I choked and gasped, trying to catch my breath, I could see long red hair streaming out beneath a helmet. Balboa! My God. She'd yanked the chain right off my neck. Someone in one of those parked cars at the container unload must have seen Santiago checking for the flash drive. If they'd watched us with binoculars—or even without—they would have seen something was up with that necklace.

"What are we going to do?" Mari cried out.

Car horns blared at us. We had to move. But where? Go straight to the starting line and the authorities with only the cash-filled bike? Or get the drive—all our supporting evidence—back from Balboa?

"You distract the spies," I decided. "Pretend like you have another flash drive. I'll go after Balboa. Without the flash drive, we can't prove anything about Preston."

And with that, I turned left, in pursuit.

58

BALBOA HADN'T gotten far; I could still hear the *putputput* of her motor. She'd made a tactical error taking that congested street. And on the bike, I was free to weave among the cars, and even hop up onto the sidewalk to try to catch up with her faster. I swerved around a street food vendor, a flower stand, and two piles of bricks. I dodged a boy carrying a huge mesh bag of soccer balls for sale. A trio of children with shoe-shine kits. *A triciclo* towing a trailer of ice cream. A group of lost Japanese tourists studying maps.

I picked up speed, as if drafting a slipstream. My legs felt so strong. Like they were part of the bike.

And then the moped came into view. It was stopped at a red light at an intersection, three blocks from where Balboa had turned on to the side street.

I wove between the waiting cars and rode up closer to her, staying just out of her line of vision. I could see the necklace chain wound around one hand. If I could only reach out and grab it. But her hand held fast to the moped handlebar.

I could poke her. Startle her. Get her to drop it.

I reached forward.

Then she saw me in one of his rearview mirrors. The light turned green and she gunned it.

Our race was on again.

I followed her for three more blocks, and then she turned down a different side street. A narrower one. With cobblestones. We were on the edge of the Old Town.

I held on tight, bouncing over the cobblestones on my dizzying descent. I didn't know how long any road bike could hold up on these cobblestones, let alone a damaged one.

I prayed that the hollowed-out bike frame would hold. I pictured the carbon tubes healthy, those threads inside thrumming with power and life. I imagined those frame joints firm, the bonds that held them secure. Juan Carlos had been a person with integrity. And even though he'd only ridden this bike once, to take it from Preston Lane's car where he'd swiped it to the hiding place in the woods, I imagined his integrity seeping into the frame and holding it all together.

At one point my wheels left the pavement. I closed my eyes, sure I was heading for a major wipeout. *I'm sorry. I tried,* I said to Juan Carlos in my head.

You're not done. You can catch him. Find your own ride.

Then I landed! I opened my eyes. I kept on riding, following that moped taillight as it turned down alley after alley, between crumbling Colonial buildings with wrought-iron balconies, deeper into a neighborhood, leading me into a labyrinth.

Was she trying to lead me? Or lose me?

And what was that sound behind me?

I glanced behind, several times, like someone in a bicycle race.

Six people on bikes were following me. Leading the pack was Pizarro. They were after the bike I was riding now. The bike with all the cash. We'd locked Preston Lane up for now, but I realized that he would still have his cell phone. He could still place orders from there, mobilizing his troops, and no doubt he had put them on our trail.

I looked ahead. The alley let out to a street where a black Ford Explorer was parked. And waiting. As I neared it, unable to stop myself on the downhill, I saw a tinted window roll down, and Darwin's head look out. The sun glanced off his sunglasses. "Need a lift?" he called out.

I glanced behind once more. Pizarro and his peloton were gaining on me. They all had two-way radios clipped to their ears, like pro cyclists. I was headed into a trap. With no hope of getting that flash drive back. I cursed myself for not having sent that email to Bianca Slade last night. Even without any attachments as proof of what we knew, at least she'd know something was up.

I turned down another alley at the last possible moment, and the peloton shot past me. This alley was so narrow I could barely get through it. And at the end, I skidded to a stop and looked down. It had let me out at the top of a staircase, where there was no fence or guardrail. If I'd kept going, I would have plummeted down to the roof of the building ten feet below. Unless I'd missed it and tumbled down the stone steps. This was urban downhill riding, for which I had no training at all.

At the bottom of the long staircase was the plaza where el Ratón had ridden his victory lap. Now it was fairly quiet, with so many people heading to the bike races. I saw some *indígena* families with blankets spread out, selling crafts. Street artists. Tourists sitting by the fountain and children playing at its base. An old man feeding a flock of pigeons, which suddenly startled at something, flew up in a cloud, and dispersed over the church.

I got off the bike and slung it over my shoulder. I'd hoof it down those stairs. If I could get to the plaza, I could find the main drag, Amazonas, and make my way back to the race starting line. I checked my watch. Fifteen minutes. I was cutting it close.

But I still didn't have the necklace. Should I go back and look for Balboa's moped? And risk facing the bicycling spies? Or bumping into Darwin in his car?

Exhaustion, nerves, everything suddenly hit me. And I had a huge stitch in my side. I massaged it and tried to catch my breath while I figured out what to do next.

Then I heard a *put-put-put* sound behind me. A moped. I turned and saw Balboa barreling toward me, her expression changing from startled to triumphant in an instant. She pulled up beside me with a squealing of brakes.

59

I GLANCED at Balboa's hands and her pockets, frisking her with my eyes. No obvious weapons bulged or poked out. But I already knew this girl was capable of doing horrible things for which she didn't need to be armed.

She looked different. Awful. Her fair skin glistened with sweat. Her cheeks were scorched pink from the harsh equatorial sun. "Great running into you here," she said. "I'm so glad I don't have to run you off the road. I kind of hate doing that."

I looked for the gold necklace around her hand, where I'd last seen it. It wasn't there. "I was following you," I said. "Give me back my necklace. I know you have it."

"I don't have it. I gave it to one of my colleagues," she said. "And now, yes, I'm following you. So I guess we've come full circle. I'll trade you that bike for this moped, and I'll be on my way."

She turned off the moped, hopped off it, and walked it toward me, fast, forcing me to the very edge of that platform before I could sidestep and get out of the way. If she took one more step, or pushed me, I'd go right over.

She put a hand on Juan Carlos's bike. "I got an instant promotion for nabbing that flash drive. I'm working in collections now. I have orders to take this bike back." Her words sounded forceful and tough, but her face betrayed her. She wasn't happy about this job.

The expression Kristen had used when she fired me from *KidVision* suddenly floated back into my head.

A chain is only as strong as its weakest link.

I'd found that weak link in Preston Lane's network. Balboa. If I could earn her trust and get her talking, I could get the flash drive necklace back. And I could still get that bike to the starting line, where hopefully Ecuadorian media, Ecuadorian government officials, and embassy bigwigs, plus a large police presence, were all assembled and waiting.

I held the bike. I stood my ground. "You could leave your job, you know," I said. "It doesn't sound so great. You could definitely use your talents for something better."

"I can't quit. Darwin will never let me."

"Then sabotage your own job. Screw up and get yourself fired."

That hesitation gave me room to maneuver. Not much, but just enough. She seemed to be willing to listen. I kept talking. "I know what it's like to get sick of a job," I said. "Like *KidVision*. It's funny. Looking back? I feel like maybe I even rode bandit on that charity ride on purpose, to sabotage my own job. I felt so much pressure to be this perfect person, always chirpy, always setting a good example for others. I didn't even know what that meant. I'd never thought deeply about it. I just felt like my life was no longer my own, like GBCN and my producer owned me or something. So I think I might have made that stupid decision as a way to get out. I didn't know how to finish that job and start something new."

Balboa nodded, scratching her neck, apparently thinking about what I'd just said.

And exposing a gold chain in the process. A gold chain tucked under her turtleneck sweater.

She'd lied to me. She did have the necklace.

So close. So close. I could rip it off Balboa's neck. I could push her down the hill. I could take the flash drive and the bike and run like hell down those stairs.

If I was that kind of person.

But I wasn't. There had to be some other path.

And I knew Balboa, for all the bravado of her explorer code name, was really just somebody lost.

"I hate this job," she said quietly.

I nodded sympathetically but said nothing, trying to gain her trust.

"It was fun at first, smuggling cash," she admitted. "I loved all the travel. Great pay and bonuses. College tuition bills paid. My family never had a lot of money. I thought I had it made, when Darwin met me at a spring break party in Florida and gave me my first assignment. And it was fun to work with these Sports Xplor agents. A lot of them really knew about sports—he'd recruited them from fantasy sports gaming sites—and it was exciting. In the early days, anyway."

I could see how tempting that job would be to someone in her situation. But it didn't excuse her role in this criminal organization.

"You can still get off this ride," I said. "It's not too late. Come with me to talk to the embassy people. Report Darwin and Pizarro. The FBI will go easier on you if you tell them the truth about Sports Xplor and its connection to Darwin, Pizarro, and Preston Lane."

She shook her head. "I'm too scared. Darwin knows everything about me. He knows about something bad I did to pay a college bill freshman year. That's the way he has power over his employees. He never has to pull a gun. He just lights up information and makes it explode. He can wreck a reputation with the push of a button. He can make sure I never find a real job."

“Balboa,” I said, “what’s your real name?”

She looked up. Her eyes glistened. “Bridget,” she whispered.

“Bridget. Listen to me. Do you understand what Preston has been trying to cover up, with Darwin’s help? What project you’re helping him with? He’s hiding a whole lot of illegal activities, including running this offshore betting business and fixing bike races. And you know he’s really the one behind Juan Carlos’s death, don’t you?”

Balboa looked down. “I try not to think about the details too much. But yeah.”

“Meanwhile, two innocent people back home are people of interest in this case: Dylan Holcomb and Jake Collier. They’re both just decent people, trying to live their lives.” I thought for a moment. Was Jake a decent person? He had his faults and flaws, like anyone, and I didn’t need him in my life. But he was innocent of the crimes and didn’t need this cloud of suspicion following him around forever. “More race fixes are being planned, on an even larger scale,” I went on. “More money will get laundered through charities and other businesses here. And cycling is going to get corrupted all over again with this scheme. You could do a lot of good, for a lot of people, by just explaining how you got dragged into this. By fingering Darwin and Preston. And by handing over that flash drive so I can take it to the people who can go after these creeps.”

Bridget’s fingers played at the gold chain, twisting it around and around as she thought.

Putputputputput.

A moped sound drew closer.

Bridget wheeled around to see who was emerging from the alley. Darwin, on a moped. Followed by Pizarro and the other five cyclists from the shadowy Team Xplor.

“Agent Balboa!” Darwin called out. “What are you doing? You

were not supposed to go after the bike until you handed off the necklace!"

Balboa clutched the necklace tighter.

"You didn't want to hand it over to them, did you," I said, locking eyes with her. "You've already gone against his orders once. You can do it again."

"This isn't funny, Agent Balboa," said Darwin. "Move away from the scene and get the flash drive away from that girl. We'll handle the bike."

"Bridget," I coaxed. "You don't need these guys anymore. Stand up for the right thing. And find your own ride."

The moped and the cyclists inched closer. Darwin revved the engine. Now both Bridget and I stood at the very edge of the platform. Bridget teetered. I grabbed her arm to keep her from falling.

"Agent Balboa!" Pizarro inched his bike forward. "Do I have to cut that necklace off you?"

"Stop calling me Balboa! I hate that name! I'm done with that name!" Bridget tore off the necklace, breaking the chain. She held it in both hands for a moment. "You want this? Go chase it yourselves!" And she hurled it over the edge.

"No!" Darwin shouted as he lunged for it and missed.

No! I wailed inside.

Pizarro and the other cyclists leaped off their bikes, and they all looked over the edge, trying to spot it on the rooftop below and figure out the best way down.

Bridget took my hand and slipped something into it. It was the flash drive. She'd thrown only the chain, to distract them.

"I'll hold these guys off you as long as I can. I think I can buy you a good lead. Now go, Tessa. Go. Ride like the wind."

/////

I DIDN'T waste any time. I shouldered Juan Carlos's bike and ran down those stone steps. I slipped twice in my bike shoes, and skinned my arm, but I got up again and kept going. At the bottom, I put the flash drive in my pocket and rode as fast as I could toward El Parque Metropolitano.

Toward the starting line of the race.

Toward the finish line of this nightmare.

Toward the starting line of the rest of my life.

I heard cheering as I neared it. I almost imagined it was for me. But the race had started. I was riding against the stream. Colorful pelotons shot past me. Including Team Cadence-EcuaBar in white and green. The Ecuadorian team followed close to their wheels, a streak of red, yellow, and blue.

I gritted my teeth and pedaled on, ignoring police who cautioned me to keep away from the barricades. Spectators scattered out of my way. Pigeons, too.

"Tessa! Over here!"

"Slow down! Slow down!"

I looked up and saw Mari and Santiago waving. Gesturing me to veer right, to a set of bleachers roped off with red ribbon. Diplomat and other government cars were parked just behind them. Police cars, too.

"You did it, Tessa! You did it! Stop!" Mari shouted.

I plowed right through the red ribbon setting off the VIP area, my arms raised up in a victory V.

60

FOUR DAYS later, I was in Santiago's Pathfinder, barreling down the Pan-American Highway. I rolled the window open and let the wind tangle my hair. I trailed my hand outside and felt the wind push back against me. I tried to grab on to that wind and hold it, to imagine it pulling me forward.

Things were definitely moving forward on the crime-solving front.

Preston Lane, Coach Mancuso, the three spies, the flash drive, and Preston Lane's bike—now emptied of cash—were all on their way back to Boston. Darwin and his crew would face more questioning there. A news story in the Ecuadorian paper said Bridget Peterson, of Ann Arbor, Michigan, had done a lot of talking already and might be able to expect some leniency from U.S. authorities compared to the other two individuals. I hoped so. Even though that article she'd posted about me still stung, I hoped she'd find a better use for her communications skills and her journalistic interest, as well as a fresh start for her life.

Preston Lane and Tony Mancuso would be taken into protective custody. They faced charges for racketeering and for conspiracy to commit money laundering, as well as conspiracy and second-degree murder charges for their involvement in Juan Carlos's death. Dylan and Jake were presumed innocent at this point, though would serve as key witnesses in eventual legal proceedings.

The FBI had swiftly tracked down and raided the homes of at least ten other businesspeople, in the United States, who were involved with Sports Xplor in some way—as investors or consultants or agents. The site was declared illegal and promptly shut down. Mari and I talked to Gage on the phone—he wanted to hear the whole story from us personally. I asked him about that Sports Xplor screen I'd noticed on his office computer. I hoped he hadn't been implicated in the gambling scheme. "No way," he said. "I knew it seemed fishy. I held on to the URL and password Preston and Tony had given me, and I kept coming back to look at the site and try to figure it out. I never would have spent money on it, as a player or as an organizer. And I'm really proud of what you girls did, reporting all this. My gut told me that site was illegal, but I never was sure of Preston and Tony's roles in it. Now I wish I'd spoken up sooner."

Next I'd had a tough video conference with my parents, where I had to tell them everything. My mom promised me "consequences galore" as soon as I got back home. They weren't at all thrilled I'd lobbied to go to Ecuador without telling them everything I was involved in. They said it was wrong to cover up so many of my own actions, even as I was trying to do the right thing and uncover the truth. If that wasn't enough, I then had pretty much an identical conversation with the Ruiz family, in Spanish. Not exactly how I'd planned to be practicing my Spanish verbs.

My dad insisted I stay out of the news, for my own safety, in case other gambling ring members surfaced and decided to retaliate on Darwin's behalf. I agreed to lay low, and turned down interviews with the media, Ecuadorian and American. I promised not to talk about the details on my vlog, once I got that going again. It wasn't hard to do. This story wasn't about me getting famous or restoring my TV persona. It was about unearthing the truth behind Juan Carlos's death. It was about owning up to the fact that while I didn't directly cause that death, I'd been wrong to bandit ride, to draft a team's paceline and pull out too fast, and to go for so long without reporting to police what I knew. It was about making sure that a handful of greedy, corrupt people like Preston Lane didn't poison the sport of cycling. Bikes could save lives, just like Mari had said once. They weren't supposed to end lives.

At the end of those tough conversations, both sets of parents—north and south of the equator—had told me they were proud of my courage. "It's a rare individual," my dad added, "who takes risks in the name of justice. I'm not saying everything you did was right, especially since you are under eighteen. But I am proud to have a daughter who's got integrity."

On Sunday, just two days after we exposed Preston Lane and the Sports Xplor scheme, Bianca Slade had actually called me at the Ruiz house. She wanted to tell me personally that I'd been courageous to tip her off about the bike sabotage in the first place, and when I confessed—off the record—what else Mari and I had done to crack the case, she expressed even more admiration. "My hat's off to you," she said. "You have the qualities of a great investigative journalist. And you know what the most important quality is?"

"What?"

"That we care enough about something to ask questions, follow hunches, and find evidence—even when it seems like no one else cares. That we keep on digging."

"Thanks," I'd managed to squeak.

"But there are ways to look for evidence and talk to sources without putting yourself at such risk," she'd continued, sounding a little bit stern. "You need to get special training for this field of work. There are journalism programs with investigative tracks, and I'll email you my recommendations. Meanwhile, I hear you're between jobs these days. There's an internship with your name on it at *Watchdog*, whenever you're ready to start."

I'd done a little dance after hanging up the phone, whooping with joy. Bianca Slade liked my work! I'd get to work with her someday! Mari and the Ruiz family had joined me in my celebratory dance. Lucia had put on salsa music—Amparo had turned it up loud—and we made our own salsoteca in the Casa Ruiz living room that night.

Kylie was less understanding at first. We had a videoconference right after my host family's impromptu dance party and she burst into tears. She said the scholarship committee had contacted her. A stop had been put on the check while investigators looked into Preston Lane's financial transactions in the United States and offshore. There were suspicious money wire transfers and more suspicious cash smuggling activities to look into, and the scholarship would likely be dissolved. I listened to her for as long as she wanted to talk. I let her cry as long as she needed. Then I explained to her, gently, why I'd exposed this scandal, how it was something bigger than all of us. She'd said she understood, but I could hear the hurt in her voice. Ending that video call was hard. I wished there were something I could do to help her raise that tuition money

Meanwhile, in Quito, the Ecuadorian police and some government officials were interrogating the local affiliates that Darwin had been working with in Quito. The affiliates were numerous, and included a mix of locals, police, and expats from the United States who were hiding out in Quito to avoid prosecution for various crimes. Even the nightclub bouncer I'd dealt with was fingered by Balboa. He was actually a police officer who moonlighted as an enforcer and a debt collector for the Sports Xplor gambling business.

The Pan-American Cycling Tour grand finale in Quito continued and came to a dramatic finish. Equipo Diablo won the circuit race, with el Ratón leading his team. He then went on to lead the team to victory on two of the stages of the four-day stage race that followed. But a Brazilian team came up out of nowhere and won the other two stages, and Team Cadence-EcuaBar—struggling without el Cóndor, reeling from the scandal, and in the absence of their head coach—placed fourth in the stage race event. After the races, el Ratón showed up at the U.S. Embassy, asking to talk to an FBI field agent. He admitted that he'd been paid off by Darwin to keep Juan Carlos's secret, and he'd been appointed the team leader of Equipo Diablo in exchange for helping to identify potentially bribable riders.

As for Juan Carlos, he had emerged from all of this more of a hero than ever. There was already talk of building a statue of him and putting it in the park where the Vuelta Youth Racing Club trained, and Wilson called for a planning meeting at Vuelta to brainstorm ways to stage a fundraising ride. The money would go to a scholarship fund in Juan Carlos's name. None of this, of course, would bring him back. But at least he'd be remembered as a person of character, as the Juan Carlos I'd known. Not just some character in a bicycle rivalry drama or a betting scheme.

And me? I still had almost two weeks at latitude zero, which I was finally free to explore. I could bond with my host family and Mari, who'd left her cousin's apartment for good and was staying at the Ruiz house with me. I could hang with the Vuelta volunteers and soak up the culture. There were cloud forests to explore outside the city. A Vuelta-sponsored jungle trek Mari and I were looking forward to. And more bike classes to teach at

La Casa and elsewhere. Even though Juan Carlos and his ghost bike would probably cast their shadow on me for a long time, I could live with that, knowing I'd taken el Cóndor's cause all the way to the finish.

"So where's this surprise place you're taking me?" I asked Santiago.

He smiled. "We are here already. An *actividad* I thought you'd appreciate."

I walked by his side through the parking lot, toward a big stone obelisk with a globe on top. The monument was surrounded by green-and-brown hills and a row of fluttering flags showing countries all over the world.

"*La Mitad del Mundo.* The official middle of the world. More or less."

"More or less?"

"Come. I will show you. Here is the equatorial line." He pointed to a yellow strip on the stones, leading up to the obelisk. Colorful flowers formed an *S* on one side, *N* on the other. I walked in the Northern Hemisphere, Santiago in the Southern. "It is a *turístico* thing to do," he admitted, "but you cannot come this far and not stand with one foot in each hemisphere."

At the steps to the obelisk, he took my picture with one foot on each side of the line. Then we climbed the stairs inside the obelisk and looked out at the view. At Quito in the distance, and the ring of velvet hills, and the line stretching out in either direction.

"So what do you mean by 'more or less' the middle of the world?" I asked.

"This isn't really the equator. The first navigators got the location wrong."

I stared at him.

He laughed. "This is the true! Modern GPS technology now

shows the early explorers were off by about a hundred meters. The line has been redrawn. Over there, by that museum." He pointed to a building a few yards away. "They will need to build a new monument, too."

I thought about this. "You know what? Maybe it's not always easy to figure out where to draw a line. Like, what's good or bad, what's wrong or right."

He considered this idea for a moment, then nodded. "We have to redraw our lines all the time, depending on situations."

"But I don't like that. How can we make good decisions and do the right things if our values aren't fixed? If our lines about what's right or wrong are always shifting?"

We'd come full circle around the observation deck of the globe. As we looked at the sprawling view below us—hills and homes and a network of narrow meandering roads—I realized Santiago had taken a step closer to me. Then another. And another. Before I knew it, he had slipped his arm around me and lowered his face toward mine. I lifted mine to meet him. Somehow, in the middle, our lips found each other.

His kiss was warm. A perfect mix of gentle and firm.

I wanted to lose myself in it. Jets of emotions that I'd turned off after Jake suddenly turned back on.

He cupped my face in his hands and looked at me. "I do not know what to do with these feelings," he said in a husky voice. "I do not know if it was right or wrong to do that just now. Maybe I hope for too much."

"I don't know, either," I whispered. I felt disoriented. Dizzy. Confused.

"The timing is terrible." He sighed. "You are returning to Boston soon. And I do not know if I will successfully get into a school in the U.S. If I do, it will not be for one more year."

"And you still have to pass that TOEFL exam."

"I will! I have been studying hard! And I have many new action *verbos* I can use."

We both smiled.

Then he grew serious again. "Tessa. I know things are complicated. But I wanted to express my feelings to you. You are the most exciting person I've ever met. The most adventurous and amazing girl."

I took a step back. I studied his face. Open, inviting. His body warm and welcoming.

I'd thought Santiago wasn't my type. But did that really matter? This was a really good guy. He'd gone out on a limb for me, from the first day we'd met. He'd gone along on my ride. And the more he revealed about himself, the more sides I saw to him. And liked.

Santiago smiled, almost sadly. "You are quiet. I understand. You are an independent American girl. You do not need a boyfriend. Especially one in another country. You do not need more complications."

He was right. I didn't need complications right now.

But maybe it didn't have to be so complicated. My future, his future—they weren't entirely charted out. Maybe what mattered was this moment, right now, and following my own heart to see where it might lead me.

As he let his hands fall to his sides in a gesture of resignation, I reached for them. I held them. Tight.

We exchanged a smile and walked back to the car together, the yellow line running between us, the strong sun warming our backs.

THE NEXT morning I woke up early, before the rest of the Ruiz house. An email from Sarita made my day right away—she told me that Cadence Bikes had heard about the frozen scholarship fund, and Chris Fitch had come through for Kylie. She'd graduate with us after all, with the gift of money from a company. A good company.

I was about to shut down my computer when another message came in.

I stared at the sender's name. Jake Collier. The subject line simply said *Hey*.

I thought of Santiago's kiss yesterday. I'd felt so free at Mitad del Mundo. Free to kiss a different guy. To go with my feelings, in the moment, and not have to second-guess everything.

I didn't want to give up that freedom.

I opened the message. It was short.

> Guess you heard they got the guys behind Juan Carlos's murder. Wild stuff. I knew there was something up with that team. Hope I can get my life back now. Started packing up for UMass this weekend, and found one of your cycling jerseys. It smelled like your soap. Made me miss you. Hope you're doing well at the middle of the world. Maybe I can see you one more time when you get back? Would be good to talk again. Like we used to.

I stared at the words on the screen for a long time. We'd never talk like we used to. We couldn't go back. But I was glad he was looking forward, too, thinking about going to college and moving on with his life.

I almost laughed at the line about doing well at the middle of the world. If he only knew how hard I'd worked here, and how my work had helped clear his name. Part of me wanted to tell him everything Mari and I had accomplished. To get some credit for saving his reputation.

But I knew what I'd done. I didn't need his validation anymore.

I smiled and typed out a fast note back, a note that would be my last, wishing him well on his new road.

AFTER SENDING that email—and deleting Jake's message—I got dressed and quietly made myself a cup of instant coffee in the kitchen. I shushed Peludo when he started to yap, so he wouldn't wake up the household.

"You're all dressed up." Amparo shuffled into the kitchen, rubbing sleep from her eyes. "You look nice." Then she gasped. "Did you stay out all night?"

I smiled. "Nope. Just thought I'd give this dress a little air." I spun around so the red skirt of my salsa dress flared. "Like it?"

"Love it!" Amparo exclaimed. "Are you going to meet Santiago? He's probably too shy to tell you he likes you. But the rest of us can tell."

"Not right now." I rinsed my coffee cup and put on a pair of espadrilles I'd purchased at a craft market—I'd given my Chuck Taylors to Rosio at La Casa, to keep.

"Hey, can you listen to my pageant speech?" Amparo asked. "I have that audition tomorrow, and I'm really nervous about it. I rewrote it last night. It's not about fashion design anymore. It's about Vuelta."

"Sure. Soon as I get back." I kept walking toward the door.

"Now? Or later?" Amparo asked, the disappointment already creeping into her voice.

I stopped walking. How many times had I said "later" to people and failed to follow through? How many "laters" did we even have in this life?

Juan Carlos had said he'd talk to me later. But we never got the chance.

I kicked off my shoes. I sat down on the couch. I listened to Amparo run through her entire speech. Three times.

Her speech was moving. It was strong. It would open people's eyes to bicycle advocacy here in Quito and what bikes could do to change lives. She'd clearly learned from Mari and me, listening to us talk about Vuelta and volunteering at the container unload that day. The Miss Earth Ecuador pageant was a good platform for her voice to be heard, and she did have a voice. I gave her a few suggestions, mostly about her eye contact, and pronounced her good to go.

She beamed.

"And now, I'm going out," I said, slipping on my shoes again. "Tell Lucia I'll be back."

I walked outside and waved a friendly good morning to Paolo in the guard booth.

"*¡Buenos días, señorita!*" he called to me, touching the brim of his black beret.

"*¡Buenos días!*" I returned, with a smile and a wave.

I grabbed a bus at the bottom of the hill and went to Vuelta, where I checked out a loaner bike. A sturdy, plain urban bike with fat wheels and three gears. I wouldn't have minded riding my old Bianchi here, but I'd already given it to Rosio along with those Chuck Taylors. In fact, the other day Mari and Amparo and I had brought a whole truckload of donated bikes to the girls and their moms. *Good* bikes, as well as helmets and bike shoes.

I wheeled the loaner bike out of the shop.

I didn't need anything fancier. I didn't need to go far or fast.

I rode down to Avenida Amazonas, to the edge of a large park. There I jumped off. Artists were setting up their stalls, crafts vendors were laying out their wares. The smell of wool mixed with the scent of street vendors cooking corn on the cob.

I was chilly in the morning air, wearing only a halter dress. I stopped at the market and bought a wool cardigan from a smiling *indígena* girl. I negotiated an excellent price, one that we both seemed pleased with. I refused the plastic bag and immediately slipped the sweater on, admiring the cream-colored wool with a design of gray llamas marching across the middle.

Then I walked the bike to Amazonas, where the Sunday *ciclopaseo* ride was getting into gear. Families, couples, friends, and solo riders were making their way up and down the street on all different kinds of bikes. Everyone looked happy.

The sweater warmed my arms. A breeze made my red skirt dance at my legs. The intense equatorial sun caressed my face as I lifted it up to the sky. I didn't know where I wanted to go or how far I'd bike today. It didn't really matter. Odds were I'd end up somewhere good.

I took a deep breath and pushed down on the pedals. I merged safely into the bicycle traffic and started my own ride.

ACKNOWLEDGMENTS

I'm so grateful to the many people who have helped me take *Latitude Zero* all the way to the finish line. I couldn't ask for a better team.

I'm so lucky to have Kirby Kim as my agent; thank you for championing my stories and for getting me in gear to write another book.

If the Olympics awarded medals to editors, Leila Sales would take home the gold. Editing this book was nothing short of an athletic event. Thank you, Leila, for your intellectual agility, your patient coaching, and your cheerleading, as well as your willingness to follow these characters down their twisting paths. I would not have found my way through without you.

Tremendous thanks to Viking and Penguin Young Readers Group—I still pinch myself and marvel that I get to be on this great team! Thank you, Ken Wright, Regina Hayes, Colleen Conway, Tara Shanahan, and everyone in marketing and sales. I'm especially grateful for the eagle eyes of Janet Pascal, who helped me avoid some plot holes, and to Lavina Lee and Tony DeGeorge for steering me clear of grammatical gaffes, timeline trip-ups, and other writing hazards. Also a big thank-you to Kate Renner for another super slick cover design.

Many individuals and organizations gave their time and expertise to help me at various stages. Tad Hylkema generously shared his knowledge of bike mechanics and the world of professional cycling. For insights into South American cycling and young cyclists, I thank Klaus Bellon of the Cycling Inquisition blog. Andrew Fischer consulted on bike crash protocol and legal matters. Bikes Not Bombs in Jamaica Plain, Massachusetts, provided insights into bike shop culture and youth programming; their store and their international bike shipping programs served as a model for Compass Bikes in the book. Corrina Roche-Cross at BNB helped me to understand the perspective of a female bike mechanic. The staff at the Belmont Wheelworks and the Pan-Mass Challenge provided valuable information about bicycle and charity rides, respectively. Paul Liberman (go, DraftKings!) advised on fantasy sports and sports betting.

Writing this book required crossing some geographic and linguistic borders. My former employer in Quito, *Experimento de Convivencia Internacional,* helped me to reconnect with my Ecuadorian experience and to connect with current young travelers there. My sister, Darcie Renn—who is ten times the explorer that I ever was—served as my avatar in Ecuador; facts and photos she supplied me with inspired several scenes. Zoraida Córdova and Lourdes Keochgerien consulted on language and culture. Lourdes, I'm especially grateful to you for spending so much time in the pages of *Latitude Zero. ¡Te agradezco mucho la ayuda!* Any errors are my own. I am also so grateful to Carlos Vivas for sharing with me some of his stories about bike racing and bike shops in Ecuador. I also must thank both Carlos and his wife, Carol Shanahan, for reading the book and helping me with bike technicalities and language issues. Finally, Martha Hauston, who was a fantastic traveling companion on my first trip to South America, had the foresight to save all my correspondence when I returned there later to work.

I have boundless appreciation for my writing group, from whom I continue to learn so much. Erin Cashman, Eileen Donovan Kranz, Patrick Gabridge, Vincent Gregory, Ted Rooney, Deborah Vlock, Rob Vlock, and Julie Wu, you guys are the best. Also Team Blue: Elle Cosimano, Laura Ellen, Ashley Elston,

Elisa Ludwig, and Megan Miranda—thank you for reading pages on the fly and providing emergency roadside assistance. Kerri Majors—thank you for helping me get past that first One Hundred Mile marker!

Many thanks are due to an elite crew of babysitters who helped me with time trials, aka deadlines: Tricia Gaquin, Lyndsey Grant, Meredith Lynch, and SpongeBob SquarePants.

I so appreciate my family and friends for cheering me on and showing up at all the water stops. Thanks, Mom, for being my best reader. Dad and Sally, thank you for always supporting my career—and for spending a birthday dinner with me hashing out evil schemes. Thank you, Rachel Liberman and Sarah Nager, for your enthusiasm—and for The Fingernail!

The yellow jerseys go to my home team: to Gabriel, who let his mother disappear into the computer for long stretches of time, and to my loving husband, who coaxed me onto a road bike years ago and introduced me to this exciting sport. He's also one cool road cyclist, and a major Pan-Mass Challenge fundraiser. Thanks for sharing the road with me, Jim. Long may we ride!

READ MORE BY DIANA RENN!

Praise for **TOKYO HEIST** by Diana Renn

"Young adult mysteries do not get any better than this."
—Peter Abrahams, author of the Echo Falls Mysteries

"Irresistible. I couldn't put it down!"
—Alane Ferguson, author of the Forensic Mysteries

"You'll want to jump right inside this book and live it."
—Kristen Miller, author of the Eternal Ones series

"An absorbing tale mystery readers will love."
—Linda Gerber, author of *Death by Latte*

"We can't stop talking about action-packed YA mystery novel *Tokyo Heist* . . . author Diana Renn's first YA novel, but we certainly hope it isn't her last!"
—HuffingtonPost.com

"It's rare for YA heroines to have such specific, developed interests, and Violet filtering her investigation through her passion for manga, art, and Japan makes her seem like a real, relatable teenager."
—A.V. Club

"This art heist has twists and turns, romance, and the happily-ever-after that many will be rooting for."
—*Booklist*

"Will enthrall readers who love action."
—Examiner.com

"A fast-paced and engaging mystery with a spunky protagonist." —*VOYA*

"Readers will cheer for Violet as she uses her wits to outsmart the adults."
—*School Library Journal*